She knew his
passion, but
his demands
were cruel

The
COACH
to HELL

Rachel Cosgrove Payes

Author of MOMENT OF DESIRE

AS THEY ASCENDED the grand staircase after the ball, Georgina's heart thudded and her pulses throbbed. Was Francis going to bed her again? Obviously he wanted her.

When they reached her bedchamber, her maid Lizzie was waiting. As Lord Francis entered after Georgina, Lizzie's eyes widened in shock.

"Oh, miss, what a disaster!" Lizzie whispered. "Charlie's here—hiding in the wardrobe—to surprise you!"

Georgina thought she would faint. She looked at the huge oak wardrobe opposite the bed. One of its carved doors stood slightly ajar, to give air to the man hidden inside.

She looked back at Francis, waiting for his valet to come and disrobe him so that he could bed her. And yet his half-brother Charles, hiding in the wardrobe, expected the same thing.

It was a nightmare. And there was nothing Georgina could do to prevent what was about to happen —nothing!

The COACH to HELL

Rachel Cosgrove Payes

PLAYBOY PRESS
PAPERBACKS

CHAPTER 1

Georgina Ryerston was so tired she could cry, but she couldn't stop work now. Although her shoulders ached from jerking the cord which sent the flying shuttle through the shed pulled open on the warp of her loom, she kept on working at the speed which had earned her enough money to pay Dr. Jennings for his visits from Exeter to try to help poor Papa in his final days. When she had first agreed to have the loom set up in the kitchen of the vicarage four years ago when she was fifteen, Georgina had not realized that she would one day count on the money she made from her weaving for essentials. Then she had only thought of money for an occasional new gown, or ribbons, or a lace pinner. A country parson didn't earn much, and the vicarage in Trindale was set in a very poor parish. Only the weaving industry in the Exeter area was lucrative. The farmers and small shopkeepers eked out as meager an existence as did their vicar. St. Edmund's was a very poor country cousin, indeed, to the great cathedral in Exeter, an hour's journey by coach to the west.

Georgina stopped her weaving briefly to rest, and to see if her father needed anything. The tumor which ate away at his vitals was killing him slowly but surely. He knew this, and did not try to hide the fact from his only child. If only her mother had survived bringing her into the world—but there was no point in dwelling on ifs. Mama had died of childbed fever, Papa had never remarried, and soon Georgina would be all alone in the world.

She crept quietly up the steep narrow stairs to the

upstairs bedroom where her father lay dozing, his pain dulled with laudanum. Dr. Jennings had tried to treat Papa with Plunkett's caustic, but it had done nothing to help him. Now only the opiate which she gave him in wine held the pain at bay.

Georgina looked at his face and at first thought that Papa was sleeping. His skin, so white she might have been painting him with white lead, was translucent, stretched taut over underlying bones. Gray hair straggled from under the nightcap he wore. Georgina turned to leave, but Papa stirred and opened pain-clouded, drug-hazed eyes.

"Has the letter come yet from the Earl of Margate?" he asked, anxiety obvious in his tone.

"Not yet, Papa," Georgina soothed. "But you know how slow the mail can be in winter. The roads are terrible. Mrs. Demsty broke a coach wheel just getting out from Exeter last week. You'll hear. Don't worry about it."

"But I do worry, Georgina," he fretted. "My time is coming soon. Dr. Jennings will no longer look me in the eye when he tells me that I am improving. I must make provision for you before I die. I don't want you trapped into the life of a weaver, growing old before your time while working for Adam Fenton." He sighed, as if too tired to say more, and his eyes drooped closed again. "The earl owes me a favor," he whispered. If she hadn't heard it said so often in these past terrible weeks, Georgina wouldn't have been able to understand him. *Owes me.* Then he was asleep.

The clock on the chimneypiece said two o'clock. It was Tuesday, and Mr. Fenton would arrive promptly at three to bring more wool thread for her to weave, and to take away the wide woolen cloth she had finished. She must prepare for him. Going to her own tiny bedchamber across the hall from her father's, Georgina took a large white lawn fichu from a wardrobe and draped it around her shoulders, making sure that it came high over her full young bosom. Adam Fenton's hot eyes strayed all too often to that tempting part of her anatomy, so she had learned to cover herself well before he arrived. Glancing in the small, poorly silvered mirror, she pulled an unbecoming mobcap well down over her wheat-colored hair, which was dressed close to her head.

Then, for just a moment, Georgina allowed herself to indulge in a favorite fantasy. Her very distant cousin, the Earl of Margate, would send for her to come to Staines, outside of London, to live with him once poor Papa was dead. He must be rich. All earls were rich, in Georgina's mind, although she knew not a single one. The grandest person she knew was the local squire, a red-faced, corpulent man who rode to hounds in good weather. As for wealth, no doubt Adam Fenton was as wealthy as anyone she knew. He had hinted to her during his weekly visits these past few months that if she were "good to him," as he put it, she might be the recipient of some of his largesse. The thought was revolting to her. Fenton was an old man, no doubt nearly fifty, a skinny man with a skinny soul. She'd heard of his reputation with women, and Georgina had no intention of becoming one of his mistresses.

It wasn't that Georgina had any special horror of such an arrangement. Although vicarage raised, and without a mother's touch, she had grown up knowing something of the world. Her father had taken his religion much more seriously than most of the clergy did in those days. A gentle man, he had ministered to all who needed him, and she was accustomed to a steady stream of misfits and beggars, of those grindingly poor, and those dishonest enough to make more for themselves than they deserved, all coming through the vicarage at any hour of the day or night. Papa discussed these people with her, and Georgina had an uncommon knowledge of the temptations of the flesh which beset the mortals in St. Edmund's parish. So she knew that men had mistresses—and their wives took lovers. Such things didn't shock her, but Georgina knew one thing: she was sick to death of poverty. She never wanted to see a loom again as long as she lived, nor hear its clack as the fly shuttle whipped back and forth in its groove. She wanted to escape from Trindale, for here she could never be anything except Georgina Ryerston, the vicar's daughter, destined to marry some village fellow and live out her life in this dull village. Georgina dreamed of fine houses, large estates, gowns of silk, satin, and velvet instead of cotton and wool, the fabrics woven on her own horrid monster of a loom in her own crowded kitchen. No, if some young, handsome lord offered to set her up in an establishment, Georgina wouldn't turn him down out of hand, although she would try to get him to marry her. If, however, she found that his desires for her did not include marriage lines, she might be persuaded to accept his terms so long as they promised the good life for her.

Oh, if only the letter would come from Hellingham, the estate of her cousin. When Papa realized that he was dying, that there was nothing the doctor could do to save him, he began to fret about Georgina's future. It was then, after much thought, that he had told her of this distant connection.

"An earl is our cousin? Papa, you never mentioned—"

And poor Papa had evaded her eager gaze, mumbling something about "might not be interested in his poor relations." But, finally, he told Georgina that he had written to the earl, explaining the situation, his terminal illness, and the precarious position in which this would leave his only child. "I have asked that he take you in, Georgina. He can well afford this, being quite wealthy. I am sure that he will not refuse my request."

Georgina waited eagerly for an answer, examining each letter which came to the vicarage for the Margate seal, but several weeks had now passed with no answer.

Perhaps the earl had died. Maybe he just wasn't interested in taking in what her father, himself, had termed a poor relation. As the days went on, with no letter, Georgina began to worry. Her future was, indeed, precarious. She had no young man who wanted to marry her, for she had discouraged all the local suitors, not wanting to spend the rest of her life trapped in a poor marriage, living in Trindale. She had no opportunity to meet wealthy young men, young lords. And if she did, Georgina knew she had nothing to bring to a marriage other than her own fresh young beauty. No dowry. No title. Nothing except some expertise at that wretched loom waiting for her in the kitchen. Oh, if only a handsome knight would slay that monster and carry her off to be his bride! Instead, she had Mr. Adam Fenton arriving momentarily with his bony, grasping hands always reaching for her. All too often, after one of his visits, she was black and blue from his attentions.

A knocking at the door snapped her out of her reverie. Peeking out of the small window, she saw Fenton's coach and four, a ragged young boy scarcely into his teens posing as coachey, swathed in a cast-off coachman's coat with its tiers of capelets over each shoulder.

As she scurried down the stairs, Georgina scowled.

Opening the door to him, she stepped back, curtsying, while he came into the vicarage. The coachey, now acting as porter, carried in the large box of wool yarn which she would use next week.

"Ah, Miss Ryerston, how nice to see your charming face." He reached out with one bony hand to chuck her under the chin, but Georgina, anticipating his action from long practice, slid just out of his reach without seeming to do so deliberately.

"If you'll come along to the kitchen, sir. . . ."

As soon as the boy had set down the box of wool, Fenton waved him back outside, although Georgina knew the poor fellow would have prefered to wait in the warm kitchen with its blazing fire in the fireplace, for his perch on the box of Fenton's landau was cold.

The coachey, from past times at the vicarage, knew he was to take along the large bundle of cloth which was ready, folded on the table. He staggered out under the heavy load; Georgina, paid by the yard, wove as much fabric as she could each week. Dr. Jennings wouldn't ride out from Exeter for nothing.

"Now, my dear, I'll help you dress the loom," Fenton offered, his usual ploy for getting her trapped behind the monstrous frame which took up so much of the small kitchen.

Today Georgina was determined to thwart him. "That is kind of you, sir, but quite unnecessary today," she lied. "The butcher's wife is coming later to help me, and I shall return the favor for her."

"Then you may offer me a cup of tea," Fenton ordered. "I have something important to say to you, Georgina."

She shuddered inwardly, for when he called her by her Christian name instead of "Miss Ryerston," trouble brewed.

"How is your father?" Fenton asked as she filled the kettle with water, hanging it from a hook over the fire.

"Poorly." What else could she say? Everyone knew that her father was dying of cancer.

"What do you intend to do when your father dies?"

As she moved past him to get china cups and saucers from the walnut dresser, Georgina was forced by the narrow space between table and wall to move close to Fenton. Quick as a striking adder, Fenton's hand reached out and he caught Georgina about the waist, pulling her to him. If only she'd heard from her cousin, she'd be able to pick up the nearest thing at hand and hit Fenton with it as he backed her into that corner behind the loom!

"Sir!" she gasped, "I think I heard my poor Papa cry out. I must give him another dose of opiate. He suffers so." Then she twisted out of his grasp and flew up the stairs, knowing full well that her father still slept. Waiting a few minutes to compose herself, she went back to the kitchen where Fenton waited for her, his face avid with lust. This time she managed to keep the scrubbed table between them.

"You will not be able to stay on here at the vicarage when your father passes on, Georgina." It was as if there had been no interruption. "A new vicar will come with his family, and you will have to move."

Georgina knew this all too well and was beginning to spend sleepless nights trying to decide what to do about her plight.

"I own a small house on the outskirts of Exeter," Fenton went on. "My tenant is leaving soon. I could set up your loom there, and you could live in the cottage."

Pretending not to know what he was proposing, Georgina said, "Sir, if I worked my fingers to the bone on the loom, I'd never be able to afford the rent for a cottage, no matter how small it was."

He leered at her, his thin lips curled at the corners. "Now, Georgina, don't be coy with me. Did I mention rent? Of course not. There'd be no rent to pay. All you'd have to do would be to take me into your bed. You know that."

It was said. Georgina had been studiously avoiding this final confrontation, although she'd known for weeks just what Fenton wanted from her. She wanted to throw the kettle of boiling water in his face, but Georgina was wise enough to know that she must handle Fenton very carefully. If she antagonized him now, he might well refuse to bring more weaving for her to do. Although her father was failing fast, he might linger on for weeks yet, and she needed the money she earned from Fenton's loom.

Putting on a sad face, Georgina said, "Sir, my father is so ill that I can think of nothing else now. But when he passes away. . . ." She let her voice fade. Let him think there's hope, she thought.

Fenton smiled, a sly, triumphant twisting of his hatchet face. "Of course, my dear, I know how trying it is for you now. Be sure to send me word when the parson passes to his reward, and I shall make suitable arrangements."

This time when he left, Georgina had no choice but to let him embrace her. His hot, dry lips moved on hers and he tried to force the tip of his tongue between her lips. She pulled away from him, trying not to show her revulsion, saying, "Sir, you are too eager by far!"

"I can't wait for you, Georgina," he said, his voice hoarse with desire.

"For shame! Do you wish my poor Papa dead?"

"No, no, but he is ill and dying. No one would want to prolong his suffering."

Finally she managed to show Fenton to the door.

"I shall see you next Tuesday," he told her, trying to snatch another kiss.

He had scarcely gone when Georgina, getting ready to fill a bobbin for the shuttle, heard a hesitant tapping on the kitchen door. It couldn't be Fenton back again. He always came to the front door and knocked with great authority. This would be someone wanting the services of the vicar, although surely, by now, everyone in Trindale knew that Papa was confined to bed.

She opened the door to find a little girl bundled up in a shabby red wool cloak just raising her chapped hand to tap again. The peaked little face peeping out from the shadow of the hood was tearful.

"Gracie, what's wrong?" Georgina asked the child. "Here, come in and get warm by the fire."

"Thankee, Miss Georgina. It's Tuppence."

"Your ginger kitten?"

Tears filled Gracie's pale blue eyes. "Yes, miss, he's

gone, he is. Since Sunday." Then, moving closer to Georgina and taking her hand shyly, the little girl asked, "Could you find him for me, Miss Georgina? Harry said you found their heifer when she strayed." Then, digging deeply into a pocket tied around her waist, the child said, "I brought you some hazelnuts, miss. Harry said I should give you something for finding Tuppence." She proffered a grubby, cold-reddened hand clutching a few nuts.

"You didn't have to bring me anything," Georgina said, stooping to embrace the little girl. "But I do love hazelnuts," she added, pleased to see the child's smile. "First let me see if I can't find a sugarplum for you." She went to a blue Delft ginger jar and brought a sweetmeat for the child who took it eagerly, popping it into her mouth. "Now, did you bring anything for me to hold in my hand, Gracie? Something Tuppence touches, perhaps?"

Gracie nodded vigorously, delving into the deep pocket again. "Here's a ball of wool he plays with. Will that do, miss?"

"Admirably, Gracie. Now, you sit there by the fire on that little wooden stool, and be very quiet. I can't promise anything. Sometimes I can see things which are lost, and sometimes I can't. I never know until I try."

The child perched on the little three-legged stool while Georgina held the ball of dirty yarn in her hand. She stood there, eyes closed, and tried to blank out all thought. At first she was acutely conscious of the sounds in her kitchen, the crackle and hiss of the fire, the faint sound of steam escaping from the tea kettle, and even Gracie's muted sniffles. Then, gradually, these sounds faded from her conscious thoughts. She concentrated on the yarn she held, the bit of wool which Tuppence, the missing ginger kitten, had used for a toy. She felt as if she were swaying slightly, as a young willow tree sways in a gentle summer breeze. All of her being concentrated on the wool in her hand, and on the kitten. It was as if she were calling, in her mind, "Tuppence, where are you, you naughty kitten?" For what seemed a long time, although later she always found it had only been moments, Georgina stood there, relaxed, seeking the little cat. And this time she saw it, faintly at first. It was confined somewhere, for she could almost feel the tiny, sharp claws as they dug frantically, trying to make an escape route. Then the picture in her mind sharpened, became clearer, more defined. The kitten was in a box of some sort. Had some other child, wanting a pet, stolen Tuppence? Then Georgina saw the stick and the string and recognized the kitten's jail for what it was.

"Tuppence is caught in a snare, Gracie," Georgina said, her voice dreamy with the vision. "A trap set to catch a hare, I think."

"Where, Miss Georgina?" the child whispered.

"I—I'm not sure, Gracie." Trying to wash all thought from her mind again, Georgina held the picture of the clawing kitten and the wooden snare in her mind. Then, slowly, so as not to lose the picture she saw, Georgina let her thoughts range outward from the simple snare, to take in the surrounding field which led to a sluggish brook with stepping-stones across its width. "The brook which flows alongside Squire Trelawn's south boundary. Where the stepping stones go across. The snare is near there."

The child's eager voice brought Georgina back from the almost trancelike state in which she'd been.

"Is he all right?"

"I daresay he's hungry by now, if he's been gone two days. But take someone with you before you go to open that snare, Gracie. Whoever set it might not like to find you meddling with it."

"I'll ask my big brother to go along," Gracie promised, hopping up from her cozy seat in front of the fire. "And thankee kindly, miss."

She flew out the door, racing away to find her lost pet. Georgina was happy that she had been able to find Gracie's kitten for her. She'd been finding things for years, since she was about twelve. Georgina couldn't understand her gift, nor could her Papa explain it to her. She only knew that there were times when things disappeared and she was able to "see" where they were. Once word spread through Trindale, there were extremes of reaction. Some of the parishioners of St. Edmund's were scandalized and didn't hesitate to tell their vicar what they thought of his daughter's most unnatural behavior.

"You should beat her soundly with a strap," one old man had suggested. "Drive this devil out of your own child, Vicar Ryerston, else you'll never be able to drive him out of your flock."

But Papa was a kind, gentle man, not one to strap his child, nor to recommend that any child in his parish be beaten.

"The gift is not evil, Georgina," he explained when she came to him in tears because the other children had taunted her about her strange powers. "Use it only for good, and you need never worry about it."

"But Teddy Beacham called me a w-witch!" she'd wailed.

"Only because I told him he had not studied his catechism sufficiently," Papa said drily. "Ignore Teddy."

So, through the ensuing years, Georgina had become well known in Trindale for her strange gift of "finding." The ability was something over which she had no control. Perhaps half of the time, Georgina had no success. Those for whom she had found lost objects swore by her ability. The ones who came to her in vain were apt to say derogatory things about her, or to call her a witch. This disturbed Georgina a great deal, for the penalties for witchcraft were severe. She had no desire to be executed as a witch because she had the misfortune to be possessed of this uncanny ability.

"You aren't a witch, dear daughter," her father would always reassure her when he realized that she was worrying, or when he learned that yet another disgruntled member of St. Edmund's had accused her of being a witch. Then he would smile fondly, adding, "Someday you'll bewitch some young man, just as your dear mother bewitched me, but that is the nearest you'll ever come to being a witch."

With little Gracie happily on her way, she went back to her loom, struggling with the hateful job of dressing it, tying on the warp threads, making sure the tension was even and daydreaming the while to make time pass more pleasantly. The letter would come soon from this distant cousin. He must be as old as Papa. Would he have a daughter her age? Or perhaps a handsome son? Papa had not spelled out the closeness of the relationship, but Georgina assumed from what he'd said that the Earl of Margate was a very distant cousin, far enough removed so that there would not be any problem marrying the earl's son. Countess of Margate! How good that sounded, and if the earl were her father's contemporary, then his oldest son might well become earl before too many years passed. Oh, why didn't he write? Papa was so sure that he would, and that Peter Hardy, Lord Margate, would take her into his home and under his protection. The yarn made her fingers rough, and she hated the arduous work required in every phase of weaving. When she went to live at Hellingham, there'd be no loom for her to face each day, with only Sunday to rest. And lately, with the doctor's bills mounting, and the cost of laudanum for Papa, there were many Sundays when Georgina wove until exhausted.

CHAPTER 2

That night, wakened by her father's moans, Georgina struggled up from sleep. She was on a pallet in his bedroom so that she would hear him if he needed her during the night. Sometimes he talked during the dark hours. At times he seemed quite rational, at other times she knew that the drug was making him hallucinate.

She leaned over his bed to bathe his face, for he felt uncommonly feverish. He reached up and seized her wrist in a grasp as tight as the irons which were hammered onto the arms of pickpockets, a terrible grasp, brought on by his fever. These last few days usually found him as weak as Gracie's kitten.

"It was a true marriage!" he cried in a loud, terrible voice. "I wrote it down."

Not comprehending what her father meant, she tried to quiet him. "Yes, yes, Papa. Do not worry about it," she begged. She tried to loose his grasp on her wrist so that she could pour him a draught of opiate in some wine, but her father clutched her even tighter.

"May God forgive me, I should never have agreed," he said. "I profaned my holy calling. I went to make amends, when I saw the notice of his betrothal in the paper—but she had died. I—God help me—I kept quiet."

He fell back onto the pillow, his face a glistening sheen of sweat, and his fingers fell from her wrist. She thought surely he was dead, and she was glad he must suffer no more, but then his chest heaved, and breath rattled in his throat. In the morning he was weak but

17

lucid. He didn't mention the strange episode in the night, nor did she. Georgina was distracted from the things he had said by her usual tasks of weaving and caring for him, so she did not ask her father what his urgent cries had meant. Indeed she thought it all induced by the laudanum which he took in ever increasing dosages for the pain which now consumed his spirit as the tumor consumed his body.

And still no letter came from the Earl of Margate. There was, instead, an official letter from the Bishop of Exeter, informing the Reverend Mr. Jonathan Ryerston that, due to his prolonged illness, a new vicar was coming to minister to the needs of the parishioners of St. Edmund's. He would not, of course, displace Mr. Ryerston, but would assist in any way he could during these trying times. Georgina did not even show the letter to her father. He didn't need this final acknowledgment that he would not recover. It was bad enough that Papa was troubled that the letter did not come from Staines.

Finally, when Georgina knew that her father would not live more than another day or two, this terrible knowledge being confirmed by Dr. Jennings on his visit from Exeter, she decided that Papa must die in peace. When, his voice only a faint whisper, he asked, "Did the letter come?" Georgina looked him in the eye and lied valiantly.

"Yes, Papa, in today's mail."

"What did Peter say?"

"He says that I must come to Hellingham to live when—when—" Her voice broke, more from the lie than from sorrow. Papa would be at peace when he was gone; he now suffered so that Georgina could only pray that the end came quickly.

Papa asked no further questions, nor did he demand to see the letter. Obediently he swallowed the drugged wine and then he drifted off to sleep. This time he did not wake but lapsed into a coma from which

Georgina couldn't rouse him. Quickly she ran to the nearest neighbor and asked if Mrs. Wilkin's oldest son, Sam, could ride to Exeter for the doctor.

"He's going, Miss Georgina?"

She couldn't answer, only nodded.

"I'll come and keep watch with you," the plain, heavyset woman promised, "soon's I get Sam off to Exeter."

It was during the deathwatch that the new vicar, Mr. Owens, arrived at the vicarage. He was a kindly man who did his best to comfort Georgina, even assuring her that she might stay on at the vicarage until she could make other arrangements.

"Have you someone who will take you in?" Owens asked.

And Georgina, knowing full well that he had a wife and a large brood of children who would fill the vicarage to overflowing, assured him that she had a cousin who would give her a home.

It was a Tuesday, a fact Georgina had forgotten, in her vigil, and Adam Fenton arrived with the weekly consignment of wool for her loom. When the man realized that Ryerston's end was near, he tried to get Georgina to one side to repeat his offer of the cottage near Exeter—with himself as a bonus—but Georgina made sure that the Reverend Mr. Owens was with them at all times.

Finally, in frustration, Fenton left, promising Georgina that he would return on the morrow to inquire as to her father's condition.

The moment the vicarage door closed behind Fenton, Owens said, "I don't much care for that man, Georgina. Is he courting you?"

She gave a bitter laugh, too tired from nursing her father to dissemble. "Mr. Fenton is my employer, sir, and a much married man. He has made me a fine offer. When Papa dies—and Mr. Fenton can scarcely wait for the last breath to be drawn—he will move me into a cottage he owns on the outskirts of Exeter, and there I can work all day at my loom, weaving for him. And at night I can warm his bed."

"Georgina! That is scandalous. You aren't considering—" The poor man broke off in confusion.

She sighed. "Dear Mr. Owens, forgive me for being so blunt. I am weary to death, and I find that I say things best left unsaid. But what I have told you about Mr. Fenton is, unfortunately, the truth. Do not trouble yourself, though. I have no intention of accepting his offer. I should as leave take an adder into my bed as Mr. Adam Fenton."

"This cousin in Staines. He will give you a good home?"

Now that the fiction was started, Georgina had to go on with it. "He is a lord, sir. Papa wrote some time ago, when he realized that his illness was fatal. I shall be quite well taken care of, believe me. I will be leaving very shortly—just as soon as poor Papa is safely in his tomb."

In truth, Georgina was terrified of what the future held for her. Each day she waited eagerly for the letter from the Earl of Margate, but still it did not come. As she had told Owens she was going there to live, she would have to leave the vicarage soon. His entire family and all of his belonging would be arriving in a few days, and there would be no place for her here. Georgina knew that she would not live as Fenton's mistress. So she had no choice. She would have to go to Staines and throw herself on the mercy of this distant cousin. How else would she live? Now, early in the year 1737, Georgina began to realize how poorly prepared she was for life without her father's kindly hand. She could earn a meager living at the loom, but in the Exeter area, Fenton controlled all of the weaving. If she moved elsewhere, she might not find a job as a weaver. Being well educated—as Papa had been something of a scholar and he'd tutored her far beyond the normal education for a country parson's daughter—she might have tried to get a position as a governess to some lord's children, but Georgina did not know how to go about obtaining such a position. Her lack of formal schooling would make it difficult to obtain a job teaching in a young ladies' school. It was this education, though, which made Georgina sure that she did not intend to spend her life in Trindale, married to one of the local lads, trapped in the drudgery of being a poor wife to a poor laborer. No, she would go to Hellingham and present herself to the Earl of Margate, letting him know that, as kin, she expected him to look after her. It was a terrifying thought, but Georgina, looking at the alternatives, which included the odious Mr. Adam Fenton, was determined that she would better herself. The glamor of life in the dizzying circles of the nobility beckoned, and Georgina, weary to death of the clacking loom and the grinding poverty of life in Trindale, knew that she would conquer her terror and embark on this new phase of her life.

That night, during those hours when life seems to cling most tenuously, her father died, never regaining consciousness. An embalmer came from Exeter with his alcohol, his oils of lavender, camomile, and Venice turpentine. Georgina tried not to think of what was happening in the bedchamber upstairs, spending her time preparing the funeral repast. In the midst of all this activity, the heavy waggons came with Mrs. Owens and their brood, and their household possessions. Mrs. Owens, a motherly woman, walked into the kitchen and began helping Georgina without any ado.

"Mr. Owens wants you to know you are welcome to stay here until you can make arrangements to go to this cousin—where did he say, now?"

"Staines. Just this side of London," Georgina said.

"Such a long journey by coach. You can afford it?"

"Yes, I think so. I won't have need of money after

I get there," Georgina said, lying valiantly. "My cousin is well to do, I believe."

"A lord, my husband said." The country woman said it almost reverently.

"Yes, Earl of Margate. The estate is Hellingham."

"Imagine that. And this loom. Is it yours?"

"No, it belongs to a Mr. Adam Fenton, from Exeter. He provides the loom and the wool, and I was paid by the yard for my work."

"Is it difficult?" The vicar's wife looked at the monstrosity in the corner with eager eyes.

"Not too difficult to learn, but very tiring."

"Could my Marie learn? She's twelve. And the extra money would be such a help."

Georgina sighed, knowing all too well that feeling. "Children younger than Marie are weavers. Mr. Fenton comes on Tuesdays—although he may well come sooner, when he learns of Papa's death." Her mouth twisted with distaste. "Mrs. Owens, if you should let Marie take up weaving, be sure you are always here on Tuesdays when Fenton comes to collect the cloth and bring more yarn."

"Georgina! Marie is only twelve!"

"But a budding beauty, Mrs. Owens. And I know that old man. He's a lecher. And the fact that Marie is only twelve might not deter him."

All Georgina knew was that she must escape Fenton, even if it meant riding by stagecoach the width of England to get away from him. As soon as Papa was buried, she'd pack her few clothes and catch the London stage at The Bee and Thistle.

Papa was buried on a cold, blustery day in early February, with Mr. Owens reading the familiar words from the prayerbook. The tears on Georgina's cheeks nearly froze, the wind was so bitter out of the east. Adam Fenton was there, a crepe weeper conspicuous on his sleeve, but his concern was for the living, not the dead. He couldn't keep his lusting eyes from

Georgina's face, even during the prayer. The minute the graveside service had ended, and the first shovelful of earth hit hollowly on the pine coffin, he made his way through the crowd of parishioners to where Georgina stood with Mrs. Owens and her shivering children.

"Ah, poor, dear Georgina," he greeted her, making as to kiss her cheek.

Georgina, now adept at avoiding his unwanted caresses, hastily turned to the vicar's wife to introduce the owner of the loom, explaining to him that Marie, eldest of the Owens progeny, might want to learn weaving.

"Fine, you can teach her, Georgina. I can arrange to have you brought out from Exeter several times a week until little Marie is well versed in the techniques."

Georgina stared at him, her face as cold as the chill wind which plucked at his black tricorne.

"I shall not be available for teaching weaving," she said with authority. "My cousin, the Earl of Margate, has offered me a home, and I will be leaving for Staines as soon as I can pack."

"But—but—" he spluttered, "we had an arrangement."

Georgina smiled sweetly. "*You* had an arrangement, perhaps, but I did not ever agree to it. Good day, sir." She turned her back on him, not even inviting him to partake of the funeral meats laid out in the vicarage for the mourners.

Two days later, Georgina was ready for her great adventure. Out of the night, faint yet clear, came the lilting notes of "Blackeyed Susan" played skilfully on a brass horn.

"That's the stage, Miss Georgina."

She felt incipient panic at young Ned Owens's words. Already she could hear the pounding of hooves on the hard-packed road as the Exeter-London stage rattled toward The Bee and Thistle. It was cold and raw at six o'clock on this February morning. London seemed to Georgina to be as far away as the American Colonies. She'd never gone so far away from her home before. Once, when she was twelve, she'd traveled with Papa all the way to Bath for a special service at the Abbey to celebrate the coronation of George II. It had been an incredibly ardous journey by flying waggon, those great, lumbering, broad-wheeled conveyances which went at two miles an hour over the execrable roads. She and Papa had been on the road three days that trip, and it had taken four days to return, as rains had left the roads between Exeter and Bath a ribbon of mud through which they wallowed. Although she was not taking the coach for the entire run to London, riding only as far as Staines which was about seventeen miles this side of the great city, Georgina dreaded the journey.

Ned was pressing something into her hand. "Ma put bread and cheese in the basket for you, miss," he said shyly, "She says the inns may be terrible dear."

"Thank your dear, kind mother for me, Ned." As a vicar's daughter, she knew that even this modest lunch meant a sacrifice on the part of the new vicar's wife, for St. Edmund's was a poor parish and the vicar's salary hopelessly inadequate. Mr. Owens had been good to her, allowing her to stay on in her room until she'd made preparations for the journey. He had even offered to ride into Exeter to book a seat for her in the stagecoach, but she assured him that she could join the coach here at Trindale.

Now, clad in her mourning costume made from black serge woven on her own loom, her black traveling bonnet covering her pale hair, she snugged her heavy winter cloak of maroon wool closer about her neck. The damp cold chilled her feet, and she wished that she'd accepted Mrs. Owens's offer of a hot brick to keep her feet warm in the coach. She shivered, and Ned noticed.

"Soon you'll be snug inside the stage, miss."

As he said it, out of the gloom came the coach, side lamps aglow, showing the coachman in silhouette as he hauled up the team of four grays outside the inn.

She picked up her valise and stepped forward.

"Coach to London, miss?" the coachman asked.

Georgina was surprised at his accent, for he spoke as the gentry did, as a man of education, and not as most of the coacheys on the stage runs.

"I'm going as far as Staines."

He swung down off the high driver's seat, his long whip still in one hand. Now she saw that he was tall, and his shoulders were broad, made broader by the triple capelets on his heavy coat which came almost to his ankles.

"Ah, a charming addition to our little group!" and he made a leg, surprising her still further by sweeping off his black tricorne with a flourish, showing dark red hair pulled back with a black ribbon at the nape of his neck. "But," he added, "I have no passenger in the book to leave from The Bee and Thistle and travel to Staines."

"The book?" she asked in dismay.

"You haven't booked for the journey?"

"I—I didn't realize—I'm sure that passengers have gotten the coach here—"

The passengers on the roof of the coach shouted rudely, "Hurry it up, coachey! Do your courtin' some other time. Let's roll! It's mighty cold and uncomfortable here."

"But—I thought——I'm expected in Staines," she said for Ned's benefit. "Can't I book now?"

"Coach is full, miss," the handsome coachman said.

Now the guard, brass trumpet slung at his side, swung down from his own high perch. "What's up, Charlie? Another little beauty waiting to see you go by?"

Until now she had held up splendidly. Although

desolated by her father's death, Georgina had managed to hold herself together, even at the funeral. Now faced with this dismaying situation, the grief that she had successfully bottled up for days burst forth. Tears slid down over her cold cheeks and threatened to freeze into droplets of ice on her chin.

The handsome coachman whipped out a lace-edged kerchief from one of the deep pockets of his greatcoat and murmured, "Allow me, miss," as he gently wiped away her tears.

One of the coarse oafs on top of the mud-spattered coach yelled, "Turn off the waterworks, miss, and let the coachey get on with his job!" The rudeness of the remark stiffened her spine. When the fellow added, "You can bed down with him at the inn tonight, but let's get there first!" she was so indignant that the tears stopped flowing.

"Thank you, sir, but I am quite all right now."

"But what are we to do with you, eh?" The coachey turned to the guard. "Robin, me lad, she's a wee thing. Do you think we could squeeze her onto the box with us?" In an aside to her, he suggested, "A penny or two would help him make up his mind—and you can afford it," he added, "for it costs only half to ride outside."

This decided her, for she had little ready cash in her pocket. The coachman handed her up into the box, mounting after her, while Robin scrambled up on the other side after tying her valise and small trunk atop the coach. There was a heavy robe of tattered bearskin which the coachman pulled up over their laps.

Leaning forward, she waved to the shivering Ned, calling, "Don't wait, Ned. You'll freeze."

Beside her, the coachman picked up the reins, while on her other side, the guard put his brass trumpet to chilled lips. He blew one long, lingering note as the coachman whipped up the horses. As they passed beneath the archway from the inn courtyard, the sign, with its crude painting of a purple thistle head over which a garish yellow bee hovered, creaked in the fresh morning breeze.

She felt a mixture of emotions. She still grieved for dear dead Papa, she felt sad at leaving the village which had been her home for nineteen years; yet these feelings were underlaid with an excitement which Georgina couldn't prevent, and all of it was tinged with fear of the unknown. Staines was so far away in more than miles. She had no idea of the wealth of her cousin, but it must be considerable. He was a peer of the realm, Fourth Earl of Margate. Hellingham would be grander than the local squire's home, she was sure, and being so close to London, the society would be vastly more sophisticated than the people of Trindale.

Georgina was distracted from her musings by the gentleman coachey. "As we're to be such close associates for several days, may I introduce myself, miss? I'm Charles Collins, at your service. Our guard is Robin Adair, and we hope we have more need for his trumpet than for his blunderbuss."

Georgina had not been raised as strictly as many young women her age. Motherless, she had developed an independence not often seen in a young woman of her tender years. Because of her liberal upbringing, she did not remain aloof from the coachman, although in ordinary circumstances young women did not engage in conversation with such men.

"My name is Georgina Ryerston." In a few short sentences she explained her circumstances, the death of her father, and the fact that she was traveling to the estate of a "friend of Papa's from Oxford." She hesitated to say they were related, as the connection was so distant and the coachey might think her boastful.

"You are very fortunate, Miss Ryerston, to have been invited to live there," Collins said.

"His lordship hasn't exactly invited me. Papa wrote to him some weeks back, when he realized that he couldn't live much longer, for he was gravely worried about my prospects. We had not heard by the time Papa died. He was so worried toward the end that I'm afraid I bent the truth a bit and told him that his friend had invited me to live with him."

"What will you do if you find that you aren't welcome?"

It was a fear Georgina had been fighting for weeks. Perhaps the cousin had died. Maybe he wouldn't think he owed Papa a favor, even though poor Papa had been so sure of his ground. "He owes me—he must do this to make amends," she heard Papa mutter more than once. But Papa never told her what favor he'd done for his cousin, the earl.

As the coach jolted along over the badly rutted roads, her face got colder and colder. The passengers riding on top of the curved coach roof had to cling with frozen fingers to the securely strapped luggage.

"Takes a pretty face to ride in comfort," one complained.

A fat man grumbled, "We paid as much as she to ride on top, but she's snug and warm, while we freeze."

"If you don't like the service, you can leave my coach at the first inn we come to," Collins offered cheerfully.

"I'll protest to the coaching company," the fat man sputtered.

"Much good it'll do you, so don't bother. Handsome Charlie makes the Exeter to London run faster than any coachey on the line, and the owners know it. They'll not fire Charlie."

"I've heard that this coach makes it to London in three days. I do hope this is true," Georgina said.

The coachman hesitated just a fraction of a second before saying, "I've made it in three days."

"Not in February," the fat man chortled, "in the rain!"

"You're in a rush, miss? Don't like our company?"

"It's not that." She was embarrassed. "The quicker the journey—" She stopped short, not wishing to mention money.

"The quicker the trip, the thicker the purse, eh?"

Georgina smiled at Collins's understanding. Such a well-spoken man. In other circumstances, he could pass for a gentleman, even a peer. Yet here was this man of obvious education and good manners driving a common stage. She could ask him how this came about, but it would be unseemly to ask personal questions of a coachman.

He asked, "Are you tired, Miss Ryerston?"

"Travel is wearying, sir."

"Going to Staines, you say. Nice town."

"Actually the earl does not live in the town but on an estate outside the town limits."

"An estate outside Staines, miss?" the guard cut in. "And it's owned by an earl?" He leaned forward to ask the coachey, "That couldn't be 'ellingham, could it, now?"

"Hellingham? Oh, do you know it?" she asked eagerly.

"Do we know it! Why, Charlie, here, is—"

"That's enough gossip, Robin!" the coachman snapped.

Georgina felt that she was at fault for the reprimand. What had she said to turn the affable coachey into this stern, angry man? He sat beside her, eyes straight ahead, face grim, so different from his earlier pleasant demeanor. What was there about Hellingham to turn this man into someone else entirely? For the first time since she'd known she was to make her new home with the Earl of Margate, she felt fearful. But with the coachman in this strange mood, Georgina did not dare ask him, nor the guard, any further questions about Hellingham.

CHAPTER 3

They topped a rise, and as the guard hauled on the brake for the descent down the muddy, rutted road, a cheer went up behind Georgina. In the valley lay a tiny hamlet. The largest building was The King's Arms, the staging inn. Once he had the brake set, Robin lifted the long trumpet to his lips and played a rollicking tune. The team clattered up to the inn, a two-storied building of wattle and daub, the high-pitched roof thatched with the best reeds. The stables, similar but only one story high, were set at right angles to the inn, and the courtyard they formed was cobbled with local stone.

Robin hopped down from his perch to open the coach door. Now, for the first time, she saw the six who had been crowded into the airless body of the coach. The only woman, a buxom lady of middle years, looked positively green. The men who'd ridden with her hadn't fared much better. The passengers on the roof were clamoring for the wooden steps to be set for them, although one intrepid young man slid to the ground.

Collins said, "Allow me, Miss Ryerston." He swung to the ground, then reached up and lifted her as easily as if she were a doll. After the long, cramped ride, her legs almost gave way, and the coachman supported her with an arm about her waist, holding her more tightly than was necessary.

Moving away, she said formally, "Thank you, Mr. Collins."

There was a twinkle in his bright blue eyes as he assured her, "My pleasure, miss."

She followed the straggling group of travelers into the taproom of The King's Arms. The innkeeper, a wizened little old man, his apron far from clean, ushered her to a settle at right angles to the enormous fireplace and seated her with the woman who'd ridden inside the coach.

"How did you ever endure it outside?" the woman asked.

"The coachman was kind enough to allow me to ride on the seat between him and the guard, and they had a bearskin robe. I pulled my hood over my face and managed, but I must admit that this fire feels very comforting."

"Are you going all the way to London?" the woman asked. She patted her own face in dismay, imagining her makeup of white lead, caked in a thick mask, washing away in the rain.

"I'm only going to Staines. And you?"

"London." The woman sighed. "Such a long journey, but my daughter expects her first, and wants me with her." She took off her red traveling cloak, showing a dress of fine green wool, flounced on the skirt and trimmed with dark red velvet ribbon. Georgina recognized the superior quality of the cloth.

"Are you visiting—or off to a position in Staines?"

"I'm going to live with a friend of my father's. Papa just died."

"Sorry to hear that, miss, although I'll admit I did notice the mourning. Sad, sad. But you are a lucky young woman to have someone who'll take you in. Many in your shoes go off alone to London, hoping to find a decent position. And most of them end up at Moll Bailey's."

Not versed in the more worldly aspects of life in metropolitan London, Georgina asked innocently, "Who's Moll Bailey?"

"Who's Moll Bailey, indeed?" the loudmouthed passenger who'd ridden outside guffawed. "She's the most notorious brothel keeper in all of London, young miss. Surely you aren't going to the city to look for work with her!"

Georgina's companion patted her hand. "Don't pay attention to the likes of him," she said. "He's no gentleman. But the truth is, young women shouldn't go off alone to the city, for old Moll Bailey gets them in her clutches all too often. There are those who say she buys girls from unscrupulous blackguards who lure them to the city with lies of love and marriage. The young rakehells of noble birth use the poor servant girls in their own great houses, then take them to Moll in London to help pay off their gambling debts."

Georgina was beginning to realize that she'd led a very sheltered life indeed in the village of Trindale.

"As we're to travel together for several days, and no doubt sleep together at inns between here and Staines, I should introduce myself. I'm Mrs. Fenton—Mrs. Adam Fenton. Mr. Fenton's in wool—Fenton and Sons, in Exeter."

"What a small world! My name is Georgina Ryerston. My Papa was vicar of St. Edmund's in Trindale until his recent death. And I have been weaving for Mr. Fenton—your husband—for several years."

Mrs. Fenton looked at Georgina with narrowed eyes. "Your father just died? The vicar in Trindale? Do you have a sister?"

Georgina, puzzled at this strange line of questioning, assured Mrs. Fenton that she was an only child.

"It must have been some other vicar, then, and another daughter," the hefty matron muttered.

Georgina couldn't stand not knowing what this was all about. "I don't understand, Mrs. Fenton. Why do you ask if I have a sister?"

"My husband mentioned a poor young woman, whose

father had just died tragically, leaving her all alone, with no way to support herself, except by the loom. But he said you—she—had to vacate the vicarage for the new man."

Now Georgina was more confused than ever. Why would Fenton ever have mentioned her to his wife, when he planned to set Georgina up in his cottage in Exeter as his mistress?

"I did have to make room for the Reverend Mr. Owens."

"Have you heard of any other local vicar who died, leaving a lone daughter?" Mrs. Fenton persisted.

"No, I haven't."

"It couldn't be a coincidence." Confused, the woman's face was flushing so much that now the color showed through the heavy whiting she wore on her coarse skin. "But he told me you were a plain, homely girl——unattractive. He said he felt sorry for you and wanted to offer you the cottage at cheap rent, so that he could set up your loom there. As a kind of charity."

She bit off that last word as if it were a spoiled pheasant leg.

Now Georgina saw what the dastardly Mr. Fenton had been up to. He would tell his wife he'd rented the cottage to an unatractive woman for whom he felt sorry. But Mrs. Fenton had done Georgina no harm and had been pleasant and friendly, so she didn't want to inform her as to what a lecher her husband was.

"He generously offered me work and a place to live," Georgina acknowledged, ignoring all of the talk about a plain, homely young woman, "but my Papa had already made arrangements for me to live with this friend in Staines."

The look Mrs. Fenton gave her was disbelieving, but the woman said no more about the matter, perhaps thinking that the less said about her husband's charitable offer, the better.

Then Sylvester, the innkeeper, came with pewter

mugs of mulled wine and offered game pie. To save pennies, Georgina took only the hot wine and ate bread and cheese from her basket. All too soon Charles Collins made the rounds of the taproom calling, "All aboard the London coach. Horses are changed, and we're ready to roll. Drink up and pay up!"

"I do wish there was room for you inside, my dear," Mrs. Fenton said. "It must be beastly riding outside."

"Ah, ma'am, what a thing to say!" Collins joked. "She has the privilege of sitting alongside the handsomest coachey on the Exeter to London run."

The man continued to puzzle Georgina. He had all the earmarks of a gentleman. His manners were more suited to the drawing room than to the driver's box. His clothes, although not of fine fabric, were well cut, and he wore them with that nonchalant air which bespoke money. Yet he was only a driver, although he seemed to be a good one.

Apparently Mrs. Fenton was thinking similar thoughts, for she murmured to Georgina, "Very strange man, our coachey. Bit of a mystery about him. Some of the gentlemen are guessing he's a nobleman who's lost his fortune at the gaming tables in London. Oh, they do gamble wickedly there. Stacks of gold pieces wagered on a single game of whist! Or they bet on whether or not the criminals who hang in Tyburn go to their Maker with a smile or a curse."

"That's terrible!"

Mrs. Fenton's remarks about Collins gave Georgina food for thought. Brought up in a vicarage, her life had been sheltered in some ways and exposed to the coarsest side of life in others. She was used to the seamier aspects of life because of the constant stream of derelicts and sinners who came to the vicarage. Yet all this talk of losing fortunes on cards seemed tales from one of the naughtier novels which she occasionally read. Could her handsome coachman be a lord? Did you lose your title if you lost your money? *How naïve I am,* she thought. *I know nothing of life away from our village.* Then a horrid thought came to her, sparked by Mrs. Fenton's gabbling. Could Collins be one of the men who lured young girls to London and then sold them to the brothel keepers?

"Now what have I done, Miss Ryerston? You're looking at me as if I'd sprouted the horns of Satan," Collins joked.

"Oh!" Her cheeks grew warm. She must remember that her face always gave her away. "I'm sorry, my mind was—wandering."

He pulled a long face. "Did you hear that, Robin my man?" he said to the guard who had come to help the passengers back into and onto the coach. "She looks at my handsome face and her mind wanders. It's enough to make me want to jump off London Bridge." But Georgina saw the wicked twinkle in his blue eyes, eyes that glittered with mischief, and knew he was joking.

Once more seated on the box between Collins and Robin, Georgina steeled herself for the rigors of the trip. There was a dreary sameness to the road which lulled her into a kind of stupor. Then the clatter of horses' hooves on the rocks of the road alerted her, and the jolting reminded her that she was awake and uncomfortable. It was nearly dark, but with the rain, the sun had never come out at all. They passed a tiny thatched cottage, its shutters latched against the wet of the day. A gleam of candlelight showed through the chinks around its edges. Georgina might this minute have been in such a cottage in Exeter, awaiting the arrival of her new lover, had she been a bit more desperate. Poor Mrs. Fenton. Did she have any idea that her husband was unfaithful?

"How much longer?" Georgina asked Collins wearily.

"We're coming into Honeton," the coachey assured her. "Tired, miss? There'll be a hot meal waiting. The innkeeper expects us, so the mutton joint will be ready and the tea strong."

There was some traffic on the road now. A light gig passed them, and the driver, a natty gentleman, waved his whip at Charles, who greeted him in return.

Curious, she asked, "A friend?"

There was a moment's hesitation before he said, shortly, "I know him."

"Charlie knows all the dandies," Robin said slyly. "Nearly in now, miss. Soon you'll hear me blowing for the ostlers at The George, so they'll be ready to stable our horses. Have to make an early start tomorrow."

Georgina was now so fatigued that the thought of another day such as this, of jolting along the winter-rutted roads, of freezing in the rain, of being crowded on this seat which was made for two, not three, nearly overwhelmed her. No one had fallen off the roof of the coach, as frequently happened, but all levity was long since frozen out of the clinging outside passengers.

The cottages were closer together now and were interspersed with some two-story homes, some roofed with mossy slate rather than the ubiquitous thatch. Then Robin lifted his trumpet to blow the approach to The George. Even the hapless outside riders cheered. They clattered into the courtyard through an archway over which a room had been built, so that from the front the main inn building with its ivy-covered tawny brick façade joined in one piece to the stables. Gray slate gleamed dully near the lamps hung outside the oak door with its tiny panes of glass.

Good smells of roast mutton and beer made Georgina realize that she was famished. She made for the long bench beside a well-laden table, choosing a place as near the blazing fire as she could get. Mrs. Fenton seemed near collapse as she fell into the place next to Georgina.

"Everytime I go by stage to London, I swear it is

the last trip," she wheezed. "These roads are an abomination."

One man spoke up, his English accented so that Georgina had difficulty understanding him. "The roads in England are far superior to the roads on the Continent. Your coaches, also, are more comfortable."

"Comfortable!" the stout woman cried, incensed. "Sir, my poor backside is one solid bruise from a day's travel in one of these 'comfortable' stagecoaches."

Georgina was too tired and hungry to comment. When the maid set a plate of mutton and turnips before her, and poured beer into her pewter mug from a brown glazed pitcher, all she could think of was the exquisite pleasure of food and warmth.

Collins came stamping in then, calling out, "Mulled wine, Dolly, and fast!" to the serving girl.

"Charlie lad, I've heard a rumor about Hellingham," the landlord roared. "Fellow rode through yesterday. Says the old man won't be with us for long."

The word *Hellingham* caught at Georgina. Why would the coachman be interested in Hellingham? Here it was again, this mysterious connection. Robin Adair had hinted at it before. And who was the old man the landlord was referring to? Was he dying—or moving to some other place from Hellingham? Tired as she was, it was all a muddle in Georgina's mind.

CHAPTER 4

The stage left Honeton at six the next morning. Georgia had shared a narrow lumpy bed with Mrs. Fenton and hungry bedbugs in a tiny room under the slate roof. Bleary-eyed she swallowed hot chocolate, ate heartily of bread and jam, knowing it would be a long time to another meal. Only Collins seemed rested and eager to resume the journey. But, oh, how wearisome the trip became. Crows walked on the red Devon earth, flapping into the air as the coach rattled along the road. A weak sun shone giving little warmth but brightening their spirits. Mile after endless mile of rocky, muddy road rolled beneath the coach wheels. Collins came out of his reverie as they neared Chard to call Georgina's attention to Ford Abbey.

"It's been here since the twelfth century. Built by Cistercian monks. Lovely gardens, come summer."

"We stoppin' soon for a meal?" one of the outsiders called.

"We'll stop later, at The Dolphin, beyond Chard. I've had a complaint that we're not making good time, so it'll be longer between inns today, sir."

There was a chorus of groans at his answer, but one soul consoled the others with, "Then the time to London will be less!"

The Dolphin's half-timbered Tudor styling of honey-colored brickwork and tiny leaded panes of wavy glass might have seemed charming under other conditions. Now it was only a place to rest briefly from the torture of the road. As they ate the game pie and drank tankards of ale, the buxom serving maid, her dark hair

38

covered with a white mobcap, her bosom nearly exposed because of the low-cut neckline of her tightly laced gown, said, "Ah, Charlie, back again, I see." She was coy and bold all at once. "Have you met up with the highwayman who's been holding up stages between here and Sherborne? They say he's a wicked one with the ladies. Known to carry them off bodily."

"Wanton slut!" Mrs. Fenton murmured to Georgina. "Look at her throwing herself at the coachey's head."

"He doesn't seem to mind," Georgina said, the words coming out sharper than she intended as she watched Collins catch the girl about the waist and give her a kiss. What did it matter to her if their handsome driver dallied with a serving wench?

Mrs. Fenton, wiser in worldly matters than Georgina, gave her a discreet jab with her elbow and slyly smiled. "Lucky you, sitting up there by him all day long."

"All aboard," Collins called. "We're going to make Sherborne tonight, God willing and the horses able."

"You'll like Sherborne, miss," the guard confided as Collins cracked his whip and they creaked out of the courtyard. "Very old town. Two castles there, and an abbey church. Sir Walter Raleigh lived in one castle, they say."

But by the time they pulled into The Unicorn and Maiden in Sherborne long after dark, Georgina was past caring about anything except food and bed. Even the next morning it was too dark to see much of the honey-hued local stone which was used in the beautiful abbey church, and she couldn't see Raleigh's castle for the mist.

Collins was in one of his friendly moods and kept up a steady stream of chatter to her, with occasional joking remarks to the passengers on the roof.

"Shaftesbury is a lovely town," he told Georgina. "We'll have our dinner there at The Castle and Falcon. They do say old Henry the Eighth stopped sometimes at that very inn. Of course, every inn in England likes to make such claims. It's market day, so there'll be crowds of people in Shaftesbury. Maybe even a traveling troup of players."

Normally the prospect of such a treat would have been tremendously exciting, but as the miles ground away behind them, Georgina longed only for the end of the journey. Yet she knew that when she alighted from this stagecoach in Staines, it might be the last time she would ever see Charles Collins.

Silly goose, what do you care about a common coachman? Once settled in Hellingham, you'll meet the young lords of the area, the friends of your cousin, the earl, she told herself. But when Collins drew her away from the others at the inn where they dined on a haunch of venison, her heart beat so hard she thought he surely could hear it.

"Tonight we'll be in Salisbury, Miss Ryerston. We'll stay at The Red Lion, but there's another inn on New Street where I'd like to take you for supper. Two hundred years old, they say—half the age of The Red Lion. The roast goose there is the finest in England."

Now's the time to put this upstart in his place, she decided and then heard her own tongue accepting the invitation, ". . . although I am in mourning." Even to her ears it sounded hypocritical and self-righteous.

"Yet you must eat, even though you mourn your father. And more reason that we dine privately, away from the clacking tongues of the passengers."

Georgina wondered how she'd escape from Mrs. Fenton, but that good matron was so exhausted by the journey that she declared, while they dined, that she would retire to her bedchamber the moment they arrived in Salisbury.

Although Georgina still ached in every bone from the rough trip, somehow the afternoon did not seem to drag as had the morning. Supper with Charles Collins! It was wicked of her to accept his invitation. What would the Earl of Margate think of such wanton behavior? Well, he needn't ever know. When the coach reached Staines, it would be good-bye to Charles Collins, but until then, she intended to enjoy his company. What harm could there be in supping with him in a public inn?

They were still miles away from the town when she got her first glimpse of the towering spire of the Salisbury Cathedral silhouetted against the sunset sky.

"Reaches up to Heaven more'n four hundred feet," Robin confided. "Tallest church spire in all England."

Inspiring as the sight was, all Georgia could think of now was that Salisbury meant supper with Collins. Oh, what would Papa have thought, to find her so casually accepting invitations from such a fellow? Yet Collins had been the complete gentleman with her. Carefully she closed her mind to his easy manner with that serving wench at The Dolphin.

The gray stone heights of the cathedral dominated the entire town of Salisbury. The nearer the coach drew to the town, the more awesome was the towering mass of gray limestone, casting its long shadows over the cathedral close. By the time they threaded their way through the heavy carriage and chair traffic of the town, night had fallen, hiding the huge building from their eyes. What a far cry it was from the squat little Norman church of St. Edmund's in Trindale.

The sign of The Red Lion was on a standard which crossed the street, its crimson rampant beast well lit by lanterns. Once again Mrs. Fenton and Georgina were to share a room, to which that worthy matron retired immediately.

"The maid says she'll carry up some supper to me. I could not negotiate those spiral stairs again tonight. Dine well, Georgina."

"Thank you, Mrs. Fenton." No need for her roommate ever to know that she supped with the coachman.

For the first time since Papa died, Georgina had a

moment's rebellion at having to wear strict mourning. Her plain black gown was not very festive, but at least she could leave her black mourning bonnet in the bedchamber. She wished she could powder her hair, but the ever watchful Mrs. Fenton would ask too many questions. Well, if Charles Collins did not like her pale blond locks, he needn't have invited her to sup with him. Georgina slipped away from Mrs. Fenton in search of her escort of the evening.

Hesitantly she entered the taproom, not sure where she would find Collins. He always had to see that the ostlers took proper care of the horses, and that Robin brushed out the coach for the next day's journey. The taproom was crowded, for Salisbury, with its magnificent cathedral, was an important center of travel. Many pilgrims came to worship.

As if drawn by a magnet, Collins's eyes met hers immediately, and his smile was heart-melting. He made his way through the crowded room, exchanging greetings with a few other coacheys. Then he was towering over Georgina.

"I have a chair waiting, else you'd muddy those pretty little feet, Miss Ryerston."

Her eyes widened at this extravagance. For a moment she almost turned and fled back up the spiral staircase to the safety of Mrs. Fenton and their tiny room. If Collins was investing this much for the pleasure of her company at supper, what would he expect in return? Yet he was the most decorous of escorts, with tricorne tucked under his left arm, freeing his right hand which he extended palm down, so that she could lay her hand on his for support.

Collins handed her into a plain varnished wood chair, then kept pace with the bearers, although it was too hectic to try to keep up any semblance of conversation. The streets were a madhouse of traffic, with chaises pulled by high-stepping matched teams dodging in and out around the slower coaches and the heavy, lumbering waggons with their wheels so wide that they were useful in rolling the roads. The streets of the town were cobbled, but the rain which had made the roads into Salisbury seas of mud had helped that mud cling to carriage wheels and horses' hooves, so that the streets were almost as muddy as the country roads. Add to this the mounds of garbage, as well as the offal from so many horses, and Georgina had to admit that she was glad not to have her feet touch the cobbles.

It was only a short way to the other inn, a picturesque old-fashioned half-timbered building, listing drunkenly to one side. The sign showed a lurid, red figure of Lucifer cringing, wings half outspread, on a bed of glowing coals. The lettering spelled "Fallen Angel" for those who could read.

"They make a wonderful steak and kidney pie here," Collins confided after he'd paid off the chair, "as well as their roast goose." He led her through a heavy oak door scarred and darkened by the centuries into a cozy taproom with a beamed ceiling and two small leaded windows. There was a vacant table beside one of these windows, and when they were seated, Georgina saw that it overlooked the cathedral close. Collins kept up a steady stream of small talk while they ate the meat pie washed down with ale. The sweet was plum pudding, and he insisted that they have coffee with it.

It was during the last of their meal that Collins turned the conversation to Hellingham at long last.

"So the Earl of Margate is your late father's friend?"

That was when Georgina felt she should have owned to the truth, that he was her distant cousin, but something made her hold her tongue.

"That is why Papa, when he knew he could not live much longer, wrote to him, asking him to take me in." Georgina sighed, murmuring, "Perhaps the letter was lost."

"And you've never met the earl, or his son, Viscount Quincy?"

"Viscount Quincy? I didn't even know the earl had a son. Do you know him?"

Georgina was surprised and a little frightened at the look of hatred that flashed over Charles Collins's mobile face. What connection was there between this coachey and her cousins at Hellingham?

"Oh, I know the viscount. Francis Hardy. The earl's only son—only legitimate son, at any rate." Suddenly he reached across the table, catching her hand in his own, startling her by using her Christian name. "Georgina, watch out for Viscount Quincy."

Worried, now, she asked, "What do you mean?"

As quickly as the mood had come on him, it was gone. Collins gave her hand a squeeze, then loosed his hold on it. "Oh, pay me no heed, Miss Ryerston. It's just that young Francis fancies himself with the ladies."

Then there was a voice behind her, a man's voice, very genteel and affected. "As I live and breathe, if it isn't Charlie. Is that a coachey's coat, my good fellow?"

A long, ebony walking stick prodded Collins's many-caped greatcoat, the unofficial uniform of English coachmen.

Again she saw rage sweep across his face, to be erased in a moment by an arrogant, supercilious look.

"You know I've always handled horses exceptionally well, Amesford. Why else would your late father have hired me to teach—or try to teach—you to drive?"

Georgina heard a hiss of angry breath, and the man moved from behind her to a place beside their table, standing over Collins, his weak, dissolute face twisted with anger.

"You always were jumped up above your station," he sneered. He had one of those long, thin, overbred faces typical of a certain type of English nobility. His pale gray eyes were flat as slate with his rage. His powdered curls fell onto the shoulders of an elegant embroidered coat of pale blue, and Amesford's waistcoat was of a darker shade of blue, also embroidered in the same pattern. Fawn trousers were buckled at the knee with diamond-studded silver buckles, matched by similar buckles on his gleaming black shoes. A lace kerchief hung from one cuff, and his neckcloth was edged with lace of the same pattern. A fop. Georgina had read many romantic novels featuring just such a popinjay as this.

Now Amesford allowed those cold gray eyes to flick over her. It annoyed Georgina to be looked at as if she were merchandise in a shop, so she sat a little straighter, and let her face show just what she thought of this unpleasant man. To her great pleasure, she saw that this Amesford had gotten her message. A faint look of respect subtly changed his expression.

"My word, Charlie, how do you do it?" Now he was looking at her—really looking at her. "A barmaid wouldn't surprise me. I know your reputation with women. But this young lady—" He bowed prettily. "Your servant, ma'am. As Charlie won't introduce me, may I present myself? Howard Dubonnet, Marquis of Amesford."

She acknowledged his self-introduction with the tiniest inclination of her head but gave him no hint of a smile. She did not like this man. True, she had led a sheltered life as the daughter of a country parson; yet she'd met a wide variety of types which many young women would never encounter. Papa had been most conscientious in discharging the duties of his calling, dealing not only with the faithful of his parish but also with the sinners. As her father's hostess, she learned to recognize readily the less attractive characters.

Collins did not give Georgina's name to the marquis, nor did she. He did not, however, take the hint. Instead he said, a shade too heartily, "Aren't you going to invite me to join you and your charming companion, Charlie?"

For one terrible moment she thought her escort might do physical harm to Amesford, but he controlled himself.

"We're just leaving," he said, his voice curt.

"What a pity. I'd thought I might fill you in on the latest gossip from—home."

Georgina hadn't the slightest idea what Amesford was talking about, but she could see that Collins knew. She saw, also, that he was interested in what the young marquis had to say, although he affected disinterest.

"My home's now on the Exeter Road," Collins said. The bitterness in his voice puzzled her, for he'd seemed quite happy, content with his lot as coachman for the stage. But there was the matter of his well-bred accent, his air of having known better times.

Now the Marquis of Amesford laughed, almost a sneer. "So the son isn't as lenient as the father! Well, what did you expect, Charlie? He's learned to hate you over the years. And why not? All he had was the name. You had everything else the old man could offer."

Georgina saw that Collins's fists were clenched at his sides. Rather than have this nasty character provoke him into starting a tavern brawl, she rose quickly, suggesting, "It's getting late. Perhaps we should go back to the inn."

Amesford caught up her cloak and gallantly wrapped it about her shoulders, letting his hands linger so that she felt obliged to move quickly to avoid his touch. Then Collins was by her side, crowding the smaller man to one side. He took her arm protectively, leading her through the crowded taproom, yet the marquis was right on their heels, standing by while Charles paid their bill.

It was at this moment that the women at the table nearest to them screamed loudly, "Me brooch! It's gone! Me gold brooch what was me mum's."

Attracted by the loud shouts, Georgina and the two men turned to see what was wrong. There was a long trestle table with a group of men and women sitting there eating. Georgina was beginning to learn the look of travelers, so she identified the motley crew as passengers from one of the stagecoaches. The woman who was making such a racket was perhaps in her late twenties, plump as a partridge, her dark hair neatly dressed and covered with a very full mobcap. Her gown was of better quality than some of the others at her table, being of heavy silk, dark blue, with a bit of lace at the neck and elbow. She was clasping a plump hand to her bosom where, Georgina supposed, the gold brooch had been pinned.

"Maybe it fell to the floor," one of the men in her party suggested, and immediately several of the group started crawling about the table and benches, lifting the flounces of the ladies' skirts without so much as a by your leave.

Charles Collins was urging Georgina to walk out, but she had an overriding compulsion to stay there. Almost without conscious volition, she moved closer to the woman who now was sobbing loudly, declaiming over and over that it had been a gold brooch, very valuable.

"Madam, may I take your hand?" Georgina said to her. No one was more startled by this request than Georgina, herself, for until the words were said, Georgina had no idea that she was going to say them.

Startled out of her histrionics, the woman looked round-eyed at Georgina. Apparently there was something in Georgina's face which commanded obedience, for the distraught woman held out one plump hand which Georgina clasped tightly. Then Georgina stood there, eyes closed, and let the images wash over her mind. This was one of the times when her gift of "finding" was working. First she saw the brooch the woman had lost.

"Is the brooch about an inch long, and half again as wide, with something . . . a stag? . . . on it—raised? And a border about it all like an ornate picture frame?"

"That's it! Me mum's brooch!"

Two others at the table were nodding vigorously, one older woman muttering about having noticed it at dinner that midday.

Another picture was forming in Georgina's mind now: a coach, large and mud-spattered, with lettering which she couldn't read on the door. And then it was as if she were inside the coach, jolting along on a terribly rough road, so that she had to cling to the sides, holding on wherever she could wedge her fingers, to keep from being hurled onto the floor.

"The brooch fell off during the trip in the coach," Georgina said as the pictures kept coming into her thoughts. "It fell—it fell into—there was something there—a basket?"

The older woman, the one who'd remembered the brooch, cried, "I 'ad a basket on the floor, tucked in by me skirts."

The woman who'd lost the brooch snatched her hand away from Georgina and said, "Look in it, granny. Is it there?"

Once the woman's hand was taken away, all of the pictures were gone from Georgina's mind. She was terribly tired, as so often happened after she'd found something this way. Feeling faint, she fumbled in her pocket for a small vinaigrette of smelling salts she carried, and sniffed quickly to revive herself.

At her elbow, Collins urged quietly, "Let's get out of here. Quickly, before they turn this into a carnival."

He wasn't quick enough, though, to forestall a few shouts of, "Trickery! They made it up beforehand!" and from somewhere across the room, one ugly word, "Witch!"

Trembling, Georgina allowed Collins to hurry her out of the taproom to the inn court where the fresh air helped to restore her, although her head ached abominably.

Behind her, the marquis said, "My dear young lady, you should have waited a moment for them to throw pennies. That was a remarkable performance."

Georgina shuddered, wishing the gift would never come again, for it was more of a curse to her than a pleasure.

Collins seemed to understand her feelings, for he looked about at once for a chair. There was a gilded sedan chair with a coat of arms blazoned on the door waiting in the courtyard. As the trio neared it, the bearers sprang to attention.

"May I offer you my chair?" the marquis asked.

Just then Collins saw an empty chair and signaled, those bearers swinging toward them.

"Thank you, no," Georgina said to Amesford, her voice cold and distant. She got into the hired chair without a farewell to the marquis.

Collins motioned for the bearers to move on, but Amesford had the last word.

"The old man's dying, you know, Charlie. Soon the earldom will pass to his—son!" He laughed so loudly that people in the courtyard of The Fallen Angel turned to look.

The chair was an open one, and Georgina had not drawn the curtains. She could see Collins's bleak face by the light of the many torches borne by linkboys to light the way for the ladies and gentlemen in chairs. She wondered what Amesford's message had meant to her escort. Why would the death of some earl affect a common coachman? No, not common. That was wrong. Charles Collins might be a coachman, but common he was not, nor could he ever be.

Georgina wished she could reach out, touch him, comfort him, but of course such action was out of the question.

Finally, she wondered if the earl Amesford had

spoken of could be the Earl of Margate. If so, if he were near death, what would be her fate at Hellingham? And why didn't Collins tell her, if this were the same man? He knew her destination, her situation. A pall fell over her evening. There were things about Collins which she did not understand. Although he was vastly attractive, in truth she knew almost nothing about him. For the first time, she realized what an appallingly naïve and stupid thing it had been for her to accept his supper invitation so eagerly.

Now he strode along beside the chair, not even glancing at her, lost in his own thoughts. First, Amesford's intrusion, then the "finding" experience, now this change of mood in her escort. What had started out to be an exciting evening had turned into a minor disaster.

CHAPTER 5

If Georgina had expected her private supper in Salisbury to lead to anything, she was mistaken. On the road once more, Collins was just the coachman. There certainly was no opportunity for questioning him about their encounter with the unpleasant Marquis of Amesford. He did bring up the episode with the lost brooch.

"I've heard of 'finders' before, Miss Ryerston." He was back to formality; there was no "Georgina" today. "I must admit that you are the first one I've ever seen practice it though, and it did seem to be work for you. You looked exhausted after you'd found that gold brooch for the woman."

Georgina thought about that. "It is tiring," she admitted, "although I've never before thought of my gift as work. It's just—something I can do sometimes."

Robin Adair, who'd heard about what had happened, asked her, "Can you find anything that's lost?"

"Oh, no. I never know before I try—maybe half of the time I'm able to see where the object is. Not always. And sometimes the picture is so dim, or so distorted, that I cannot interpret it." She shuddered. Georgina didn't like to talk about this unwelcome talent.

"People must be very grateful to you when you find something for them. Do you—do they—pay you?"

This shocked Georgina. "I could never charge for finding anything. Papa explained to me, when my gift became apparent, that it was just that—a gift—and I must use it only to help others, and that I must never charge them for that help." She had to add, though, honestly, "Sometimes they give me something—and I've learned to accept that. If I don't, they feel beholden to me, and sometimes, later, they are unfriendly."

Collins nodded. "No one wants to be owing another."

They rode in silence for a time, then Collins said, as if they'd kept on with the conversation without pause, "Sometimes people get ugly with you about your talent, don't they, Miss Ryerston?"

"Yes, I fear that they do." She remembered too many instances.

"And they call you a witch?"

"Sometimes. You heard the man at the inn last night."

Apparently one of the passengers, ears stretched to the limit, was trying to hear their conversation.

"What's this about a witch?" he called. "Say, Charlie, don't tell me that your lovely companion has bewitched you?"

And the coachey, his usual debonair self, turned, smiled, and said, "Wouldn't she betwitch you?"

The fat man cautioned, "All witches aren't old and ugly, coachey. Some are young and beautiful. They're the ones you'd best watch out for. Sleep with the devil, they do. And drag any mortal man who consorts with 'em down to hell."

Georgina, despite the cold rawness of the day, felt her cheeks burn with embarrassment.

Collins, his ready smile replaced instantly with a cold, deadly look which turned his merry blue eyes to ice, said, "No more talk of that kind in front of a lady, sir, or I shall stop this coach on the road and heave you off into the mud."

The fat man muttered, but he kept his remarks quiet enough so that Charlie couldn't hear the words.

Adair, his manner warm and sympathetic, leaned close to Georgina to murmur, "So that's what it's like for you? I'll bet you wish you never found nothin', right, miss?"

"I often think of it as a curse, not a gift."

After the exchange with the boor on top of the coach, Collins lapsed into a pensive mood for the rest of the day. Even Robin noticed it and later mentioned it to Georgina in private.

"I'm sorry, miss, not meaning to pry, but a lot depends on the coachey on these runs. If Charlie's out of sorts, it helps if I know about it. Charlie's the best on the line, but he has his moods. And it's no wonder, considering."

She was at a loss to know what to say. Why should Robin Adair question her? How would she know of Collins's moods? And what did he mean by that last odd remark?

Then Collins called, "Blow the trumpet, Gabriel. Time we were on our way. London and its pleasures await us."

When they stopped for dinner at The Old Cock Inn at Andover, Robin maneuvered Georgina to one side. "Wouldn't want Charlie to know I was inquiring into his business—nor you, miss—but I couldn't help but see you go off together in Salisbury."

"He took me to supper at The Fallen Angel."

"Did anything untoward happen? He's been in such a mood—"

As Robin had been included in their discussions of the "finding" episode in Salisbury, she knew he wasn't referring to that as something untoward which had occurred.

"We encountered a thoroughly unpleasant young blade." Her mouth pursed as if she'd eaten a green persimmon. "The Marquis of Amesford. He seemed to know Mr. Collins."

"That'll be it. Young rakehell, if you'll pardon me, miss. His father came over from France years ago. The old marquis let him run wild. He was killed in a hunting fall, the father was, and the young one inherited. A bad fellow." Then, conspiratorially, "But what did he have to say to Charlie to make him so glum? Or did the marquis play up to you, miss?" He grinned knowingly.

"He's not the type of man I admire," Georgina said primly. "As to what he said, I didn't understand it at all. He twitted Mr. Collins about being a coachman." Georgina smiled, remembering. "Mr. Collins put him in his place."

"I should think so, miss! The marquis has a heavy hand with horses. Did he mention—anything else?"

"He did mention that someone—an earl—was dying, as if it might be of interest to Mr. Collins."

Adair sucked in his breath. "So that's it," he muttered.

She could control her curiosity no longer. "What is this all about, Robin?"

Before Adair could answer, Mrs. Fenton came around the side of the coach. "Ah, there you are, Miss Ryerston. I have been waiting for you."

"I'm coming, Mrs. Fenton," she said, trying to sound enthusiastic, but not succeeding too well.

"My dear, your mother has been dead a long time, hasn't she?" Mrs. Fenton asked when Georgina was by her side.

"Yes, but—"

"I thought so. And no older sisters? No aunt to raise you? No grandmama?"

On the defensive, recognizing the tone if not the reason for it, Georgina said, "Papa raised me, madam, with care."

"Of course, my dear. My, this heavy oak door. . . ."

Georgina opened the heavy door into the taproom. The inns were beginning to run together in her mind, now. All the serving girls looked alike with their rosy cheeks and plump, bare arms, their sparkling eyes and saucy smiles. And they all liked Charles Collins!

Mrs. Fenton led her to a small table near the fire. "Ah, it warms my old bones." Then she turned to Georgina, her face sober. "When I saw you were traveling alone, my dear, I was worried; a young woman alone on the road is prey to all kinds of unpleasant characters."

Georgina knew this tone all too well. There had been several good ladies in Trindale who, feeling that she needed a woman's hand in her upbringing, gave her unwanted advice on every possible occasion. She was nineteen, a grown woman. Why shouldn't she be able to make her own decisions? Why be badgered by a chance acquaintance—particularly one whose lustful husband had tried his best to ruin her? Ah, wouldn't Mrs. Fenton smart if she told her that!

Aware of Georgina's resentment, Mrs. Fenton said, "I have a daughter just a few years older than you. I raised her very strictly. Now she is married to a good man, but if a young woman is not careful of the company she keeps, she can ruin her reputation. Once ruined, there's no mending it. This coachman—my dear, you must not become familiar with him. He is beneath your station."

Stung to speech, Georgina snapped, "If it weren't for his kindness, I'd be hanging onto the roof of the coach."

"I'm only trying to help. You young people—no respect for your elders these days."

Georgina didn't like to quarrel. "I'm sorry, Mrs. Fenton, if I spoke unkindly. I am so very tired. . . ."

"True. As am I. But not too tired to give you needed advice. This Collins—how do you know he doesn't augment his pay as a coachey by luring young, unattached women to London, selling them to Moll Bailey?"

"Oh, that's a wicked thing to say!" Georgina was even more vehement than she might have been because she'd thought just such things about Collins

earlier. "He's been a perfect gentleman the entire
trip."

"Even when he took you off somewhere last evening?"

Not deigning to ask how Mrs. Fenton knew of her
supper engagement, she struck back, pandering to her
companion's inherent snobbishness. "Mr. Collins knows
some very important people, Mrs. Fenton. While at
The Fallen Angel last evening, I met the Marquis of
Amesford, one of his acquaintances."

"A marquis? You're making this up."

"I don't lie, Mrs. Fenton. The man obviously knew
Collins well, for he chatted for some minutes with
him—and me."

"No doubt Collins said the man was a marquis to
impress you."

"As a matter of fact, the marquis, himself, gave
me his rank and name."

"An imposter! Ah, Georgina, you are so gullible."

"If you had seen the diamond buckles on his
breeches and shoes—or the coat of arms blazoned on
his gilt sedan chair—you'd not doubt my word, Mrs.
Fenton. Who knows, he may even be acquainted with
my cousin, the Earl of Margate. Of Hellingham. Near
Staines. Where I'm going to stay." There! That would
put Mrs. Fenton in her place forever. Yet Georgina
immediately regretted telling the lady her secret, which
she had so far kept hidden even from Charles Collins.

"You never mentioned that you were kin to an
earl."

"You never asked me." The barmaid had brought
tankards of ale, and Georgina had drunk hers much
too fast, so that it went to her head. Why else would
she be making such outrageous remarks to kindly but
nosy Mrs. Fenton?

"I suppose you're going there as a—a governess. Or
a companion. Poor relations get such positions when

they are forced to rely on wealthy kin for their living."
Mrs. Fenton obviously relished putting her down.

Thoroughly angered now, and feeling the heady
brew, Georgina said, "No, my cousin recruits young
women—attractive young women—for the notorious
Moll Bailey. I'm sure he'll find me suitable."

If she thought she'd gotten the best of her companion, Georgina was mistaken. First the older woman
ate, mopping up the juice from the roast beef with her
bread. Then, while waiting for the sweet, Mrs. Fenton
said, "I know you are just joking with me, Miss Ryerston. But you should be careful with that tongue.
There are some who might not realize you are just a
young lady full of high spirits—and ale—and believe
you. In polite society, Moll Bailey and her profession
are not mentioned—and certainly not jested about by
ladies."

"Yes, Mrs. Fenton." Georgina looked about guiltily,
hoping that no one else had heard her rash statements.

"You were telling me about this Earl of Margate.
Your cousin, you say?"

"Truly, Mrs. Fenton. My father entrusted me to
his care when he knew he was dying."

Mrs. Fenton said, "It's hard to be left alone in this
world. I'm glad that you have someone to care for
you." She made no further mention of menial jobs
doled out by rich relatives to poor orphans.

Her earlier unkind remarks stayed in Georgina's
mind, though. Was that to be her fate? Until today
she'd thought of living at Hellingham as a lady, surrounded by wealth, dressed in satins and lace, courted
by eligible young lords. How she wished that there
had been an answer to Papa's letter. What would she
do if they were not expecting her? Or, worse still, if
they had received Papa's letter, but had chosen to
ignore it, not wishing to be saddled with some poor,
distant cousin? She shuddered at the bleak prospect.

Georgina woke next morning to the sound of rain

pouring down on the slates and beating against the tiny window. Today would be sheer misery. Even before they pulled out of the yard of The Boar's Head here in Basingstoke, the road was a ribbon of mud embroidered with rain-slicked stones. The coachey was in fair humor for so foul a day, but the poor miserable souls on top of the coach clung doggedly in grim silence, enduring.

Finally Georgina plucked up enough courage to ask Collins, "When will we reach Staines?"

Collins shrugged, the capelets of his greatcoat scattering droplets of water onto her cloak. "Depends on how hard it rains and how deep the mud gets, miss. I hope to make London tonight, but it might well be tomorrow before we see The Bull and Mouth in St. Martin-le-Grand." Then, quietly, so that even Robin Adair couldn't hear him, Collins added, "I've been worrying about you, Miss Ryerston. You say you've had no answer from Hellingham, so you can't be sure they're expecting you. Will you be all right?"

"I'm sure I shall." Was he hinting that her cousin might deny her sanctuary? There was something here she didn't understand. Maybe he'd worked at Hellingham, and her cousin had dismissed him. She couldn't picture Collins kowtowing to any lord. Probably he'd been the earl's coachman. Yet she dared not ask him anything.

"Miss Ryerston, be careful there. I can't come to Hellingham for various reasons. But if you should ever need me, you can reach me by leaving a message at the inn near the estate. It's called Ye Grape. Just tell the innkeeper to deliver a letter to me. He's honest —and discreet."

"It's kind of you, Mr. Collins, but I don't expect trouble."

"I hope you get none. Yet sometimes, when we're alone in the world, it helps to know that there's someone who is available to help." Then he flashed that devastating smile. "And I'm available, Miss Ryerston."

Georgina was touched, for under the brashness, she sensed sincerity, a good quality in any man. "Thank you, Mr. Collins. You have helped make a long, hard trip bearable."

It was dark when they drove through Staines. "Where are you planning to stop, Miss Ryerston? In Staines? Or at Ye Grape?" Collins asked. "Or—we drive right past the gates of Hellingham. I can drop you there, if you think it is advisable to arrive unannounced."

All this talk of not being expected bothered her. Collins seemed to have knowledge of Hellingham which he didn't impart to her, although he kept hinting that things might not be well with her there. It was possible that he had a grudge against the Earl of Margate for something which had been Collins's own fault. Well, the earl was her blood kin. Collins was a stranger. She would give Hellingham a fair trial. Perhaps all of these oblique references to undefined problems were attempts to lure her away from the safety of her cousin's house, tempt her to London. Georgina knew enough of the world to have a healthy suspicion of a glib man. She had no intention of winding up in a London brothel, sold there by a charming rogue!

"Thank you. I shall take you up on your offer to drop me at Hellingham Mr. Collins. On such a rainy night, the nearer I get to my destination, the better."

Georgina knew from his silence that he disapproved. Well, let him. She was a grown woman, and could make decisions without the help of a stagecoach driver.

"How soon?" she asked.

"Less than an hour even in the rain."

The rain came down harder than ever, and she was miserable. She felt hot tears mingle with the cold raindrops on her face. Why was she crying? The seemingly endless trip was nearly over. She'd soon be surrounded by the kind of luxury she'd only read about. But why the tears? Surely not because of Charles Collins. Yet in her secret heart, Georgina had to admit that this handsome coachman was the most exciting man she'd ever met—the only man she'd met who made her heart beat faster just sitting beside him. The air of mystery surrounding Collins only added to his attractiveness. She'd met no one in Trindale who interested her at all. Adam Fenton, the only man who had made overtures to her, was absolutely repulsive. She had decided, when she found out that there was an earl who was a cousin, that she would find a handsome, rich lord with whom to fall in love. Her future would be full of luxury such as she'd never known. Georgina still wanted these things. Why, then, was she attracted to this coachman? What kind of life was that, always on the road between London and Exeter? She must be mad to be unhappy that the journey was nearly at an end. Georgina remembered all of the brazen serving wenches at the inns the past days, how they hovered about Charles Collins like bees around clover. And he didn't mind their attentions. Why would she want such a man as that, with her prospects just now showing great promise? She was a fool to think about him further.

Then there was a light ahead, on the left, and Collins pulled hard on the reins, slowing the horses to a walk.

"The gatehouse at Hellingham."

"Is this an inn, coachey?" one passenger asked.

"Not likely," Adair answered. "It's the grand house of the Earl of Margate. Not for the likes of you."

"Then why're we stopping?"

"The young lady is going to Hellingham."

"Say, miss, have you a position there?" one bold young fellow asked. "Housemaid, maybe? Wonder if they need a footman? I'm so cold and wet I'd rather stop here than go on to London."

The coach was now stopped in the road directly in front of high, ornate, closed gates of intricate iron grillwork set under a massive brick arch with a marble carved coat of arms as keystone. Georgina could see in the dim light a bird, perhaps a falcon, on the shield. The gatehouse was built right into the wall.

"Get her cases, Robin." Collins ordered as he swung down from the high seat and reached up, for the last time, to help her down. At his touch, Georgina caught her breath. She wanted to throw her arms about his neck and beg to stay with him, to go on to London in the rain, just to be able to spend more time with Collins. It was madness, and she knew it, but for one moment, she almost gave in to her rash impulse. Fortunately, it was a momentary thing, which soon passed. Georgina turned resolutely away from Collins, facing her new home.

The guard handed down her luggage, but Collins left the cases standing on the muddy road. "I'll have Robin take you to the gate, and summon the keeper," he muttered. "Robin! Hurry it up. Miss Ryerston will be soaked. Ring for the gatekeeper, there's a good man."

The wag on top of the coach called, "Did you say this great place is called hell, miss?" The outsiders guffawed at his wit. "Men, we're at the gates to hell," he went on. "Didn't know you'd been riding the coach to hell, did you?"

Then Robin was beside Georgina, picking up her cases.

"Goodbye, Miss Ryerston. Remember—Ye Grape, if needed," Collins said quietly so that Adair couldn't hear him, taking her hand in his for one thrilling moment.

"Thank you, Mr. Collins. It has been an interesting

journey." She would not cry, she would not! Resolutely she turned away from the exciting coachman.

Then there was a call from inside the coach. "Miss Ryerston—farewell! I trust all goes as you hope at Hellingham."

"Thank you, Mrs. Fenton. And with your daughter."

Then Robin led her to the heavy iron gates where he rang the bell. For a long moment Georgina thought that no one was coming. Soon a door in the gatehouse opened, and the keeper hurried out, pulling his hat down about his ears to keep off the rain.

"Yes?" he grumbled, not unlatching the gate.

"Miss Ryerston to see his lordship, the Earl of Margate," Georgina stated clearly, in a tone of authority.

"You was expected, miss?"

"I have written of my arrival." Well, it was only stretching the truth a little. Papa had written, but she had no way of knowing whether or not the earl knew she was about to appear on his doorstep.

Finally, reluctantly, it seemed, the man creaked open the heavy gates, and Georgina stepped through to Hellingham.

CHAPTER 6

The saucy maid, saying something about finding Mrs. Pruning, left Georgina standing in the enormous hall. Wet, bedraggled, Georgina felt overwhelmed by Hellingham. From the outside it had seemed huge and gloomy, the red brick dark with rain, heavy with twisted vines. Once through the great carved double doors, her senses were stunned by the size of the hall. Although only a few candlestands had lighted wax tapers, so that the high, vaulted ceiling and the corners of the room were in deep shadow, the highly polished blocks of white and black marble which made up the floor caught and reflected the flickering flames. On the long wall opposite the entrance a small fire burned in a huge fireplace.

Chilled through. Georgina tiptoed across the seemingly endless checkerboard to the welcome warmth of the fire. The chimneypiece was of pale tan marble, with carved busts of classical figures flanking the fire. Above the marble was a shelf of carved oak, more intricately designed than the oak paneling which lined the entire room. At one end of the room was a minstrel gallery, with delicately carved wood fretwork hiding the interior. Georgina shivered. It was a cold, forbidding room, not lightened by the faded Brussels tapestries hanging on the walls from the high ceiling.

A shrill yapping announced the entrance of a fat little black spaniel who came padding into the room, nails clicking on the checkered floor. Georgina, who liked animals, bent to pet the dog, but it snarled at her and looked up with rheumy eyes before snuffling at her draggled skirt.

The sound of heels tapping on the marble floor made her look up from the curious dog. A woman entered, walking quickly across to Georgina. She was middle-aged, her hair drawn off her ears, with tight little sausage curls on either side. Tall, very thin, with facial features sharp as a hawk's, the woman said, "Come here, Puffy." Staring down at Georgina, she added, "He's getting old, and often he doesn't take to strangers." Then, giving Georgina a long, intent look, she said, "Lizzie said you were asking for his lordship."

The woman, in her gray ribbed silk with lawn fichu and apron, a frilled lawn pinner on top of the gray, unpowdered hair, was probably the housekeeper.

"I sent a letter—"

"His lordship is ill. If Viscount Quincy received your letter, he did not inform me." Her hard green eyes looked Georgina up and down. "You appear to be suitable. Have you had experience in caring for the elderly ill?"

Her heart fell. Mrs. Fenton had been right. She was being taken in only as a poor relation, to nurse someone—certainly not the earl!

"Well, miss, what have you to say? We can't tolerate a simpleton. His lordship has periods of lucidity and when that happens, he insists on a companion who can read to him and converse with some intelligence. You can read?"

Incensed, Georgina spoke more sharply than she intended, so that the spaniel, whose unpleasant smell now filled her nostrils, growled again and snapped at the hem of her gown. Mrs. Pruning's eyes widened with shock as Georgina announced, "Of course I can read. French, some German, Latin, and even a bit of Greek. My father was only a village parson, but he went to

Oxford with his lordship, and saw to my education himself."

At the mention of Oxford, Georgina detected a slight thawing in the frosty Mrs. Pruning.

"I hadn't realized—most remiss of his lordship— he must have forgotten to show me the letter, but with the earl ill—responsibility rests heavy on a young gentleman."

So she wasn't expected. At least by the housekeeper.

"Very well then Miss—Ryerston, is it? Come along. The earl is asleep for the night. We must give him a sleeping draught, you understand. I shall show you to your room. In the morning, I'll see to it that you meet his lordship if he is lucid. You won't do the actual nursing. We have village women to do that, and one who sleeps in for nights. But his lordship will be your responsibility."

As tired as she was, Georgina didn't try to explain who she was. Tomorrow would be soon enough.

"Would you like some supper, Miss Ryerston?"

"That would be lovely. I'm quite exhausted."

"And very damp. How did you get here at such an hour?"

"The stage from Exeter. The coachman left me at the gates when he found I was coming to Hellingham."

"Extraordinary!" Mrs. Pruning frowned as if puzzled. "The coach from Exeter. You have traveled that far?"

"Almost. Trindale is about an hour this side of Exeter."

With a shrug of bony shoulders, Mrs. Pruning said, "We can sort it all out tomorrow, I suppose. Leave your bags," she added as Georgina started to pick up the smaller case. "One of the footmen will bring up your cases. You'll be in one of the lower tower rooms. His lordship is in the top suite."

Georgina followed the sweep of gray gown across the marble floor into a dimly lit corridor. At the end of this long hall was a spiral staircase so narrow that she had to tilt her hoops slightly to follow Mrs. Pruning up and up, with Puffy scrabbling along behind them. Finally Mrs. Pruning opened a door and Georgina found herself in a tiny vestibule with two doors opening off it.

"Your room will be this one. The night nurse has the other, smaller, chamber." The housekeeper opened the door and ushered her into a curiously shaped bedchamber. The room was more than half a circle, with the inner wall a very small arc to allow for the stairwell. There were three long, narrow windows on the outer wall, but heavy blue curtains of velvet covered them now. A small fireplace in one of the side walls had a newly laid fire just catching nicely. The bed was massive, with a canopy of the same blue as the curtains, and the side drapes were fringed on the bottom. There was a fine chest of mahogany, and a small mirror on the wall over a dressing table which matched the bed. The upholstered chairs had ornately carved wooden arms, legs, and headpieces in the Kent style, the fabric a gold floral design. One had a matching footstool. On the other side wall there was a desk with a chair.

Mrs. Pruning lighted the candles from the one she carried. She motioned to a three-paneled screen of China silk and bamboo which hid one corner. "Your washstand is behind the screen. Lizzie will be along with a pitcher of hot water, and while you wash, she will get some supper for you. I shall see you in the morning, at breakfast."

When the housekeeper left, Georgina sat down before the fire, not even taking off her traveling cloak, she was so exhausted. She must have dozed, for the next thing she knew, there were hands at her throat. Not fully awake, she shrieked. Then she saw that Lizzie was standing in front of her, eyes wide under the ruffle of her mobcap.

"Sorry, miss, I was trying to undo your wet cloak."

"I must have dropped off." The maid giggled at Georgina's words. "I've just traveled for five days on the coachey's seat of the stage. There was a lot of talk from the outside passengers about dozing and 'dropping off.' "

"Well, miss, I'm not much for travel. I've seen that stage race by with Mr. Charlie on the seat." She shook her head. "What a comedown for him. Seems a pity."

Obviously Lizzie was talking about Charles Collins. Coincidence couldn't stretch far enough to have another coachey named Charlie on the London-Exeter run. How Georgina wished she could ask Lizzie what she meant by Collins's comedown.

"Now, miss, you get a bit of a wash behind the screen while I bring your supper."

When Georgina finished her ablutions, she found that Lizzie had unpacked her meager wardrobe. On the bedtable she had put the family Bible Papa had used. Georgina had her own Bible with her, also. Since Papa's death, she could not bear to open the larger Bible as it brought back such painful memories of him. His most recent journal lay beside the Bible. That, too, brought back such vivid thoughts of Papa, so feeble he could scarcely hold the quill, still writing daily in his journal as long as he'd been able, just as he'd done for all the years she could remember. Georgina had left the older journals at the vicarage with Mrs. Owens for the time being. She would send for them when she was sure of her welcome here.

A small table held a chased silver tray with a light supper of cold pheasant, a bowl of very welcome steaming broth, some fruitcake, and hot tea in a squat silver pot. After her repast, Georgina drank the last of the tea gratefully, and then climbed into her high bed.

"Goodnight to you, miss." Lizzie whisked away the supper tray, and Georgina snuffed her bedside candle the moment the door closed behind the abigail.

Next morning, feeling somewhat rested, although she

had dreamed long, hazy, involved dreams, Georgina was up and dressed before Lizzie came to take her to breakfast. She pulled aside the heavy curtains to find that the rain had stopped, and a pale winter sun was low in the sky. Georgina looked out over formal gardens which were laid out in intricate patterns. In spring they must be lovely.

Lizzie led her down the spiral stairs. "It took me a month to find my way about Hellingham, miss. I got lost one day and they had to send an underfootman to find me."

Hellingham was larger than any place Georgina had ever been in. They followed endless passageways and finally turned at right angles toward another hall, when she came face to face with Charles Collins. She stopped short, choking back a gasp. Lizzie, sensing that Georgina wasn't following her, turned.

"That's a portrait of his lordship when he was young."

Then Georgina realized that it was, indeed, just a life-sized, full-length portrait hanging on the wall. It was a trick of the light which had made her think it was a man. But it was no trick of light which made it look like a portrait of Charles Collins in a full periwig.

"His lordship doesn't look much like that now, with his mouth all drawn down. Handsome when he was a young man. No wonder Charlie's ma warmed his bed for him."

Georgina was stunned by Lizzie's words. "Charlie?"

"Oh, I keep forgetting, miss, you don't know our Charlie. Always made the young lord furious, Charlie looking like his lordship this way—Lord Francis don't have the Hardy face nor that red hair at all. Takes after his mother."

Charlie. Charles Collins. The son of the Earl of Margate? Is that what Lizzie was saying?

"By the by, miss," the maid said, "you mentioned the stage. You came here by stagecoach?"

"Yes. From near Exeter. In Devon."

"Charlie wasn't your coachey, was he? Wasn't him you sat by all that way, was it?" She had a knowing look which Georgina resented. "Charlie Collins?"

"I believe that may have been the coachman's name," she said stiffly.

Something in her tone warned the garrulous Lizzie, for she said no more. Now Georgina was furious with herself. If she told Lizzie the truth, the girl would no doubt tell her the whole story of Collins. Well, she'd hear plenty of gossip if she stayed on here.

Georgina had finished her breakfast when Mrs. Pruning swept into the room, her back ramrod stiff, her dress plain maroon wool.

"Ah, here you are, Miss Ryerston. Nurse tells me that his lordship is fairly alert this morning, so I shall present you at once. Come along."

They went past the portrait so quickly that Georgina had only a glimpse of the man who looked so like Charles. Just before they went into the earl's tower suite, Mrs. Pruning asked, "Do you have any gowns that aren't black? His lordship seems to like color when he's aware."

"Yes, most of my dresses aren't like this one. Papa died so recently that I've had little chance to sew a complete mourning wardrobe."

"Good. Don't bother. I should have told you last night not to wear black, but perhaps he won't mind just this once."

The room was almost identical in size and shape to Georgina's, but although the furnishings were more luxurious than her own, the room had a sickroom odor which almost gagged her. Reluctantly she approached the bed. Having watched Papa die slowly this past year, she had grown to hate the sight of illness. The stroke had left the right side of his lordship's face drawn, the eyelid drooping. His head was covered with a green silk nightcap, but straggles of white hair crept from under it. His eyes were closed, and she thought he was sleeping. Beside him sat the nurse, her hair completely covered by her mobcap, her white apron spotless over a gown of dark blue cotton.

"I thought he was awake, nurse." Mrs. Pruning's tone was accusatory.

The nurse, broad country face placid, said, "He comes and goes, Mrs. Pruning." Then, leaning over him, she said loudly, "Your lordship, are you awake?"

His eyes opened, and for the first time Georgina saw a strong resemblance to Collins in this wreck of a man.

Mrs. Pruning drew her closer. "Your lordship, Miss Ryerston, your new companion."

There was no awareness in his faded blue eyes.

"He doesn't see me," Georgina murmured, trying to edge away.

Mrs. Pruning said sternly, "Give him time." Then, to the patient, "Your lordship, this is Miss Ryerston. She says you knew her father at Oxford." Turning to Georgina, she hissed, "Your father's name? What was it?"

"His name was Jonathan. Jonathan Ryerston."

"This is Jonathan Ryerston's daughter."

It was as if someone had lighted a candle inside his skull. His eyes cleared, and Georgina knew he was seeing her. His mouth opened, the corner pulled down grotesquely, and sounds came out, but no words that she could understand. Then, quite plainly, the earl said, "Georgina."

Startled, Mrs. Pruning looked at her. "Is that your Christian name?"

Georgina nodded.

"Then he remembers you."

Georgina started to say his lordship didn't know her, then held her tongue. He must have received Papa's letter. No doubt his illness accounted for his not having answered Papa's request for him to care for her. Georgina smiled at the ravaged features. With awareness brightening his eyes, the resemblance to Collins was even more apparent.

Again the old man tried to speak, but no more words came. Then, as if someone had snuffed a candle, the light went from his eyes, and he dozed off.

"Well," Mrs. Pruning said briskly, "you'll do. Come along, now. He won't be awake again for some time. After dinner is the best time for her to read to him, isn't it?"

"He's often a bit more awake then," the nurse agreed.

"Very well. Now, we must see to your wardrobe. If you haven't proper dresses, I'll have the dressmaker from Staines make you suitable attire. Bright colors."

"I'm not sure I can afford a dressmaker." Georgina made her voice firm. "I haven't much money. Papa was vicar at St. Edmund's in Trindale, a very small village."

"A vicar's daughter?" Mrs. Pruning sounded puzzled. Then she shrugged. "Obviously his lordship approves of you. Don't worry about money. The gowns will be paid for by Hellingham."

Now was the time for Georgina to tell Mrs. Pruning that she was a distant cousin, but something made her keep silent. It really was no concern of Mrs. Pruning's. Later, when she met the viscount, she could explain herself to him. Perhaps even he was unaware of Papa's letter to the earl.

Mrs. Pruning examined Georgina's wardrobe. "Woefully inadequate." She flicked the skirt of Georgina's best gown, a watered silk copied from a picture she'd seen of a Parisian fashion. It was a pale blue, most becoming, and the sleeve frills were of Belgian lace which she'd found in a trunk of Mama's clothing.

"Do change into something else," the housekeeper ordered. "Mourning is quite old-fashioned."

Georgina was putting on a sprigged muslin with apple green ribbon trim when Lizzie came in carrying a large box. "Paints, miss. Mrs. Pruning said you didn't seem to have any of your own."

"Paints?" Georgina picked up one of the little pots, took off the silver lid. Inside was bright red rouge. "I don't paint, Lizzie."

"Well, miss, they'll expect it of you here. The last companion painted. In fact these pots and bottles are hers."

"I certainly can't use someone else's paints. Why didn't she take them with her when she left?"

"Oh, she's not gone, miss. She offered these to me herself. She has ever so many more, and can buy whatever she wants." It was said slyly, with a very knowing look.

Georgina was confused. Obviously something was going on here in Hellingham which involved the woman whose job she now had.

"Was she dismissed from her post of companion?"

Lizzie grinned. "You might say, miss, she got a better job."

"A better job? Doing what?"

"I can't say, miss." But it was obvious that Lizzie knew more than she was willing to tell. Instead, she suggested, "You sit down and I'll do your hair. I'm really quite good at it. I help do the hair for Miss Nugent, too. I used to do Lord Francis's young ladies when they were here, but of course they don't come around the way they did."

"Miss Nugent?"

"The one who was companion to his lordship, miss —before you, that is." She studied Georgina as an artist studies a model. "And I can paint you—just a wee bit, miss. A touch of carmine on your cheeks— and a little on your lips."

"I won't use that dreadful whiting."

"There's mercury water—but you're so fair, you don't need bleaching. Just a little color. And a beauty patch just here." She touched Georgina's face at the corner of her mouth. "And I'll powder you. Oh, miss, you have the makings of a lovely lady. His lordship may take to you."

"His lordship?" Georgina thought of that ravaged face upstairs. "He's much too ill to pay attention to anything, Lizzie. Certainly not to me."

"Oh! Not his lordship, the earl, miss. No, I meant Lord Francis, the viscount." She paused. "You said you were a vicar's daughter?"

"Yes, but believe me, Lizzie, vicars' daughters aren't the innocents the silly novels portray them to be. I've seen all kinds. My Papa ministered to the good and to the bad as well. His favorite scripture was the story of the prodigal son."

Georgina could see the maid's sparkling eyes in the mirror. Lizzie was dying to gossip, she just knew it. And if there was anything she'd learned in the years of vicarage living, it was that the gossips knew what was going on; they knew the things the "nice" people wanted to know! Properly handled, Lizzie could keep her in the know here at Hellingham. Georgina said no more, but waited. Lizzie couldn't wait to tell her.

"I—I shouldn't say this, miss." Georgina had difficulty keeping a straight face—nothing would keep the little abigail quiet. "Don't ever tell Mrs. Pruning, or I'll get the sack." Georgina made soothing, encouraging noises. "But the young lord—well, just don't let him get around you, miss. A vicar's daughter. No matter what kind your Papa had in his parish, I doubt they were rakehells the likes of Lord Francis. He's a real devil with the women. And while Charlie was still here!" She rolled her eyes expressively. "Take after their father, both of them. They do say the earl was a ladies' man when he was younger. Oh, miss, it was very lively at Hellingham while Charlie was still here, and both he and Lord Francis chased after Miss Nugent. First the talk was that she was warming his lordship's bed—Lord Francis, that is—but then Charlie made a big play for her."

Georgina wanted to scream at her, "Stop! Not another word!" Yet she listened avidly, torturing herself as she heard Lizzie talk about Charles Collins. Ladies' man. Well, she knew that. She'd seen all of the barmaids between here and Exeter throw themselves at him, brazen things that they were, and he welcomed it.

"The stableboys were all betting on which one would have Miss Nugent," Lizzie went on, enjoying immensely her role as gossip.

Georgina couldn't help it. As aloof as she'd pretended to be, she had to ask, "Who won?"

Lizzie let her eyes flick about the room as if expecting to find Mrs. Pruning hiding under the canopied bed. "Well, miss, Charlie's gone and Miss Nugent now has a room in the wing with the viscount. And she doesn't have to read to the earl these days. They've hired you to do that."

Determined to stop the gossip which had taken a turn she didn't like, Georgina said, "Perhaps Miss Nugent just didn't like reading to the earl."

"Oh, she did little enough of that, miss. Always off in a corner somewhere with one or the other of them. And when she was with Charlie, the viscount was in a terrible rage."

"And when she was with his lordship, what did—" Georgina couldn't say his name, couldn't bear to.

"Charlie? Oh, he just went around smiling. Then he'd make an even bigger play for her." She sighed. "Think of it—the two handsomest men in the county after you."

There was a tap at the door, and Mrs. Pruning swept in with Puffy snuffling along behind her. "Ah, I see Lizzie's been doing you. You really are passably attractive, Miss Ryerston, once you attend to your looks. I'm sure you'll cheer his lordship considerably." She turned to leave. "And no gossiping, Lizzie. Your tongue wags at both ends. Just finish up and get back to Miss Nugent."

Meanwhile Puffy had left a puddle on the hearth. So, when the housekeeper and her pet were gone, Lizzie had to mop it up. "Horrid little monster," she complained. "I hope he gets into some rat poison." But she said nothing more about Miss Nugent and that triangle which included Charles Collins and Viscount Quincy.

CHAPTER 7

En route to the tower suite of the earl, Georgina met a lovely young woman coming down the spiral stairs. She was dressed *en déshabillé,* a beautiful velvet robe of emerald green falling loose from the low-cut neckline, with her firm, full bosom rising in a white swell from the top of the robe. Her hair, not yet dressed, flowed like black silk down over her shoulders, a slight wave giving it the look of a midnight waterfall. Her eyes were a startling green, with a hard look, as if they were carved from shiny gemstones. She smiled at Georgina, although the smile didn't quite reach those cat-eyes.

"Ah, you must be the new companion." Her voice was low and throaty. "I'm Olivia Nugent. Before you go up to the earl's bedchamber, let me have a little chat with you. I can give you pointers on how best to handle him." Again the smile flashed, but the eyes were avid with curiosity.

Georgina, not wishing to seem unfriendly, agreed. Turning with some difficulty on the narrow stairs, she led the way back to her own room, gesturing for Miss Nugent to come in.

"I'd quite forgotten how small this room is," Olivia said, a note of smugness creeping into her interesting voice. "It was mine—for a while." She had a little smile on her face, and Georgina was reminded of a sleek cat who had just lapped up a saucer of heavy cream. "I didn't much like being companion to a sick old man," she added with great candor. Then the smile flickered

76

across her face again. "But it did lead to better things —for me."

Georgina decided that she didn't much care for Olivia Nugent. The woman was a blatant opportunist. If it were true that she was the viscount's mistress, Georgina thought that the woman had not been at all reluctant to accept such a role at Hellingham. She found herself eyeing the beautiful woman as closely as Miss Nugent was observing her. This, according to Lizzie, was the woman Charles Collins had wooed. It stunned Georgina to realize that she was decidedly jealous of this raven-haired beauty.

"I am happy that you have bettered yourself, Miss Nugent."

"Oh, please call me Olivia. And you are Georgina, are you not? Is it true that your father was his lordship's friend at Oxford?"

"Yes, that is quite true," Georgina acknowledged. My, gossip went like wildfire here at Hellingham. No doubt Lizzie had told Olivia everything she knew about Georgina, and might well have added things she guessed, as well.

This was borne out by Olivia's next words.

A bit too casually, she said, "I understand that you came by coach from Exeter. Riding all the way on the coachman's box!" There was an undercurrent in her tone which puzzled Georgina. "Did you have an interesting coachey? Or was he some old man with a nose like a turnip and rheumy eyes?"

Ah, now Georgina recognized that tone. Olivia was jealous! She knew very well that Georgina had ridden beside Charles Collins all those long, wearisome miles, and she was beside herself with envy. Why? She had another handsome man to dance attendance—hadn't Lizzie mentioned that he and Charles were the best-looking men in the county? He was rich, too, and his prospects were dazzling. So why, if she were the mistress of the viscount, was Olivia Nugent jealous of those days when Georgina had sat beside Collins?

Because Georgina was equally jealous of the luscious Miss Nugent who had given her favors to Charles—if Lizzie could be believed—she chose not to answer. She just sat and smiled back at the woman, an equally smug smile. Let Miss Nugent interpret that any way she wished.

The temperature seemed to drop in the room. "I must be getting back to my bedchamber. Lord Francis will be wanting breakfast soon."

"But I thought you wanted to give me advice about how to care for his lordship, the earl," Georgina reminded her, keeping her voice honey-sweet, with just a threat of bee sting in it.

The hard green eyes narrowed. Georgina hadn't fooled Olivia for a moment. Nor had she made herself a friend.

With an indifferent shrug, Olivia said, "It doesn't really matter what you read to the old man. He's past hearing you or understanding." Her mouth twisted with revulsion. "All he does is to live on, cheating the viscount out of his inheritance." Then she swept out of the room.

Stunned at the ugliness of this final remark, Georgina sat there for a few moments until she had composed herself. Contrary to the words of Olivia Nugent, Georgina knew that the earl was aware of his surroundings, at least part of the time. He had known who she was, had spoken her name. She'd read aloud with the idea in her mind all of the time that he might be listening. If it gave him comfort, or helped to relieve the anguish of his condition, then she would read herself hoarse to help him.

Once more she went up the spiral stairs, finding the same nurse that she'd seen the day before. His lordship lay there, eyes closed, apparently asleep.

"Should I read now?" Georgina whispered to the

country woman. "I know it's early, but I'm free this morning, it seems."

"Might as well. He might be awake. He might not. The other one read regardless." The woman reached to a book lying on a walnut table near her chair. "This is the latest book, miss. If you read that French." Her tone made it plain what she thought of the French.

"I do. And I enjoy French novels." Georgina sat down on a Queen Anne chair of mahogany and opened the novel. She started at the beginning, so that she'd have the pleasure of following the story, even though the Earl of Margate seemed unaware of her presence. The nurse had him propped with three down pillows, but his eyes were closed. When Georgina started reading aloud, though, he opened his dull, lifeless blue eyes, but he did not try to talk. At least she didn't have the sickroom care of the feeble old man. Georgina thought she heard the door behind her open and close, but she had become so engrossed in the romantic novel, she kept right on reading.

Then Georgina felt a hand on her shoulder, in a much more than casual caress. Startled, she lost her place in the book and looked over her shoulder to see who was so familiar with her. A young man stood behind her, a man quite handsome, a veritable fashion plate. His wig was in the new, short style, with curls over the ears and an elegant pompadour, while the ends were pulled back into a small black silk bag. The man's complexion was olive with a hint of paint on his cheeks. His eyes, so dark a brown as to appear black, were worldly, his full, sensual lips pulled into a knowing smile. The young gentleman's morning suit was of pale green satin, with a contrasting embroidered waistcoat of deep wine worked in gold and silver thread. His knee breeches were faun, with bows instead of buckles, and his legs were encased in white silk hose with red clocks. His black leather slippers had red high heels.

From snowy neckcloth and lace cuffs to the shoes, he was a blood.

Pulling slightly away from his caress, Georgina said in what she hoped was a chilling tone, "Yes?"

"How nice to see that my father's new companion is hard at work," he said negligently. He touched her powdered hair. "And such an attractive young woman. Don't you think so, nurse? Dear Olivia didn't tell me how luscious the new one was!"

The nurse's broad, country face was blank. Village reared, Georgina knew that look. The nurse didn't care to be drawn into anything not her immediate concern.

"If you say so, milord." The nurse picked up the silver water pitcher and moved stolidly toward the door.

"I say so. I forget your name," he added to Georgina.

"I'm not sure you ever knew it," she said with some spirit, envying the nurse who could walk away from this arrogant blade. So this was the Viscount Quincy of whom Collins had warned her. He was smug and insufferable, she decided, but there was no denying that the viscount was handsome and Georgina felt drawn to him even as she felt that she must show her annoyance at his familiarity.

Further conversation with the viscount was cut short when the earl began making the distressing sounds he'd made yesterday. His son's face twisted with disgust.

"You're wasting your time reading to that," he said, scorn in his voice. "He's a vegetable."

Shocked by this lack of filial regard, Georgina was about to make a sharp retort when the earl spoke.

"Georgina." He said it quite distinctly.

"There's no Georgina here, old man," the viscount said. "Another of your fancy women, no doubt."

This outraged her. "My name is Georgina. He spoke it yesterday, too," she said curtly, liking the young lord less each minute.

"Cousin," the old man mumbled. Once he'd said an intelligible word or two, his consciousness drained away. His head lolled back, and his twisted mouth hung slack.

"Cousin?" Lord Francis asked. "What does he mean?"

"He and my Papa were distant cousins. Papa wrote to his lordship when he knew he was dying. So the earl knows who I am."

"The old man knows nothing. I told you, he's a vegetable. The nurse cares for him as if he were an infant."

Again there was that amazing transformation in the earl's ravaged face, intelligence suddenly returning. Quite distinctly he said, "I should have married Rebecca."

There was a hiss of anger from the younger man who took two steps toward the bed, his face a mask of rage and hate. "But you didn't, you old lecher. You married the Honorable Agnes Bouchard, daughter of the Duke of Wilmouth. My mother! I'm your only legal son and heir. Someday I'll be Fifth Earl of Margate. And it can't happen too soon."

What a shameful way to treat one's own father! Georgina remembered how loving her own parent had been, and tears burned her eyes.

The earl didn't seem to hear the vituperation from his son's lips. Once again he slumped into a torpor.

"He's delirious," young Viscount Quincy said. "Pay no attention to his maunderings."

Georgina didn't trust herself to answer. The viscount turned his back on the sickbed, and smiled at her as if nothing unpleasant had happened. "So we're cousins!" She was surprised he acknowledged his father's comment, but let the matter drop. He eyed her appreciatively, and she felt flattered, despite her distress at the viscount's attitude toward his father. The young lord was most attractive, and Georgina felt herself responding to his attention despite her feelings of distaste. "And your father is dead?" Georgina nodded, the tears still ready to fall. "How sad for you, dear Cousin Georgina. No mother?" His bantering had turned into concern.

"Mama died when I was born. I'm—I'm all alone in the world now. That's why Papa wrote to his lordship about me."

"And rightly so," Lord Francis said, surprising her. "It would never do for a young lady, even distantly related to the house of Hardy, to be left to her own devices. It is a wicked world, Cousin Georgina. You'll be safe here at Hellingham." Then he gestured to the French novel she'd been reading to his father. "But what's this? Why are you doing the work of a companion? You are a lady of the house, my dear. Such occupation is unsuitable for you."

"I—Mrs. Pruning—"

"Leave her to me. I can't imagine what got into her."

Just then there was a discreet tapping at the door. A liveried footman stepped inside. "Milord, Mrs. Pruning wishes to see Miss Ryerston in the office."

"Well, run along, my dear. But don't take any guff from old Pruning. If you get into difficulties, just call for me." He made a leg, bowing prettily.

"Thank you, milord."

"Please, cousin, no formality. I must be Cousin Francis."

Perhaps I misjudged him, Georgina thought. *He was very familiar with me when he thought I was just a servant; but once I established my* bona fides, *he has been exemplary in his behavior.*

Georgina found Mrs. Pruning in a small, austere room, seated behind an oak desk. Puffy lay sleeping in front of the fire. Another woman, thirtyish, was sitting on a plain chair. She wore a traveling suit of tan merino trimmed with deep brown braid, while her cloak, thrown back over the chair, was of a dark brown matching the trim. Her bonnet was small, with lappets tied under the chin.

Buoyed up by her conversation with Cousin Francis, Georgina said, without a trace of subservience, "You wanted to see me, Mrs. Pruning?"

"Indeed I did. You seem to have tried to deceive me."

"Deceive you? Not at all, Mrs. Pruning."

"You passed yourself off as the new companion his lordship has engaged. What is your game, Miss Ryerston? Are you in league with one of the notorious highwaymen, insinuating yourself into the homes of your betters to spy out the hiding places of the jewels, the silver?"

Indignant, Georgina exclaimed, "That's a wicked accusation!"

Mrs. Pruning rose, her height awesome. "That's enough! Here's Miss Twistle, out from Staines, with his lordship's letter giving her the position of companion to the earl. And here you are, insinuating yourself into the family with tales of your father's being up at Oxford with his lordship. Came here, pretty as you please, butter wouldn't melt in your mouth, all demure in black—mourning, you claim."

"It's true," Georgina cried hotly. "My Papa died less than a fortnight ago. And he was at Oxford with his lordship, the Earl of Margate. In fact—"

Then Miss Twistle spoke up. She was short and dumpy, her gown unflatteringly styled so that it emphasized her bulk, instead of minimizing it. She had that haughty look assumed by so many gentlewomen forced to earn their livelihoods.

"I have the letter, Miss—uh—Miss—"

"And you presented no letter to me, Miss Ryerston," Mrs. Pruning cut in smoothly. "An imposter."

"It's all a misunderstanding," Georgina declared.

"Indeed!" Miss Twistle said sharply. "You are trying to take the position which has been given to me."

"I suggest that you pack your cases and leave at once," Mrs. Pruning said, her eyes cold, her lips thin.

"We'll let Viscount Quincy decide that," Georgina said.

"The viscount, indeed! I handle such matters as this."

Sure of her ground, Georgina insisted, "He told me particularly that if there was any difficulty, to call him."

"I shall do no such thing. Go pack at once, or I shall have Lizzie dispose of your meager wardrobe and you shall leave with only the clothes you wear."

This was too much. Georgina turned and marched, not to the door, but toward the tapestry bellpull. Unfortunately she did not notice that Puffy, roused from his slumbers by the raised voices, was waddling away from his cushion by the fire. As the path to Mrs. Pruning led right across the line Georgina was following to call for the viscount, she inadvertently stepped on Puffy's paw. With a shrill yelp, the nasty little spaniel bared his yellowed teeth at her.

"Oh, the poor little doggie," Miss Twistle cried. She popped up and rushed across the room, scooping up the angry dog before a flustered Georgina could move. "There, there, the bad lady stepped on poor little doggie's paw, did she?" the woman murmured.

"I didn't mean to step on him," Georgina said on the defensive.

"See, he likes me," cooed Miss Twistle, cuddling the smelly little beast.

"At Hellingham, especially in dealing with a sick old man, we must all exercise extra care," Mrs. Pruning said, her eyes darting from the woman to Georgina, her voice cold with dislike.

Georgina had no intention of being deflected from her plan to summon the viscount to help her. Ignoring both Mrs. Pruning and the simpering Miss Twistle, she tugged firmly on the bellpull. When the footman arrived, she said, "I wish you to tell his lordship, Viscount Quincy, that Miss Ryerston needs him here."

"Very well, Miss Ryerston, you'll see how his lordship handles imposters. He may have an eye for a pretty face and a tempting bosom, but he has a quick temper if he thinks someone is trying to put something over him," Mrs. Pruning said stonily.

Miss Twistle sat there looking distressed. Mrs. Pruning had a smug look on her haughty face. Georgina had an attack of the jitters. Perhaps Cousin Francis had only been polite. Would he side with her or with his housekeeper?

"He won't come here, you know," Mrs. Pruning said. She glanced at Georgina, her face triumphant. "Enough of your insolence. Remove your belongings from the tower room at once, so that Miss Twistle can be lodged there."

It was on this speech that Viscount Quincy made his entrance. His dark eyes took in the scene immediately.

"Problems, dear Cousin Georgina?" he asked solicitously.

Georgina saw Mrs. Pruning's eyes widen with shock. "Milord, this young woman is an imposter!"

"Please, Mrs. Pruning, do not speak so unkindly of Miss Ryerston. She is a member of the family. I am most displeased that you have put her to caring for his lordship, the earl. Why was I not informed of her arrival? This is most remiss." Then he turned and gave Georgina an outrageous wink.

Mrs. Pruning spluttered, utterly confused, but to no avail.

"And who is this poor creature?" he asked carelessly, waving a languid hand at the unfortunate Miss Twistle, who flushed, indignant at such treatment.

"This is Miss Twistle, the lady you engaged to be a companion to his lordship." Mrs. Pruning wasn't finished with Georgina yet. "This snippety miss came in on us in the dead of night, pretending that she was expected. As the only woman we were expecting was the new companion, I assumed it was she. Milord, she did nothing to correct that impression, but moved in as if it were her right."

"As it is, Mrs. Pruning, you do not seem to be hearing too well today. Perhaps we shall have the doctor bring his leeches and bleed you, to cure your deafness. Now, move Miss Ryerston out of the tower into a more suitable room. Appoint one of the maids to be her abigail. Have the seamstress out from Staines. She needs gowns more suitable for life at Hellingham."

Miss Twistle, through all this, looked more and more indignant. As the viscount turned to leave, offering his hand to Georgina, she burst out, "But what about me, milord? I have your letter—the position as companion—"

"Oh, settle all that with Mrs. Pruning. It's her job."

"You mean—the position *is* mine?" He gave a negligent nod. "Oh, thank you, milord." She bobbed him a curtsy.

His lordship escorted Georgina from the room. "My, my, cousin, you've made an enemy of Mrs. Pruning. Old Pruning doesn't like to be bettered in an argument."

Georgina felt quite bad about the whole situation. "She just started talking as if she expected me," she explained, "and Papa had written . . . and I was so weary from the journey . . . and then, just before you walked in, I had to step on that nasty little spaniel."

"Spare me the boring details. As to Puffy, someday I may decide he has to go. Meanwhile, it is enough that you are here, such an attractive addition to Hellingham. Sometimes Olivia gets a bit trying. You are much too attractive to be wasted on my ailing father."

Georgina was again shocked at her cousin's attitude, but he had taken her in, offered her all she'd dreamed of since Papa first said they were related to the Earl of Margate. She'd reserve judgment until she knew the full story.

"We'll give a ball," Cousin Francis was saying, "to introduce you to my friends. They'll all envy me."

"But I'm in mourning," Georgina reminded him.

"There is no mourning at Hellingham." He said it lightly, but there was a hint of underlying iron in his voice. "It reminds me of death, and I choose not to think of that."

She found they were in the corridor where the earl's portrait hung, the one so strikingly resembling Charles Collins. As they came opposite it, Viscount Quincy stopped short and glared at the painting.

Perturbed at his abrupt change of mood, at the dark flush on his olive cheeks, and the eyes narrowed in anger or hate, Georgina said, "He certainly was a handsome man in his youth."

"The Hardy look!" Francis almost snarled it. "I look like my mother's family, the Bouchards. He's never forgiven me for that, as if I had anything to do with it. While that bastard—!" He didn't go on, so Georgina could not know of whom he spoke. Charles Collins? Or was Lizzie's story just one of those snippets of gossip circulating around every country house in England? Still, with the marked resemblance, Georgina could well believe that Collins was the illegitimate son of Peter Hardy, Fourth Earl of Margate, who lay chained in the tower as surely as if iron held his limbs, not paralysis.

Her cousin threw off the rage and smiled at her. "But that's nothing for you to worry about. Forgive me, Cousin Georgina, a private thing. It doesn't concern you."

Or does it? she asked herself. *If it is true about Collins . . . .* She mustn't think so much about him.

She had been accepted by Viscount Quincy. She'd no longer associate with coacheys now that she was to be part of the family at Hellingham.

Later Georgina was installed in a new room on the main floor, away from the tower. It was spacious and luxurious. Lizzie presented herself, almost bursting with excitement, as her new abigail.

"See, miss, it was the new hairstyle. I knew it would impress his lordship. He does have an eye—" Then she caught herself, stopped short. "Miss, is it true that you are related to his lordship?" Her manner was much subdued.

"Yes, distantly. But I've never met this branch of my family, Lizzie. It's as if they were strangers." She was very curious, though, that Lizzie had been given to her as her personal maid. "I thought you were Miss Nugent's abigail. What will she do, now? Or do I share you with her?"

Lizzie didn't look Georgina in the eye. "She will get a new abigail, miss. I'm for you."

"Didn't she like your work, Lizzie?"

Defiantly, Lizzie said, "Well, miss, she came here as a companion and didn't rate an abigail. Now that she is his lordship's mistress, she forgets that we once were friendly, when she was lowly hired help like me."

"I see." Georgina did see. And she realized that she might have an ally in Lizzie. All too well she remembered Olivia Nugent's hard green eyes which had looked her up and down, not liking what she'd seen. And she recalled Cousin Francis's remark that Olivia hadn't mentioned to him that the new companion was so attractive. "Well, Lizzie, I think we'll get along splendidly. But I hope you don't get into any trouble with Miss Nugent. It might be well not to say anything about her outside of this bedchamber."

"I know, miss. I should hold my tongue, not gossip about folks here. Mrs. Pruning would have my hide if she heard me say anything." Then she lowered her voice to a conspiratorial level. "She's all on Miss Nugent's side. Thinks dear Olivia will marry his lordship and become the Viscountess of Quincy—and someday Countess of Margate. Old Pruning knows how to play house politics."

Georgina saw Lizzie as a fountain of information about everything here, so she hinted that she wasn't averse to listening to an occasional tidbit of gossip if it weren't malicious. She would dearly love to ask Lizzie point blank about Collins, but she felt it better not to seem too curious. Lizzie might well gossip about her in the servants' quarters, and word would filter back upstairs to Cousin Francis.

She might find out more about Olivia Nugent, though. If that charmer were, indeed, Cousin Francis's mistress, as Lizzie said, then why had her cousin been so solicitous of Georgina? He'd even said she was a refreshing change from Miss Nugent! How the green-eyed beauty would love that!

It was with great apology that her cousin summoned her that evening.

"Cousin Georgina, it is in shocking bad taste for me to ask this favor of you, but apparently you have managed to penetrate the mental fog in which my father has existed since his attack of apoplexy. The nurse says that my father is calling for Georgina. Would it distress you too much to visit with him briefly?"

"I'm happy to be able to do anything to repay you for your kindness to me. Shall I attend his lordship now?"

"If you would. And dear Cousin Georgina, he fell ill while we were in the midst of certain discussions of importance. If he says anything coherent to you, would you carefully take note of it, so that you could repeat it to me? It might well be the key to some of these matters."

His smile was so charming, his manner so diffident,

that it took his request out of the realm of asking her to spy on his father, so she was willing to agree.

"If he talks no more than he has to me already, I'm afraid I won't be much help to you, though."

"Your father—was he ill for long before he died? Was his mind clouded, as my father's is?"

"Only toward the end, when the doctor had to increase the dosage of laudanum. Then he had periods of confusion—something troubled him. Sometimes he'd blurt out coherent sentences, but I didn't know to what he was referring. It was so very frustrating, for I felt he needed to tell me something, yet he never did. Just hints—words—perhaps only drug-induced hallucinations."

"Did you expect him to recover?"

Georgina shook her head, unable to speak.

"My father might as well be dead." His voice was bitter, his face sullen. "His Majesty even sent out his own personal physician, Dr. Ward, to see my father. Ward bled him until I thought he would drain him dry of blood, but it did no good. He prescribed physicks and draughts, including his own famous drops and pills. Nothing helped. Nothing can. Yet while he lies there, his mind dead but his hulk of a body still breathing, I cannot assume my rightful title. And every day that passes, that bastard of his tries to wrest my title away from me! But I am the only legitimate son of my father, and when he dies, I shall be Fifth Earl of Margate."

Did he mean Charles? Was Collins trying to claim he was the legitimate son of the earl? Georgina wished she knew the whole story, yet she hesitated to ask her cousin. Perhaps, if she kept her ears open, she'd learn what was going on here at Hellingham.

CHAPTER 8

"Miss, here's a letter for you, delivered by hand."

Georgina was surprised. Who would write to her here? If it were from friends in Exeter, it would come by mail. A name leaped into her mind—Charles Collins. Lizzie stood there, all eager eyes, hoping her mistress would tell her of some romantic lover, but Georgina had no intention of opening her mysterious letter until she was alone.

"Thank you, Lizzie." Georgina took the letter, addressed to her at Hellingham and closed with a blob of wax without any seal on it. She wanted to read it immediately, but Lizzie told her that the dressmaker from Staines had just arrived, so she put the letter in a drawer of the elegant little French desk and told her maid to show the dressmaker in.

What seemed hours later, when Georgina was exhausted from standing still to be measured, after looking at endless fashion plates just over from Paris, and selecting fabrics from swatches Mrs. Ealing carried along with her, she finally had a chance to read her letter. Sitting on the padded window seat, the late afternoon sun coming through the mullioned windows to light the paper, she broke the seal and opened the letter. A quick glance showed that it was, indeed, from Charles Collins, and Georgina felt her pulse quicken.

My dear Miss Ryerston, It is urgent that I see you on a matter of the greatest gravity. Could you take supper with me on Friday at eight at Ye Grape? It is imperative that no one from Hellingham knows

91

*you are meeting me. There will be no opportunity
for me to have an answer from you. I shall be at
Ye Grape, and hope that you will find it in your
heart to see me. Yr. obedient servant, Charles
Collins.*

Friday evening. How could she hope to go to Ye
Grape without anyone's knowing of it? Yet Georgina
knew that she would make every effort to meet Collins.
She told herself that curiosity alone was driving her,
that she must learn what ties he had with Hellingham,
but she knew that she wanted desperately to see the
redheaded, volatile coachman again. Just thinking about
him, remembering how thrilling it was to sit beside
him in the coachman's box for the long drive from
Trindale, made her heart race.

By the greatest good fortune, Viscount Quincy told
her on Thursday that he must go up to London the
following day to see to some business affairs. "I may
even have an audience with the king," he told her, "to
personally thank him for sending Dr. Ward to see
father. He dosed that dying hulk with his famous
pills made of antimony and dragon's blood, for all
the good they did. Next time, perhaps you can come
with me to London. I could have you presented at
court."

"Oh, Cousin Francis, that would be so exciting!"
To see London, to be presented at the Court of St.
James, to personally meet King George II and Queen
Caroline, was beyond her wildest dreams. For minutes,
these pleasant prospects completely drove all thoughts
of Collins from her head.

The viscount's trip gave Georgina ample chance to
plan for her supper at Ye Grape. First Georgina told
Lizzie that she could have the night off to visit her
mother in the nearby village. Then she pretended a
headache, and left word that she wanted no supper,
nor did she want to be disturbed. Georgina wished that

Mrs. Ealing had finished at least one of the new gowns, but then her good sense prevailed. If she went to Ye Grape all decked out in the finery of a noblewoman, all eyes would be on her, and the wagging tongues would clatter so loudly that everyone at Hellingham would know where she'd been, and whom she'd seen. No, one of her frocks from Trindale would be more appropriate. She even brushed the powder from her hair, once Lizzie had gone to see her mum. She did dress with care, however, and used a tiny bit of carmine on her cheeks and on her lips, to give herself a little color. Georgina's gown was of a soft blue Exeter wool, so fine that it draped like heavy silk. The bodice was fitted, and she tied a lovely lace kerchief about her neck in place of a fichu. She wore a white lace cap, with lappets tied under her chin, her golden hair showing above her smooth forehead. Her traveling cloak would make a good concealing garment with the hood pulled well forward.

Lizzie had told her there was a small door in the wall further along the road from the main gate.

"Mrs. Pruning would skin me if she knew I slipped out to see my Neddie," she giggled. "You'll not tell, miss?"

Now Georgina, herself, would use Lizzie's escape route.

The great clock standing on the landing of the main staircase was whirring in preparation for striking eight when she slipped past it and flitted like a ghost to the side door which led to the back courtyard and the path to the gate. She was late, but surely Collins would wait for her, knowing she might have difficulty in getting away. Georgina almost had heart failure as she neared the side door, for Mrs. Pruning's tall figure appeared down the hall with dumpy Miss Twistle beside her. Fortunately the housekeeper turned to say something to the companion, and Georgina eased out of the door, pulling it shut quietly behind her.

It was a blustery night, but the moon shone fitfully through the high, scudding clouds, lighting the road. Ye Grape was actually within sight of the estate walls, so she had only a short walk once she was through the little door.

Georgina stood for a moment in the castellated entrance porch of the whitewashed brick inn. The pantiled roof shone in the moonlight, and the sign, hung over the door of the porch, showed a large bunch of gaudy purple grapes. She felt that the small, diamond-paned windows were watching her. Georgina opened the heavy, black-painted door and stepped into the main taproom. Here the stone slabs of the three-centuries-old inn were worn smooth with the patina of age and untold restless feet. The tiny windows in the thick walls gave a sense of security inside, and great open fireplaces at either end of the room had roaring fires which lighted the room full of travelers and locals drinking ale.

Georgina hesitated beside an enormous oak settle which must have been built inside the room, for it would never go through the door. A crowd of boisterous ostlers and grooms were playing shove-ha'penny on a table whose polished surface was marked out for the game.

One of the rude fellows noticed her and called out, "What have we here, men? Come, girl, take off that cloak and give us a look at you!"

Georgina was ready to turn and flee back to Hellingham, but the innkeeper, a short, pudgy fellow almost as wide as he was tall was at her side at once. "Miss Ryerston?" he asked so quietly that only she could hear him. She nodded. "This way, miss." He led her across to a small door at one end of the serving bar. "Go right in, miss."

It was a cozy private parlor, with its own fire burning on a small hearth. A bearskin rug lay before the fire, brown fur thick and luxuriant, not like the mangy, moth-eaten rug they'd covered themselves with on the coach box. There was a table already set for a meal, with a tall candlestick, its wax taper burning. Collins was waiting for her, wearing his plain coachman's clothes in that elegant way he had.

"I was afraid you couldn't get away, Miss Ryerston." Quickly he helped Georgina with her cloak, led her to a seat at the table. "Thank you for coming tonight. I—it's a difficult story I have to tell you. And I hope, when you've heard it, that you will find it in your heart to help me."

Not knowing what he'd ask, Georgina committed herself only to the extent of smiling, which won a smile in return from Collins. "It was kind of you to invite me, Mr. Collins."

A discreet tap on the door signaled the arrival of their meal, thin slices of roast beef beaten tender, sprinkled with bread crumbs, grilled over the fire, and served on a silver dish with fine large potatoes seasoned with salt butter. There was cabbage with turnips, boiled together, and they washed down the meal with good English beer. Collins did not mention his problem while they ate, but kept up a light patter about his travels as a coachey. Pouring honey sauce over her meat, Georgina allowed herself to enjoy the supper as if it were entirely an occasion of pleasure, a man and woman supping together. The maid carried in a saffron cake and a bottle of Bordeaux wine with two glasses. Collins asked for cheese, but Georgina had cake for dessert. When the girl had cleared, leaving only the wine, Collins finally broached the problem.

"Miss Ryerston, have you met the Earl of Margate?"

"If you can call it that."

He looked at her sharply. "What does that mean?"

"The earl is very ill, Mr. Collins. He suffered a stroke some months ago, and is partially paralzyed. He speaks only a little—and seldom is his mind clear."

Collins hid his face in his hands. "He had that stroke

the day before I left Hellingham. If he had remained healthy—" He broke off, overcome by emotion.

Collins lifted his head and said with pride, "He is my father. You may have guessed."

"I saw the portrait of the earl. It could be you."

"Let me tell you the story, Miss Ryerston, before you make any judgment about me. My mother was Rebecca Collins. Her mother was cook at Hellingham, and her father the head groom. Mother lived there all her life. The Fourth Earl, Peter Hardy, was in his early thirties when my mother was sixteen. You've seen his portrait. He was a fine figure of a man, unmarried, and he had a way with women. Mother was very lovely." He reached into one of the large pockets of his plain brown waistcoat, brought out a miniature. It was of a pretty young woman, hair dark brown and curling about her face, eyes hazel, lips laughing. "My father commissioned this done. Well, to make a long story short, the earl wanted my mother, but she was a very moral young woman, brought up strictly by her parents, and she refused to let him bed her.

"There was to be a great ball at Hellingham. The earl insisted that mother should attend, and had a ballgown of finest French satin made for her, although my grandmother disapproved. Now I tell you the story told to me over and over again by my grandmother, because I do not remember my mother. But mother told her this story, and swore on the Bible that it was true. By the end of the ball my mother, not used to so much wine, was slightly tipsy, although she was not drunk; she knew what went on. The earl said that he had a surprise for mother. He took her into the small chapel —have you seen the Hellingham chapel?" Georgina shook her head. "There they were joined by a clergyman who was a friend of the earl's. He gave my father a document. Father told her that it was a special license. 'We'll be married here and now,' the earl announced. The clergyman went through a short ritual and pronounced them man and wife, even signing the marriage document."

Caught up by the narrative, Georgina asked, "Then what?"

"What do you think? Mother thought they were married, so she went to bed with him. First she exacted a promise from him that she could show the marriage lines to her parents, and he laughingly consented, knowing they could not read."

Having heard Collins called a bastard, Georgina asked, "But if they were married, why aren't you Viscount Quincy?"

Collins flushed a dark red, got up and paced the small parlor. "I should be. God knows I should be. But I was cheated out of my inheritance."

"How? A marriage license, a wedding. Didn't that make it legal?"

He sat down, slumped dejectedly, stretching his booted feet toward the fire. "When mother knew I was on the way, she was delighted, and assumed the earl would be, too. But she began hearing rumors that he was courting a fine lady, the Honorable Agnes Bouchard, daughter of the Duke of Wilmouth." He almost snarled the name. "The Fourth Earl of Margate, master of Hellingham, had no intention of making my mother his countess. She was just a serving girl he lusted after."

"But you said—a license—"

"He laughed at mother, said it was all a hoax. His friend had not married them at all. The license was a fake. He burned it in the fireplace of their bedroom. Mother was heartbroken. My grandparents were not surprised. They knew that a nobleman, an earl, doesn't marry beneath him." Now he was blackly bitter.

"But what did they do?"

"Do? What could they do? Nothing. They couldn't even leave Hellingham. Where else could they get such good positions? My mother—poor, deluded mother . . . ." He took out the miniature once more, looking at it sadly. "She died having me. My grandmother insisted that she grieved herself to death. And not long after her death, the earl married again, with all suitable pomp, in Salisbury Cathedral, with an archbishop officiating. And the following year, dear Francis was born."

Collins poured another glass of wine for himself, motioned toward her glass with the decanter, but she declined.

"Do you know what the worst part of the story is, Miss Ryerston? I look like my father—Francis doesn't. You've met Francis?"

Should she tell him that she was a distant cousin of the Hardy family? The further Collins got into his narrative, the more uncomfortable Georgina felt. Cousin Francis had taken her in, given her a lovely home; she felt it was disloyal to listen to Collins talk this way against the earl and his rightful son. Yet so great was Georgina's attraction to Collins—she could well understand Collins's mother's infatuation with the earl—that she wished she could do something to help him.

"I've met the viscount," she said noncommittally.

"I warned you about him. Do be careful. He has a vicious reputation with the ladies, much worse than the earl."

In all good conscience, Georgina felt she must speak up for Cousin Francis. "He has been quite gentlemanly to me, Mr. Collins."

She saw he felt the rebuke by the way his mouth tightened.

"I don't trust him—and you mustn't, either."

"He has given me a home, Mr. Collins," Georgina reminded him gently.

"Just watch out for him."

She waited, not replying. What favor did Collins

wish of her? It had to have something to do with his status.

"Until the moment she died, my mother insisted that her marriage to the earl was legal, that I was his legitimate child. I believe her! Somehow, somewhere, there has to be proof. If only I could find the man who married them!"

"You have no clue? Your mother did not know his name?"

He frowned. "She told my grandmother a name, but gran can't remember what it was. She saw the marriage lines—or a paper my mother said was the legal document—but gran can't read. Nor could my mother. It could have been anything. And yet—and yet, Miss Ryerston, I feel that I am his legitimate son, his heir. He raised me as a son. Once he saw that I had the Hardy looks, while miserable Francis looked like a Bouchard, he pampered me, petted me, kept me in the drawing room more than in the kitchen and stables. He even had the same tutor for me as for Francis."

It was so frustrating for Georgina. Her heart went out to this man; yet what could she do about this sad affair?

"For years, Miss Ryerston, I've waited for Peter Hardy, Lord Margate, to acknowledge me as his legitimate issue, as his eldest son, heir to his title and to Hellingham. He doesn't even like Francis. I'm the Hardy! I'm his true son. Francis may be the son of Agnes Bouchard—while my mother was Rebecca—"

"Rebecca!"

He caught Georgina's hand in a grip so hard it pained her, but she wouldn't have withdrawn her hand for the world. It seemed so right that her small hand should be caught by his large, masculine one.

"Why does that name surprise you?" he demanded.

"The earl—at times he seems lucid. And the other day he said, quite plainly, 'I should have married

Rebecca.' Cous—Viscount Quincy," she amended hastily, "was livid."

"I'll wager he was! You can help me, Miss Ryerston." He still held her hand in a burning grip. Then his eyes softened, and his voice took on a timbre which thrilled her to the depths of her heart. "May I have the honor of calling you Georgina? I believe I did once, but without your kind permission, at The Fallen Angel. It is such a lovely name, and you are such a lovely young woman." He paused, then added, almost embarrassed, "Do you now find that too forward of me, Miss Ryerston—Georgina?"

It was quite forward, but throwing caution to the winds, she said, "If you wish, you may call me Georgina."

He smiled, squeezed her hand, then took his away quickly as if afraid she'd retract her permission if he became too bold. "And I am Charles—or, if you prefer, Charlie."

With quiet dignity, trying to quiet her pounding heart, Georgina said, "I shall call you Charles." Not for her the familiarity with which every barmaid from here to Exeter greeted him! Now that she knew that good blood flowed in his veins, albeit illegitimately, her feelings about Collins were justified. He was just as much a Hardy as was her Cousin Francis.

Charles was her cousin! Distant, of course. A little imp whispered, *No problems with the church concerning consanguinity.* Georgina longed to tell Charles this, but some inner caution kept her silent. Now was not the time to tell him that she was related by blood to the Earl of Margate.

Collins busied himself pouring more wine for them.

"About the favor I beg of you, Georgina," and he flashed that devastating smile at her, "I keep thinking there must be proof somewhere in Hellingham of my legitimacy."

It grieved her for him to beat his head against a

stone wall. Obviously, if his marriage to Rebecca Collins had been legitimate, as he was the favorite son of his father, the earl would have acknowledged him long since.

"Charles," Georgina ventured timidly, "does it matter so much—"

"Does it matter?" he blazed, frightening her with his burst of temper. "Of course it matters! Do you think I like to be called a bastard? Do you think I like all the sniggers—'there goes the old earl's by blow'—do you think I like driving a stagecoach day after weary day, making a pittance, when all Hellingham should be mine when father dies?"

Georgina was stunned by the outburst. "I didn't mean. . . ."

Instantly he was contrite. "I shouldn't take out my frustration on you, dear Georgina. But will you help me?"

"How?" She was ready to promise him anything.

"Keep your eyes open. You say that my father is lucid at times? Listen to what he says. Already you've told me one important thing, that he said he should have married my mother."

Sadly she reminded him, "If he says that, it can mean only one thing, Charles: he didn't marry her."

"No, I won't believe that. He did. I know he did!"

"Give it up, Charles."

"Never. Francis kicked me out when father became ill. He pensioned off my grandparents, gave them a little cottage on an estate owned by his mother in Kent. He wanted them out of the way."

"But why?"

"He knows that gran always believed my mother."

"But they stayed on here, worked at Hellingham for years after your mother died. If they'd thought that—"

"Where else could they go?" he asked savagely. "They wanted to be near me. And the earl kept me about—I told you that. So they swallowed their great hurt and stayed on, working for him. Once he was stricken, though, Francis got rid of me and them."

Georgina felt impelled to defend her cousin. "But if he gave them a cottage, it was quite handsome of him, Charles."

"Listen to me, Georgina. My brother"—he gave a bitter bark of a laugh at the word—"my dearly beloved younger half brother does nothing unless he, personally, gains from it. He sent them off to Kent, gave them a cottage and a pension, to keep their mouths still."

"They took it," she said reasonably.

"What else could they do? Gran wouldn't tell me what Francis said to them, but it was some threat, at least implied. I know it. Remember, he's a lord. He could accuse them of stealing, have them hanged, and they know it."

"That's wicked! The law wouldn't allow—"

"Georgina, Georgina, how innocent you are. The law is concerned with the rich, not the poor. Master wins over servant every time."

"Now you're being cynical." It broke her heart to see him in such a mood.

"I've learned that lesson well." He was so bitter. "Will you help me or not? I thought you were my friend."

"What do you want me to do?" Georgina asked reluctantly.

"Listen. Listen to what my father says when he is lucid. Try to find out where he keeps important papers, try to look at them—"

"Charles!" She was shocked. "You want me to spy on them, after they've taken me in, offered me a home?"

"Ha! They'll use you. You'll have to nurse the earl, or be a housemaid, or—"

"Not so! The viscount was very annoyed when he

found that Mrs. Pruning had put me to work as a companion."

He eyed her, his face cold. "And just what is your position in that house? I know what most young women have to do there—the last companion my father had, the one who came just before Francis gave me the boot—is my sweet brother's mistress. I still have friends in the stables, even if I don't have an ear in the big house. Is that your position there?"

Terribly hurt that he should think such a thing, Georgina overreacted, flaring, "That's a dreadful thing to say, sir." She sprang to her feet, looked about. "Where's my cloak? I shall not stay here and be insulted, Mr. Collins."

CHAPTER 9

When Georgina indicated that she meant to leave, Collins was instantly contrite.

"Please, Georgina, I apologize." Collins was abject. "The only other personable young woman at Hellingham is Olivia Nugent, and she is Francis's creature. I don't want you to fall under the influence of my brother. He can be most charming if he chooses. Don't leave—please don't. You can't know what a state I'm in constantly, wondering if my father lives or dies, knowing I ought to be the next Earl of Margate, wondering how to prove my claim." He had taken her hand and drawn her back to the fireplace. Georgina, loath to leave, allowed him to hold her hand while he pleaded his cause with her. Just being near him was so thrilling that she had difficulty in keeping her mind on what he was saying to her. Georgina reacted instead of thinking. She felt. Her emotions were slowly coming to a boil. Never in her nineteen years had she been near a man who had this effect on her. Cousin Francis was charming, attractive, and interesting, but beside Charles Collins, he faded to a pale excuse for a man. Then Collins went on, his voice low and hoarse with emotion, "You are my only hope, Georgina. Somewhere in that vast house must be a record of that marriage."

Feeling betrayed, she tried to pull away from him. "That's all you're interested in, isn't it?" she demanded bitterly. "Your legacy. The proof that you should be the viscount, not Francis. You want to be Earl of Margate when your poor, sick father finally dies." She snatched her hand away from him, and turned to run from the room.

Collins caught her and turned her to face him, his hands like iron on her shoulders, bruising her flesh.

"Georgina, how can you think that? Don't you understand what I want? Of course I want my rightful legacy. Hellingham should be mine, and the earldom. But, now that I have met you, it isn't just for me that I want these things. It is for you, too." He pulled her to him in a rough embrace that took her breath away, and when his lips found hers, they were hot and demanding. Some of the village boys back in Trindale had kissed her, and Mr. Fenton had soiled her lips with his own on occasion when he had trapped her behind the loom and she couldn't escape, but nothing in her life had prepared her for the burst of passion loosed in her when Collins's lips met her own. Her bones seemed to melt, and she swayed against him, her face lifted to his to accept his demanding kisses.

"Ah, Georgina," he groaned as his ardent lips found her throat, the hollow of her shoulder, and then moved down to the swell of her bosom.

"Don't," she begged. "Please, Charles, don't."

But he paid no heed at all to her pleading. Georgina seemed to be two people. One was a woman she didn't recognize, a creature full of fire and passion, who was yielding herself to this demanding male who had set her emotions ablaze with his ardent lovemaking. The other was, perhaps, the Georgina she knew, the familiar girl, the vicar's daughter. This Georgina looked down from somewhere above, seeing the drama that was being played out in the private parlor of Ye Grape before the blazing fire. This girl wanted to cry out, "Stop, stop, Georgina, before it is too late!" but she was mute, her tongue paralyzed. She watched as the man's knowing hands undid the fastenings of her gown, moving skillfully from much experience. The watching Georgina acknowledged bitterly that he had undone many a maid's gown in his travels on the London-Exeter road, but even as he was removing her clothing, she could not protest. With ever-increasing ardor she returned his kisses, and even found her own fingers swiftly unbuttoning his plain brown waistcoat and untying the white lawn neckcloth he wore.

Then they lay on the bearskin rug in front of the hot fire, but the flames that danced in the fireplace were never as hot as the passions that flamed between the man and woman on the rug. His eager hands caressed her lovely bare breasts, and when his lips kissed them, Georgina heard someone moaning, not recognizing it as herself in her ecstasy. She had prided herself on being a virgin. She had intended to remain so until she married. Now all she wanted was to give herself to Charles Collins, to please him in any way he wanted. What she was most unprepared for was the discovery that she was as eager for this pleasure as he was. As their bodies joined in love, she matched his rhythm with her own, until finally, in a wave of sensation so acute that she felt she could not bear it, she achieved that ultimate in sensations, crying out from the intensity of her pleasure.

They lay on the soft fur rug, their limbs still entwined, and Collins murmured endearments to her which she listened to, starry-eyed.

"You will help me, won't you, my dearest Georgina?" he begged, his lips caressing her bare shoulder, the words so soft that she scarcely heard them.

Sated with love, holding this passionate man in her true woman's embrace, she was ready to promise him anything, anything. "What can I do?" She sighed as waves of feeling still swept over her body in lingering reminders of the joy she had created with him. "You've lived in Hellingham for years. If you haven't found evidence that your mother's marriage was legal, how do you expect me to succeed?"

He groaned and buried his face in her bosom. "You're right," he murmured. "There's no hope."

Caught in the trap of her feelings, she said, "Charles, I can't promise anything, but if his lordship, the earl, does say anything which might be a clue to your status, I shall surely remember and get word to you."

"Ah, that's my darling Georgina." His kiss was all the thanks she wanted.

They lay there, relaxed and happy, while the fire burned down. Finally, reluctantly, Georgina said, "I must get back to Hellingham, dear Charles. No one knows where I am."

She could feel his muscles tense. "Francis—where is he? What excuse did you give my dear brother for your absence?"

"He's gone to London to see His Majesty, King George."

"Well, remember he has spies. The servants report to him."

She shivered in spite of the warmth thrown out from the fire and the more intimate warmth of the nude male body embracing her. "If he should find out—he'd be furious."

"Just be careful when you go back. Did you come out through the little gate in the wall?"

"Yes, Lizzie mentioned it to me. She slips out through it to see her young man." *And so do I,* Georgina thought, smiling a little secret smile, *and so do I.*

She moved as if to get up, but Charles held her so that she couldn't leave his embrace. "Georgina?" There was a questioning note in his voice which cut through her blissful haze, alerting her senses, pulling her away from the comfort of her love.

"Yes, what is it, Charles?"

His fingers caressed her flesh, but suddenly Georgina felt that he was doing it automatically, that he wasn't thinking of her at all, but of something entirely different.

"When you found the gold brooch for the woman at The Fallen Angel—how did you do it?"

"I thought I told you. I don't really know. It's a gift which comes and goes. I don't like to think about it, Charles. It has often brought me more unhappiness than it is worth." She sighed, then said bitterly, "It isn't nice to be called a witch." This time when she shivered, it was because she remembered that they still burned witches at the stake.

"Could you—no, that would be asking too much of you." Now his hands were carefully caressing her breasts, rousing her again so that she found it difficult to think.

"Could I—what?" Did he want to make love again? Georgina had no experience with men. She'd heard the whispers from other girls her age. Village life could be very blunt and earthy at times. But she didn't know what to expect of Collins.

"Could you try to find the proof I need?"

Her voice was now hoarse with desire as she said, "I told you I'd listen to the earl—"

"No, that's not what I mean, Georgina. Can you try to use that strange gift of yours to find proof that I am truly the firstborn legitimate son of the earl?"

His hands closed on her flesh so hard that she cried out with pain. "Sorry," he muttered. "I am so desperate, Georgina—please, can't you help me?"

"I don't know," she cried in protest. "I can't control my gift. I never know. Sometimes I can find things, and sometimes I can't. Now—I don't even know what it is that I'm supposed to look for."

"Oh. You have to know the exact object. I should have thought of that."

"Charles, I'm sorry. If I thought that it would work—"

"Will you try? Couldn't you just—think of my great

need? It would have to be a paper of some kind, I should think. A legal document."

"But you said the license was burned."

"There must be something else. There *has* to be!"

Georgina was frightened by the intensity of his words. His blue eyes, so close to her, glittered with reflected firelight. The planes of his face were like granite. All of the warm, relaxed feeling was gone, replaced by something frightening in its intensity.

"It would have been associated with your mother?" He nodded. "Then it would help if I had something of hers to hold in my hand. Do you have anything of your mother's?"

He frowned, thinking. "The miniature! Would that do?"

"It was hers?"

"Yes, father had it painted and gave it to her." His eagerness frightened Georgina.

"I—I don't know," she wailed. "It may not work."

Suddenly the whole lovely experience with him was marred by his insistence on this. He got up from the bearskin rug without even kissing her, and quickly drew on his clothing which he had discarded so recklessly earlier. Biting her lips to keep from crying in disillusionment, Georgina dressed, her shaking fingers fumbling the fastenings of her dress.

Meanwhile Collins had gotten the miniature of his mother from his waistcoat pocket, and was waiting impatiently for her to be ready to try to use her powers to find the proof he so ardently wanted. If he noticed how unhappy she was, he gave no evidence of it.

Georgina reached for the miniature with reluctance. It was all wrong—the setting, the emotional climate, the reason for trying to find the proof for Collins. Even before she tried, Georgina knew that she would fail. But with this vibrant, exciting man standing here beside her, demanding that she try, there was nothing else for her to do. Even though she felt as if she'd been used solely to get her cooperation, Georgina couldn't deny the tremendous attraction Charles Collins had for her.

She studied the pretty face with the hazel eyes, then her own eyes went to Charles's face. There was no look of his mother there. He was a Hardy, every feature a mirror of his father's looks. Trying to compose herself, Georgina closed her eyes and breathed deeply. She folded her fingers around the small picture of Rebecca Collins. With an effort she washed her mind clear of all thoughts of Charles, all emotions, all images. For the first time since she had become aware of her gift for "finding," Georgina tried to force the gift to work for her. Nothing happened. Concentrate as she might, she was unable to pierce the curtain which separated her from the visions which might help the man standing there beside her, so eagerly awaiting her words. Georgina felt herself swaying, and then his arm was about her, supporting her.

"Georgina, are you all right?"

"I—I feel faint," she managed to say, fumbling in her pocket for the plain glass vinaigrette in which she carried smelling salts.

Collins, realizing what she wanted, uncorked the bottle and waved it under her nose until the fumes of the sal volatile brought tears to her eyes, and she pushed the vinaigrette away, her fainting spell now driven away by the ammonia.

"What did you see?" he demanded. Not a word about how she felt.

Georgina's eyes prickled with unshed tears. Blinking furiously, keeping her head averted so that Collins would not see how distressed she was, she murmured, "I'm sorry. Truly I am, Charles. I didn't see anything." Then, angrily, bitter that he should put here in such a position, she cried, "How can I find something that isn't there—how can I see anything when you don't even know what you want me to look for? I'm not a magician. Nor a witch." The scalding words fell from her lips as she thrust the miniature back into his hand.

Collins seemed to realize that he had handled the situation badly, for he now caught Georgina in his arms, laying his cheek against her golden hair, murmuring endearments. She struggled against his superior strength in vain. Even though she was enraged at him, and furious with herself for giving in to his demands, his very nearness set her blood to singing through her veins, and she was sure he could hear the pounding of her heart.

"Dearest Georgina, I shouldn't have asked the impossible of you." With one of his mercurial changes of mood, he flung back his head, smiling that heart-turning smile of his. "Ah, dearest love, how can I ever thank you enough for what you have given me tonight? You have made me the happiest man in all of England. Tonight." His kiss was so inflaming that all Georgina could do was react, feel—she was completely unable to think.

"Don't feel distressed that you weren't able to find the proof I so desperately need," he murmured, his lips close to her ear. "Just listen to my father. If he does say anything which you think might help me, remember—leave word here with the landlord. He can be trusted. He'll get word to me."

Georgina's emotions were at war with her strongly nurtured conscience, with her strict moral values. Still with some qualms about what Collins wanted her to do, yet knowing that she could not refuse his request, she reluctantly said she must go back to Hellingham.

"If the earl should call for me, as he does from time to time, it would be very bad for me to be gone. I'm sure Mrs. Pruning would tell Viscount Quincy." She shivered. That was a situation she wouldn't relish.

Again Collins kissed her until her knees felt weak. If he had asked her to spend the night there at Ye

Grape with him, Georgina would have said yes, but if she expected him to beg her to stay longer, she was to be disappointed.

"I wish I could see you back to the gate, Georgina, but no one must know you have seen me. Francis hates me enough as it is. If he should find out you've been with me. . . ." He didn't finish the sentence. He didn't have to.

Now she felt that Collins, his mission accomplished, wanted to be rid of her. Although the walk to the little door in the wall was short, she did not like to travel alone this late at night. The innkeeper hurried her to the door of Ye Grape, and she kept her face concealed with her hood as before. Once outside the porch, Georgina was dismayed to find that the moon was behind the clouds which had boiled up. It was dark, and the wind had risen, swirling dead leaves about the road and plucking at her cloak.

Georgina got back through the gate and the garden without mishap, but when she slipped into the house, Puffy came waddling out of a room down the corridor and yapped at her. Instantly Mrs. Pruning appeared.

"I thought you were ill!" the housekeeper said sharply, not trying to hide her dislike for Georgina.

Although reluctant to lie, Georgina knew she must hide her assignation with Collins from the woman. "I felt some air might clear my head," she said glibly. How easy it was to learn to lie! "So I went out in the garden briefly, but the wind has come up, and I regretted my decision to take the air."

There. Let Mrs. Pruning disprove it.

"I wish you would let me know when you go out of the house, Miss Ryerston. If his lordship should call for you, I need to know where you are."

Rather than antagonize her further, Georgina said, "Of course," and swept past the housekeeper without another word.

But no summons came from the tower room that

night. Georgina lay in her curtained bed for hours, sleepless. Over and over she reviewed what had happened in the parlor of Ye Grape. Bitterly she regretted succumbing to Charles's sweet seduction. Yet even as she berated herself for listening to his blandishments, submitting to his desires, Georgina had to admit that she would do the same thing again, at any time, as eagerly and willingly as she had tonight. She loved Collins. Her virginity meant nothing to her. If she could please him as he had pleased her, she was his for the asking. Aching with desire, she tossed and tumbled in her lonely bed.

It troubled her, too, that Collins expected her to find out something about his status. How could she? She didn't even see the Earl of Margate except when he asked for her, and then Miss Twistle guarded him jealously every moment that Georgina sat with him, lest she usurp the companion's position. It was hopeless. Yet Georgina knew that she would do everything in her power to help Charles Collins.

CHAPTER 10

"Oh, I'll never learn piquet!" Georgina wailed, laying down her cards.

Across the inlaid gaming table from her, Olivia Nugent smiled, shook her head. "I cannot get used to the idea of a woman who doesn't play cards! Everyone plays, Georgina."

"Not where I come from," Georgina muttered, rebellious.

Olivia Nugent had invited her to play piquet, and when Georgina told her she didn't know the game, Francis's mistress, bored with inactivity as Francis had not yet returned from London, offered to teach her some card games.

"Didn't people play whist?"

"Perhaps at the squire's house," Georgina conceded, "but people in my village were poor, Olivia. The poor have no time for such foolishness as card games. They are busy from dawn to nightfall working for a living. Their pleasures are few, believe me. They may see an occasional performance by a traveling troup of actors, and they have Maypole dancing, or Morris dancing at appropriate times. The men play shove-ha'penny at the taverns. But the ladies don't sit around a card table playing whist or piquet or any other games."

"What did you do in your spare time, Georgina? You are well educated, so I assume you went to school."

"No, my father tutored me at home. He was an Oxford scholar. As to spare time, Olivia, I was the

114

vicar's daughter, with no mother. I acted as hostess for my father, and did the things usually done by the vicar's wife. Then I had my loom." Candidly she declared, "If I never see a loom again, I shall be blissfully happy."

"You are a weaver?" Olivia's eyebrows went up. "How droll. And yet you are Francis's—cousin?"

"A very distant cousin, Olivia, but yet, a cousin. I wove to make a bit of pocket money for myself. St. Edmund's was not a wealthy parish, Olivia. Father had little of this world's goods. But we had enough," she added loyally, and she meant it. "We never went hungry. Papa had a bit for books. We managed."

"But to work at a loom—that's not easy, is it?"

"No. It is very tiring. But I could do it at home. It paid me more than I could have made otherwise." Then she grinned, and confided in her companion. "The man who owned the loom wanted me to become his mistress when Papa passed away. You don't know how much delight it gave me to be able to tell the skinny old lecher that I was leaving Trindale to stay with my cousin, an earl."

"Was he rich, this man who owned the loom?"

"I thought so then. Now that I'm at Hellingham. . . ." Georgina rubbed one hand over the beautiful fruitwood inlay of the card table. "Mr. Fenton probably would never be able to buy such a table as this."

"One need never worry at Hellingham," Olivia said smugly. "The Hardy men are rich, and keep getting richer. Francis gambles, of course. Who doesn't? But he never loses huge sums of money as some do." She leaned across the table, her ample bosom rising in white mounds above the tightly-cut bodice of her pink morning dress. "Francis told me that the Duke of Edgerson killed himself last week—stuck a duelling pistol in his mouth and blew out his brains—when he lost his last ten thousand pounds on the turn of a card in faro. It was at Miller's gambling hell off Lincoln's Inn Fields."

Aghast, Georgina exclaimed, "How dreadful! Suicide!"

"It was that or debtor's prison," Olivia said, shrugging. "But come, we must get back to our game. I'm sure that Francis will expect you to learn whist, but we need four to play. I suppose Miss Twistle could sit in. Even old Pruning holds a hand occasionally, in a pinch. But you need the game socially. So we start today with two-handed piquet. You can graduate to whist a bit later. Now, remember, if you are dealt a hand containing no face cards—you know which ones they are, don't you?—you declare *carte blanche* and it gives you ten points."

The game went on until Georgina insisted that her head was aching so abominably that they must stop. At least she had learned the names of the face cards; it was a start.

Olivia was loath to let her leave, though, being so bored without her lover there. "Francis says he plans to give a huge ball—a masquerade—to introduce you to local society," she told Georgina. "It should be very amusing. I love masques, don't you?"

"I never went to one," Georgina had to admit.

"Never? Georgina!" There was proper horror in the woman's voice. "Do you dance?"

"I've done a few folk dances on the village green."

"But the gavotte—the minuet—the mazurka—the waltz. Can you do them?"

Feeling more countrified by the second, Georgina shook her head. She wished the dressmaker from Staines would arrive for some fittings. Or the earl would wish to see her. Anything to rescue her from this inquisition. She wished she knew Olivia's background, but Georgina felt too shy to retaliate with personal questions of her own. So she had to sit there in silent agony as she owned up to the fact that she knew none of the current dances.

"Well! The minute Francis returns, I'll tell him that he must get a dancing master in. There's no other way for you to learn in time for the ball. There's a good one—French—in Staines. We'll have him teach you." Then, with uncommon perception, she added, "You must forget your vicarage upbringing, Georgina. Francis likes sophisticated women, my dear. As you are family, he'll expect you to be adept in all the social graces, so as to show him to good advantage. Our Francis is very vain. Remember that. And as his cousin, anything you do will reflect on him."

Georgina had never acted in a play, but she had seen performances, and she was familiar with the concept of stage fright. She was sure she'd be afflicted with it when she first went on display at some social function here at Hellingham.

"No doubt the viscount will try to arrange a good marriage for you, too," Olivia went on, for all the world as if she were his viscountess, and not his mistress.

This frightened Georgina. Marriage. It had never occurred to her that her cousin might suggest any such thing. En route to Hellingham, and at the vicarage during those last sad and dreadful weeks while she waited in vain for the letter to come from the earl, Georgina had indulged in much daydreaming about meeting and marrying a rich young lord. But that was all before Charles. After last night, Georgina could not bear to think of marrying any other man.

"Woolgathering, Georgina?" Olivia asked, her voice sharp.

"Sorry," Georgina said too quickly. "I—I didn't sleep too well last night." She was on the defensive, saying too much.

"Pruning said you were ill. But I heard a juicy little

rumor about a mysterious young lady who was at Ye Grape last night." Her smile was hard and glittery.

She can't know for sure, Georgina thought, her mind racing frantically. *If I don't admit anything, Olivia can't prove anything.*

"Ye Grape?" she asked, hoping her face was as innocent as her voice, which she kept under the strictest control. "What is Ye Grape?"

For a long moment Olivia stared at her, green eyes narrowed. Then she gave a little shrug as if to say, *I tried,* and told Georgina, "It's an inn just outside the gates. Surely you've seen it."

"It was long dark when I arrived," Georgina reminded her, "and by then I was so weary from the coach ride that I'm not sure I'd have seen Exeter Cathedral if it had been just outside the gates of Hellingham. Besides, it was pouring rain. Did we pass the inn on our way from Staines?"

"No, it is just beyond," Olivia conceded.

Georgina didn't know whether it was best to let the subject of the mystery woman drop, or to ask Olivia questions, pretending interest. It might be more natural to ask. "A mystery woman—that sounds exciting, Olivia. What did she do at Ye—Ye Grape?" She gave a slight smile, although it felt wooden, as if carved on her face. "Why did anyone notice her? Surely inns have so many people—we were crowded at every inn we went into on the trip—what did she do to cause comment?"

Had she thrown Olivia off the scent? She didn't know.

Olivia shuffled the cards expertly, although she did not deal out another hand of piquet. "She was so muffled in a hooded cape that no one saw her face." Then she paused for effect. Narrowing her green eyes, Olivia said too casually, "They say Charlie was at Ye Grape last night."

"Charlie?" Georgina widened her eyes in innocence,

and prayed that her voice didn't quaver to give her away.

"Your coachey, my dear. Charlie Collins."

"Oh, that Charlie." *Don't say more,* Georgina cautioned herself. *It's so easy to say too much in lying. Let Olivia do the talking.*

"You must have had a lovely trip, sitting beside Charlie all the way across England."

Georgina shrugged. "It was bitter cold, Olivia, and it poured rain a good deal of the time. By the time we were ready to stop for the night, I could scarcely stand up, I'd been so cramped for room, crowded between the coachey and the guard. But it was that or cling to the luggage tied on top of the coach. Next to him was the only place available on the coach, and I was glad to get it."

"Did you find Charlie—attractive?"

Georgina did some lightning-fast mental gymnastics. What was the best approach to use with this avidly curious woman—and why was Olivia so curious? She'd had Charles for her own, if Lizzie was to be believed, yet she'd abandoned him for Cousin Francis. Why would she care what he did now?

"Mr. Collins was a perfect gentleman. I did wonder at him. He was so obviously well educated. It seemed strange to find such a man driving a stagecoach." She had no intention of letting Olivia know that she was aware of Charles's history.

"Oh, didn't you know?" Those lips smiled, but the hard green eyes were glittery and unreadable. "He's the earl's bastard. I would have supposed that Lizzie, whose tongue wags at both ends, would have told you all about him."

Hoping to change the subject, Georgina said easily, "Oh, she is a little chatterbox, but I don't pay much attention to what she says. I do feel badly, though, that she was taken away from you and given to me as my abigail. However do you manage without her?" Inside, Georgina was giggling. All her life she'd done for herself, with no maid to do her hair or to help her dress. Having her own abigail was an experience! And there was something in Olivia Nugent's manner which told Georgina that dear Olivia had not been raised in a noble family, a member even of the gentry. She'd not been used to abigails until she came to Hellingham, of this Georgina was sure.

Looking up at a lovely gilt clock on the marble chimneypiece, Olivia said, "I'm expecting a new abigail to arrive shortly. She's from Staines, and comes highly recommended. Mrs. Pruning heard about her. Marie. French."

My, my, a French abigail. Georgina wondered how little Lizzie would react to that.

But she said politely, "I do hope that she works out well. I find that Lizzie does hair beautifully." She patted her golden locks lightly.

"You should powder," Olivia said, pursing her lips and looking at Georgina as if she were some kind of museum exhibit. "Francis likes powder."

"I've tried it, but I didn't have her bother today." And I didn't have my hair powdered last night for dear Charles.

As if picking the thought right out of her mind, Olivia went back to her discussion of Collins as if there had been no intervening conversation. "Charles Collins—the earl's bastard—was living here until recently. Francis can't abide him, of course. And why should he? Collins is trying to cheat Francis out of his rightful inheritance. As long as the earl was well, he pampered Charlie—made him think he'd be legitimatized. But there never was a chance of that. These old families don't mind bastards, but they call them bastards and they don't let them inherit. Charlie's insane to think that he'll ever get the title. He's more likely to wind up in Bedlam than in Hellingham!"

"It sounds like a cruel fate to know you have a peer for a father, but that you can't be acknowledged."

"Charlie will survive," Olivia said cynically. "I do wonder who the mystery woman was, though. She spent the evening with Charlie. There's no question about that."

Although she hated herself for it, feeling that she was betraying her love, Georgina said, "Well, the coachey didn't seem to lack for barmaids to amuse him en route. No doubt his companion last evening was some dollymop he knows in the local village."

"Perhaps. Perhaps not. Charlie can be quite devious. Francis got rid of him, and not a moment too soon. With someone like that around, a bastard with overweening ambition, life can be dangerous for the legitimate heir to the earldom."

Georgina was shocked. "You make it sound as if Char—Mr. Collins was trying to kill Cousin Francis."

"It would remove the competition."

"But it wouldn't make the coachman any more eligible to become Earl of Margate than he is now," Georgina reminded her companion.

Olivia shrugged. "Charlie has a vast reservoir of misplaced hope, Georgina. And he is bitter. Beware a bitter man, Georgina. He can be dangerous."

"I scarcely see how all this talk of the coachey concerns me." She must allay Olivia's suspicions. If she talked to Cousin Francis, passed on the gossip, made him suspect that Georgina had met Charles . . . it didn't take a vivid imagination to know what the viscount's reaction would be. Georgina had already seen him in a rage at his sick father. She certainly didn't want him angry at her.

But oh, how could she bear not to see Charles again, to lie in his arms, to have him make love to her? Even though she had left Ye Grape convinced that

Collins had only used her to further his own selfish interests, Georgina knew that he had only to send for her again, and she would move heaven and hell to go to him. The ecstasy she had enjoyed last night, that taste of heaven, had only made her hungry for more. It was unbearable to think of her Charles in bed with some serving wench along his coach route. Georgina knew, though, that he wasn't going to enter a monastery because he had bedded her, and was waiting only for her. He was a lusty man, full of fire and vigor, and he would take his pleasure where he could find it. And after seeing all of the barmaids at the inns between Trindale and Staines falling over each other to attract his attention, Georgina knew there would be no dirth of beds into which he could climb for his enjoyment. She was consumed with jealousy. Even Olivia, here, had been one of his women, galling though it might be to Georgina.

Now I'm in the same class with Olivia, she thought. *It should appall me to be so judged, but I would rather share him, even with Olivia, than never to be with him again.*

Where was all of her good upbringing? The years in the vicarage, with her kind, gentle Papa as her mentor? Vanished, washed away in a tide of consuming passion. She had thought of love as something on a high plane, as romantic, noble, and now she learned that love was a physical experience so all-consuming as to change her instantly into a woman she could scarcely recognize. Where was the Georgina Ryerston of the first nineteen years of her life, raised in a vicarage, looking forward to marriage? Gone. In her place was a woman no better than the lowliest barmaid, one who wanted nothing more now than a chance to lie in Charlies's arms, to feel the heat of his passion, to have his eager, skillful hands caress her flesh, rouse her to heights of rapture that made every other emotion seem pallid.

Georgina had not even suspected that she had such a passionate nature, for until she met Charles Collins, this nature had slumbered.

How was she to endure being separated from him?

CHAPTER 11

Francis returned from London two days later. Shortly after his arrival, a footman came to tell Georgina that his lordship wished to speak with her. Expecting word of a future audience with His Majesty at the Court of St. James, Georgina was completely unprepared for Francis's tirade which he unleashed against her the moment they were alone.

"Cousin Georgina, have I taken an adder into my nest?"

Georgina could see that Viscount Quincy was barely able to control his rage, and she trembled. She felt guilty, even without knowing what troubled Cousin Francis, for she had pledged herself to help Collins oust this personable young man from Hellingham and the peerage.

Trying, though, to dissemble, Georgina asked, her voice quavering in spite of her efforts to keep it steady, "What do you mean, Cousin Francis? Have I displeased you in any way? I go to your father whenever the nurse calls me—"

"And to the pretender to my title whenever you can slip away! Planted on me—a spy in my own family."

Now Georgina feared for her physical well-being. The young lord, clad in a black velvet riding habit, tall black knee boots clacking on the parquet floor, came toward her, flicking a riding crop against one boot. Would he dare strike her with the whip? Slowly, step by step, Georgina backed away from Francis, and inexorably he matched her steps, advancing as she retreated. Then, when she had backed to the wall and manhood, seen him seduce the kitchen maids first, then the housemaids, and finally I saw him try to ruin poor Miss Nugent, my companion. She was father's companion before you arrived here, but obviously she was wasted on him!" He gave a secret little smile which Georgina had no trouble interpreting. She knew exactly what Olivia's position was here at Hellingham.

"Miss Nugent is indeed lovely," she said noncommittally.

"Charlie thought so, too, but Miss Nugent chose me over him, not wanting to be allied with a bastard pretender to the Margate Earldom. Charlie tried to take her to London with fine tales of love, a discreet establishment in Grosvenor Square. He attempted to lure her with lies of his inheritance; told her, from what she has said, that he would one day be Fifth Earl of Margate. But she wasn't taken in. Olivia had heard tales of our fine Charlie, how he tired of women and then discarded them. And when he did, he'd take them to London and sell them to Moll Bailey so he'd have money in his pocket. You've heard of Moll Bailey, little cousin? She's the infamous London procuress."

"No!" Afraid she would be physically ill, Georgina gulped at the remaining Madeira in her glass, then put down the crystal goblet with trembling fingers.

"I am sorry to have to be so blunt, to tell you such an ugly, sordid story, Cousin Georgina. It is for your own good. I know how charming Charlie Collins can be. I've watched him polish that charm over the years. But you are my own kin, and I cannot let him use his wiles to win you. Seduction is all he is interested in, dear Georgina. I beg your forgiveness for having to introduce such a coarse subject into our conversation; it is to your advantage to know the man behind the charming façade."

"I—I don't know what to say."

"Say nothing, little cousin. Just be wary the next time Charlie invites you to sup with him. Weren't you supper, I might add—in the private parlor. Don't try to deny it."

Trapped, Georgina only nodded mutely, still terrified. She had lied to Olivia, but she had not the will to lie to Francis. Georgina was much too afraid of him. Would her cousin cast her out? Would she have to find some other home, now that she'd come to think of Hellingham as her haven?

"I think it would be wise if you told me all about it, cousin. What's Charlie's game now?" His smile was even more terrifying than his scowl, making her tremble. "Come, come, speak up, Georgina! How did you meet Charlie?"

Georgina managed to control her voice as she answered, "He was coachman on the stage from Exeter. I hadn't booked in advance, not being much traveled, so when the stage stopped at The Bee and Thistle in Trindale, there was no room for me in it. I was much distressed, for the new vicar had no room for me in his home. Charl—Mr. Collins offered me a seat in the box with him and the guard." Ingenuously she added, "And it was only half fare outside."

"So you rode all the way from the outskirts of Exeter with Charming Charlie, God's gift to the ladies." He nodded. "How many days?—five?—six?—plenty of time for him to cast his spell over you, my innocent little Georgina."

Stung to the quick because it was partly true, she forgot her fear to say, "You make me sound like some ninny of a country maid." And she'd acted just like one lying with Charles on that bearskin rug.

Instantly Francis changed his tactics. "On the contrary, I admire your pluck immensely, Georgina. It must have taken a great deal of courage to leave your home and travel here to Hellingham as you did. But you see, I've known Charlie all my life. He's been here, underfoot, raised with me, given most of the privileges I've had—except the name! I've watched as he reached put her hands flat on the red silk wall covering, he stopped.

With the same kind of mercurial mood change she had seen in Collins, the young lord of Hellingham laughed. "Poor little Cousin Georgina." He smiled his most charming smile for her. "I'll swear, you remind me of a sparrow confronted by the big tomcat in the stables. Very well, I'm not going to eat you—at least not immediately." He held out a hand to her. "Come, cousin, let us sit down and discuss this matter with civility."

"Wha-what matter?" Despite all her efforts, Georgina's voice squeaked, making Francis laugh even more heartily.

He reached over, took her hand, and drew her toward a heavy Kent settee. "Sit down. Your hands are like ice!" He went to a sideboard and poured two glasses of Madeira. "Here, Georgina, drink this. You're like a ghost."

Obediently she sipped the wine, striving for composure.

"Now, what's this about your slipping away at Ye Grape to meet that bastard, Charles Collins?"

Georgina choked on the wine, and Francis patted her on the back solicitously until she recovered, even handing her the lace-edged kerchief which dangled from his sleeve. Georgina patted her lips, playing for time. So Olivia Nugent had tattled on her the moment that Cousin Francis walked in the door.

Waiting until she was composed, Francis said, "Sorry. I didn't mean to upset you so." He sat down beside Georgina, turning to face her. "Little goes on at Hellingham or its surrounds that doesn't come to my ears, little cousin. And when Charlie is in the vicinity, I get word quickly." He sipped wine delicately, then said coldly, "I know you met him at Ye Grape while I was away, and had supper with him—a lengthy alerted when he did not offer to escort you from Hellingham? Surely you do not think that gentlemen expect ladies to attend them at local taverns?"

Georgina felt her face grow hot with shame. "He said—he couldn't come here—I didn't know why—"

"Put it from your mind, dear Georgina. You don't have to explain Charlie to me. I can even guess what he wanted from you—other than the pleasure of your company. I don't wish to offend you. You are an extremely attractive young woman." He smiled appreciatively, his dark, satanic face lighting up as he let his eyes drift over her. "I don't wish to imply that Charlie does not find you attractive. He'd be blind if he didn't—and Charlie's never been blind to a lovely woman! But he has an ulterior motive, I fear, in his attentions to you. Be honest with me, Georgina. He wanted something from you, didn't he? No, not the usual, vulgar desire—I don't mean that. Charlie wants you to do something for him here at Hellingham, something to further his insane ambition to become earl when my father dies. And as that moment could arrive soon, Charlie's getting frantic in his ambition."

Again Georgina's mental distress was so extreme that it made her feel nauseous. She groped for her wineglass, forgetting that it was empty. Without a word, the viscount took it, and poured the rich amber-colored wine into it from the cut glass decanter.

She sipped at it, grateful for a moment's respite. Her family loyalty forced her to speak at last. "He did tell me about his mother." Georgina looked Francis in the eyes. "Charles says that his mother was legally married to his lordship."

"And he wants you to find that elusive magic paper, the wedding lines. Ah, I see by your face that I'm right. Let me save you much time, Georgina. The license isn't elusive—but illusive, a figment of his imagination. A sop to propriety offered by his mother to her parents to account for her bastard. Do you really imagine, if they had thought their daughter the true wife of my father, wrongfully kept from her position as wife, do you truly believe that if they believed Charlie, their grandson, to be the heir to Hellingham, that they'd have stayed on here all those years, silent?"

"Charles—Mr. Collins—said—"

Viscount Quincy waved a languid hand. "Spare me Charlie's arguments. I've grown up with them. He lies. Or perhaps his mind is turned, maybe he truly believes what he says. Georgina, do you think that if there had been a grain of truth in his allegations, something would not have emerged during the more than twenty years since my birth? My father would not deny the title to his beloved Charlie if he were legitimate." Again she saw a glimpse of that wicked temper. "I've never been father's favorite. But even he cannot deny me my rightful heritage. When he dies, I shall be Fifth Earl of Margate. And my son, the Sixth." As quickly as his temper had flared, it was gone. Georgina's cousin smiled at her. "So, no need for you to rummage through the attics which are full of dust and cobwebs, nor to search the volumes in the library. You won't have to examine the dressers and desks for secret drawers, nor the paneled walls for sliding doors leading to priestholes. There is no marriage license."

Then Georgina remembered what Collins had told her. "He said that your father burned the license in his mother's presence, telling her it was a fake."

Francis shrugged. Then he smiled, changing his entire expression. "I'd not heard that version of Charlie's story." He shook his head, amazed. "Indeed, he becomes more inventive as the years pass—or madder." He poured more Madeira for himself, offering it to her, but she refused the wine. "If true, and I'm not saying it mightn't be, it just shows how clever father could be when he wanted a reluctant woman." His face sobered. He sat beside Georgina, putting down the crystal wineglass and taking her hand between both of his. "Father had a way with women, and Charlie inherited that trait. Don't trust him, Georgina. He means you no good. If you were someone else, I wouldn't bother to warn you, but you're my cousin, and a lovely, innocent young woman. I can't allow him to use you shamefully to act as his spy, when he's thinking only of himself, not of you."

Georgina tried to speak, found herself choked with unshed tears, and kept silent. It was cruelly hurtful to find she'd been duped by the man she found so devastatingly attractive, to know she had given herself passionately to a glib deceiver. It was a shattering revelation. Georgina's cousin seemed to understand her emotional upheaval. He gave her hand a warm little squeeze, a little shake, then relinquished it, taking up his wine and sipping. Hoping the painful interview was at an end, she was just gathering up the courage to ask to be excused when Francis Hardy began to speak quietly, not looking at her.

"For your own safety, Georgina, I must ask you to promise me something. If Charlie approaches you again, if he sends messages secretly, you must tell me. Only if I know what that scoundrel is planning, can I thwart him." He turned to face her, and his eyes burned into her soul. "You have become very dear to me in the few days you have sheltered here at Hellingham, Georgina. I am not going to let Charlie ruin you. If necessary, I shall protect you from him, and from yourself. I know how devilishly attractive he is to women. I can't blame you for being drawn to him. But I warn you, nothing but sorrow can come to you from any association you have with Charles Collins. So, be a good girl, and promise me that you won't be taken in by him."

Georgina owed so much to Viscount Quincy that she had little choice. She promised what he asked, although it grieved her to do so. The weight of guilt and revulsion which she felt for having submitted to Charles's carnal desires flooded her with shame. Georgina had to atone, somehow, for her foolish, wanton actions. What better way than to help her dear Cousin Francis thwart the bastard Collins in his attempts to gain Hellingham and the title for himself?

CHAPTER 12

The Hellingham landau, its yellow and purple body gleaming with polish, pulled by four matched chestnut geldings, rattled along the rough road which led from the Margate holdings to the estate of the Marquis of Amesford. Although a little apprehensive on the occasion of her first social event since leaving Trindale, Georgina was full of excitement, too, as affairs at Paladino Manor were reputed to be splendid.

She, Olivia Nugent, and Cousin Francis were invited. The dressmaker from Staines had created a marvelous gown for Georgina from cloth of silver imported from the Continent. The décolletage was shockingly low, even for evening, but Georgina's firm young bosom took well to exposure. Lizzie had laced her so tightly that she thought she might faint. The abigail had only grinned and said, "It makes your bosom stand up even more, miss," and kept hauling on the laces while Georgina clung to the upright of her four-poster to keep from being pulled across her bedchamber. The overskirt was divided in the center and looped up, caught in place with bunches of silk posies of ruby red, with green leaves embroidered in tiny beads. The under petticoat was of the same rich red as the flowers, with an overall design of embroidery and beading. Silver shoes with high red heels peeped out from beneath the hem. Lizzie had dressed her hair with soft curls hanging down over one bare shoulder, all heavily powdered, and had insisted on painting her lightly, although Georgina would not let her use the white lead to cover her naturally pale skin. She did agree to a tiny black beauty spot beside one corner of her mouth, quite agreeing that it was most fetching, calling attention, as it did, to her nicely shaped mouth with its full, sensuous lips.

Her cloak was of sable lined with white satin, a luxury which she could scarcely comprehend. Cousin Francis, himself, had draped it over her shapely shoulders as they were ready to leave. Georgina had seen Olivia's mouth thin and her hard green eyes glitter in the candlelight of the entrance hall at Hellingham when Francis gave her the cape.

"I found this in London," he said. "My cousin mustn't get chilled in the night air."

Olivia, whose cloak was of rich velvet trimmed with ermine, said, "It is lovely—but such a bulky cape for someone so small."

Georgina recognized the sour grapes, but held her peace. She had no desire to quarrel with her cousin's mistress. Perhaps the sable wrap would have looked better on the more stately Olivia. However, Francis had not chosen to give it to his light of love, but to his churchmouse kinswoman.

Caressing the silky fur, she murmured, "Cousin Francis, it is much too fine for me."

He made a leg, elegant in his scarlet satin suit. "My dearest coz, nothing is too fine for you."

The look Olivia gave her—and Francis—was lethal, yet the viscount seemed not to notice it. In fact, Georgina felt a bit embarrassed that Francis seemed to be paying much more attention to her than he did to his own true love.

Olivia, gowned in moss green velvet laced with gold, looked magnificent. Her new French maid, Marie, had dressed her hair much higher than the current fashion in England, insisting that all of the Parisian ladies now wore more elaborate hair styles. She was painted dead white, with heavy rouging on lips and cheeks, and dark shadowing about her green eyes, showing them off to good advantage. She, too, wore a beauty patch, a large, spectacular design of a coach and four which reached from the corner of her mouth almost to the lobe of one ear. Her drop earrings were diamonds which glittered as much as her eyes.

Now, as they rode through the winter twilight, Francis kept up light, witty conversation mainly, Georgina thought, to put her at ease. At times Francis was capable of little kindnesses which surprised her, doing much to counter the rages he had at his poor, paralyzed father. The earl still lay in his sickbed, wasting away by the hour; yet he lived on, frustrating Francis in his desire to inherit the earldom.

Georgina pulled Francis's gift cloak about her. Despite his generosity, she was sure Francis would toss her out of Hellingham without a qualm if she betrayed him by spying for Charles. The thought of that, of returning, perhaps, to Trindale to work at a hated loom again, to be forced to submit to Fenton's lechery, was a frightening prospect. She liked living here with her cousin, pampered, with her own personal abigail, with no duties other than reading occasionally to the earl. Georgina loved the beautiful clothing she now had to wear, beginning with shifts of finest linen or Lyons silk trimmed with delicate Belgian lace. Her hose were knitted of silk, her shoes were of the finest Italian kid, and her gowns were all cut from the latest styles just over from Paris. And now she had a magnificent sable cape to wear over them. Life was very good to her, and Georgina wanted to keep it that way.

She tried to tell herself that the passionate scene on the bearskin rug in front of the fire in Ye Grape's private parlor had never happened. She tried to force Charles Collins from her mind, but at night as she lay in the high, canopied bed alone, Georgina ached with desire for the man her cousin warned was so dastardly. If Charles sent for her again, would she be able to resist the summons? She prayed she would not be put to the test; yet even as she hoped for this, Georgina bitterly resented the fact that Charles had not made any attempt to contact her since that fateful night.

"There's talk that the king may begin forcing landowners to keep roads on or along their property in good repair." Francis clung to a strap hanging on the side of their carriage to keep from being thrown to the floor when they hit an unusually bad bump.

"Oh, there are always such rumors about," Olivia said. "You know nothing ever comes of them. I think we have the worst roads in the civilized world, but no one does anything but talk about them. Every year the ruts go deeper."

"When I was coming from Exeter," Georgina said, "one of the passengers, a foreign gentleman from the Continent, said our roads here were excellent—and that our coaches were models of comfort."

She had just said the last word when they were rocked to and fro like passengers on a Channel packet in a mid-winter storm.

"The man must have escaped from Bedlam," Francis averred.

"Or if not, that's where he should have been sent." Olivia groaned. "I shall be bruised all over."

Fortunately the ride was soon at an end. The coachman turned from the road through the arched stone gateway with its capping pediment, and drove past a round stone building where Amesford's grooms exercised the horses in bad weather. There was a gibbous moon riding high in the sky, and by its light Georgina was able to see the outlines of Paladino Manor, one of the showplaces of the area. The three-storied main block of lovely gray granite was flanked on either side by curved colonnades leading to two other, smaller blocks. The proportions were Palladian, the effect graceful and elegant, light and airy. The driveway was lined with huge old beech trees, their bare limbs now silhouetted against the moonlit sky. The entire house was ablaze with light, outside torches lighting the main entry. The driveway curved around the front of the house, and was already full of all manner of landaus, berlins, chaises, and other coaches discharging passengers for the festivities.

"Everyone is here!" Olivia said, pointing out first one carriage and then another. Most carried coats of arms blazoned on the varnished doors. "There is the Duchess of Timberlake, with her new lover, the Duke of Asley," she said, pointing to a tall, thin woman and a giant of a man who were just entering the Manor. "I daresay her husband is in London. He can't stay away from the gaming tables. And there's the Marquis of Amseford, our host."

Georgina was so caught up in the excitement of the occasion that she forgot how unlikable the marquis was. She remembered, though, as her Cousin Francis presented their host who was in brilliant peacock blue with a waistcoat of palest robin's egg blue embroidered all over with seed pearls. Those cold, opaque gray eyes stripped her naked.

"Your cousin, Francis? How amazing." He took up the quizzing glass hanging on a gold chain about his neck, and peered once more at Georgina. "We have met before, Miss Ryerston." His mouth twisted in a sardonic smile. "You seem to like the Hardy men."

"I say, what does that mean, Howard?" the viscount interjected. "Georgina, where did you ever meet the marquis?"

Trapped, she had to tell the truth. "He was at an inn where we supped en route to Hellingham from Trindale."

"The Fallen Angel in Salisbury, to be exact," Amesford said, almost smirking.

Georgiana prayed that he would not divulge further details, but she should have known that a man as unpleasant as the young marquis wouldn't allow such an opportunity for spite and mischief-making to go unused.

"She was with your dear brother, Francis. He seems to be working as a coachey on the stage these days. But he still has an eye for a lovely lady." Then he smiled at Olivia. "And how are you, my dear?" It was almost as if he were including Olivia in Charles Collins's women. "Have you found anything since you came to Hellingham, Miss Ryerston?" he went on.

"Amesford, you are excessively cryptic tonight," Francis said, somewhat annoyed. "What was Georgina supposed to find at home?"

The pale eyebrows went up, making the long face seem even longer. "My dear fellow, didn't you know? Your charming cousin has special powers—she can find lost objects just by doing nothing but looking off into space. I saw a most marvelous demonstration at the inn in Salisbury." He turned to Georgina. "Surely, my dear, you told your cousin of your extraordinary powers."

Her evening was ruined already. "No, I did not." She was furious with the marquis, and let him see it. "It is not a subject on which I like to discourse."

Olivia's eyes widened, looking enormous with their dark rims of cosmetic. "Are you a witch, Georgina?"

"No, I'm not," she said crossly. "I do wish you hadn't brought up the subject," she told her host.

"But it is such a handy art," Amesford said. "Perhaps you could give a demonstration tonight. The guests would be most interested."

"I'm sorry," she said, her voice curt, "but it is not a parlor trick which I can do at will. It is a gift which comes to me occasionally, not something I can call up whenever I wish."

They moved away from their host into a magnificent saloon where the guests were assembled, bright as summer butterflies in their elegant attire of silk, satin, velvet and lace. The room was huge, with fluted columns of brown marble rising to a high mahogany dado. Over this, smaller flat columns of darker brown marble supported the coffered ceiling done in a brown plaster, with ornate chandeliers hanging at intervals. The chimneypiece was of carved white marble with a gilt-framed mirror over it which reflected the light of hundreds of white wax tapers which lighted the room. The floor was an intricate parquet pattern of vari-colored oak. In one corner was a small platform for a string orchestra. Along the end of the huge room was a larger platform, presumably for the players who were to perform later.

Leading the two women to a bench padded with pink brocade, Francis sat down.

"Now, what is this business of finding things, Georgina?"

Unhappily she told him the story as briefly as possible.

"Ah, so that's what the bastard wanted with you. He thought to make use of your gift to find this proof he's been searching for year after dreary year."

It cut Georgina to the quick to have her cousin say this; it was painfully true.

"I didn't realize that dear Georgina was such a friend of Charlie's," Olivia said spitefully. "I thought he was just her coachey." Georgina once again that evening sensed Olivia's jealousy. "Such a quiet little minx, aren't you?"

Defensive, Georgiana said, "He kindly invited me to take supper with him, because The Fallen Angel is an inn of great charm."

Francis added, quite coldly, "And what business is it of yours, Olivia, who sups with my cousin? You certainly know how appealing Charlie can be."

Realizing her error, Olivia tried to make amends, but Georgina knew that Francis was angry with his mistress. Off to a bad start, the evening was rapidly deteriorating.

Fortunately the musicians struck up a gavotte, and Francis, rising and bowing, asked Georgina to have the first dance with him. She knew that Olivia was fuming at this insult, but what could she do? She accepted, hoping that the few dancing lessons she'd had time for with the French master, M. Dupree, would keep her from disgracing herself and Francis.

"Olivia can be tedious at times," Francis murmured, as they moved through the figures of the dance. "She takes too much for granted. She really is rather common, though she likes to put on the airs of a great lady. But the blood in your veins, dear cousin, is much more noble than that which courses through hers." He gave her hand a squeeze.

Georgina scarcely knew what to say to Francis. She didn't want to be the cause of a rift between Olivia and her cousin, but sensed that Francis might be tiring of his mistress. These were hardly the first unkind comments about her to fall from his lips.

"Olivia seems well-spoken," she said neutrally.

"Oh, yes, she has learned well," was his careless reply, "but blood tells, Georgina." He said it with consummate arrogance.

"We cannot help who we are, cousin."

"True, but some try to rise above their stations in life. I should have let Charlie have her. She's more his level," and he laughed. "Charlie's not for such a lovely as you, dear cousin. But he's quite good enough for Olivia."

Poor Olivia, Georgina thought. *Does she realize that Francis is tiring of her? What will she do, where will she go, when Francis no longer wants her in his bed?* Then a most awful thought came to her. Would Olivia turn again to Charlie if Francis tired of her? But she mustn't think of Collins. He wasn't interested in her, only in what she could do for him. How bitterly she regretted giving herself to him! What would her cousin do if ever he found out what a fool

she had been? Would he throw her out of Hellingham?
It was a dreadful thought.

"Why so pensive, Georgina?" her cousin whispered.
"You must smile. You have a lovely smile, dear
cousin."

Obediently, Georgina smiled brightly and said, "I
must concentrate on the dance steps, Cousin Francis,
for I am new at this."

"No one would ever guess," he complimented her.
"I am the envy of every blood here. I see that I'll have
a steady stream of callers at Hellingham in the future
—all coming to pay court to my lovely cousin."

When the dance came to an end, Olivia was nowhere in sight. Francis scowled, but said nothing.
Georgina supposed that the other woman, furious that
Francis had not danced first with her, had gone off
somewhere to sulk.

This was indeed the case, as Georgina discovered
when, later, she went to the ladies' boudoir along a
curved passage from the crowded hall. Olivia was
there, sitting in front of a large mirror, daubing more
whiting on her already chalky face from an alabaster
pot with a gold lid. She saw Georgina in the mirror.
Looking at the mirrored reflection, she said, "Don't let
him turn your head, little country girl." It was in a
vicious undertone, but Georgina heard it all too well.
"Francis is interested in only one thing—bedding you.
So be prepared to accommodate him when we return
to Hellingham tonight. If you refuse him, he'll probably
send you packing. And come back to me. You're just
a novelty—a new face—rather pretty, but so unsophisticated. For the moment he thinks that's what
he wants. But your inexperience will bore him. Francis
was never one to want virgins in his bed. He likes
experience." Then, with consummate malice, she turned
and looked directly at Georgina, those hard green eyes
full of spite. "I'm sure you are a simpering virgin, my
pretty vicar's daughter. You're much too goody-goody

to bed a man." Her laugh was harsh and hateful. "Poor Charlie. I daresay you were a great disappointment to him the other night at Ye Grape. He's used to having women fall into his arms like ripe pears dropping from their branches. Although a vicarage-raised maiden might be quite a challenge to our Charlie." She gave Georgina a shrewd look. "He quite turned your head, didn't he, our handsome coachey? Were you shocked, little Georgina when ardent Charlie tried to get you out of your clothes? He's quite skillful at it, believe me, my dear. There's many a chemise he's seen, and what's under a chemise, too."

Georgina wanted to pick up the silver skirts of her gown and flee the boudoir, but then Olivia might guess the truth. At least she could be thankful for one thing: Francis's mistress had no idea that she had submitted to Collins with only the barest token of resistance. *Oh, how could I?* she thought. *I was sure he loved me. What a little fool I was. Love. Mister Charles Collins doesn't know what the word means. Lust he understands. Lust is all that he knows. And lust was all that he felt toward me.* Georgina could only hope that Collins, having been raised as a gentleman, would behave like one, and never tell anyone that he had seduced her so easily.

To Olivia, though, Georgina put on a deceiving face. "I saw all the serving wenches throwing themselves at Mr. Collins. What do you expect of him, Olivia? Men are men. If you think that being raised in a vicarage protects one from such knowledge, then you know nothing of the duties of a vicar. I grew up knowing of all the vices, all the sins, the human failings, the foibles of people. I know that men seldom turn down pleasure when it is offered."

"My, my! Quite the little philosopher, aren't we!"

By now Georgina was furious with Olivia Nugent. Casting caution to the winds, she snapped, "I find it strange that, being mistress to my Cousin Francis, you still seem to spend a lot of time talking about Charles Collins. Are you regretting your choice, Olivia? Do you wish now that you'd settled for Collins and his coach instead of for Francis and his earldom?"

Olivia's face turned so blotchy with rage that it showed even under the layers of paint with which she covered her skin. "You little hussy! Wait until the rotten old man dies, and Francis comes into his inheritance. Once I'm the Countess of Margate, don't think that you'll be staying on at Hellingham. I'll see to it that Francis sends you far, far away, Georgina. Or marries you off swiftly to one of his friends. I do not think that two beautiful women can live under one roof, no matter that the roof is as large as the one at Hellingham."

No more pretense of friendship, Georgina saw. She studied Olivia, whose beauty was already tarnishing very slightly. *Will I look like that someday?* Georgina asked herself, appalled at the prospect. *Is this what happens to a woman who allows any ardent male to occupy her bed? Will one slip place me forever beyond the pale of gentility?*

Fortunately further acrimonious discussion was prevented when an elderly maid in the maroon livery of Paladino Manor bustled into the boudoir. "Ladies, ladies," she cried, "the theatrical entertainment is about to begin. If you do not wish to miss the opening scene, you must hurry."

Glad of an excuse to get away from Olivia, Georgina quickly left, not waiting for the other woman. Cousin Francis was waiting impatiently. And for her, she discovered, not for Olivia.

"Amesford has arranged seats for us on the edge of the stage, so that we can see and hear everything. It's a traveling troup of players doing a shortened version of Gay's *The Beggars' Opera*. I understand they are quite clever."

There had been few theatrical performances at

Trindale. Occasionally at the fair there had been traveling players of mediocre ability, and once in a great while there was some Shakespearean drama produced, usually sponsored by the squire. Papa had even taken Georgina into Exeter on rare occasions to see some play, but this was a great treat for her. She noticed that there wasn't a vacant seat for Olivia. Georgina was seated between her host and her cousin, and she was vain enough to realize that they made a striking trio, the viscount with his dark good looks, the marquis with his fair skin and pale gray eyes. Once she caught a glimpse of Olivia, sitting with the other guests in the rows of chairs the footmen had quickly arranged at the end of the dancing. The orchestra remained to play for the opera.

To Georgina's untutored eye, it was a marvelous performance. She wept real tears when poor Polly Peachem pleaded for the life of the highwayman, and she clapped with great enthusiasm when the play was over.

"I've asked the two principals, the highwayman and the luscious little beauty who plays Polly, to mingle with the guests for a time," Amesford murmured. "I thought it would amuse everyone."

"Clever, Amesford, very clever," the viscount murmured. "Come, my dear cousin, meet a highwayman!" He held out a hand to Georgina, and they followed their host to the front of the stage, where the actors waited.

Close up, some of the glamor dissipated. The man who had been such a swashbuckling Captain Macheath had shifty eyes, while his pretty Polly was coarse and cheap. Still, they were actors, and Georgina was impressed with them.

Amesford called for more dancing, and the two members from *The Beggar's Opera* went through figures, dancing with lords and ladies as if it were an everyday occurrence.

They were still circulating among the guests when the butler, an impressive figure in maroon and silver, rang a small brass gong to signal that the repast was ready for the guests.

The state dining room had two long tables at either side, with an army of serving maids and footmen to load the lovely china plates with delicacies. At either end of one table were a pair of roasted swans, all feathers back in place, each resting on a "pond" of blue grapes. The other table boasted suckling pigs, while the tables groaned with a vast variety of other foods in between. There were roast beef, joints of mutton, hams, fowl of every description, both domestic and wild, with silver side dishes piled high with candied carrots, turnips and potatoes boiled together, great bowls of fresh peas grown in the estate hothouses, and even dishes of the lowly asparagus, usually served only in the cottages of the farmers, now embellished with special sauces which one guest said were direct from a famous chef at the palace of Versailles. There were sweets of all kinds, from treacle puddings to elaborate molded confections shaped to represent all kinds of animals, both real and mythical. The showpiece of the repast was a griffin molded of a stiff custard and covered with slivered almonds. Wine flowed, and the punch bowl was constantly replenished by kitchen boys who rushed in with full pitchers and rushed out with empty ones.

It was during the latter part of the meal that the Duchess of Timberlake let out such a screech that the hall came to an aching silence.

"My diamond necklace!" she cried. "It's gone!" She clutched frantically at her scrawny neck, patting down to her almost invisible bosom as if to find the necklace somehow embedded in her flesh.

Her escort boomed, "You were wearing it during the theatricals, my dear Duchess. No doubt it has dropped onto the floor. Perhaps the catch was not well fastened."

There was an immediate search launched, but when ten minutes passed and no necklace materialized, the atmosphere in the great hall of Paladino Manor became so tense it was almost tangible.

"Silly cow, she's worried because her husband paid a fortune for that bauble. If it's gone, he may inquire too closely for comfort into why she was here, and who escorted her." Francis had not bothered hunting, and he'd kept Georgina out of the thick of the crowd. By now Olivia had rejoined them, apparently realizing that by staying away from the viscount, she was merely playing into his hands if his intent was to get rid of her.

"It looked stupid on her scrawny neck, anyway," Olivia said cattily. "Now, if I had such a necklace. . . ."

Georgina's eyes were drawn immediately to Olivia's lush bosom and lovely white throat. She noticed that Francis wasn't bothering to look at Olivia at all. No doubt by now he knew every inch of her white skin by rote.

Their host, seeing the three of them off to one side, came gracefully but quickly to their sides.

"Gad, what bad luck to happen tonight! Drat the duchess, anyway. What could she have done with the diamonds?"

"Surely someone will find them," Georgina said. "I know she was wearing them earlier. I saw the gems." It was such a spectacular necklace that no one could have missed noticing it.

"It should have turned up immediately."

Francis said, "You're worried, aren't you, Amesford?"

"Of course I'm worried," the marquis snapped, his brow furrowed. "It'll be the talk of the *ton* that such a valuable thing disappeared at my rout. Would you want it to happen at Hellingham?" He scowled, spoiling his good looks, showing his petulant nature clearly.

"They'll all say that one of my servants stole it, no doubt."

"I shouldn't be surprised, Amesford. You know how people like to gossip."

"But that's terrible," Georgina cried. "There's no proof of theft, is there? No doubt the clasp came undone, and the necklace fell down somewhere."

The Marquis of Amesford looked at her, gray eyes widening, and then he grinned an almost wolfish grin. "As I live and breathe, dear Miss Ryerston, it is almost like the situation at The Fallen Angel.

"I say, my dear Quincy, why doesn't your lovely cousin help us?" Even as Georgina was shrinking back, wishing she could hide behind one of the marble columns, Amesford was advancing, a hand held out, gray eyes alive for the moment.

"Georgina?" Francis asked.

"I told you—she can find things. I saw her do her pretty little parlor trick in the inn at Salisbury. Come, come, my pretty, do help me out. The consequences may be disastrous otherwise."

"But I can't control my gift!" Georgina wailed. "I never know—"

Then Francis cut in, and Georgina knew that she was lost. "Surely you can try, dear coz," he said quietly; he left no room for refusal. "Amesford, here, is really going to be in bad shape if that valuable necklace doesn't turn up soon."

Bowing to the inevitable, she said, "Very well. I'll try. But you mustn't blame me if I don't succeed."

"My, your little witch trick!" Olivia said spitefully. "Maybe I'll see how it's done. It should be a great attention getter at any gathering."

Amesford ignored the remark, and Francis turned on her with such a black scowl that she retreated into sullen silence, hiding her face behind a dainty fan of carved ivory.

"What do you need to do, Georgina?" Francis asked.

"It helps if I hold the hand of the duchess," she admitted, somewhat daunted at the prospect.

Just then the butler approached, bowed, and said, "Milord, the players are ready to leave. Shall I pay them?"

"Oh, yes, and compliment them for me. They did a good job. Perhaps we can use them again."

Then he led Georgina across the huge hall to where the Duchess of Timberlake stood fuming; her lover, Asley, was by her side.

"My dear duchess," Amesford cried before she had a chance to launch into a tirade, "we are in luck. Miss Ryerston, here, has a gift for finding things. She has graciously agreed to try to see if she can locate your necklace."

The duchess, raddled face now streaked with sweat which had cut runnels through the white paint with which she had tried to hide her wrinkles, peered closely at Georgina from beady eyes set too close to her great beak of a nose.

"Indeed. And how does this young lady accomplish such a feat?" She rounded on Amesford, accusing. "Is this some parlor trick you've thought up to enliven your rout, Amesford? Did you have someone slip off my necklace, so that this pretty young chit could 'find' it? If so, I find it most unamusing."

"Most!" the Duke of Asley echoed, his voice booming.

"No, no, I assure you, I am at a loss to know where your lovely necklace has gone, dear duchess. And Miss Ryerston, here, is quite reluctant to perform. She says that she is often unable to see where lost things are. It is a gift over which she has no control. But I hope we shall be lucky tonight, and that she will see your diamonds."

He motioned Georgina forward, and she asked, "May

I hold your hand, your grace? It helps me if I have contact with the person who has lost something."

"Oh, very well," the duchess said ungraciously, extending a bony hand for Georgina to take in her own soft hand.

"Everyone, quiet!" Amesford ordered. By now the guests realized that something special was going on, although few of them knew what. However, seeing their host, the duchess, and this lovely young woman together, they crowded around, eager to see what new entertainment the marquis had thought up for them.

Georgina was stricken with terror. For the first time in her life, she was under terrible pressure to use her gift. If no vision came to her, she probably would be disgraced, and Cousin Francis as well. What would he do if she did not succeed? Would he be so angry with her that he would send her away from Hellingham?

Even as she thought this, though, the vision was forming in her head. At first Georgina thought that her senses were playing her false, that she was seeing the first thing that her subconscious hit on, the entertainment of the evening; Captain Macheath loomed in her mind, the gentleman-highwayman of *The Beggar's Opera*. Then Georgina realized that what she was seeing was not a scene from the play, but a scene from real life. As if she were actually watching it happen, she watched the actor approach the Duchess of Timberlake, bow, and offer his hand to escort her into the dining hall. The minx who had played Polly Peachem quickly captured the Duke of Asley, distracting him while the sly actor, in true highwayman fashion, managed to undo the clasp of the diamond necklace. As it came unfastened, the actress dropped a plate of food, causing great commotion. As the duchess turned to see what was happening, the actor slid the glittering necklace into the top of one of his thigh-high swagger boots. It was as if she were observing it through the wrong end of the old spyglass Papa used to have in his study.

Georgina felt herself sway, and she might have fallen, but the duchess had a deathgrip on her hand.

"What is it, girl, what is it?" she cried. "Where is my necklace?"

Someone cried, "Sal volatile!" and Georgina smelled the sharp odor of the ammonia, which cleared her head.

"My dear, what is wrong?" Amesford demanded, worry in his voice. "What did you see? You are pale as a ghost."

"It's the actor and his lady friend," she gasped. "Macheath and Polly. They stole the necklace. He dropped it down into his right boot."

"You heard her!" Amesford shouted. "Don't let those players leave Paladino Manor. Hurry. Apprehend them!"

CHAPTER 13

"What will they do with the pair of them?" Olivia asked avidly as the coach rattled back toward Hellingham. "Will they hang? Or will they just cut off their hands?"

"Oh!" The words suddenly made Georgina so queasy that she feared she might be ill. Frantically she fumbled in the satin pocket hidden under the edge of her silver overskirt for her own silver vinaigrette of smelling salts, sniffing deeply until tears came to her eyes to fight off nausea.

Cousin Francis, getting a whiff of the pungent salts, said sharply, "Olivia, you are ghoulish tonight. Can't you see that Georgina has had quite enough for one evening?" Solicitously he leaned toward his cousin. "I'm sorry that I forced you into that situation, my dear. Can you forgive me?"

Olivia laughed, a harsh sound in the confines of the landau. "It attracted an enormous amount of attention to her, Francis. What woman hates that? I think this all is playacting, now, just to gain your sympathy."

"Be quiet, Olivia! Jealousy does not sit well with you. Georgina has been through a trying time, and she deserves sympathy, not the edge of your viciously sharp tongue."

"Please, don't quarrel over me," Georgina begged, near tears. It had been a horrible evening. The "finding" had tired her terribly, even more than it usually did. Then to see the two criminals dragged back into the great hall, caught just as they were leaving Paladino Manor, had been a completely unnerving experience. Apparently one of the footmen had told the two miscreants that it was Georgina who had been instrumental in their apprehension.

Hauled up before the irate Duchess of Timberlake, the actress who had played poor Polly Peacham cried, "There's the witch who done us in, love!" and the actor, still in his highwayman's costume, had cursed her so viciously that the Duke of Asley cuffed him hard enough to send him sprawling onto the parquet floor, blood streaming from his nose.

The necklace, glittering in the light of the hundreds of wax tapers, was recovered from the thief's right boot. A rider was dispatched at once for the constable, and the thieves were hauled off to be guarded until the minions of the law arrived. Georgina was acclaimed as the heroine of the evening by Amesford and many of his guests. Being sensitive to such things by now, she sensed that others in the crowd were afraid of her, or were convinced that her powers smacked of witchcraft. Cousin Francis, seeing that she was so upset, had taken leave of their host, the Hellingham coach was called, and they had left immediately, before the end of the festivities.

"Georgina, Amesford is eternally thankful to you for your help tonight. It would have been a terrible blow to him if that necklace had not been found. Once the troup of players left Paladino Manor, the diamonds would have been lost forever."

Georgina shuddered, and huddled into the warmth of the sable cape. "I feel so responsible. Because of me, those two will have terrible sentences imposed on them."

"Georgina, they are common thieves. They are not deserving of your sympathy."

She could not be comforted, though. This was the first time that her gift had put anyone's life in jeopardy. It was a crushing feeling to know that she had spoken words which might lead two people to the gallows.

Once back at Hellingham, Cousin Francis insisted on escorting Georgina to her bedchamber, making sure that Lizzie was there, ready to undress her mistress.

Although she'd been dozing before the fire, the abigail was quickly alert, with a suppressed excitement which made her eyes sparkle in the light of the small fire.

"Your mistress has had a very trying experience, Lizzie. Get her ready for bed quickly, and see that she has a glass of claret to help her sleep." Turning to Georgina, he asked, "Would you like a sleeping draught, dear coz? We always keep opiate for father."

"No, no, I'll be quite all right, thank you, Cousin Francis." All she wanted was to crawl into her bed and try to lose herself in sleep.

The minute that the viscount had gone, Lizzie said, in an excited whisper, "Oh, miss, you had a visitor."

Shocked awake by the undercurrents in her abigail's voice, Georgina asked sharply, "A visitor? Who on earth would have come calling to see me? Everyone I know was at the Marquis of Amesford's rout."

"Not everyone, miss." Lizzie's smile was sly. "Not a certain tall, handsome gentleman. He was most disappointed to find you gone."

Charlie? Could it have been—

"Lizzie, who was it?"

Leaning close, as if the walls had ears, Lizzie whispered, "It was Charlie, miss, slipped into the house, he did. Cornered me in the pantry and asked for you especially. When I told him you was out, he was in a high temper. Asked when you'd return, and he hung about for ever so long, dodging old Pruning and her new shadow, Miss Twistle."

Georgina felt faint with excitement. "Is he still here? Where is he, Lizzie?" She looked all around the room, as if expecting to find Charles hidden in the huge oaken wardrobe, or under the high bed.

"Well, miss, I had to come up to check your fire. When I went back, Charlie had disappeared. I'm not sure where he went to. Sometimes I think he sleeps with the ostlers when he's around Hellingham. Of course if his lordship, the viscount, knew, he'd sack the lot of them. He wants no part of Charlie."

Then he still might be somewhere on the estate. What was she to do?

"I must get you ready for your bed, now, miss. His lordship was quite definite about that. And the claret— I'll pour a glass for you to sip while I help you disrobe."

Clad in a flowing gown of palest peach silk, Georgina finished the wine and got into the high, lonely bed. There had been no sign of Charles. Probably he'd given up in disgust and was not even at Hellingham now. Georgina didn't know whether to be glad or sad. She knew he had used her shamefully; yet in her heart of hearts, she longed to see him again, to feel his strong arms about her, to have his eager hands fondle her and bring her to blazing passion.

"Shall I snuff the candle, miss? And do you want the curtains dropped about the bed?"

The claret had been stronger than she expected, and the effect of the wine was making her very drowsy. "Snuff the candle, but leave the bed open. Goodnight, Lizzie."

Georgina expected to lie awake, fretting about the episode at Paladino Manor, and thinking about missing Charles. Instead she drifted off to sleep almost immediately. She dreamed that Charles Collins came into her room, quietly, carrying a shielded candle in his hand which he blew out as he approached her bed.

"Georgina," he whispered. "Georgina, are you awake?"

In her half-dreaming state, she was not sure whether

she was awake or asleep. Had she heard Charles call her name? Her eyes flew open, and she looked wildly into the dark of her room, trying to see whether or not she was alone. She must have dreamed—but then a dark shadow beside the bed moved, and in the faint light from the banked coals in the fireplace, Georgina saw the outline of a man standing beside her bed.

Normally she would have been terror-stricken to wake and find someone in her room, but she was so sure that it was Charles Collins, who had been hiding somewhere in the house waiting for her return, that she was not afraid. All she felt was a great wave of desire. She didn't care what Cousin Francis had told her about Charles. She knew he was using her, but it didn't matter. Nothing mattered but that he was here, and she could share her bed with him.

The shadow leaned closer, and once again the whisper, "Georgina, are you awake?" filled her eager ears.

"Yes, oh, yes," she breathed, welcoming him into her bed, reaching her arms to hold him close, so close. With one quick movement he slipped out of the robe he wore, and moments later she felt his nude body in the bed beside her, eager arms pulling her to him so that she felt his maleness, ready for love. In the next moment, though, she was shocked completely awake, for this was not the body she had caressed and submitted to on the bearskin rug in front of the fire at Ye Grape.

"Who are you?" She thought it was a scream, but between the time that her mind registered that some stranger was in bed with her and the actual utterance of the words, terror so froze her throat that it came out a quavering whisper. "No! No!" she protested, struggling against the man's grasp, but to no avail. "I'll scream," she warned, the initial terror now giving way to a fierce rage. Who dared invade her bed thus, to force her?

Georgina opened her mouth to cry the alarm. An

iron-hard hand clamped on her lips, bruising them against her teeth.

"Who were you expecting?" the man demanded, his harsh whisper grating in her ears. "Who was coming into your bed? I thought you were the pure, innocent little girl from a country village vicarage—and I find, instead, an experienced trollop. Very well, I shan't have to teach you anything, then, shall I?"

Georgina fought fiercely, burrowing her head back into the soft down pillows to escape the suffocating hand over her mouth. Then she bit, hard, drawing a loud curse from her unseen assailant.

"Who are you?" she hissed in the moment's respite from his silencing, as he snatched back his bitten hand.

For answer she was cuffed so hard in the jaw that tears welled in her eyes, and she gasped with pain, sure that he had broken her jaw.

"Who do you think I am?" For the first time he spoke in a normal voice, and, stunned, Georgina realized that it was her Cousin Francis.

"Cousin Francis! What is the meaning—" she sobbed.

"Don't play the innocent maiden with me, Georgina. When I got in bed with you, you turned to me quite eagerly, those lovely hands of yours reaching for me as if it were the most natural thing in the world."

"But I thought. . . ." Too late she saw the folly of her words. To tell the viscount what she'd thought would surely infuriate him further. Her jaw ached unbearably.

"You thought I was someone else? Who?"

"I was asleep, dreaming," she said quickly, trying to undo the damage she'd already done with her unruly tongue. "I wasn't sure I was awake or asleep. I thought—"

His laugh was lewd. "So you dream about men, do you? Well, little cousin, I'll be the answer to your dreams." His hands moved over her body, caressing her.

Terrified, Georgina realized that nothing she was going to say would stop Francis. He was determined to have her, and have her he would. Still, she begged him not to violate her.

"You aren't a virgin, my dear, don't tell me that. Not after the welcome you gave me when I climbed into this bed. Someone else has been here before me. Now you'll learn what a real man is."

Georgina knew that she had only two choices. She could scream and scream, rouse the house, hope that someone would come to her aid in time, or she could submit to her cousin's ardor. If she did get help, there would be such a scandal, such laughing in the servant's quarters, such anger from Francis at his humiliation, that she would be expelled from Hellingham. Surely this couldn't be any worse than that. So she stopped struggling and lay there, passive, while Francis took her.

He was not pleased with her performance. "You have a lot to learn, little cousin, and if you are at all interested in staying on here at Hellingham, I advise you to be a good pupil."

"Oh, Francis, how could you treat me this way?" she said sadly.

"Come, my dear, everyone in the *ton* does it. Don't be such a naïve little girl. You are a lovely, desirable woman, and I have gotten tired of Olivia. I like a fresh face, and a new woman to love." His hands caressed her flesh again, intimately, and Georgina shivered. To her horror she found that her body was responding to his skill, even while her mind rejected him utterly.

She felt that she was betraying Collins completely, for with him she had given herself willingly, glorying in the ecstasy he had roused in her, yielding to the physical raptures he had been able to give her. Now, feeling her body responding to Francis's demanding hands on her breasts, feeling her pulses pound at his kisses, Georgina hated both her cousin and herself. If she loved Charles, how could she feel passion with another man? But she did. This time, against her will, her body matched his rhythm, and she came to a blazing climax even as she had done with Collins.

This time, there were no abusive words from her cousin. He lay, relaxed and sated, murmuring endearments to her. At this final betrayal of herself, Georgina lay and cried silently, tears slipping down over her cheeks onto the linens. What would Charles Collins do if he learned that she had lain in his half brother's arms, had responded as fully and wildly as she had to his own lovemaking? *What is wrong with me?* Georgina thought, her mind frantically looking for excuses for her behavior.

It had been an emotionally exhausting evening. The episode of "finding" had depleted her severely, and realizing that she was responsible for the thieves' apprehension—and probable severe punishment—almost made her ill. Then there was the terrible disappointment of missing Charles Collins. All of these factors had contributed to her receptiveness when the man she thought was her lover had invaded her bed.

She was spared the final degradation. Francis did not stay with her for the rest of the night. Georgina did not have to have Lizzie's sly, knowing eyes find her in bed with the viscount. He finally left her to herself, going back to his own suite.

Georgina lay awake for hours, until dawn was faintly pearling the sky. What was she to do? Could she stay on here now, after this episode with Cousin Francis? Would he expect her to give her favors to him every night? Oh, why couldn't it have been Collins who had stood here beside her in the dark?

She wondered what would have happened if she'd heard Francis come into her bedroom, had known who he was. If she had not been heavy with sleep, if she'd not been hoping for Collins, would she have been able to prevent what had happened? As it was, she had so obviously welcomed him into her bed, thinking that it was Charles, that it was no wonder Francis expected her to submit to him.

And what was Olivia Nugent going to do now? Georgina prayed that Francis would be discreet, that he wouldn't tell Olivia where he had spent the night. She would guess, though. She had spitefully warned Georgina that Francis would expect to bed her, and Georgina, in her stupidity, had ignored the warning. How right Olivia had been, how well she knew the young viscount.

It had all started with the broken wreck of a man up in the tower room, with his desire for Rebecca Collins. He had wanted his women, and his two children had inherited this trait from their lusty father. He had bred two equally lusty sons, who seemed to delight in bedding the same women.

I have been feeling superior to Olivia Nugent, Georgina mourned silently. *Now I am no better than she.*

CHAPTER 14

Georgina decided to have a breakfast tray in her room, for she did not think that she could face her cousin if he were up at this hour breakfasting. Nor did she want to chat with the catty Olivia. Olivia. What was there about the two of them that attracted both of the sons of the Fourth Earl of Margate, Peter Hardy? *Am I like Olivia?* Georgina asked herself as she lay in the high bed where she had been taken, last night, by the wrong brother. There was no seeming resemblance between the two women, one dark, one fair, one an avowed trollop, and one raised in innocence. But no more! Georgina had left her innocence behind her. She had given herself freely to Charles, and had submitted in despair to her Cousin Francis, and then had acted as abandoned as any wanton woman from the streets of London.

Lizzie brought her chocolate and toast at her request, and asked about the rout at Paladino Manor.

"I hear that it is a fine mansion, even finer than Hellingham, miss. Is this so?"

"It is larger," Georgina acknowledged. "And there is no question that it is one of the showplaces of the area."

"Was the entertainment something special?" the little abigail asked wistfully.

Remembering what had happened·last night, Georgina shuddered. But Lizzie waited, eyes bright and avid, for news of the evening. Suddenly Georgina realized how little amusement the servant girl had.

"There was dancing, with a string orchestra. Then

a group of actors, a traveling troup, put on a short performance of *The Beggar's Opera.*"

"Oh, miss! About the gallant highwayman?"

"I'm not at all sure that highwaymen are gallant," Georgina said drily. "They are thieves, Lizzie. And murderers. There's nothing glamorous about the knights of the road." She could see, though, that the abigail didn't believe her for a moment. Many people looked on highwaymen as heroes, not rogues.

"It all sounds very grand, miss."

"The actor who played the part of Macheath stole a very expensive diamond necklace from one of the guests." Georgina hadn't meant to tell Lizzie about this, but it slipped out, for she was so disgusted with the hero worship of these desperados.

"And they caught him?" Lizzie's eyes were saucer-round. "Oh, miss, will he get the gallows?"

Wishing now that she'd not mentioned the theft, for Georgina still felt enormous guilt at having helped apprehend the thieves, she said, "That is up to the magistrates, Lizzie."

"They'll stretch their necks, I'd wager."

"Let's not talk about such dreadful things at breakfast!" Georgina cried, frightening the maid.

Lizzie was not one to stay silent long, though. As she poured a second cup of chocolate from the silver pot into the china cup for her mistress, she asked, almost in a whisper, "Did you see him," with great emphasis on the pronoun, "after I left you last night, miss?"

Georgina, swallowing a bite of toast, almost choked. Did Lizzie know that the Viscount Quincy had come into her bed last night?

Coughing at the crumbs in her throat, Georgina had a moment of panic. "Did I see—what do you mean, Lizzie? I was in bed when you left me."

Lizzie grinned impishly. "Yes, miss, I know that. But at breakfast in the kitchen this morning, one of the kitchen lads whispered that Charlie had spent the night in the big house last night."

"Not with me!" A wave of jealousy rushed over Georgina, surprising her with its intensity. Charles hadn't shared her bed last night. If he had stayed inside Hellingham, had he been with Olivia? At that moment, she despised her Cousin Francis. He had slithered his way into her bed, when she was half asleep and expecting Charles. Had Charles known that she was not alone in her room? Was that why he had not returned to see her?

"I didn't mean to upset you, miss," Lizzie said contritely. "I just thought that you liked our Charlie."

"Don't think such things," Georgina said crossly. "And don't talk about them, either, Lizzie. If I find out that you are gossiping about me in the kitchen—"

Lizzie paled visibly. "Oh, no, miss, I couldn't do that, truly I couldn't. Miss Twistle pries and tries to find out all manner of things—I think she tells Mrs. Pruning. But I never let on. Never!"

Reluctant to get up, dreading to face the others in the household, Georgina lay in bed reading until a footman came saying that his lordship, the earl, was asking for her.

"Tell the nurse I'll be along as soon as I dress," Georgina said. And as soon as the footman had gone, "Hurry, Lizzie. I should have been up before now. Get the green muslin morning dress out for me. And the matching kid shoes. I must get to the tower room as soon as possible."

By the time she was dressed and presented herself at the earl's bedchamber, however, he had slipped back into his usual stupor.

Miss Twistle, in a gown of heavy blue brocade which made her look as broad as she was tall, smirked at Georgina in a very self-satisfied way. "Poor man, he kept calling for you earlier, but I guess you were still in bed." She made it obvious what she thought of such sloth.

Georgina, getting very tired of Miss Twistle's innuendoes, said with some asperity, "As his lordship is your job, not mine, Miss Twistle, I wouldn't want you to think I was trying to usurp your place in the household by spending too much time with him."

The look of hatred from those beady eyes chilled Georgina.

"I hear you were out witching last night," the companion said softly, virulently. "There are some who don't hold with witchcraft, Miss Ryerston. And the magistrates are very hard on witches."

"I am not a witch." She said each word distinctly, biting them off. "I have a gift, Miss Twistle, which I use only to help people who have been unfortunate enough to lose things. Witches are in league with the devil, as you well know, while I am the daughter of a vicar, raised in the Church of England, properly baptized and confirmed. I'm sure you know that, too, as you seem to know a great deal about me."

"Well! I never! If you are such a fine Christian lady, why do you associate with such low characters as coacheys?"

"My friends are my own business, Miss Twistle. I don't care to discuss either them or theology with you this morning."

Miss Twistle smirked. "Anyway, your fine, handsome coachey wasn't with you last night, was he? Perhaps he finds your goodness too sugary for his lusty tastes." She tittered. "I daresay my friend Olivia is more to his liking."

Ah, so it was now "my friend Olivia," was it? Georgina seethed with anger, and with jealousy. Was Miss Twistle telling her that Charles spent the night with Olivia? Georgina began to see the voluptuous Miss Nugent as an arch rival. She was not, however, going to allow this nasty woman to see how she felt. Instead,

Georgina smiled her most contemptuous smile and said, "If you expect to keep Miss Nugent's friendship, you should refrain from such scurrilous gossip about her. I daresay she might not be happy to know that you are saying she shared her bed last night with such a common fellow as this notorious Charlie."

Realizing her error too late, Miss Twistle turned an ugly red. "I didn't say any such thing."

Fortunately the nurse came back into the earl's room just then, and Georgina said to her, "If his lordship calls again for me, please let me know. I'm sorry I missed his call this morning."

For one moment the stolid woman's eyes widened a fraction, the only sign she ever gave of surprise. Shooting a swift look at Miss Twistle, she said quite matter-of-factly, "He hasn't been aware at all this morning, miss. Someone must have called you by mistake." There was no room for doubt. The nurse knew very well that Miss Twistle had lied to Georgina.

Smiling grimly, Georgina gave Miss Twistle one hard look, then swept out of the sickroom.

She hurried down the spiral staircase, planning to find a novel in the large library, and then retire to her room. At the foot of the stairs, she met Olivia Nugent, and for a long, tension-charged moment the two women stood there, eyeing each other. This morning Olivia was in a Watteau sacque of soft lime green silk, the flowing lines well-suited to her statuesque beauty, and to her coloring. She was unpowdered, her dark hair flowing about her creamy shoulders.

Olivia recovered first. "Ah, bewitching the earl, my dear Georgina? Perhaps, if you are lucky, you can find the poor man's wits, which he seems to have mislaid."

Keeping her voice even, Georgina said, "He is my cousin, and I was just visiting him."

Olivia Nugent wasn't to be bested this morning. "It must be dull to have to spend time with a sick old man. I prefer the company of a lusty young one."

"Indeed. It is strange, Olivia; I thought you were almost betrothed, if that is the proper term, to the viscount. I should think you'd have spent your night with him."

"And what makes you think I didn't?" Too late Olivia realized the mistake of her question.

Georgina just stood there and smiled.

The other woman's face was a study in seething, conflicting emotions. She was furious that Georgina knew Francis had rejected her last night—and clever enough to know how Georgina had come on this fact. On the other hand, she had probably spent the time with Charles Collins. Realizing that Georgina was infatuated with the handsome redheaded coachman, she wanted to let the younger woman know that she had enjoyed his love last night.

"Francis likes variety," she said finally, spitefully. "But he'll come back to me. He always does. In the meantime, I won't be lonely. Isn't it nice that Charlie found me last night when he was so alone?"

"You're playing a dangerous game, Olivia. What would Francis say if he knew you'd spent the night in bed with the man he so loathes?"

"He'll not know."

Georgina was surprised to find how infuriated she was at the idea of Charles Collins and Olivia Nugent in bed together. She knew they'd been lovers, but after the night she'd been with him at Ye Grape, she thought —what exactly did she think? That Charles would remain celibate? Even as she lay in the arms of his hated half brother?

"I wouldn't be too sure that Francis won't know you were bedded by his favorite coachey last night," Georgina spat at the other woman. "I might mention it, myself."

Did Olivia look afraid? If so, she recovered so quickly that Georgina couldn't be sure. Smiling a knowing smile, Olivia said quietly, "Did you know that foolish Charles was looking for you last night? He hung about here, risking discovery by Francis, hoping to see you when you came home. He might have come slipping into your bedchamber, if I had not stopped him, Georgina. What a shock it would have been to Charles to find Francis in your bed." She laughed, then, throwing back her head so that the long, smooth line of her white throat arched prettily. "What would you have done then, Georgina? One brother in your bed and the other at your bedchamber door? It plays like a French farce!"

"You are despicable." Georgina caught up her skirts and moved to pass Olivia, but the other woman stood her ground.

"Be warned, little country lass. Francis is only playing with you. You are a novelty—an inexperienced woman he can have for a pupil. He'll come back to me. I know what he likes, how to please him. As to Charles, he's using you. He wants someone inside Hellingham to tell him the gossip, help him find whatever it is he thinks is here to prove him the rightful heir to the earldom. You're just one more wench for him to bed —no more important to him than a barmaid at one of the inns where he stops."

"And what do you think you are to him?" Georgina said angrily. "What kind of woman are you, that you'd invite a man into your bed when he wanted to see another woman? Me! How does it feel to be second best?"

This time she did push past Olivia, but the woman caught her arm in a painful grip.

"Watch your step, little churchmouse! You are playing for high stakes—and you haven't a penny in your pocket. You can't win. When the time comes for you to pay up, you are going to find yourself in trouble."

Georgina pulled her arm from Olivia's grasp and hurried away from the other woman, her emotions seething. She was tempted to say that Francis was bored with Olivia, but some tiny measure of good sense kept her silent. Olivia might well be right. Francis might be using her only as a toy, a passing fancy. He might return to Olivia or he might find another woman. And what of Charles? How could he fall into the arms of the woman who had rejected him in favor of his half brother who had prospects of becoming the Fifth Earl of Margate?

Finally, Georgina acknowledged her jealousy. It infuriated her that Charles had spent the night with his old love instead of with her.

Georgina fled to the large library for diversion. The high-ceilinged, beautifully proportioned room was lined with book shelves from floor to ornate ceiling, the wood enameled a brilliant white. There were rolling steps so that she had access to the very top shelves. A rich-hued Turkish rug worked in an intricate Eastern design glowed on the floor, and the massive furniture was surely by Kent.

She looked through the latest novels, for Francis had a large collection sent from France, as well as a good selection of the finest English fiction. But she could not concentrate on the books. Why had Charles not waited somewhere near her room so that he could see her when she did return from Amesford's rout? How had knowledgeable Olivia lured him into her bed? Had she told him that Francis was with Georgina? How had she known? Oh, it was making her head ache.

Briefly she wished she were back in Trindale where life was simple and safe. Angrily she thrust the novel she held back into the bookcase. Life was much more complicated than even the most convoluted plot in a book of fiction. Why read such things, when the drama unfolding here at Hellingham far surpassed anything she could find on these shelves?

She could always flee, but Georgina knew that she hadn't the willpower to do this. She liked it here, liked the feel of real silk next to her skin, liked the gowns her cousin paid for, liked having her own abigail, liked lying in bed until noon if she wished. The ugly loom in the vicarage kitchen of St. Edmund's was not what she wanted to go back to—nor was Adam Fenton. If she had to be bedded by someone, let it be Charles Collins—or even her Cousin Francis. At least he had rescued her from a life of poverty. Having tasted wealth, Georgina could never go back to a diet of hardship. Never.

CHAPTER 15

Georgina spent the day in dread, wondering what she would do or say when she saw Cousin Francis. Would he make reference to bedding her last night? Would he expect to do the same tonight? She was nearly ill from the turmoil of her thoughts. At one time during the afternoon, she put on her old, heavy traveling cloak, avoiding the lovely sable wrap which the viscount had given her, and went out to walk in the gardens. It was dreary; the flowers were dead, the beds covered with straw by the gardeners to protect them from the winter cold. Georgina walked down the long driveway to the main gate and stood there, looking out through the ornate grillwork as if peering out of a prison cell. The little gnome who tended the gates came out once to see if she wanted him to open the heavy portals so that she could go outside.

"Although there's a wee door in the wall further on," he told her. "The maids all use it to save opening the big gates here."

Georgina remembered that little door in the wall all too well, for it was through it that she'd gone to meet her darling Charles at Ye Grape.

Shaking her head, she told the gatekeeper, "Thank you, I am just out to get a bit of fresh air. I have no wish to go through the gates."

She turned to leave, but just then Georgina heard a familiar sound: the sweet notes of a trumpet played as only Robin Adair could play it.

Noticing that she had heard, the gatekeeper muttered, "Must be the Exeter stage, miss, headed out from London. Sometimes they stop at Ye Grape. I daresay they did today, to pick up the coachey. He was around Hellingham last night, the ostlers say."

Did he look at her slyly, from under his bushy brows? Georgina didn't know. She wanted to flee from his knowing stare, yet wanted to stay and watch the stagecoach go by in hopes that she would get a glimpse of Charles. If he were driving, would he stop when he saw her here at the gate? Indecision made her delay until the gatekeeper shrugged and went back into the snug gatehouse built into the brick wall.

Now she could hear the pounding of horses' hooves, and the rattle of the coach wheels on the rough road which ran beside Hellingham. In an agony of desire, she slipped to the side of the huge iron gate, half concealing herself behind the brick archway. She heard the crack of a long coachey's whip, and the stage came into sight, the horses going at a gallop. Was it Charles on the box? Georgina peered at the muffled figure, catching a glimpse of that red Hardy hair. Although the guard turned and looked directly at the Hellingham entrance, Charles rode by without even a glance in her direction. It broke her heart. She knew that it would be days before he could be back in the vicinity of Hellingham.

Oh, Charles, she mourned silently, *why couldn't you have waited a bit more patiently for me last night? Why did you go to Olivia, when I was aching to hold you in my arms, longing to have you make love to me? If you had been with me, then Francis would not have*—But it was all fruitless. Charles hadn't waited. And Francis had come into her bed. As he well might tonight. Would he take her for a mistress now instead of Olivia? Was this why she had come all the way to Hellingham? Was she destined to be a rich lord's mistress rather than someone's wife? She shivered, more from the bleakness of her thoughts than from the chill in the cold winter air.

Finally, when the faintest sounds of the passing stagecoach were long gone, Georgina turned and slowly made her way back to the great house.

That afternoon, even though she had vowed to herself that she'd not go near the earl again unless Francis asked her to, Georgina found herself climbing the spiral stairs to the sick man's tower room. If she stayed downstairs, she might run into her cousin, and she still didn't know how to react to him after last night's passionate encounter.

When she went into the sickroom, the nurse was nowhere in sight. Miss Twistle looked up almost apprehensively, knowing that she had stepped far over the bounds of proper conduct this morning. Georgina, however, chose to ignore the incident.

"If you want a moment's respite, I'll stay with his lordship for a time," she said, keeping her voice neutral.

Miss Twistle gave her one quick, suspicious look as if trying to find the trick. Then she smiled and jumped up from the small Queen Anne chair on which she had been sitting. "I would enjoy a cup of tea with Mrs. Pruning, if you'd be so good as to stay until the nurse comes back." Then she relinquished her charge with alacrity, hurrying from the room in a swish of starched petticoats, her pinner bobbing on top of badly powdered sausage curls.

Georgina sat down, picked up the book which Miss Twistle had marked with a goose quill, and began reading. The earl lay back on his pillows, apparently asleep. Soon Georgina lost herself in the story she was reading.

"Get Sir Barnaby Kane!"

She stopped in mid-sentence, startled by his lordship's voice, not realizing that he had waked and was lucid.

The Earl of Margate had not improved since her arrival at Hellingham. Usually Georgina felt defeated by his blank stare, even when he was awake. Once in a while he regained his senses and spoke to her, but the lucid intervals were short. When he was having a good spell, he did seem to remember her, know who she was and the connection she had with the family, so she tried to visit him daily, reading to him from this novel said to be the current rage on the Continent.

Now, hearing his words, Georgina laid down the book and went to stand beside the high bed. "Sir Barnaby Kane? There is no one by that name here, your lordship."

He beckoned for her to come closer. With his one good hand he seized her wrist in a grip that frightened her with its power. For a feeble, sick old man, his fingers were surprisingly strong, biting into her flesh.

"My s-s-s—" The intensity of emotion blocked his speech. This time he was so determined to communicate something to her that his eyes bulged with the effort. Afraid that he might suffer another stroke, Georgina seized the little brass bell from the walnut nightstand and rang it.

Before the nurse came hurrying in, the earl's iron grip relaxed, and he fell back against the mound of down pillows, his face blank, his eyes dull.

"Yes, miss, what is it?"

Quickly Georgina told the nurse of the earl's strange behavior.

"Well, it's over now," the stolid woman said. "He does this now and then. He's not aware of his actions." She dismissed the episode with a shrug.

Georgina wasn't as sure that the earl's mind was completely blank. He knew her sometimes. And the name Sir Barnaby Kane. He'd said it quite distinctly. But she was reluctant to discuss his lordship's words with the nurse.

Later, as Georgina went back into the paneled library to see if there might be other novels for her to read, she found her cousin sitting there before a small fire, his feet propped on an ottoman to warm them. He was leafing through what appeared to be a handwritten journal. When he heard her, he quickly put down the volume.

Leaping up, he bowed over her hand, carrying it to his lips. Then he turned Georgina's hand over and kissed the inside of her wrist, much to her consternation. Again, to her utter dismay, she found her pulses quickening at the touch of his lips.

"I have been looking for you, my lovely cousin," Francis said. "Have you been hiding from me today?"

"Hiding?" Her voice betrayed her, rising almost an octave, eliciting a knowing smile from her cousin.

"Some women are shy after their first bedding," he said. "I would not want you to be embarrassed with me, my lovely Georgina."

She didn't know what she would do if he should choose to take her in his arms, but he relinquished her hand, with that knowing smile still on his dark, exciting face.

With mockery in his voice, he said, "Ah, cousin, looking for romance among the books instead of with me?"

Flustered, she said quickly, "I want to find another novel to read aloud to his lordship. I've almost finished the one from France."

"Georgina, it really is a waste of time to read to father. He doesn't understand a word you say. He's a vegetable."

"Not always," she protested, glad to have the conversation turned away from herself. "I sometimes think he may hear and be able to understand more than we suppose. Think how terrible it must be to know what's going on around you, but to be unable to communicate your thoughts. Just now, your father tried to tell me something. I was frightened that he'd bring on another spell of apoplexy, he tried so hard to get out words."

There was a sudden heightening of awareness in her cousin, yet his voice was casual when he spoke.

"What did he want? What did he say to you, Georgina?"

She sighed, sinking down in a Kent chair. "That's the terrible thing. I don't know. He asked for someone, a Sir Barnaby Kane—or that's what it sounded like."

"Sir Barnaby? What did he want with him?"

"I don't know. He became so excited trying to tell me. Then he sank back, as he does, all awareness gone."

"If he says anything more about Sir Barnaby, you must tell me, Georgina. It's important."

"Of course." Georgina wanted to ask who Kane was, but she hesitated, as the viscount hadn't volunteered the information.

Later, in her bedchamber, while Lizzie powdered her hair, she asked, "Do you know anyone named Kane, Lizzie?"

"Kane, miss? Well, there's a farmer near Staines by that name. Cook gets turnips and potatoes from him. Is that who you mean, Miss Georgina?"

"I—no, probably not." She didn't want to probe further for fear it might excite Lizzie's curiosity.

"There, miss, all powdered." She set down the silver powder can and took off the pink silk powdering cape from around Georgina's shoulders. "Or there's his lordship's solicitor."

"Solicitor?"

"You asked about Kanes, miss. Comes to Hellingham now and again—Sir Barnaby Kane. Not so often these days. I think the young lord doesn't like him much."

So the earl wanted his solicitor. Georgina wondered why. And she wondered why Francis hadn't told her who Kane was when she mentioned his name. Should she take it on herself to try to contact the solicitor for his lordship? No, that would be presumptuous of her. Cousin Francis knew that his father wanted to see the man. He'd make the arrangements. Although how any solicitor could make heads or tails of poor Lord Peter's attempts at speech, she didn't know.

For several days Georgina tried to spend more time than usual with the sick man, hoping that he'd say more to her, but he was sunk in an uninterrupted torpor. It was as if the tremendous effort he'd exerted trying to communicate with her that day had sapped all of his strength and his will.

As Georgina left the tower room, she met her cousin on the spiral stairs. It had been a strange few days. He had made no further attempt to bed her. In a way Georgina was relieved; yet secretly she was hurt, too, wondering if she had been so inept, as Olivia had insinuated, that she had driven him away. Remembering her passionate response to his second lovemaking, she blushed from the edge of her low-cut gown to the roots of her blond hair. Were all women this way? Was it natural to behave in such a wanton manner with any man who bedded you?

"Ah, what a lovely blush, dear Georgina. It is nice to know that I have such an effect on you." He drew so close to her that she found she was backed against the stone wall of the staircase. "One of these nights I shall want a change from Olivia again," he said softly, watching her as a cat watches a mouse. "Then I shall come calling, little country cousin."

She was speechless. What could she possibly say to a statement of this kind?

Trying to hold her skirts aside so that Francis could go up to his father's room, Georgina sidled down the stairs hoping to escape from any decision-making about a further relationship with her cousin. Francis, though, was not finished with her yet.

"How's father? Has he said anything today?"

"Nothing, Cousin Francis. He's completely unaware."

"No more requests for anyone?" Francis eyed her closely in the dimly lighted staircase.

"If you mean his solicitor—"

Quick as a snake his hand flashed out and caught her wrist. "Who said anything about a solicitor?"

Startled, Georgina defensively insisted, "His lordship did. I told you. He asked for his solicitor."

"You told me—" He checked, as if determined not to lose his temper. "How did you know Kane was a solicitor?"

Now Georgina thought fast, even more on the defensive. She didn't want to involve Lizzie. If she said her abigail had told her, he'd know she'd been gossiping with the servants about his father's affairs. Feigning nonchalance, Georgina gave a little shrug, murmured, "I heard it somewhere," and moved to go on down the stairs.

"I'll go with you," her cousin said. "If the old man's lying there like a vegetable today, there's no point in my wasting my time visiting him."

Then with one of his quicksilver changes of mood, Francis suggested, "Come, let's stroll through the Long Gallery. I want to discuss plans for the ball with you."

She wondered why he didn't include Olivia in such talks, but again she felt silence to be important. If he turned his affections to her and abandoned Olivia, life here at Hellingham might become very unpleasant. She knew that Olivia was friendly with Mrs. Pruning, and the housekeeper had a lot of power in such an estate as this. Miss Twistle had already allied herself with Mrs. Pruning and Olivia. The only friend Georgina felt she had at Hellingham was her own little Lizzie, who had no standing at all in the servants' quarters. No doubt the new French abigail, Marie, would be completely loyal to Olivia. It made Georgina feel very alone. She would have to tread warily if she were to keep herself out of trouble.

The gallery was spectacular, carved marble arches intersecting it at intervals. The white marble, showing off the Grinling Gibbons touch, lent a light and airy look, even though there were high windows only on one side of the gallery. Members of the Hardy family peered down at her from their frames on the walls, many of them with the red hair and bright blue eyes which reminded Georgina of Charles Collins. They sat by one arched window on paired upholstered chairs done in light tapestry.

"A masked ball, I think," Francis said without preamble. "Small, intimate—I think only about one hundred guests."

Georgina looked at him closely to see if he were jesting, but he seemed quite serious, as if one hundred guests were a mere handful. "I heard quite a good orchestra last time in London. I'll have them play for the dancing. Now, what shall we wear? Something charming for you, dear Georgina. You shall be the belle of the ball. I have it! A shepherdess." He reached and tipped her chin up so that the light fell on her face. "Yes. Unpowdered hair, in long ringlets. Can your woman manage that?" He leaned over and kissed her on the lips, but lightly, with no passion.

Ignoring the casual kiss, Georgina assured him, "Lizzie is absolutely fantastic with hair."

"And that little dressmaker from Staines—can she do your gown, Georgina, or should we order something from London?"

The prospect of a London gown almost overwhelmed Georgina, but good sense made her say, "If Mrs. Ealing has something to copy, I'm sure she can cope."

He rose gracefully, walked to a glass-fronted case built into the opposite wall of the gallery, and brought out a delicate porcelain figure of a shepherdess done in soft pastel shades.

"Here, this should do quite nicely."

"And will you come as a shepherd?" Georgina was surprised to hear herself asking such a question. Already she was thinking of Cousin Francis and herself as a couple. And what of Charles? She didn't want to think about that now.

Francis grinned engagingly. "No, I think I'd make a better Mephistopheles." He smiled, a hint of wicked fun in his eyes; Georgina could easily see him in that guise.

He set the date, told Georgina to have Mrs. Pruning summon the dressmaker, and the plans were put in motion. He did not mention Olivia's costume, and Georgina did not ask. She felt that the subject of the voluptuous Miss Nugent was one better left undiscussed at present.

The ball was to be held in the magnificent hall which had been her first view of Hellingham. The musicians would be out of sight, but not out of hearing, in the minstrel's gallery. All of the furniture was moved from the marble checkerboard floor, and an army of servants spent days polishing and decorating the room.

Refreshments were to be served in the state dining room, a magnificent buffet which Mrs. Pruning planned under Georgina's watchful eye. "Spare no expense," was the young viscount's order. "This will be the most talked-about ball of the season, rivaling balls held at Kensington Palace or the Court of St. James."

She could well believe it. Elegant invitations went out to a host of the nobility. The gardeners were told that the flowers growing in Hellingham's greenhouses must be in profuse bloom for the ball. No excuses would be accepted for less than a bower of blossoms. The kitchens hummed with activity, and the butler spent hours with the young viscount planning the wines for the affair.

Through it all, Georgina maintained her reading schedule with the earl. The day before the ball she was sitting beside the sick man, who had not shown any evidence of awareness since the day he'd asked for his solicitor. As far as Georgina knew, Sir Barnaby Kane had not yet put in an appearance. Well, with his lordship sunk in this torpor, a trip from London would be a waste of time. She was reading, hoping that the sound of her voice might penetrate the hidden recesses of the man's locked brain, when she sensed a presence in the room. It was Cousin Francis, elegant in a satin coat of pale gray with hammered silver buttons and silver braid.

"Why bother, Georgina? He can't hear you. Come see how the hall is going to look."

Georgina laid down the book and rose, only to hear, behind her, the harsh, gargling sounds the earl made when he was trying to talk. Instantly Francis was beside his father's bed demanding. "What is it you want with Kane, Father?"

Georgina was stunned by the malevolent look the earl gave his son. Even discounting the drawn, twisted face, there was no mistaking the hate blazing from those blue eyes.

"No business . . . yours," the old man spat at Francis. "Get Sir Barnaby."

"Not unless I know why you want him. Demand that he make the long trip from London on the whim of a sick, dying—already half-dead—man? Even if you are the Fourth Earl of Margate, Sir Barnaby Kane is a man of power in London. You can't expect him to give two or three days to you unless he knows why he's making the trip. If he comes and finds you lying here like a log, the way you usually do, then what?"

The elder man's eyes began to bulge, and his mouth worked frantically, but nothing but guttural sounds now issued from that ravaged throat.

"See!" taunted Francis. "You can't say two sentences together." He turned, the red heels of his shoes flashing, and said to Georgina, "Sir Barnaby won't waste his time on that." He took her arm, not too gently, and pushed her toward the door. "You've spent enough time here today. We've a ball to plan, dear cousin."

Nor did he let loose her arm, even at the door to the spiral stairs.

But the sick man had the last word, after all. With a tremendous effort, he said loudly, "I'll recognize him as my s-s-s—"

Stunned, Francis turned so fast that he almost pulled Georgina off her feet. She caught frantically at her blue taffeta overskirt, to keep it from under her kid slippers.

Still tugging her after him like a Thames river barge, the viscount strode back to the high, canopied bed.

"What do you mean? You'll recognize—"

It was too late. The earl had already collapsed onto the mount of pillows, his face blank, eyelids drooping over dull eyes. For one moment Georgina was afraid that his lordship had killed himself with the exertion of trying to talk. Then she saw his chest moving up and down with shallow breaths.

"I should ring for the nurse, Cousin Francis."

He stared at his father, frustration turning his face into a hideous mask. He reached out and caught the man's wasted shoulder in a harsh grip, crushing the linen nightshirt.

"What were you trying to say?" He almost screamed it, and shook the inert body so hard that the old man's nightcap fell off.

Georgina could stand it no longer. She picked up the bell and rang loud and long for the nurse.

"Stop it, Francis! Stop shaking him! You'll kill him!"

"I wish it were as easy as that," he muttered, but he left off shaking the sick man who then fell back limply.

The nurse came bustling in, exclaiming, "Whatever's the matter, your lordship? Heavens! The earl's nightcap is off. What happened?"

"He had another of his ranting spells," the viscount said, giving Georgina such a cold, hateful look that she didn't dare tell the nurse the truth. "Take care of him." Then, as if nothing had happened, he said, "Come along, Georgina. Help me decide what prizes to give for the cleverest costumes at the ball."

Later, in the middle of trying to decide whether to award dainty, painted etuis or scent-flasks decorated with miniature cupids to the ladies, Francis asked, "What do you think my father was trying to say, Georgina?"

"I—" She was frightened by the intense look Francis gave her. She had been thinking about those garbled words, even while she tried to keep her mind on her cousin's suggestions for gifts. Had the earl meant to say that he would recognize someone as his son? If so, it could mean only one thing; he meant to acknowledge Charles Collins. Yet Georgina knew instinctively that this was the wrong thing to say to the viscount. It wasn't quite a lie to insist that she didn't know what the earl had attempted to say.

Georgina was bold enough, however, to ask Francis if he thought it wouldn't be better to send for the solicitor. "His lordship seemed so agitated about it, Cousin Francis. Maybe he'd be calmer if Sir Barnaby came to see him."

"Sir Barnaby is much too busy to travel here from London just to see a vegetable. I don't want to hear any more nonsense from you, Georgina. I'm the one who provides for you, gives you a home, not my father."

"I'm sorry," she mumbled, fully aware that she had overstepped her place. For the first time since Francis Hardy, Viscount Quincy, had welcomed her to Hellingham, she feared that he might, just as easily, toss her out as she'd arrived, practically penniless. In the short time Georgina had lived here, she had learned to prefer the luxury which went with the house of the Earl of Margate. She must be very careful not to anger her volatile cousin, if she wished to remain here at Hellingham.

CHAPTER 16

In her bedchamber, Georgina paced back and forth, her full skirt sweeping the floor. She would have to tread very gently with Cousin Francis. He had made it abundantly clear that he controlled her destiny. By now Georgina was becoming a bit more sophisticated. What could she do without her cousin's help?

She thought hard about what the sick man up in the tower had said. If he meant to recognize Charles Collins as his legitimate heir, the Earl of Margate had waited far too long. No matter what he said now, Georgina did not think there was a court in England that would pay any heed to an old, apoplectic man's mutterings. If Charles were ever to inherit the title and the estate, it would have to be through some other means than his father's word.

Proof. Charles Collins was convinced that there was proof here at Hellingham that he was the legitimate heir to all this wealth and power. Poor Charles. The longer she spent here with her cousin, the less Georgina believed that Collins would ever find any proof of his legitimacy. It didn't exist. She thought of the glimpse she'd had of him as he drove past the gate at breakneck speed, as if determined to set a new record for the run from London to Exeter. For a breath, she longed to be with him, sitting beside him on the crowded box, warmed by the ratty old bearskin robe. The entire trip had receded in her mind so that now it seemed a dream. Had she actually ridden there beside him for all those long, rough, wearisome miles? Had Mrs. Fenton been her companion, criticizing her, trying to advise her, a poor, motherless, fatherless young woman? Georgina's lips thinned in memory. If the self-righteous Mrs. Fenton could see her now.

To date she had submitted to not one, but two, men. Brothers. Or, at least, half brothers. Each exciting in his own way. *Wanton, wanton!* her conscience cried. Georgina knew, though, that if either man tried to bed her again, she'd probably submit, having learned the joys of lying with a lusty young man, of submitting to his ardent lovemaking, of the blazing passion which he could arouse in her.

Georgina stopped beside the delicate French desk done in gilt and white, and her hand caressed the worn volume which had been her father's journal. The leather binding was smooth from wear. As her fingers felt the satiny leather, an astounding thing happened to Georgina. She knew she still stood there, one hand on the journal, yet at the same time, she seemed to leave her body, to lift from the floor of the bedchamber, and to rise slowly to the high ceiling where she hung, lighter than air, looking down at herself. She saw the flowing folds of the silk gown she wore, the brocade cuffs just below her elbows, long frills of Belgian lace billowing over her forearms. Her hair was unpowdered today, the pale tresses dressed close to her shapely head, a lace pinner topping it. Then the scene changed abruptly. The disembodied Georgina could still see her corporeal self standing, one hand on the leather-bound journal, but the place was no longer Hellingham; it was the bedchamber where her Papa lay suffering in the vicarage of St Edmund's in Trindale. The family Bible was there, too, opened. Georgina found the vision fading rapidly, and she could not see the page nor the text.

She swayed, almost falling, and her fingers clutched at the back of the dainty little gilt and white chair, losing contact with her father's journal. Abruptly the strange vision faded, leaving Georgina clinging to the back of the chair, her whole body cold and trembling violently. With difficulty she stumbled across the room to the bellpull and gave one frantic tug to the tapestry pull, summoning her abigail. Then she made her unsteady way to her bed and fell across the counterpane.

Lizzie, hurrying in, cried out, "Miss Georgina! What is wrong? Are you ill?" With one quick swooping motion, she caught up Georgina's feet and swung them up onto the bed. Then she had out the bottle of sal volatile, holding it under Georgina's nose.

In desperation, Georgina finally pushed away the smelling salts, averring weakly, "I shall surely die of an overdose of ammonia fumes, Lizzie."

"What happened, miss?" She withdrew the vinaigrette, but kept it handy in case Georgina had another faint spell.

"I—I don't know. I just suddenly felt faint." Georgina was too upset by the strange thing that had happened to her to want to discuss it with anyone. Was she losing her mind? Is this the way that madness came on you? Would she be sent to the dreadful Bedlam hospital, to live out the rest of her days with the mad? She trembled at the thought.

Quickly Lizzie pulled a blanket over her mistress, tucking the soft woolen folds about Georgina, thinking she shivered from a chill.

"Oh, miss, you aren't sickening for something, are you, with the grand ball tomorrow?"

Georgina had completely forgotten the ball. "No, no, I just had a faint turn, Lizzie. No doubt something I ate."

Softly Lizzie said, "I thought that game pie yesterday was a bit high, miss. Perhaps it poisoned you."

"I feel all right now." To put the lie to her words, Georgina shivered again, remembering the strange sensation of being out of her body, watching herself.

"Let me pour you a bit of claret, miss. It will help

to settle your stomach." She poured a generous glass of the rich red wine from a decanter on a side table.

Sipping the wine, Georgina felt much better.

"I was just coming to tell you that Mrs. Ealing is here with your costume for the ball tomorrow. Shall I tell her to wait? Do you feel like seeing her?"

"I think so. Have you seen the shepherdess dress?"

Lizzie nodded eagerly. "Oh, miss, it is lovely. You will be the most sought-after lady at the ball."

"Do you know what Olivia—Miss Nugent is wearing?"

Georgina had scarcely seen Olivia in the past few days. She assumed that the other woman and Cousin Francis had made up their quarrel, whatever it had been, and that he was once more sleeping with his mistress, for he had not come to Georgina again.

Lizzie said, "I've tried to quiz that stuck-up French maid, Marie, about Miss Nugent's costume, but she just smiles a snippy little smile and won't tell me a thing —rotten little frog!"

"Well, it doesn't matter," Georgina soothed. "We shall all see her soon enough, I imagine. Now, let me get up and bathe my face, and then I'll see Mrs. Ealing in here. I'll want to try on the gown. I may even have you do my hair the way it's to be done tomorrow night, so we'll be sure the complete effect is good."

Lizzie poured water from the china pitcher into the washbasin, so that Georgina could splash the cool water on her face. It was refreshing. She felt now that she had fully recovered from the odd episode which had occurred earlier. It was somewhat like the visions she saw when she was "finding," but it wasn't quite the same. And this was the first time Georgina had ever experienced the sensation of being out of her body, looking at herself, as if she were two people, or two parts of one person. She hoped she had no more such seizures. It had frightened her more than she wanted to admit.

Fortunately the seamstress was now ready to show Georgina the costume, so her mind was quickly distracted from the earlier strangeness.

"I do hope this fits, miss," the little dressmaker said, bustling into the room, an assistant carrying the costume. "Spread it out on the bed, Tess. Let Miss Ryerston see it."

"Yes'm," the adenoidal girl said, laying the gown of velvet and taffeta, done in shades of blue, across the coverlet.

"Oh, Mrs. Ealing, it's a dream!" Georgina cried when she saw the exquisite creation. She lifted the flounces on the skirt, and saw that they were lined with a midnight blue.

"Do you wish to try it on now?"

"Of course." Quickly Lizzie helped her out of her dress and into the lovely shepherdess costume, pulling the bodice laces tight to make her bosom stand up high, two lovely white mounds rising from the velvet ribbon which edged the deep décolletage.

"Do you have the porcelain figurine, Mrs. Ealing?"

The pouter pigeon woman clapped her hands sharply. "Bring in the basket, Tess." She explained to Georgina, "I have it well packed, miss, as it probably is very valuable."

"I'm sure it is."

Tess brought in the basket, and Mrs. Ealing produced the figurine from which she had copied the gown.

"Lizzie, can you do my hair the way it is on that shepherdess?" Georgina asked her maid, handing her the china figure.

Lizzie turned it about in her hands, examining the head carefully. "Oh, I think so, miss. It won't be hard."

"His lordship, the viscount, wants my hair unpowdered."

Lizzie nodded agreement. "Yes, miss, it will look much more rustic. Too bad that you don't have a shepherd's crook to go with the gown, like the one the china girl holds."

Tess tittered, then looked frightened when the little dressmaker turned on her.

"That's enough from you, my girl. Go out into the passageway and bring in the rest of the costume." She turned, a smug smile on her rather plain, round face. "You wouldn't be a shepherdess without the crook, miss."

Tess came back in, carrying a lovely concoction of satin and ribbons, a genuine shepherd's crook which had been wound about with ribbons in shades of blue to match the gown, with long rose-colored streamers falling gracefully from a large rosette of blue and rose.

"Mrs. Ealing—it's perfect!"

"Glad you like it, miss."

"Now let me do the hair, miss. Here, I'll brush out the powder first." Lizzie threw a large silk powdering cape over the gown to protect it, then she brushed vigorously at Georgina's fine, silken hair until it was natural shining wheat color. Deftly Lizzie wound two long curls down over Georgina's bare shoulder.

"Your hair curls so well, miss."

"Now give me the crook." Georgina crossed to the freestanding walnut-framed mirror and looked with pleasure at her reflection. Cousin Francis would certainly be pleased with how well his suggestion worked. It was indeed a most becoming costume for Georgina, perfectly suited to her blonde loveliness.

"Do you know what Miss Nugent is wearing?" Georgina asked the dressmaker.

"No, miss. I was not asked to do Miss Nugent's costume." It was obvious that Mrs. Ealing was put out about this slight.

"It was ordered from London," Tess put in quickly, eager to show that she knew what was going on in the great houses. "That foreign maid of hers told me so."

"That's enough gossiping, Tess." Mrs. Ealing shook her head. "I try and I try, but these girls!" She rolled her gray eyes expressively. "Impossible. Their tongues clack like a lot of silly geese."

"Then you don't know what the costume is for Miss Nugent?"

"It's scandalous!" Tess cut in before Mrs. Ealing could say once more that she didn't know what Olivia would wear.

"Tess!"

"Yes, Mrs. Ealing." She was much subdued.

The dressmaker left with her assistant in tow, giving Georgina no opportunity to quiz the girl further about Olivia's costume.

"I can't wait now to see Olivia at the ball," said Georgina. "Scandalous. I wonder what that means?"

"With Miss Nugent, it could mean anything. She might appear in her bare skin," Lizzie said. "If she thought it would cause a sensation, miss, she'd do it."

"Oh, Lizzie, you're exaggerating."

"Well . . . maybe, miss, but not too much. You don't know Miss Nugent the way I do. I've been around her longer than you have."

"We'll just have to wait for tomorrow, I guess."

Lizzie helped her out of the beautiful costume and hung it carefully in the wardrobe.

How Georgina wished that Charles could be here tomorrow night to see her in the costume. Georgina knew that she'd be beautiful in it. Surely she'd be able to lure him away from Olivia, no matter how scandalously the other woman would be garbed.

There was no way, of course, that the coachman could attend the ball. Driven away by his half brother, his father lying paralyzed—there was no one who would be foolhardy enough to try to get Collins into the house. Georgina knew that he had been here that one night, smuggled in by someone—perhaps one of the maids, for he seemed a great favorite with all of the servants—but unfortunately there was no way for him to come to such a splendid function as this ball Viscount Quincy was giving to introduce his cousin Georgina Ryerston to the local society.

CHAPTER 17

The day of the ball dawned bright and clear, a good omen, for the roads would not be so bad that their guests could not get to Hellingham. All day the house was a beehive of ordered activity. The gardeners had forced blossoms, so that the floral bower Cousin Francis envisioned was a fact, turning the rather austere Great Hall into a veritable fairyland. Extra help had been brought in from the nearby village, for Francis wanted plenty of maids and footmen to wait on his distinguished guests, some of whom were coming from as far away as London and the Kentish downs.

Mrs. Pruning was busy supervising the preparation of the food which was lavish in kind and variety; the punch and wines were enough to form a small sea.

It was Georgina's first ball, for Trindale had no such amusements, and the rout at Amesford's had been just that, a small social gathering with dancing and entertainment, in no way to be classed as a major ball. Georgina could now dance quite well, thanks to the continuing lessons with M. Dupree. She knew that she would not shame Cousin Francis. Not sure of her dancing ability, Francis had practiced with her several evenings, using a makeshift orchestra of various servants who played instruments. He was delighted with her ease and grace and she felt greatly relieved.

When Georgina was finally dressed, Lizzie declared, "Oh, miss, you'll be the belle of the ball. Not one of those countesses or duchesses will hold a candle to you."

Georgina was pleased with her reflection in the long

mirror which stood in her bedchamber, but the look in her cousin's face when he saw her descending the main staircase told her more than any mirror could ever say.

"You'll put our guests to shame, dear Georgina," he declared, bowing over her hand.

Then she saw his eyes widen in shock. Turning to see what it was that had attracted Francis's attention, she watched a tall, statuesque Juno come down the stairs. She was all white, as if she were a marble statue. Her face, including the tiny satin eye mask, was dead white from a heavy layer of white lead covering it completely. Her gown was the simplest of Grecian robes, skillfully draped so that one magnificent breast was bare. This, too, was white, as were her bare arms. Her hair, dressed in the Grecian style so often found on marble statues, was powdered white as snow, and her bare feet, peeking out from under the hem of the flowing gown, were bare except for very scanty white kid sandals.

"Good God! It's Olivia."

Georgina, stunned by the bare breast with its whitened nipple so prominent, asked, "Didn't you know what Olivia was planning to wear, Cousin Francis?"

"She refused to tell me. Insisted it was to be a secret."

Georgina had to know. "If she'd told you ahead of time, would you have allowed her to show herself so—so—"

He quirked up an eyebrow. "So magnificently? You'll be the most beautiful woman here, Georgina, but Olivia will certainly be the most spectacular. Every man will notice her."

"And every woman," Georgina said drily. "Enviously."

Francis, in his devil's costume, was strikingly handsome. The black suited him well. But Georgina realized how clever Olivia had been in choosing her costume, for she went so much better with Francis than did Georgina in her sugary blue and rose shepherdess's costume. The three of them had little time to admire each other, though, for the first guests were arriving, the musicians were tuning their fiddles, cellos, and flutes in the minstrel gallery, and the evening was about to begin.

Because the ball was in her honor, Cousin Francis led Georgina to the first dance, as he had done at Paladino Manor. This time Olivia accepted it more gracefully, acquiring a hot-eyed partner almost immediately. Georgina thought the men would be lined up, vying for a chance to dance with the half nude Miss Nugent. But the little shepherdess did not lack for partners, and it was a heady pleasure, indeed, to see the men look at her the way they did. Many scolded Francis for keeping her hidden away at Hellingham and Georgina felt, for the first time in her life, that she was a social success. She'd made a vivid impression on the guests at Paladino Manor, but that had been because of the "finding." Tonight she was being judged on her own merits, without the supernatural overtones lent by her strange gift.

The ball was in full swing when Georgina was led onto the dance floor by a tall man dressed like a highwayman. He could have doubled for the character in *The Beggar's Opera*. His face was covered by a red silk scarf, and his black tricorne, which he did not remove even when bowing to Georgina, was jammed down so far onto his forehead that his eyes were in deep shadow. He didn't speak a word, but Georgina knew it was Charles Collins.

Georgina went through the figures of the gavotte as if in a dream, a delicious dream, but one with fringes of terror just out of sight. If Cousin Francis saw her partner, there would be trouble; he'd be sure to recognize him, just as she had, no matter what his disguise. Frantically her eyes searched the dazzling crowd of Cathay princesses, Persian potentates, fairy princesses, knights, and devils. Nowhere did she see the slim, elegant figure of the viscount, in his fitted black garb and swirling scarlet-lined cape. As part of his disguise, he'd left his black hair unpowdered, pulled back sleekly into a black silk bag on his neck. His man had attached tiny horns at his hairline, and the effect was devastating. Now he was temporarily out of sight, as was Olivia, the white Juno.

Georgina and her partner were separated by the dance. As they came back together, she whispered, "You're mad! Someone else is bound to recognize you."

He was so distinctive in height and looks, Georgina was sure that everyone at the ball knew she was dancing with the uninvited Charles Collins.

If he smiled, she couldn't tell because of the concealing scarf. He made no answer, but the moment the music stopped and the figure ended, he swept Georgina through a doorway into the corridor which led to the tower stairs.

Her heart was thudding so hard that she was sure he could hear it beat. What was Charles doing here? It was insane for him to risk this. Had he come just to see her? In the past week, Georgina had almost persuaded herself that she no longer cared for the tall, handsome, redheaded, devil-may-care coachey. She told herself that her distant cousin, the Viscount Quincy, was a much more suitable companion for her than this pretender to the title at Hellingham. She had convinced herself that the evening of blazing passion with Collins had been a one-time encounter, a terrible mistake on her part, that she had been innocence personified and he the skillful, glib seducer. Now, with him once again so close to her, Georgina's pulses throbbed and she was almost weak with desire. She only prayed that he would never find out that she had allowed his hated half brother to share her bed and her favors. How could she have allowed it!

"Charles, you're insane!" she breathed.

"You're repeating yourself, dear Georgina." It was his beloved voice, full of amusement.

In a state of terror for fear someone had recognized Collins and was even now whispering into the viscount's ear, Georgina cried, "Why are you here? And how did you get in?"

"Why am I here? To see you, of course. I missed seeing you the other time."

No word that he'd spent the night in Olivia's arms. Nor any indication that he knew she'd done the same with her Cousin Francis. Perhaps Olivia hadn't told Charles that Francis had gone to Georgina's room.

"And I want to see my father," Charles added, sober now, his voice low with emotion.

Georgina closed her eyes, sure she would faint. See his father! "Please, you must leave," she begged, "before Francis discovers you."

"I don't fear my brother!" His eyes blazed above the scarlet of the mask.

"Well, I do! If he finds me with you, he'll send me away from Hellingham."

There was a change in Collins, perceptible even though his face was still masked. Georgina could sense it immediately.

"He'll send you away? What makes you say that, Georgina?"

"Charles, he knows that I met you at Ye Grape." Her voice stumbled over the name of the inn where she'd lost her virginity to this exciting man. "Someone spied and reported to him. He—"

"He warned you not to associate with me? Is that it, Georgina? Did Francis fill your head with stories about how terrible I am, what a rakehell?"

Her silence was all the answer Collins needed.

"That decision is for you to make, Georgina." He

caught her to him, held her close so that her senses reeled. "If you don't want to see me, go back to the ball. Mingle with all of Francis's fine guests. Dance with him, not me. I'm going up to see Father."

"But—the nurse—"

"—is my friend. She won't tattle. Will you tell Francis that I'm here, Georgina? Will you betray me?"

What could she say? With Charles here beside her, radiating that fatal charm, Georgina was powerless to do what she knew she should. Instead, she said, "I must tell you something before you see his lordship."

Catching up the voluminous skirts of her gown, Georgina sped up the spiral stairs, taking him past Miss Twistle's room on tiptoe, a finger to her lips.

There was a small storage chamber off his lordship's room. She slipped inside, silent as a wraith, with Charles right behind her. Georgina dared not light a candle, but some moonlight crept in through the long window.

"What's happening here at Hellingham?" he demanded.

Quickly she told him of the earl's wish to see his solicitor, and repeated the old man's words to Francis.

"Georgina, he wants to recognize me as his legitimate son! If he does that, I inherit. The title. Hellingham. Everything. My dear brother will get nothing." He tossed back his head in that familiar gesture, and his laugh rang out in the small room.

"Hush, Charles!" It made her cross for him to be so reckless. "Francis refuses to send for Sir Barnaby Kane."

"I must see my father. I must, Georgina. It's imperative now—surely you see that it is."

"Charles." How she ached for him. How she longed to touch his dear face, to feel his arms around her again. It grieved Georgina to have to tell him that his chances of talking with his father were almost nonexistent. "Most of the time your father just lies there. He may not even know you're in the room."

"He'll know," Charles insisted, his voice fierce.

Georgina sighed. He was so stubborn—so sure of himself. "Then let me lure the nurse away," she coaxed. "Remember, Francis pays her wages. You might think she's your friend, only to find, to your sorrow, that she has betrayed you. Wait here until you hear her go downstairs."

Georgina hurried out, pulling the door almost closed, leaving only a crack so that Collins could watch and listen. Inside the sickroom, she smiled at the surprised nurse.

"I thought you might like to see the ball for a bit," she said. "I'm willing to sit with his lordship briefly."

The country woman's blue eyes widened in surprise. "But miss, you're the hostess. Lord Francis—"

"With all those people, he'll never miss me. And I've danced so much that my feet ache. I absolutely must rest a bit. Go on—you can slip into the end of the minstrel gallery and watch the dancing. The costumes are really wondrous."

The nurse's eyes lighted up. "What a tale I'll have to tell in the village!"

"But don't mention it to Mrs. Pruning," Georgina warned.

"I won't, miss, never fear. Nor to that Twistle harpy. She wouldn't have offered to spell me for a few minutes not the way you have, Miss Ryerston. She's got a vantage point at the door of the butler's pantry where she's watching. She bragged about it to me earlier."

"Well, run along and watch the dancers," Georgina urged.

The nurse hurried out with a swish of dark skirts and starched apron. Almost immediately, Charles was in the room, closing the door behind him. He'd shed scarf and tricorne so that his father could easily recognize him.

Georgina's heart ached at the look of expectation on his face. Already she had seen that the earl lay still, eyes closed, unaware of anything around him.

In a few strides Charles was across the room and bending over the inert form on the high, canopied bed. "Father!" His voice was low-pitched but urgent. "Father, it's Charles."

The old man lay there, not stirring.

"Father?" Charles laid a gentle hand on the old man's forehead, but even this brought no response from the patient. Then Charles turned to Georgina, anguish on his face. "Is he always like this?"

"Usually. Charles," and her voice was distressed, "I told you. He has spoken only a few times in the weeks I've been here. And since that time when Francis quarreled with him, he's been like this."

"He has to talk to me—he must!"

Something, perhaps the urgency in Charles's voice, reached the sick man, and he stirred restlessly, tossing his head on the pillows so that his nightcap was pushed awry.

Bending over him, Charles said, yet again, "Father!"

The waxen, blue-veined eyelids fluttered, then opened, revealing the blank, lusterless eyes Georgina was used to seeing. But Charles, who'd not seen his father since the night of his stroke, was appalled.

"He's blind, Georgina!"

Timidly she laid a gentle hand on Charles's arm. "No, it is only the stroke, Charles. Occasionally, when he has a lucid interval, his eyes light up."

Even as she spoke, the amazing transition came again. The earl's eyes took on life and color, and Georgina knew that he was looking at Charles. Did he recognize his son?

"Charlie?" No preliminary noises this time. The word was strong and clear.

Overjoyed, Charles cried, "Yes, father, it is I."

"Is Kane here?" The old man looked around wildly,

and Georgina feared a repeat of the last time he'd spoken, when he became so excited that he lost his power of speech again.

Quickly she moved into his range of vision. "I am sorry, milord. Sir Barnaby is not here tonight." No need for lengthy explanations.

"Not here." He closed his eyes, and she thought that his lucid spell was over.

"Charles," Georgina whispered, "it's no use. He's gone again."

But without opening those blue eyes, Peter Hardy, Fourth Earl of Margate, continued speaking. "Jonathan didn't want to do . . . said . . . wicked. . . ."

"Who's Jonathan? What's father talking about?" Charles's face was a study in frustration. "His mind's wandering."

"I warned you, Charles," she whispered. "He's like this most of the time. Jonathan's my father. His lordship sometimes remembers him, and realizes I'm Jonathan's daughter."

"Jonathan?" The old man's voice rose, his eyes flew open, there was a wild look to his face which Georgina didn't like. Should she run, bring back the nurse? His lordship might have to be given more opiate. Then the old man spoke again. "Jonathan . . . were right . . . I shouldn't have forced you . . . should have been a true mar. . . ." Again he stopped talking, much to Georgina's relief. His eyes were closed now, but his breath was harsh and rattling in his throat from the intense effort of speech.

"Charles, come away," Georgina begged. "I'm afraid he'll kill himself—"

"I must hear it for myself!" Charles snapped. "Father!" His voice was sharp. For the first time, she saw some resemblance between him and his half brother, the viscount. "Father!" Charles said again. "Do you wish to acknowledge me, make me your heir?"

The old man lay there as if dead.

Charles turned from the bed, caught her shoulders in a painful grip. "You heard him the other time. Would you swear in a court of law——"

"Swear what, you imposter?"

Georgina snapped her head around, looking over her shoulder in terror. There in the open doorway stood Mephistopheles, himself. Francis Hardy advanced in ominous silence. Charles let go of her so abruptly that she almost fell.

"I thought I made it clear that you were not welcome here, Charlie. Do you leave peacefully, or must I call the King's men to take you off in chains?"

"I have a right to visit my sick father."

"Bastard!" The word was a scream of rage.

And into the silence following it, came the gargling, forced sounds of the Earl of Margate, trying to communicate. All three froze. The earl's eyes opened and once again he was lucid.

"Charlie," he said, voice quavering. "Where are you?"

The spell broken, Charles moved to the bedside. "I'm here, father."

"Should . . . married Rebec . . . Jonathan told me. . . ." His voice trailed off, his eyes closed, and he seemed to sink into the mound of pillows.

"Father!" Charles's voice was anguished.

"Thought you'd get the old man to acknowledge you, Charlie? It would never stand in a court of law, even if he does manage to get out the words. He's *non compos,* you know."

"With Georgina as a witness——"

"Ah, yes, Georgina. I assure you, my dear Charlie, little Georgina knows which side her bread is buttered on, don't you, Georgina?"

His dark eyes blazed, and Georgina felt an hypnotic quality to Francis. She stood there, unable to speak, terrified of the glitter in his eyes. He'd warned her.

Now, would he cast her out, too, when Charles was forced from Hellingham?

"See, Charlie. Georgina won't say a word to help you."

"I want Sir Bar . . . Kane!"

The loud, sepulchral voice stunned them to silence.

"Charlie . . . my son . . . oldest . . . inherits . . . title."

"Father!" Charles clasped the earl's hands in his, but the sick man once again slumped into his oblivion. "Father?"

Georgina was watching, not Charles in his triumph, but Francis in his rage. The viscount looked ready to erupt at his father's words.

"Get away from that bed!" the viscount ordered, his voice trembling. "Get out of Hellingham! I never want to see you again. If you set foot on my land, I'll have you arrested, and you'll wind up in Tyburn!"

Charles straightened up, standing tall and arrogant, an imposing figure against his half brother's slim elegance. "You heard him, dear brother. I heard him. And, most important of all, Georgina heard him. My father wants to see Sir Barnaby Kane, and he shall. I'll ride to London and fetch him."

"Get out of here!" The viscount's voice rose to a scream. "Father's no longer competent. I'll petition the king. He's already sent Dr. Ward to see father. He'll declare him incapable of functioning. No, Charlie, you'll not usurp my place. And Georgina—" He turned, and she was frightened by the look he gave her. "Georgina didn't hear anything. Did you, little homeless cousin?"

Numbed by the terror of the moment, Georgina couldn't force her lips to form the words to deny this.

Charles gave her one long, penetrating look. "Cousin? You didn't tell me you were kin to this popinjay, Georgina. So we have secrets?"

Still Georgina couldn't answer Charles, although she died inside at the cold, cynical look he gave her.

Then he shrugged. "Everyone knows I'm the earl's son," he said easily. "Kane will fix it for me to inherit Hellingham." He glanced at his father's inert form. "Kane can sit here beside the bed for days, if necessary, to hear my father acknowledge me as his heir."

"Not while I'm here," Francis threatened.

"Come, now, Francis. While father lives, he's still Earl of Margate. It's his authority, not yours. And when I tell Kane that father wants him, but that you forbid it, you'll need all the influence in court your position can muster! The king upholds the law of the land." His tone was insolent.

Charles, Charles, Georgina cried silently, *don't push Francis too hard!*

Then, without even a look at her, Charles strode to the door, and she could hear the diminishing sound of his footsteps as he ran lightly down the spiral staircase.

"Where's that woman?" The viscount caught up the bell and jangled it loudly. "Where is she, Georgina?"

"W-watching the dancing," she whispered, her mouth dry with fear so that her tongue slid over her lips to wet them. "Don't blame her, Cousin Francis. I told her I'd sit here—"

"To give your lover a chance at my father." It wasn't a question, the way he said it. "Well, Georgina, we must decide what to do about you, mustn't we? It would seem I have nurtured an adder in my bosom. Isn't it lucky that Miss Twistle just happened to see you and Charlie on the stairs?"

Georgina expected him to order her out of the house at that moment. Instead, he smiled at her, and held out a hand, but the smile reduced her to jelly, and she thought she'd faint. Was this the Francis who had held her in his arms, who had aroused such rapture in her? Now that Charles had returned, Francis seemed like some alien soul.

"Our guests will wonder where we are." There was cold steel under the smile. "We must go back to the ball."

Then the nurse came hurrying in as if pursued by Furies. She checked when she saw the viscount. All he said to her, though, was, "Good, you're back. Come, Georgina."

Her icy fingers were caught in his hand, and he almost dragged her down the spiral stairs past the crack in Miss Twistle's door. The music of a minuet swept up to meet them, and at the bottom of the stairs stood a masked man dressed as a pirate, his satin costume of carefully contrived tatters. The moment he spoke, she recognized him as the Marquis of Amesford.

"I might have known you'd be dallying somewhere, Francis. And with your pretty cousin, too." He made a leg, smiled mockingly. Georgina was too terrified to acknowledge his salute with an answering curtsy.

"My, my, she does find the Hardy men attractive!" And at Francis's sudden, alert look, "Didn't I see Charlie here? I'd not expected that. Come to see Miss Ryerston?"

"I think we must have a long chat later, Amesford. But at the moment, please escort Georgina back to the ball. And stay with her, Howard. There's a good fellow."

"My pleasure." Lord Amesford tucked Georgina's unresisting hand into the crook of his elbow and led her away from her cousin, back to the great hall.

CHAPTER 18

The rest of the ball was a blur to Georgina. How she longed to slip away to her room, to leave the merriment and the music behind her, but Francis gave her no opportunity to escape. In her charming costume, she was much sought after as a dancing partner; but as each new blade bowed his thanks for the privilege, Cousin Francis was there eager and ready to keep her from disappearing.

There was no further sign of Charles. Georgina wondered if he was still somewhere in the house, hiding, perhaps, in the servants' wing where he had friends. Or had he slipped away from Hellingham as quietly as he had arrived? There must have been many of the servants who knew Charles was there. It was nothing short of a miracle that Francis hadn't spotted his hated half brother while he was on the dance floor earlier. Georgina shuddered at the thought. What a terrible commotion Francis would have raised if he'd caught Charles dancing with her. It was bad enough that he'd found them together in the tower room with the earl.

In the giddying whirl of guests, Georgina got glimpses of Olivia in her revealing costume. Did she, too, know that Charles Collins was at Hellingham? A wave of jealousy swept over Georgina. If Francis had not cut short Charles's visit with his father, what would have happened later? Would the handsome coachman have tried to bed her had they not been interrupted? *What would I do if I found him waiting for me in my bedchamber tonight?* Georgina asked herself, knowing full well what the answer was. She could not turn him away. When she was away from Collins, Georgina could think rationally about him, could acknowledge that he possibly cared not a whit for her but was only using her as a means to his own private ambitions; but when he was beside her, all she could do was to react to his attraction.

Now, with the ball drawing to a close, Georgina couldn't even think, for the imported orchestra was large and played loudly, and during any lulls in the dancing, the guests, who had consumed gallons of punch well laced with gin, and innumerable glasses of wine, were giddy and boistrous. The swirling dancers, the hundreds of flickering French wax candles, the tension and fear of wondering if Charles would be foolish enough to come back to the dance floor, coupled with the tightness of her stays which Lizzie had laced unmercifully snug, made Georgina feel faint and feverish, alternating with dizziness and chills. The tall clock on the landing was chiming three before the musicians put away their instruments and the guests began leaving. Through the farewells, the viscount insisted that she stay with him as hostess, although Georgina, unaccustomed to such lavish and lengthy festivities, would have been ready to drop from sheer exhaustion even if she had not been emotionally depleted from the terror of trying to guess her fate once the hall was clear of guests. Would Francis spend the few remaining hours of the night with his mistress, who now was much in evidence, slightly tipsy and glowering at Georgina, or would the viscount come into Georgina's bed? No doubt Olivia was wondering exactly the same thing. *Ah, Olivia, we are sisters under the skin,* Georgina thought ruefully.

Finally the last coach clattered away from Hellingham. In desperation Georgina begged, "Will you excuse me now, Cousin Francis? I am weary to death."

"Yes, do let poor Georgina go to bed. She's so very young for such late hours," Olivia suggested sweetly, moving close to the viscount and slipping her arm through his. By this time the white lead paint was beginning to wear off, and the rosy nipple that was exposed was peeking through the paint.

The Marquis of Amesford, who was staying the night, was lolling against one of the buffet tables, now a shambles of leftover delicacies and empty bottles. He was drinking another cup of the potent punch. His bloodshot eyes kept going from the voluptuous Olivia to the weary shepherdess. Now, hearing Olivia's pointed remarks, he smiled slyly.

The viscount was having none of it, though. His sardonic face darkened. "Georgina is no doubt weary from climbing those spiral steps to the tower. But she looks fresh as a daisy, doesn't she, Amesford?"

The marquis made a leg, his sly smile chilling.

"Charming. Fully as delicious a morsel as dear Olivia, here. Ah, Quincy, how lucky you are to have two such delectable ladies at your beck and call. However do you manage? Do you have them cut the cards to see who will be your lady of the evening?" He was quite drunk now, weaving slightly as he stood there leering at both women.

Although more than a little drunk herself, Olivia was infuriated by Amesford's remarks. "Francis loves only me," she said, speaking slowly and distinctly to keep from slurring her words. "Don't you, Francis?" She twined herself around him lasciviously.

Francis, in a sudden fit of revulsion, caught Olivia's hands and forcibly removed them from around his neck.

"You're the one who needs to go to bed—to sleep off the punch you drank too much of," he snapped at Olivia.

"And you'll bed little Miss Wheyface? You'd better hurry, then, Francis, or Charles will be there before you. He was much in evidence tonight." She laughed, an ugly sound, and looked pure hate at Georgina. "Didn't you see your dear brother dancing with your little country cousin?"

Francis turned on her, forgetting Georgina for the moment. "And why didn't you report to me that Charlie had come uninvited to my ball, Olivia?"

Olivia realized too late that she had trapped herself with her words which were meant to damage Georgina.

"I thought surely you had seen him yourself, Francis. He was outstanding, dressed as a tall highwayman—"

Francis advanced on her, and she retreated until she was cowering beside Amesford, her escape blocked by the table.

"Of course you would be inclined to see him, wouldn't you, having shared his bed so often of old. Well, tell me!" he thundered. "How did Charlie get in here unnoticed?"

Georgina trembled at her cousin's burst of anger, and hoped that it would not be directed at her when he was through with Olivia Nugent. But he looked at her, now, as he asked, voice icy cold, "How did he get in?"

Inspired by malice at Olivia who had been tormenting her, Georgina smiled a tiny smile and suggested, "Ask Olivia. She knows Mr. Collins far better than I do."

Amesford laughed loudly and long at this, and clapped his hands. "Well said, little Miss Ryerston. Answer that, Olivia of the bare bosom."

Pulling some of the draperies of her gown around her to hide her breast, Olivia said, "I have no idea how Charlie got in here. The maids all adore him. No doubt he services them regularly, and for this they grant him favors."

"Not just the maids," Francis said darkly.

Again Georgina tried to excuse herself from the company.

"Not so fast, little cousin," Francis said, his eyes devouring her. "I shall see you safely to your bedchamber."

"That's not necessary," she said.

"I think it is."

Olivia looked daggers at the younger woman. Walking unsteadily to Francis, she laid one white-painted hand on his arm. "Don't be long, dear," she said in a stage whisper.

"You're tipsy, Olivia. Go to bed and sleep it off," Francis said cruelly, pulling away from her touch.

"So! You're going to bed the little cousin!" she spat, her green eyes glittering dangerously.

"What I do is no business of yours, Olivia. Now, do as I tell you. Go to bed."

Defiantly she moved away from him and turned to the drunken Marquis of Amesford. "Howard," she cooed, "do you want to share my bed tonight?"

Deliberately he reached over and pulled the drapery away from her bared bosom. "Delectable," he said, caressing her. "Do you mind, old man?" he asked Francis.

"Not at all," the viscount said, not even looking at the couple. "Come along, Georgina." He held out a hand, palm down, and she had no choice but to place her hand on it and be led away from the banquet room, through the great hall where the servants were snuffing out the hundreds of candles which had lighted the room brilliantly. Others were dismantling the floral bowers which the gardeners had so cunningly contrived.

As they ascended the grand staircase, Georgina's heart thudded, and her pulses throbbed. Was Francis going to bed her again? Obviously he wanted her. They passed a footman in the long corridor leading to her room, and the viscount sent word that his valet should attend him in Miss Ryerston's bedchamber. He meant to spend the rest of the night with her. She was trembling now, from fatigue and emotion. Francis, feeling her hand shake, said, "No vapors, please, Georgina. You aren't a simpering virgin, you know. I've had you before, and you enjoyed me as much as I enjoyed you. Admit it."

She didn't answer, but walked along with him, eyes downcast. It was all too true that her body had betrayed her, and she had been consumed with lust as she lay in his arms. She hated herself for it. Georgina thought that she truly loved his half brother, Charles Collins. Yet her woman's body had responded to his maleness with abandon. Would it be that way again tonight?

When they reached her bedchamber, Lizzie was waiting. As Lord Francis entered after Georgina, her eyes widened in shock. It annoyed Georgina. Lizzie knew perfectly well what had happened between her cousin and herself that other time. Why should she be surprised tonight?

"Get your mistress ready for bed," Francis ordered.

In a show of modesty, Georgina retreated behind the screen which hid her washstand from the rest of the room, with Lizzie right behind her.

"Miss," Lizzie whispered, her lips so close to Georgina's ear that she could feel the breath from the abigail's mouth. "Oh, miss, what disaster!"

Disaster? Now what? Georgina knew that Lizzie was given to flights of fancy, and saw great drama in the slightest thing. As tired as she was, and as tense from the knowledge of what was coming, Georgina was more provoked than interested in what her abigail had to say.

"Charlie's here."

Georgina, who had been slipping out of her costume with her maid's help, stopped stock still. Turning to face Lizzie, she leaned close and asked, "What do you mean, Lizzie?"

"He's hiding in the wardrobe, miss. To surprise you."

Georgina thought she would faint. Charlie here, in this room, crouching in the huge wardrobe—with Francis waiting for his valet to come and disrobe him so that he could bed her.

"What will I do?"

"Is—is his lordship—?"

Georgina nodded, not trusting her voice to stay whisper-soft and unheard. As it was, Francis was becoming impatient.

"How long does it take you to get out of a few petticoats, Georgina?"

There was a knock at the door, and the low murmur of male voices, so his man had arrived.

"Georgina! Have you gone to sleep behind that screen?" Francis demanded. "Don't dawdle. I'm impatient for you in my arms."

She closed her eyes, sure she would not survive the night. What was she going to do? How could she get Francis out of the room long enough for Charlie to escape?

Quickly it became obvious that there was no way out of this horrible dilemma. When Francis said that if she didn't appear from behind the screen, he was going to knock it over, Georgina gave in to the inevitable and went to her bed, the soft folds of her nightdress clinging to her youthful, womanly curves.

"That's all," the viscount said brusquely to Lizzie and his valet.

Georgina thought frantically, trying to come up with a solution to her intolerable situation. Could she pretend that she heard someone in the passageway outside her bedchamber door, and ask Francis to investigate? That would not give Charles an opportunity to escape, unless he went out the window and grew wings for flight. If she suggested that she heard a disturbance in the garden under her window, would

Francis go to the window to look, making it possible for Charles to slip from the room? Not a chance, she realized. Francis would surely hear his half brother tiptoe across the floor.

Then it was too late, for Francis was getting into bed beside her, throwing off his robe to reveal his nude body.

"Snuff the candle, Francis," she begged.

"No, I want to be able to watch your face," he said, his voice husky with desire. "Here, take off that ridiculous nightdress, Georgina. Why did you bother to put it on?" His impatient hands reached for the silken folds, pulling it roughly over her head.

Her eyes strayed to the huge fumed oak wardrobe opposite the bed. One of its carved wooden doors stood slightly ajar, to give air to the man hidden inside. It was a nightmare! There was nothing she could do to prevent what was about to happen—nothing. Francis would take her, and there was not a thing in the world she could do to prevent it. And Charles would be a witness to the entire performance. She closed her eyes, hoping to shut out this unthinkable situation, but Francis's hands moved over her body, and she could not ignore him. All too well Georgina remembered the other time when Francis had joined her here in this bed, remembered that her body had betrayed her at the last, responding to his talents as a lover. Was that what was going to happen tonight, with Charles as a captive audience?

Georgina shuddered, and her lover chose to misinterpret her reaction. "Do you like that?" he murmured. "Does it please you when I touch you there, Georgina?"

The most awful thing about what was happening was that Francis was very skillful in his lovemaking, and it did please her, even though she hated herself and him for making this true. When Francis had roused her to a fever pitch, she forgot all about Charles crouched in the wardrobe, and knew only the sensations which Francis gave her, the wild and sensual feelings which were her unwanted response to his demands. Her eager body joined with his in passion, and her mind forgot everything except her pleasure. When it was over, and Francis lay beside her, relaxed and smiling, Georgina suddenly remembered Charles. Oh, God, what would happen when Francis left her for his own room? Or did he intend to spend the rest of the night in her bed? There was no longer any need to pretend, even with the servants. Oh, what would Lizzie think, knowing that Charles had hidden, waiting for Georgina's return to her bedchamber after the ball? What was Charles thinking now as he hunched inside that wardrobe? Georgina felt that she could almost see those bright blue accusing eyes through the crack in the door. It was Charles she truly loved, it was the handsome bastard with whom she longed to share her bed; yet here she lay, sated with love, with another man beside her. How could she be truly in love with one man, yet still so enjoy the bliss of physical love with another? Truly she was wanton. How her poor dead Papa would mourn to know that his carefully reared daughter was no better than any common tart.

Now Francis raised himself on one elbow and looked down at her, a little smile on his handsome face. "You're tired, aren't you, my lovely little country cousin?"

"Yes, I am."

He leaned over and kissed her, gently, with no passion. "Then I'll go back to my own room and let you sleep. If I stay here, you may get no sleep at all." His hands slid down along her smooth, white flesh, from the hollow of her throat over her lush bosom, across the soft roundness of her belly, to her more womanly charms. She felt a stir of passion, but Georgina did not make any indication to Francis that she was willing for more of his lovemaking. By now she was almost desperate for him to leave, so that Charles could be released from his self-imposed prison inside the wardrobe.

"Goodnight, Francis. Or, more accurately, good morning."

It would soon be dawn. Charles would have to be away during the dark hours, or he might be found by Francis. Georgina didn't know what would happen at such a confrontation, nor did she want to find out.

"I'd really prefer to stay right here," Francis said, lying back down beside her. "You make a man feel very drowsy, little Georgina," and he laughed, an intimate sound which she found both pleasing and disturbing. "But," and he sighed, sounding quite aggrieved "no doubt Isher will be expecting me to sleep in my own bed at least a little while tonight." Again he laughed, but this time there was a jarring note in his humor. "Who knows, I may find dear Olivia in my bed, waiting for me. Amesford was so drunk that he may have given her very little satisfaction."

To her horror, Georgina found that she was filled with an irrational jealousy. It bothered her more than she'd have dreamed possible to think that Francis might go from her bed to one containing Olivia. But she said nothing. She wouldn't give Francis the satisfaction of knowing that she resented his mention of Olivia after having made love to her.

Again she said, "Goodnight, Francis."

This time he left her bed, pulled on his robe, put on the kid slippers Isher had brought for him, and picked up the candle which was burning so low that it was starting to gutter, the flame casting weird shadows on the ceiling.

Not wanting to be left in the dark with Charles, Georgina begged, "Light another candle for me, Francis. I—I wish to put on my nightdress before I go to sleep."

He lighted a taper on the chimneypiece and brought it to the bedside, setting the silver candlestick down on the small bedside table. Then he leaned over, kissed her lightly, and finally left her to her fate.

CHAPTER 19

Georgina was frantically slipping into her nightdress as Francis left her bedchamber. The moment the latch clicked, she was out of bed, running barefoot across the room to the huge wardrobe. Before she reached it, however, the door burst open and Charles climbed out, his posture still contorted to fit his height into the space.

She stopped short, not knowing what to say to him, not sure of his reaction. He straightened slowly. Charles had discarded the red kerchief with which he had hidden his face at the ball, and he no longer had the big black tricorne pulled over his red hair to conceal it. The rest of his costume was the highwayman's garb he'd worn to the masquerade ball.

"Oh, Charles!" Georgina held out her arms to him more in supplication than in passion, although she was flooded with desire at the sight of him.

He stood there, unsmiling, cold, looking at her from those blue eyes which could be so warm and alive, but which now looked like blue ice in the flickering light of the one candle flame.

Then Charles spoke one word. "Slut!"

"Charles!" Her voice was anguished. Suddenly Georgina felt exposed, standing there in her sheer nightdress, her bare feet cold on the oak floor. She crossed her arms over her bosom in a gesture of concealment. The cold of the floorboards penetrated into the bones of her feet. The fire had died down in the fireplace, and Georgina shivered from cold. She knew why Charles had called her such an ugly name, but it hurt dreadfully. The chill she felt was from more than the cold air of the bedchamber.

For an interminable moment they stood there like two statues, Charles disgusted and irate, Georgina crushed at his reaction to her.

Then he turned and strode to the door. At the last possible moment, Georgina cried, "Please, Charles, let me explain!"

He turned, his hand already on the brass doorknob. "Explain? What is there to explain, Georgina? Are you forgetting that I've been here in this room for the past hour? Do you think I'm deaf? Or perhaps you have me down as the village idiot, one who can't comprehend what goes on right under his nose."

She walked toward him hesitantly, still with her arms wrapped about herself, shivering, frightened. Georgina knew, though, that she mustn't let Charles leave this way. He must listen to her, he must let her explain—oh, God! How could she ever explain what had happened in her bed tonight? Yet she had to try, she must make Charles realize that she was trapped, that she had no choice, it was go to bed with Francis, or be forced to leave Hellingham. Charles certainly hadn't offered her any security, he hadn't proposed marriage, he hadn't even suggested setting her up in an establishment somewhere along the stagecoach route, so that he could be with her whenever his work made it possible. Didn't he know how difficult it was for a woman alone, a woman with few skills, who'd tired of the drudgery of weaving woolens for a lecherous old man, who wanted some of the nicer things in life?

"Charles." Her voice shook with cold and with fear. She was sure she would be rejected, but Georgina had to try. She let her arms fall to her sides, then lifted them to him in entreaty. "Charles. Won't you listen to me, let me explain?"

His laugh was low and bitter. "Explain! Oh, indeed, you need to be very clever, Georgina, to explain to me about your bed and your bedfellow!" He turned to her, caught her arms in a grip so hard that she winced with pain. "Do tell me, little slut, how much you enjoyed my half brother's attentions. I could hear you. I recognized those sounds. I'd heard them before—remember? Those sounds of passion, the little moan of fulfillment! I thought that they were for me, Georgina —for me alone. When you gave yourself to me that night, I thought that I was the only man in your life. You are a marvelous actress, little vicar's daughter. You should consider a career on the stage. John Rich might hire you for one of his productions. You'd be the toast of the Haymarket—there'd be thunderous applause at the Drury Lane Theater—you could tour the continent, be the darling of Paris as well as London."

"Stop, Charles. You—you're hurting me."

His fingers bit even deeper into her flesh, but it was his words which wounded Georgina sorely, more than his harsh hands. It was true, what he said. She knew it. There was nothing she could say to refute that. Still, Georgina had hoped for some understanding, some sympathy. Charles knew what his half brother was like. He knew how Francis could rage if he were crossed, how dangerous it was to oppose him. Charles had been driven out of Hellingham by his half brother. Why couldn't he be a little more generous with her? Was there no sympathy, no understanding, in his heart?

"You made me think that you were mine alone," Charles went on. "I trusted you. I told you things I might better have left unsaid. I daresay by now you've told Francis everything about our talk at Ye Grape."

"Not everything." She didn't dare say more, for she had told Francis most of what had happened. Georgina had not, of course, let her cousin know that she had lain in Charles's arms before that fire, that she had let him take her, that she had responded to his love-making with abandon. She had told him, though, that

Charles was still trying to find proof of his legitimacy. It was no secret. Francis already knew it.

Now Charles shook her as a terrier would shake a rat, so that her long, fine, silken hair flew about her in a shimmering rain of pale gold, the lone candle flame picking out highlights in it.

"Did you tell him that I was here tonight? Did you?"

"No!" She reached out for him and clung to him, even as he shook her. Although Charles was her tormenter, he was also the rock to which she turned for support. "He knows, though. Olivia Nugent couldn't wait to tell Francis that you had danced with me."

That stopped him short. "Olivia?"

It gave Georgina great satisfaction to be able to say, "Yes, Olivia. Did you think that she cared anything for you, Charles? Olivia cares for no one but herself. I should think that was abundantly evident, even to you. I know you are used to having women throw themselves at you, but Olivia is using you only for her own purposes, even as you've tried to use me for yours."

"And what does that mean?"

"What do you think it means?" she cried bitterly. "You aren't interested in me—only in the fact that I'm here at Hellingham, an inside source of information for you."

"Do you believe that of me, Georgina?" His voice was low, troubled. "Didn't our lovemaking mean anything to you?" Then he added, his voice as bitter as hers had been, "But I guess you were just dallying with me. You seem quite happy with my rotten brother in your bed."

"Charles, what choice do I have?" she cried. "Don't you understand that? I am here only because Francis allows it. If the earl were not ill—but he is. I am lucky to have a place to live."

"You could get a position somewhere, a decent job, not be the doxy of a rich man, who'll keep you as his

toy only as long as you please him. He's tiring of
Olivia, isn't he? She made the same choice you've
made, Georgina. She chose Francis because he was the
Viscount Quincy, heir to the Earldom of Margate.
You've heard all of the gossip, I'm sure. A house such
as Hellingham is always rife with gossip, speculation.
I'll wager that every servant in the house knows that
you entertained the young lord in your bed tonight.
So you know that Olivia was my mistress. She loved
me, or so she claimed; but when Francis offered her
the lure of becoming a viscountess, and eventually a
countess, she turned from me with never a backward
look."

"If that's so, why did you spend the night with her
when we returned from Paladino Manor?" Georgina
spat, tired of having this rakehell make her feel cheap
and inferior.

"Who told you—"

"Olivia, herself. She bragged to me that she'd had
you in her bed. She knows how I feel about you."
There, she'd said it.

"I noticed tonight how you feel about me," he
said, voice dry. "I had a box seat for the entire performance."

"You say I should leave here, get a position. Doing
what? Shall I go back to Exeter and take up my loom
again?" Her laugh was harsh, remembering. "Do you
recall the stout matron who rode the coach when I
came here?" Charles nodded. "Her husband owns all
the looms in that area. I worked for him, the loom
set up in the kitchen of the vicarage. Once poor
Papa became so seriously ill, I dreaded Tuesdays, for
that was the day that Adam Fenton came with more
wool, to collect what I'd woven for him during the
week, and to pay me the few shillings I'd earned from
hours of backbreaking labor. Have you ever woven at a
loom, Charles? Have you ever listened to the clack of
a flying shuttle hour after hour, while your feet ache

from working the treadles, and your arms feel like lead after pulling on the strings and pulling the bar so steadily? With a chance to be pawed by Fenton when he arrived? Do you think I liked that? If I had wanted to stay in Trindale, Mr. Fenton, fine Christian married gentleman that he was, offered to set me up in a little cottage he owned on the outskirts of Exeter, where I could slave my fingers to the bone through the day, weaving fine woolen cloth for the Fenton firm, and then entertain him in my bed evenings." She made a little moue, remembering. "That's what I could look forward to if his lordship hadn't given me a home—a good home, too, Charles. Lovely gowns, fine food, no work—"

"Indeed not. What you just did with him in bed wasn't work at all, was it, Georgina? It was pure pleasure."

If he had slapped her full in the face, it couldn't have hurt more.

"That's right—judge me! You can bed every serving wench between London and Exeter, you can warm Olivia Nugent's bed even though she is betrothed to your half brother, and it is perfectly all right. Don't tell me that you love all of them! When you had me there at Ye Grape, was it love, Charles? Another four letter word, starting with the same letter—not love but lust. And you have the audacity to throw my conduct in my face! If I don't accommodate Francis, I must leave Hellingham."

He shrugged. "I left."

"You're a man. You have no problem finding gainful employment. You are a coachey."

"That's right, a coachey! You think I like that job, Georgina? Do you think I enjoy driving hack horses over rotten roads day after weary day from London to Exeter and back again to the Big Smoke? Do you? Can you imagine what it's like to have no more intelligent conversation than what I have with Robin

Adair? Do you honestly think I enjoy all of those complaining, carping, miserable passengers? I hate every minute of it, Georgina, because I was raised for better than that. I was raised a lord's son in everything but name. I had a fine education. I drove the best horseflesh that money could buy. I had my own coaches—I didn't stoop to the public stage. And I had expectations. I've had them for years. Do you know what that does to a man, Georgina, to know that he's entitled to something which someone else has! I've resented Francis from the time I was old enough to understand who I was—and who he was. I've hated him, just as he's hated me. He stole my birthright, and I want it back."

"And you'd use any means, no matter how underhanded to get what you claim is yours," she reminded him bitterly, "even if it meant the seduction of a young woman who'd been raised in a decent home by a saintly father. Admit it, Charles. Admit that you have no interest in me except for what I can do for you—in bed and out of it." Now she reached up and took his hands from her shoulders as if they were dirt. "Very well, Charles, you want back into Hellingham, and you are willing to go to any lengths to get here, no matter that you hurt me. All right, I want to stay here. You can understand that—surely you of all people must know how I feel. I like living here. So I guess I must go to any lengths to stay here, mustn't I? And if it means bedding your hated half brother, then you prepared me for that, didn't you?"

He walked out then, without a word, without a backward look at her. Georgina, the moment the words were out of her mouth, regretted them bitterly. She loved Charles, truly she did. What made her be so antagonistic to him? She longed to run after him, throw her arms about him, beg him to forgive her for her harsh, bitter words; but her pride kept her there in her room, shivering with cold and emotion, for too long. When she did open the door, the long passage-way was empty. She had no idea where Charles had gone. No doubt by now he was well away, knowing the house so thoroughly. It was too late for her to apologize to him, make amends.

Slowly Georgina returned to her high, lonely bed. She crawled into it and huddled under the quilts, her feet lumps of ice, her flesh all over her body a mass of goose bumps. The tears came then, hot tears gushing from her eyes to rain down over cold cheeks and nose. Angrily she dashed them away, wiping her eyes on the soft linen sheets. She wouldn't weep for Charles Collins, she wouldn't! He wasn't worth her tears. He'd used her despicably, and she resented it. Even Cousin Francis was more honest about their relationship. Francis desired her and said so quite openly. He didn't pretend love. He just wanted to bed her. Very well, she would not say no to him. Georgina knew that he was already tiring of Olivia Nugent, that he thought the woman's low birth unsuitable for a viscountess. As for Georgina, her bloodlines were as good as his own, for they were cousins. She knew Francis found her attractive, and she had to admit that he could be very interesting if he chose to be. She could do much worse than try to become the Viscountess Quincy—and later, when Francis's father died, as he was sure to before too much longer, she would become Countess of Margate. It was a far cry from the vicarage of St. Edmund's in Trindale to the estate known as Hellingham. She would forget Charles Collins. He'd never be anything but a coachey, and Georgina wanted more than that out of life. She'd been poor for nineteen years. Now she wanted to be rich—and if that meant being nice to her Cousin Francis, then so be it. She would make him forget Olivia.

Finally she drifted off to sleep as dawn lightened the windows. But she didn't dream of Cousin Francis. She dreamed that she lay once more on the bearskin rug in front of the fire in the private parlor of Ye Grape, and Charles Collins was the man who lay there with her, loving her.

CHAPTER 20

"It is lovely to have you here gracing my home," Cousin Francis said, smiling at Georgina over the laden dinner table. Olivia looked up quickly, her face closed, her eyes shuttered. Georgina wished that Francis had chosen another time to tell her, for she knew that she'd already earned Olivia's enmity several times over since the masquerade ball. Francis paid excessive attention to her, practically none to his supposed lady love. He had spent several nights in Georgina's bed, and she stopped worrying about what Charles might think. Charles was in the past. She'd thought she was madly in love with him, but his actions toward her had not been conducive to much ardor. She now was convinced that Charles had seduced her only to get her to cooperate in his mad scheme to claim the earldom for himself when his father died.

"A little country maiden is scarcely sophisticated enough for your tastes, my dear," Olivia said spitefully. "You've always preferred someone with more experience."

Francis smiled his most satanic smile at Olivia. "And you, my dear Olivia, certainly are experienced, aren't you? My bastard brother—and others. No doubt you find any number of men to amuse you—perhaps Amesford will come over from Paladino Manor again to keep you company. Did you enjoy him the night of the ball? Or did Charlie warm your bed again? I always thought you had a soft spot in your heart for our Charlie, even when you were loudly professing your

222

love for me—or for the title that would go to you if you married me."

"Francis, that's unkind," Olivia said, sullen, her face dark with anger. "You know I never cared for Charlie."

Georgina said nothing, feeling acute embarrassment that she must be a witness to this discussion. She knew that Francis was tiring of Olivia, that he had no intention of marrying the woman; and no doubt Olivia, herself, realized this, too. Georgina understood how the other woman must feel, to be rejected now, when she had been so sure of her place at Hellingham. No doubt Olivia hated Georgina. But there was nothing Georgina could, or would, do to change the situation. It was not her doing that Francis had tired of his mistress. If it hadn't been Georgina, she was sure it would have eventually been some other woman. Very well, if he prefered her to Olivia, he did. There was nothing she could do about that. It suited her fine.

It did not suit her to be in this *ménage à trois,* however. The sooner Cousin Francis made some provisions for Olivia, and sent her away from Hellingham, the better. It became increasingly unpleasant to have Olivia always angry with her, always whispering about her behind her back. Lizzie carried gossip from the servants' quarters, most gleaned from Olivia's French abigail. Olivia Nugent neglected no opportunity to blacken Georgina's name and reputation with the servants. She had both the housekeeper and the odious Miss Twistle on her side. No doubt they reveled in nasty gossip whenever they could.

"Miss, they keep saying you're a witch," Lizzie told her, worried lines on her pretty face.

"Nonsense! I'm no more a witch than you are, Lizzie."

Yet Georgina sensed a slight withdrawing of her abigail, as if even Lizzie thought the tales might have some substance.

It all came to a head a few days later when one of the kitchen maids came down with a fever.

"Have they tried any herbal teas for her to bring down the fever?" Georgina asked her abigail.

"Well, miss, no one knows just what to use. His lordship doesn't usually send for the doctor for a kitchen maid. And there's been so much talk against the granny woman in the village who usually brews up such teas, that no one wants to send for her."

With nothing to occupy her time, Georgina decided to go see the sick girl. She found her in a poky little room under the eaves in the servants' wing. Nan was only a child, probably thirteen, and her cheeks were flushed an unhealthy red from whatever fever she had contracted. Her eyes were glazed, and she seemed only faintly aware of Georgina's presence. Having been a vicar's daughter, Georgina knew more of caring for the ill than many, and she was village-raised, so she knew of the common herbal remedies.

Leaving the sickroom, she went directly to Mrs. Pruning.

"Nan is quite ill, Mrs. Pruning. Why hasn't something been done for her?"

"That is scarcely your responsibility, Miss Ryerston." There was naked antagonism on the older woman's face. "Let me worry about kitchen maids."

As if sensing his mistress's dislike of her visitor, Puffy waddled toward Georgina, snarling deep in his throat. When she ignored him, he snapped at the ruffle on the pink morning dress she was wearing.

Annoyed with Mrs. Pruning's lack of concern for Nan, Georgina said sharply, "Some day that wretched spaniel is going to nip me. And when he does, expect trouble, Mrs. Pruning."

The housekeeper smiled a chilling smile. "He doesn't like you, Miss Ryerston. They say that dogs aren't friendly to witches—witches have nasty cats for familiars."

"Mrs. Pruning, if you insult me further, I shall be obliged to report your conduct to his lordship."

"Feel free to do so. I shall tell him that you are a troublemaker. I have been at Hellingham for more years than his lordship has been alive. He couldn't manage without me. But," and she looked down her long nose at Georgina, "if you wish to test him, by all means, do ask to have me dismissed. You may be his cousin—so distant that the blood must be very thin—but when he tires of you, he'll send you packing, miss, and I'll still be here, running Hellingham for him."

Georgina was just unsure enough of her position here to decide not to carry the fight with the housekeeper further. Instead, she said, "I'm sure I saw feverfew in the herb garden. Do you mind if I brew some tea for Nan? It helps bring down a fever."

Mrs. Pruning shrugged. "Do as you like. But if she dies, I shall feel compelled to tell his lordship that you probably poisoned her."

Georgina left with as much dignity as she could muster, but Puffy trailed her, snapping at the hem of her gown. Georgina usually liked animals, but this nasty little dog was a nuisance.

Taking a small willow basket with her, Georgina tied on a widebrimmed straw hat to keep the sun from her face, and went out behind the kitchen wing to the herb garden to pick the white-flowered feverfew. When she went to the kitchen to ask for help in brewing the medicinal tea, she found that both Mrs. Pruning and Miss Twistle were there, having a cup of tea with the cook, a woman of mountainous proportions.

Anticipating her request, Mrs. Pruning said firmly, "Don't ask cook to make your witch's brew, Miss Ryerston. If poor Nan dies, the responsibility will be wholly yours."

"A little tea made from feverfew isn't going to kill anyone," Georgina snapped. "Hopefully it will lower the poor girl's fever. She may well die without any care. It would help if someone sponged her off with cool water."

"All this concern for a kitchen maid," Miss Twistle sneered. "Yet except for a bit of reading, she pays little attention to the poor earl."

"The poor earl is your responsibility," Georgina snapped.

"That's right, be sharp with me," the dumpy woman said. "Honey around the poor sick man when Lord Francis is there, to make an impression on him. And, from what dear Olivia tells me, you've certainly impressed his lordship. Don't be high and mighty with me, miss. At least I don't go hopping into bed with any man who asks me."

Goaded beyond reason, Georgina said, "And how many men have ever asked to go to bed with you? None, I'll wager."

Then she brewed the herbal tea herself, ignoring the snickers and unkind remarks the three women made about her. Ringing for Lizzie, she sent the abigail off to get a basin of cold water to bathe Nan's face and arms.

By evening, the fever had broken and the girl, weak though she was, took some mutton broth and declared that she would be back in the scullery in the morning.

Two days later Puffy was found dead in the buttery. Lizzie was gleeful as she told Georgina of the spaniel's demise.

"What killed him, Lizzie?"

The abigail was powdering Georgina's hair, and she had to sneeze before she answered. "I think it was old age, miss. Puffy was fifteen if he was a day."

"I can't say I shall grieve," Georgina said drily.

Later that day, Georgina met Mrs. Pruning in the hall. Usually she spoke to the woman, but today the housekeeper anticipated the greeting.

"Wicked! Wicked!" she said, her voice low, furious. "To kill my poor little Puffy."

There was no mistaking her meaning, for her green eyes glittered with hate.

Affronted, Georgina said coldly, "Are you suggesting that I had anything to do with the death of that miserable animal?"

"You bewitched him!" Mrs. Pruning said. "Put a spell on him. Now my darling little Puffy is dead."

"He no doubt died of old age, Mrs. Pruning. And I will thank you not to go around Hellingham spreading such a vile story about me. I had nothing whatsoever to do with the death of that dog—but I can't say I'm sorry he's gone."

"Oh! What a horrid creature you are. Everyone loved little Puffy—everyone but you. And he was so gentle and loving himself. You are the only person he didn't like."

Remembering the footman she'd seen kick at the annoying dog when it had tried to nip his ankles, knowing that Lizzie felt the same way she did about Puffy, Georgina maintained a superior silence.

"A witch! Don't think I haven't heard about you, missie. Finding things at Paladino Manor. In league with Satan, you are. It isn't normal. No Christian woman could do the things you so easily do."

Georgina swept past Mrs. Pruning, seething with rage. She was glad the nasty little spaniel was dead; but if his death was going to cause her trouble, she'd almost wish him alive again.

That wasn't the end of it. When she went up to the tower suite to read to the earl, Miss Twistle made a great show of backing away from her, hand on sagging bosom.

"Don't look at me!" she ordered nervously. "I don't want to be given the evil eye."

"It gives me great pleasure not to look at you," Georgina snapped, seeing the nurse almost smile at her riposte. She picked up the novel she was reading, sat down, and began her daily chore without another

look at Miss Twistle. Behind her, Georgina heard the
solid thump of the companion's feet as she ostenta-
tiously left the room rather than stay there with the
witch.

As it was one of the earl's more torpid days, Georgina laid aside the novel and asked the village woman,
"Do you think I'm a witch?"

Surprised out of her taciturnity, the nurse said, "Me
own dear mother, God rest her soul, had a way with
herbs, miss. And sometimes she had the sight. Saw
death, most often. She wasn't a witch. One of the best,
godliest women you'd want to know. No, Miss Ryerston, I don't think you're a witch; but what I think
don't count much here. It's that mean Twistle—and
hard-faced Pruning runs the house. Take care, miss. It
could get ugly for you."

And ugly it did get. Within a week, scarcely a servant in the place would even look at Georgina, let
alone speak to her. Every time she saw the housekeeper, the woman gave her a cold, smug stare, as
if to say, "See! I'm head of Hellingham."

Georgina said nothing to her cousin at first. She
knew that Francis did not like to be bothered by
domestic affairs. When Lizzie came to her, though, and
said that Olivia was in the thick of it—spreading stories
about her via her maid—telling the tale, with many
embellishments, of how Georgina found the necklace
at Paladino, Georgina knew it had to stop.

That night Francis came to her as he did more and
more frequently, which added fuel to Olivia's fire of
hatred for Georgina. First Georgina let him make love
to her, responding with all the passion of her young
body. Then, as they lay relaxed, sated, she said,
"Francis, I'm so unhappy these days." Feeling him go
tense beside her, she hastened to add, "Not with you,
my dear. Never with you. But Olivia. . . ." She let her
voice trail off, almost demanding a question from him.

"Now what's she done? I do wish you two wouldn't squabble."

She knew that petulant tone all too well. "Oh, Francis, I try so hard to be friends with her, but now she's telling everyone that I'm a witch, that I killed that hateful spaniel by putting a spell on it."

"For that King George should have a special medal struck."

"It's not funny, Francis. Lizzie says that Mrs. Pruning is talking about bringing in the constables. She wants to have me arrested for witchcraft."

That did get to Francis. Abruptly he sat up in bed, his bare shoulders set in a stiff, unyielding angle. "I know old Pruning thinks this place would fall into ruin if she weren't here, but this time she may have gone too far. I have no intention of seeing my own dear cousin hauled up before a judge on a witchcraft charge. I'd be the laughing stock of the entire county. I'd not be able to go into White's in London without causing comments. Isn't it bad enough that I just got you out of appearing at the trial of those two robbers who took the diamonds when we went to see Amesford? I pulled strings in very high places, Georgina."

"I know, Francis. I'm very grateful."

"Well, you should be. Once Amesford told his solicitors the whole story, they agreed there was enough evidence to convict both the actors without your testimony. In fact, Lord Mintern advised that no mention be made of your role in apprehending the thieves, lest the court be turned into a circus, with your strange powers causing a scandal."

"So you'll make Olivia and Pruning quit gossiping about me behind my back?"

"Never fear. I'll be quite firm with them. Olivia had best mind her manners. If I get too annoyed with her, I'll toss her out. She'll wind up in one of Moll Bailey's brothels, will Olivia."

Next day Francis had Mrs. Pruning in for a chat,

and she left his presence in a towering rage, glaring at Georgina when she passed her in the hall; but the witch talk stopped.

Before dinner, Olivia cornered Georgina and hissed, "All right, maybe you've won this round. But it's not over."

During the meal, Olivia was only a little subdued. Once she even dared say spitefully, her teeth poised over a pheasant wing on which she was nibbling delicately, "Take heed, Georgina. Francis can be very fickle—can't you, Francis, dear? Someday you'll read in *The Gazette* of his engagement to a fine lady."

Francis went right on eating a portion of roast mutton and boiled turnips which he washed down with gulps of claret. Was this true? Would he tire of her as he had of Olivia?

It was as if Cousin Francis could read her mind. "Don't pay any attention to Olivia, my dear Georgina. I'm not even sure she reads well enough to peruse *The Gazette* for the latest tidbits of gossip."

Olivia flushed darkly at his jibe, but she held her tongue. The look she shot at Georgina, though, was absolutely venomous. Georgina wished that Cousin Francis wouldn't try baiting his mistress—or former mistress. Georgina thought that he no longer sought Olivia's bed on the nights when he did not come to her. Yet Francis did nothing about sending Olivia away. The situation was rapidly becoming intolerable. Georgina resented Olivia as much as the older woman hated her. At times Georgina was convinced that Francis knew how much antipathy there was between the two women—and reveled in the emotion generated by them.

Sometimes she was tempted to ask Francis to send Olivia away. One thing restrained her. If he did as she requested, would Olivia go to Charles Collins? *I don't care if she does!* But there was a surprising pang which struck Georgina when she thought of the now long-absent handsome coachey. Every time Georgina passed the portrait of Lord Peter Hardy which hung in the corridor, she was forcefully reminded of the redheaded man who had seduced her and made her so blissfully happy. When she tried to erase that face from her mind, Georgina found that it was difficult. She was sure that she loved her cousin, Francis. He was a much more suitable husband—and Georgina was determined to marry him, although Francis had never actually discussed marriage with her. He did keep mentioning that she was a more well-born young woman than Olivia, being of Hardy stock; but Francis seemed content to let matters drift for the moment.

Georgina still went up most days to read to the earl, but he was seldom lucid. Francis questioned her rather closely about her contacts with his father, yet he did little on his own to see how the old man was. Sometimes Georgina remembered that she had promised Charles Collins to try to help him get evidence to prove his title to the earldom and Hellingham; but as days passed, with no further contact from the bastard son, she began to forget what had happened between them. Surely, if the earl thought that Charles was his legitimate son, he would acknowledge him. She remembered all too well the hatred which had shone in those bright blue eyes on one of the occasions when the earl was lucid and Francis was present. Francis hated his father and the old man hated his son. It was a deplorable situation, one she still had trouble in understanding, for Georgina and her own father had been wonderfully close, with a great tide of love flowing between them. Hatred between father and son was incomprehensible.

When the meal was finally concluded with a wondrous pudding cook had molded in the shape of a beehive, with bees made from currants stuck all over it on short quills, Francis suggested, "Let us walk in the garden, Georgina, to digest our meal." He did not include Olivia in the invitation.

They went out onto the slate terrace through the French windows of the grand salon, and strolled into the gardens which were green with the promise of spring.

Francis, close beside her, reached over and lifted a curl which fell down over Georgina's bare shoulder, the end nestling on the white mound of her bosom. His fingers trailed across the soft flesh, sending a thrill through her. Leaning close, Francis said, "Let's go to the folly at the end of the garden, my dear. It is comfortable there, with a spacious sofa. I want you now."

It was broad daylight, and Georgina was afraid that one of the gardeners might happen on them as they lay there unclothed, but she had learned early in their relationship that it did no good to refuse Francis, for then he would only force her. With his warm, sensitive fingers on her breast, her breath quickened, however, and she felt desire flash through her like a hot flame. If he wanted to take her there on the grass in the garden, she could not deny him. All thoughts of Charles Collins were whisked away on the balmy spring breeze as her senses responded to her cousin's appeal.

They walked along the crushed oyster shell paths which led to the folly which was built in the Palladian style, with a stream diverted to circle it, and a miniature Palladian bridge of warm brown marble leading over it. By now Francis's busy fingers were working on the fastenings of her gown, so that Georgina pleaded with him not to expose her before they reached the privacy of the folly.

He laughed, a laugh deep in his throat, and said, "I may chase you nude through the garden, Georgina. The sun is warm today, and then I could take you in some secluded spot with sun and shade dappling your lovely flesh."

Scandalized, she cried, "Francis, you wouldn't!" and hurried across the arch of the bridge to get into the small, elegant building before he had a chance to completely disrobe her and make good his threat.

The wide sofa was covered with lovely cut velvet of rich, stained glass hues, and Francis wasted no time once they were there. Deftly he stripped Georgina, caressing her full breasts while her trembling fingers untied his neckcloth and unbuttoned the hammered gold buttons of his waistcoat. His fingers sought out the pins which held her hair, saying, "I want your hair loose, Georgina." Then, laughing lewdly, he asked, "Did you know that the whores in the Bible advertised themselves by wearing their hair unbound?" He ran eager fingers through her blond tresses.

Georgina caught up her sprigged India muslin gown and held it in front of her self-consciously.

"Francis! Are you calling me a whore?" Georgina knew that it was wrong to lie with Francis without benefit of clergy. But the term "whore" jarred her sensibilities.

With one sweep of his hand, Francis pulled the gown away from her, exposing her ripe nakedness to his hot eyes.

"Of course you aren't a whore, dear little cousin," he murmured, catching her to him in his eagerness to have her. His lips slid across her cheek, he nipped the lobe of her ear, causing her to gasp at the combined pain and pleasure of his caress, then he buried his face in the soft flesh of her throat, his lips sending waves of sensation through her so that Georgina thought she might faint with desire.

Francis lifted her in his arms and laid her on the velvet of the sofa. Georgina, nearly mad now with the passion he aroused in her, reached up and pulled her cousin down onto her eager, waiting body, arching her supple young back to meet him. Now it didn't matter to her if the entire complement of Hellingham gardeners stood watching them make love. She was unaware of everything except the sensuous delight of her cousin's body as it joined with her own.

When she finally shuddered from the intensity of sensation, Georgina had a terrifying experience, instead of the rapture she had come to expect. As had happened to her once before in her bedchamber, Georgina's spirit seemed to leave her body. She was hovering in the domed ceiling of the folly, so close to it that she could see the intricate plasterwork which ornamented the small arched dome. Below her, on the velvet Kent sofa, Georgina could see two nude bodies, her own and that of Francis, writhing in the rhythms of love. Suspended above them as she was, she could see every nuance of their enjoyment of each others bodies. She was two people, the one on the sofa who was enjoying the raptures of the flesh, and the other, the onlooker. Georgina was conscious of every tingling of her body; yet her other persona, the one high above, felt nothing.

Then she was transported somewhere else. She was in a tiny, ill-lighted, slant-ceilinged garret, pressed against the dingy sloping wall, watching another couple on another bed. This time it was a mean little pallet on which the man and woman moved together. The dark red hair she recognized. The broad, bare shoulders were familiar to her. Georgina could almost feel the muscles move under her fingers, even though she was several feet above the heaving body. The girl was no one she knew, a full-blown, buxom, fresh-faced country lass, probably a barmaid. Even as she watched unwillingly, Georgina saw them reach their rapturous climax, and the waves of their delight reached up to her, engulfing her in the sensations so deeply that she cried out, "Charles!" in her joy.

Instantly Georgina was once again in her own body, lying on the velvet sofa, the soft pile of the fabric buffing her own tender flesh.

With an oath, Francis sprang away from her, standing there nude and shiny with sweat, his face dark with anger. Before Georgina could put up a hand to protect herself, Francis slapped her so hard that her ears rang.

"Whore!" he spat. "How dare you cry out for that bastard, Charlie, when you are in my arms!"

Georgina, sobbed bitterly. "Francis!" she begged. "I don't know what you mean." She had scarcely been aware of what she had said.

"You cried out Charlie's name in your joy. How do you think that makes a man feel, Georgina—I give you pleasure and you think of Charlie." Again he lifted his hand to strike her, but she pulled back, burrowing into the upholstery of the sofa to escape from him.

"You—you must be mistaken," she pleaded. "I just —I just cried out from pleasure, Francis. I didn't actually say anything."

He scowled at her, disbelieving; but Georgina, determined to maintain her position at Hellingham, smiled her most seductive smile at Francis and reached up her arms to him. "Come, don't be angry with me because I am so carried away when you make love to me," she whispered. "I want to hold you in my arms, Francis. Please."

She saw the anger fade from his face, the lust return. When he joined her again on the sofa, Georgina knew that this time she had won. But if she kept having these strange visions, what was going to happen to her? Georgina shuddered with dread, but as Francis's expert hands were caressing her, he thought that she shuddered from the pleasure of his touch.

"Do you like that, Georgina?" he demanded.

"Yes," she whispered. "Oh, yes."

CHAPTER 21

"Marie says that Miss Nugent is in a proper snit," the abigail reported to Georgina, tossing her head so that the mobcap ruffle fluttered about her forehead. "Or at least that's what the French wench says," and Lizzie giggled at her play on words. "His lordship doesn't go near her bedchamber these days." She said it proudly, as if working for the woman who now enjoyed the viscount's favors made the abigail important in her own right. Probably in the servants' hierarchy, it did give her status.

Georgina had almost succeeded in wiping all thoughts of Charles Collins from her mind by day. But sometimes, at night, she dreamed about him. She would dream that Francis was making love to her, and then his face would change from the dark, sardonic one she knew so well to the fair, debonair face with the bright blue eyes, and her rapture was from Charles, not from his half brother.

"Do you want to keep these books here on your desk?" Lizzie asked, breaking in on her thoughts. "Or shall I pack them away? They're just gathering dust here."

The abigail was holding Papa's journal, and the family Bible which Georgina had not opened since she had come to Hellingham. There was nothing at Hellingham conducive to religion. Francis, like most of the young bloods, was a skeptic about matters religious, going through the motions occasionally only for social reasons.

A wave of remorse washed over Georgina as Lizzie

236

held out the two well-worn volumes to her. Papa would be so distressed by her conduct. He had not raised her to be a wanton. Had he lived, Papa would have been baffled by her conduct with her cousin, Francis. She took the books, clutching them to her bosom. "I—I don't know, Lizzie. We'll see if there's room—" And then it hit her again, that strange, disturbing sensation of being separated from her body. Georgina could see herself stand there, holding both leather-bound books, swaying slightly so that the long folds of her Watteau sacque of pink satin brushed lightly over the patterned Turkey carpet on the wide boards of the polished oak floor. Lizzie was reaching out for her mistress, her face white with alarm. And somewhere, far away, Charles was calling . . . calling . . . calling. . . .

There was a pungent odor, and Georgina fought against the fumes which brought tears to her eyes.

"She's coming 'round now, milord," Lizzie was saying, her voice far away as if she were speaking into an empty hickory hogshead.

"What happened?" It was her Cousin Francis, his voice harsh with worry and anger. Georgina wanted to talk to him, but she seemed to have no voice at all.

"She just had a faint turn, milord. I may have laced her stays a mite too tightly." Lizzie's voice was frantic. "No doubt that's what made her come over faint, milord."

Georgina opened her eyes, seeing an image of Francis blurred by the tears in her eyes which were caused by the pungent odor of ammonia.

He smiled, but she could tell that he was worried. "You have given me quite a turn, Georgina. Are you all right? Are you sickening for something?" He turned to Lizzie. "Get a footman. I may want to send for a doctor."

"No, no," begged Georgina. "I'm quite all right. I think Lizzie's right—I'm laced too tightly."

He smiled at her. Then, turning to make sure that Lizzie had gone out of the room, he asked quietly, "Are you with child, Georgina?"

"Am I what?" She was stunned at his question.

With a shrug, he asked, "Is it such a strange question, little cousin? We've been lying together for weeks, now."

I am naïve, Georgina thought. *Such a thing never even occurred to me. What would I do if—* "No, I'm not with child," she assured him, her voice very positive.

He patted her hand, an impersonal kind of touch from him. "Don't worry about it if you are, Georgina. There's a woman in the village who makes a brew from molded grain—it's worked quite effectively with Olivia on occasion."

Georgina had to force herself not to snatch her hand away from his, the subject was so distasteful. Destroy an unborn child? As obviously he had done before. How could Olivia Nugent have allowed it?

As if guessing at her thoughts, the young viscount said darkly, "I've seen enough of Hardy bastards to last me all the rest of my life. I'll not bring any into this world, Georgina. When I marry, that will be soon enough to father sons on my lawful wife, and they'll be legal issue, with my eldest son in line for the earldom, with no nonsense about secret marriages and other such trumperies."

He didn't ask her to be his viscountess, although she thought that was what he had in mind. When the old earl died, Francis would inherit, and his wife would be Countess of Margate. Would she be Countess Georgina? Their relationship was as intense as it had been from the beginning. Georgina was positive that Francis paid no attention at all to Olivia Nugent now, if she could believe the gossip which Lizzie gleaned. Yet Francis did not ever mention matrimony.

Will he tire of me and discard me as he has Olivia? The thought was chilling, and Georgina shivered.

Immediately Francis was pulling a down coverlet over her. "I think you need some wine, Georgina. Where is that woman of yours?"

"You sent her for a footman," Georgina reminded him.

Francis tugged the bellpull impatiently. "Where did she go—clear to the stables?"

Just then Lizzie hurried in, out of breath.

"Wine for Miss Ryerston," he ordered brusquely. "Are you sure you don't need to have the doctor come bleed you?"

Georgina shuddered again, screwing her face up in distaste. "Ugh! I hate those leeches. Please, Francis, no doctors."

"Very well. But I expect you to be up and about in the morning, Georgina."

"I could get up right now." She sat up and sipped at the crystal goblet of claret Lizzie poured for her.

"Stay in bed," he ordered. "And Georgina, remember what I said. About the other matter. Just let me know, and I'll make all arrangements."

She cringed inside, hoping Lizzie couldn't guess at what his lordship meant.

"Very well, Francis, I'll remember."

When he was gone, Georgina wanted to get up, as she now felt quite all right. The strange sensation she'd had was gone. But her abigail was quite adamant.

"His lordship said for you to stay in bed, miss, and it would be worth my position if I let you get up." Then, leaning toward her mistress and lowering her voice to a conspiratorial level, she asked, "You aren't in the family way, are you, miss? If you are, I know an old granny in the village who takes care of such things. Some say she's a witch—"

Never in her life had Georgina been so close to slapping anyone as she was to slapping her little abigail. "What a hateful thing to ask me!" she snapped, more harsh than usual because she'd not been able to vent her anger on Francis, so poor little Lizzie was getting the brunt of it all. "I don't ever want to hear such nonsense from you again."

Poor Lizzie's open face was woebegone. "I—I didn't mean—I mean—it does happen, miss, and I thought—"

"And I never want to hear you use that word *witch* again," Georgina went on, plowing right over the maid's stammered explanations. "Do you have any idea what it's like to be called a witch? It's horrid, that's what it is. I know. I've had the word thrown at me for years, and I'm getting very tired of it. The old granny probably is no more a witch than you are. She's just someone who knows herbs and can brew up healing teas. Witch!"

Tears spilled out of Lizzie's brimming eyes. "Oh, miss, I'm that sorry, I am. I won't call anyone a witch ever again. Truly I won't. And I'm sorry about the other. I was just trying to be helpful. I know that Miss Nugent has had to—well—you know—and I thought—"

Georgina fell back on the pillows with a sigh. "It's all right, Lizzie," she said, her anger spent. "I know you only meant to help."

"When you nearly fainted, I only thought—"

"A natural thing to assume." It was, too. Francis had thought of it immediately. Everyone had thought of it except the principal character, Georgina, herself. Lucky for her it wasn't true—this time. She tried to shut the ugly thought from her mind, but it persisted. A child. She'd known, of course, that many a child was born out of wedlock, but Georgina had never, in her wildest imaginings, thought of such a thing in connection with herself. It would be tragic to have to destroy a life that way. Maybe, if she was unlucky enough to become pregnant by Cousin Francis, he would marry her so that she could have the child legally. Yet some

little imp whispered to her, *And maybe he wouldn't.*
Georgina was learning that Francis could easily dispose
of unwanted problems—he threw an unwanted illegitimate half brother out of Hellingham, he seemed
quite casual about abandoning Olivia, and he no doubt
would call in the granny woman to treat her should
she inconveniently find herself pregnant.

This latest problem had almost driven the original
trouble from Georgina's mind. Then she saw the two
leather volumes lying on the French desk again, and
the terror came back to her.

Lizzie, eagle-eyed, said, "Are you feeling faint
again?" and had the vinaigrette under Georgina's nose
before she had a chance to answer.

"No, no, I'm all right, Lizzie," Georgina insisted,
annoyed with the girl for her overconcern. What was
it about Papa's books which seemed to trigger this
strange phenomenon in her? They were everyday volumes—a Bible and a journal—which had been in his
room when he died. Was his spirit trying to tell her
something? Georgina had never believed in the spiritual-
istic nonsense spouted by some, nor had Papa. In fact
he had preached a very strong sermon against spiritual-
ism once, angering several members of St. Edmund's
who were firm believers in mediums and other such
trumpery. Had he been wrong? Was there something
here which defied common sense and logic? It was
a very disturbing line of thought, one which Georgina
did not want to pursue. It was bad enough that she'd
been afflicted—the only word which adequately described her condition—by her "finding" ability since
adolescence. Now, there was this new and terrifying
circumstance in which she left her body and seemed
to be several places at once. She remembered some
old religious works she had found in the library in the
vicarage once, stories of Papist saints who were reputed
to be in more than one place at a time. *But I'm cer-*

tainly no saint! Georgina thought hysterically. Far from it.

She wished that there were someone with whom she could discuss these strange occurrences, but she had no friends here. She wouldn't dare bring up such a subject to Francis. It was hard to talk of anything so strange with a man you loved, a man with whom you shared your bed. It might make him lose all interest in her. She did not even have a man of the cloth with whom she could chat, to ease her mind.

Finally Georgina convinced herself that she was only overtired, not going out of her mind. If she just ignored everything, she could relax and forget the disturbing journeys she made outside her own body.

By evening Georgina felt quite well again, impatient with being in bed. Seeing that her mistress was recovered, Lizzie asked if she wanted the two books, the Bible and the journal, left on the desk, the question she'd asked hours ago before Georgina's fainting spell.

A curious feeling of revulsion swept over Georgina. "Put them away somewhere," she said quickly, not wanting even to discuss it with Lizzie.

"Whatever you say, miss."

Trying to think of some excuse to leave her bed, Georgina said, "I haven't been up yet today to read to the earl, Lizzie. Miss Twistle will think I have deserted him."

"That spiteful toad!" the little abigail said, lips narrowed in disgust. "All she does is suck up to Miss Nugent. She's not your friend, miss," Lizzie added in a rush of emotion, "so don't trust her."

Remembering how the loathsome companion had spied on Charles, Georgina assured her loyal abigail, "I would trust Miss Twistle as far as I could throw her —and the way she eats cook's puddings, that is not far!"

Lizzie giggled in appreciation.

"But I feel quite well enough now to go visit with

his lordship," Georgina went on. "He sometimes knows I am there. Occasionally he recognizes me."

Once out of her bed, Georgina hurried to the library, looked over the shelves until she found a novel she'd not read, and skimmed up the spiral stairs to the earl's tower bedchamber, surprising Miss Twistle who was dozing in a highbacked chair beside the bed, a book open on her ample lap, faint snores coming from her bulbous nose.

Quietly, so as not to wake the companion, Georgina moved close to the nurse who sat to one side, her fingers busy with knitting, deftly shaping the yarn into mittens for one of her multitudinous children. Leaning close to the busy woman, Georgina asked, "Has his lordship been lucid today, nurse?"

Not looking up from her knitting, the nurse whispered, "No, miss, he has been like the dead all day."

"I thought I'd read a bit to him. I've been neglecting him terribly, I'm afraid."

"So Miss Twistle has mentioned, miss," the nurse said, shooting a quick look at Georgina to see how she'd take it.

Georgina eyed the sleeping Miss Twistle with annoyance. That woman wouldn't miss a chance to blacken her character to the nurse. No doubt she'd gone on at great length about how Georgina spent more time with the young lord than with the sick old earl. But Miss Twistle was the one who was paid to be his companion, not Georgina!

As soon as she began reading in her low, pleasant voice, the earl's eyes opened, bright blue in his pale face. Georgina knew that look. The old man was fully aware of her presence.

"Good evening, milord. Would you like for me to read to you?" She held up the book. "It's by Jonathan Swift."

"Jonathan? Where's Jonathan?" The earl cried out in a terrible voice, frightening Georgina and waking

Miss Twistle, who blinked in confusion, then glared at Georgina.

"Papa is dead, milord," Georgina said quietly and sadly, sure the old man had forgotten. She should never have mentioned Swift's name, but it was said before she could have anticipated its effect.

"Come here, Georgina." The terrible old man glared at Miss Twistle and asked, "Who is that poor creature? Send her away at once!"

"Well! I never! I am your paid companion, milord, while this young woman is—"

"A dear relative!" he thundered.

Then, as quickly as his lucid spell had come, it was gone. His face went blank, his eyes seemed to fade as Georgina watched, and the sick old man fell back on his pillows, exhausted.

"See, nurse!" Miss Twistle cried, her voice shrill with anger. "See how Miss Ryerston upsets his lordship? I think I must talk with his lordship, Viscount Quincy, about this. I really must. It is a disgrace that this poor, sweet, dear old man must suffer so from her presence."

"Oh, do be quiet, Miss Twistle," Georgina said curtly. "You know very well that his lordship is like this most of the time. When he is lucid, he prefers my company to yours for obvious reasons."

"Well! How dare you insult me so!" She almost hissed the words.

Georgina chose to ignore her remark, earning further enmity from Miss Twistle. She was sorry to have to leave the earl to the not so tender mercies of his paid companion but Francis had hired the woman. Georgina realized full well that the earl was seldom aware of her presence. The times when he was lucid, however, he often seemed troubled by something of which she reminded him, although Georgina had no way of knowing what this was. Perhaps he was dwelling in the far past, when he and Georgina's father had been fellow students at Oxford. Maybe there had been some uni-

versity prank of which he thought, something which
had gotten out of hand, as such things do. Georgina
heard many stories of the young men at university, and
she could guess that this great hulk of a man had been
a prize rake in his time, although it was hard for her
to think of her father in the same fashion. Who knew,
though? Papa might have been a real hell-raiser when
he was young, before he had decided to join the clergy.

Georgina didn't dwell on the matter. She saw that
his lordship had lapsed back into his torpor, so there
was no need for her to stay.

She was torn between the two half brothers. Georgina had promised Charles to help him gain what he
claimed was his inheritance—but she'd also promised
Francis to ignore Charles and his unreasonable claims.
She had lain in the arms of each of the vital, different
brothers, and had responded with abandon to the lovemaking of each man. She must someday soon make a
decision, choose between the two sons of the Earl of
Margate. Which would it be? Should she choose Francis, Viscount Qunicy, who was the legal heir to the
earldom? He had done much for her, giving her a
luxurious home, saving her from the accusations of
witchcraft brought by Mrs. Pruning. She owed a lot to
him. She was not sure, though, that he would marry
her, for he had her now, without the need of a wedding
ceremony.

Or should she return to her first love, Charles? She
was not sure of his feelings toward her. Had he seduced
her only so that she would be his spy within Hellingham? If he truly loved her, surely he would make more
effort to see her, be with her. Yet, if she chose Charles
and he could never find proof of his legitimacy, then
she was doomed to be the wife of a common coachey.
And after the luxury of Hellingham. . . .

CHAPTER 22

It was a beautiful day, the sun warm, the breeze light, the air fragrant with the odor of apple blossoms, as they cantered along the road from Hellingham to Paladino Manor. The Marquis of Amesford had invited Georgina, Francis, and Olivia for dinner *al fresco*—a picnic, he called it, the newest pastime for the *ton*. Georgina hoped that the marquis, whom she could not abide, would devote his time to Olivia. That dark-haired beauty, as if clinging to a spar, shipwrecked and near drowning, was these days clinging to Francis.

Jealousy was an ugly emotion, and Georgina tried her best to ignore the other woman. From the amount of time her cousin spent in her bed, she knew he was completely disenchanted with Olivia, yet Georgina tried not to say anything about the other woman to her lover. Francis had a spiteful streak which could be directed at Georgina as well as at those less in his favor. Never quite sure how she stood with Francis, Georgina was inclined to tread very warily with him. He might be amused at her rancor toward Olivia—and again he might find it boring, a deadly sin as far as Francis was concerned. Or he might take perverse pleasure in rekindling his affair with Olivia, just to laugh at Georgina's jealousy. But today, if Amesford would keep Olivia amused, Georgina could have Francis all to herself.

How she wished that Olivia, knowing herself displaced, would leave. Georgina refused to think about what Olivia would do, where she would go, if she left Hellingham. His former favorite had thought she was

246

going to marry Francis, that her future was assured. Now, with a younger woman supplanting her, what were her prospects?

She could marry the odious Amesford, Georgina thought. Olivia had been so hateful to Georgina, had gossiped so about her, had spent hours whispering about witchcraft, that Georgina truly hated her now. Georgina never had learned whether or not Olivia had entertained Amesford the night of the masquerade, and she didn't care to ask the viscount. Georgina preferred to forget that awful night entirely.

Georgina had not seen Charles since that night. Once she had been in the garden when the London-Exeter stage rattled past the gates of Hellingham. She had heard Robin's melodious trumpet in the distance in plenty of time for her to have picked up her skirts and run to the gates, but she had controlled the impulse to get a glimpse of Charles. He had left her in anger and disgust after being a witness to her lovemaking with his hated half brother. Furthermore, Georgina had still done nothing to try to help him find the proof of his claim to the title. Charles would have no reason to pay any attention to her the next time he saw her. It brought pangs of sorrow and remorse. Georgina knew that the handsome coachey thought she had let him down dreadfuly when she had refused to say that she had heard the earl bequeath his title to his bastard son. Couldn't Charles understand how she felt then? Didn't he know she was in mortal terror of Francis? She couldn't have gotten out a word, her mouth was so dry from fear. But he could argue that she'd not been terrified of Francis later that night when she responded to his lovemaking. What possible answer could she give to that?

"Why so silent, Georgina?" Francis asked, urging the big bay gelding he rode so that it cantered alongside her chestnut mare. Francis was very handsome today in a scarlet riding coat and tan breeches, black leather boots with wide cuffs reaching to his knees. If he'd worn a silk scarf under the cocked brim of his black felt tricorne, the viscount could have posed as a gentleman highwayman, just as his brother had the night of that fateful masquerade ball.

"I'm saving my chatter for this picnic," Georgina answered, trying to dispel her unhappy thoughts. "I've never been to one. Will the servants cook the meal outdoors? Will the marquis have tables set up under the trees in his park?"

Francis smiled indulgently, but the answer came from Olivia who had spurred her high-stepping gray hunter forward so that she was riding on the other side of Francis.

"It's much more rustic than that, Georgina. I've been to picnics before." She gave a little toss of her head as if to say that Georgina was hopelessly provincial. Olivia was looking quite elegant, until you took a good, close look at her face. She wore a beautifully fiitted basque-style riding habit of wine wool, the jacket snug over her ample bosom, the peplum flaring out from a waist which Marie had cinched in so tightly, Georgina wondered how she could breathe. But under a matching felt miniature tricorne, her face was beginning to show faint signs of sagging at the jawline, and there were tiny wrinkles at the corners of her eyes which she had tried to hide with a heavy coat of white lead paint. Her eyes were outlined with kohl to darken them, and she had bright spots of carmine on her cheeks to match the overly bright carmined lips.

Georgina, in contrast, looked fresh and natural. She had told Lizzie not to paint her at all, as she knew the ride would bring natural color to her cheeks. Her lovely golden hair was unpowdered, in contrast to Olivia's. The bright apple green riding habit she wore suited her coloring beautifully, and Georgina knew that she was the more attractive of the two women.

The felt hat perched on her head was in a darker shade of green, with her riding boots dyed to match.

Soon the graceful lines of Paladino Manor showed through the trees. The three found that Amesford had not invited any other guests to his bucolic meal. Their host was not in riding clothes, but his coat was not as ornate as he was used to wearing, being of a bright peacock blue, very plain, with silver buttons down the front and trimming the deep cuffs at sleeve and pocket. Paler blue trousers with silver buckles at the knees completed his outfit. His hat brim was curled both front and back, with a feather cockade for trim.

"We shall all go in my open carriage," he cried when he saw his guests ride up. "My grooms will see to your horses." Then he made a leg to Georgina after lifting her down from her horse before Francis had a chance to dismount himself. "And are you ready for picnicking, my dear Georgina? I think that cook has put up a basket of wondrous delicacies for us. I thought we'd drive to the lake and sit on the bank in the shade of the willows. It is such a peaceful setting."

"Georgina has never been on a picnic, milord," Olivia said, with a little cat smile, making sure the marquis knew that Georgina was quite unsophisticated.

Amesford, though, smiled at Georgina, not Olivia, and told her, "Then I am happy to be able to introduce you to this most delightful of ways to enjoy a repast."

The open coach seated the four of them comfortably, with a coachey and a footman on the box, and another footman riding clinging behind, where linen-covered baskets held their meal. When they arrived at the tiny lake, a glittering sapphire set in a ring of feathery willows which dipped their branches to meet the clear water, the servants spread damask cloths on the grass and quickly laid out a meal of cold roast pheasant, roast duck, a variety of pickles, freshly baked bread, a wide selection of cheeses, and little gooseberry tarts.

Several bottles of wine waited to be drunk with their lunch.

The four sat on rugs which the servants laid over plump pillows for their comfort. Georgina was enjoying herself immensely when Amesford turned the conversation to Charlie.

"There are rumors all over the county that Charlie is still trying to wrest the title from you, Quincy," he said to Francis between bites on a pheasant leg. "Someone told me he's threatening to bring in Sir Barnaby Kane."

Francis just scowled, not answering, pouring himself more claret which he gulped noisily.

Ever the troublemaker, Amesford went on, "Did he plant this charming little miss on you, Francis?" He smiled sweetly at Georgina, but all she saw was a shark's grin of sharp teeth. "Remember The Fallen Angel in Salisbury."

Olivia Nugent, eyes avid, said, "So your little darling has been spying on you and reporting to Charlie." She threw her head back and laughed gaily, with a forced note which grated. "Oh, Francis, how delicious!"

The viscount's face hardened, and he seemed a coiled spring, ready to lash out. "I should have gotten some answers from you, it would seem, the night of the masquerade, Georgina." Then he gave a long look at his host. "You knew more then than you told me, Amesford."

The marquis shrugged. "You were so interested in your cousin's charms that I hated to spoil things for you."

Francis scowled, his eyebrows almost meeting over his aristocratic nose. "Georgina seems to like supping with Charlie. The Fallen Angel, Ye Grape just outside my door—don't I set a good enough table at Hellingham, little cousin?"

He expected no answer, and Georgina gave none.

"You expect me to believe that you never knew

Charlie before that coach ride—yet you supped with him en route—you, a vicar's daughter?"

"It's true! He—he was kind to me. He knew Papa had just died, and—"

"See, Francis. She admits it. She'd known our Charlie before that famous ride across all England," Olivia said, spite thick in her voice. "Remember, the London-Exeter stage runs right through the rustic place where she lived."

"I never saw Charles Collins until the morning I got the coach to come here!"

It was as if she'd not spoken. Her cousin asked his friend, who was cutting off a bite of crumbly Stilton cheese with an ivory-handled knife, "What do you say, Amesford? Did Charlie plant her on me so he'd have a way into Hellingham?"

"He didn't!" Anger counteracted Georgina's fear. "I never knew him until that trip. I was coming here because Papa had died, and you know it."

"I do believe our little dove speaks the truth, Francis."

"All right, so it wasn't planned deliberately. Charlie, with his usual shrewdness—the lower classes have an animal cunning, I've noticed—learned that Georgina was coming here to live during that long ride from her village."

"So he charmed her with that way he has with women," Howard Dubonnet, Marquis of Amesford, interposed, "and she's been spying on you. Is that what you believe, my man?"

"I don't spy!"

"Very innocent, my little cousin. I'm sure that Charlie learned more than you realized you were telling. How often have you seen him, Georgina?" he barked, the change in his manner making her cringe.

"Only that once, at Ye Grape," she insisted.

"Then when did you set up that little drama played out the night of the masked ball? Do you correspond with him? Must I instruct the butler to screen your letters before he puts them in the bag for the mail coach?"

It was hopeless. They wouldn't believe anything Georgina told them. And through all this, Olivia sat there, delicately picking bites from a duck's leg with her white, even teeth.

Surprisingly, it was Amesford who came to Georgina's aid. "I think you are overreacting, Francis," his friend suggested. "Did any real harm come from Charlie's seeing his lordship? From what you tell me, the earl lies there, unknowing. If it afforded Charlie any satisfaction. . . ."

"Sometimes he's aware," the viscount muttered darkly. "That night he spoke. Several times after I got there."

"Does he say anything coherent? Come, come, Francis, if you expect me to help you, I must know what's going on. I can't work in the dark."

Suddenly resentful of the treatment she was getting, Georgina forgot her fear long enough to say, "His lordship said quite clearly that Charles is to be the heir to the title."

The minute the words were out of her mouth, Georgina regretted the rash impulse. There was a moment of terrible silence. Olivia's green eyes were round with shock. Then Lord Amesford laughed, a chilling sound.

"My word, Francis, no wonder you're all in a tizzy! So the old man's decided he'll legitimatize the bastard. You know where that'll leave you."

"It'll never happen. The old man's mad. I'll have the king, himself, send his tame doctor around to certify him, and I'll ship him off to Bedlam."

"If you mean Dr. Ward, the judges may take a dim view of him, even if he does have the king's ear. The man is in bad repute in London, Francis. He's really an impossible fraud. No more doctoring ability than my old nurse with her herbs, and she almost got herself hanged for witchcraft."

"His lordship wants his solicitor," Georgina said, again wishing immediately that she'd kept silent. It must be her nerves going to pieces that caused her to say such things.

"Sir Barnaby? Francis, you're in trouble if Kane gets his teeth into this. Remember when he advised his lordship to cut you off—disown you?"

From the black look on Francis's face, he remembered.

"I've not sent for Kane, nor shall I."

"How much of this does Charlie know? Has our little flower, here," and Amesford reached over and chucked Georgina under the chin playfully, "told him all?"

"Unfortunately she didn't have to tell him anything. He saw father the night of the ball—in one of dear father's lucid intervals."

The young rakehell opened his eyes wide at this, their flat grayness reflecting light from the lake. "Charlie actually heard himself acknowledged?"

"He heard enough to know what that old devil is planning."

Laying a hand on Francis's arm, Olivia said, "But what will you do? You won't be—"

A vicious look from Francis silenced her, and he pulled away from her touch. "Why should you worry, Olivia? If Charlie inherits, you can go back to his bed. Although then he may get highflown ideas, and not think you'd make a suitable countess."

Olivia got his message, and her face flushed with anger, but she did not dare say anything to Francis.

"Why can't father die?" the viscount asked petulantly. "Without the solicitor to hear him, who'll believe Charlie—bastard Charlie Collins, whose mother was a silly serving girl here so many years ago? The whole county knows about Charlie."

"Can your father recover from his illness?"

"He's one foot in the grave."

Amesford looked worried. "Francis, friend, I had a wicked old half uncle who had apoplexy. Lay like a log for months. Thought he'd pop off any moment. Everyone gathered around for the reading of the will. But he foxed 'em all. Recovered. Got so he could walk about, even regained his speech, after a fashion. Can be understood, at least. And he's living on and on and on. What if his lordship recovers? He can acknowledge Charlie, legally. And if he does, you've had it, old man. Cut off, no title, no Hellingham. Once the old man goes, Charlie will kick you out faster than you deposed him."

The viscount's eyes narrowed. He was, truly, Mephisto. No wonder he had chosen that guise the night of that ill-fated ball, Georgina thought.

"If father dies soon, I'm the Fifth Earl of Margate."

The way he said it chilled Georgina, and she shuddered.

"Is the breeze too chill for you?" her host asked with great solicitude. "Breezes can be bad off the water. Put your arm about your sweet coz, Francis, and keep her warm."

Georgina thought that Francis wasn't going to embrace her; but then Olivia gave her a black look, and Francis moved immediately closer to Georgina, cuddling her to him, obviously trying to annoy the other woman.

"And will Georgina be discreet?" Amesford asked.

"Georgina? She's family, Amesford." She could feel the muscles of Francis's arm tense, though. As usual, the marquis had struck a nerve with his probing question. "Georgina lives at Hellingham with me." He grinned wickedly. "Where else would a young gentlewoman go? Alone in the world, no money, no family, except at Hellingham. You're loyal, aren't you, Georgina?" There was a warning in his hard voice. "Charlie took advantage of her the night of the masked ball, but it won't happen again. I can trust my cousin, can't I?"

She couldn't answer, her throat was frozen, her tongue paralyzed; apparently her cousin didn't expect her to say anything. He knew Georgina was trapped. Nor was she a completely unwilling victim. Even as they sat there under the willow tree, his arm about her shoulders, she felt that surge of passion which proximity to him caused in her. Francis and Charles. Both brothers had this same devastating effect on her. One touch, and she melted, yielding herself to whichever one was with her.

Then Francis shattered her pliant mood by adding, a cruel smile on his handsome face, "Because if Georgina made me angry, and I threw her out of Hellingham, she might wind up in one of Moll Bailey's brothels, mightn't she?"

Olivia Nugent, annoyed now that Georgina was getting all of the attention, said, "Vicarage raised, you'd not like that, would you?" her voice treacly, yet there was more than a touch of vinegar underneath, corrosively acid. "Although you're scarcely an innocent virgin, not with dear Francis visiting your bedchamber."

Surprisingly, Francis said, voice icy, "Do not ever speak to my cousin in that manner again, Olivia."

She paled, obvious even with her whitened face. "I was only joking," she said hastily, in real panic. "Georgina knows I was only fooling."

Georgina didn't say a word, numbed by the whole conversation. Why couldn't Charles have planned to meet her again? The idea which was most galling to her now, most emotionally destroying, was that Charles had no interest in her except as Francis suggested—he wanted a listening post at Hellingham, a spy, to keep him posted on his father's health. Charles had walked out without a backward glance when he learned that she was a cousin to Francis. And what future was there with Charles, even if he returned to pay court? A coachman forever on the road. She'd see him once a fortnight, if she were lucky. What kind of life would that be for her?

CHAPTER 23

The picnic at Paladino Manor should have been a happy occasion, but there had been undercurrents all during the visit which haunted Georgina after she went to bed that night. Francis had not come to her bedchamber with her. He had, during the afternoon, taken her off into a wooded glade some distance from the lake where they had dined, and had made love to her there on a mossy bed with the sun coming through the leaves of the beach trees, dappling her skin and his with light and shade.

Now Georgina lay in her high bed, the curtains looped back so that she could see the night sky with its stars studding a field of black velvet. Her thoughts were not with Francis, but with Charles. She was frightened by what had been said—what had been hinted at—during the picnic. Moll Bailey. She remembered Mrs. Fenton's suggesting that Charles might sell girls to old Moll, and Francis made it sound as if he, too, might supply the brothel keeper.

Maybe if she had found the proof Charles had asked of her, the coachey would now see her as a woman in her own right, not just as his spy. She was in the earl's bedchamber for a while most days, sometimes without even the nurse to keep her company. She might have tried to look through his lordship's papers. There might be something, some overlooked clue, which would point the way to success for Charles. It was a slim chance, she knew, for Charles had lived in Hellingham all his life and had never found anything to substantiate his mother's claims that she and Peter Hardy, Lord Margate, were legally married.

Every time Georgina vowed to concentrate on Francis and forget Charles, Francis would do some cruel little thing, such as his veiled threat of Moll yesterday, and Georgina would wish that Charles were viscount instead of Francis. How nearly alike were the two men? Did Charles, too, have a cruel streak in him? She knew him so little, she'd been so overwhelmed by his virility, his good looks, and his personality that she had flung herself at Charles without using any common sense at all.

But her heart still turned to Charles. *Tomorrow,* Georgina promised herself, *tomorrow, when I go up to read to the earl, I'll try do something to help Charles.* Maybe that would clear her conscience, help her choose between the two brothers.

She tossed and turned for hours. The ormolu clock on the chimneypiece struck three before Georgina finally fell into a troubled sleep, for her nerves were tighter than the strings of a well-tuned lute. Then she dreamed—dreadful, frightening dreams. She knew she was dreaming, yet the terror was no less real for it, and she couldn't wake from the series of nightmares. She climbed the spiral staircase in her dream, up, up, and still higher, yet she never reached the earl's suite at the top of the tower. She knew she must get to his bedside or disaster would strike, but she found only more steps to climb, each circling higher. Then she was in a churchyard somewhere—it was Trindale, yet it wasn't. An open grave yawned in the darkness. A light from inside it beckoned and she was forced to walk to it, reluctant feet dragging in the dew-damp grass. At last Georgina was close enough to look down into the open grave, and she screamed with horror at the sight of a grinning corpse with red hair and staring blue eyes. It was Charles Collins. No, it was the Earl of Margate. Or was it an earlier face, one of the portraits in the Long Gallery?

Georgina woke with a start, cold sweat chilling her. With trembling fingers she lit the candle beside her bed, then slipped from the warm covers, pulling on her rose dressing gown. The night had turned chill, and she closed the window and pulled the drapes, shutting out the night. Carrying the candle, shielding the flame with one cupped hand so that it did not dance in the drafts, Georgina peered at the clock. Four-thirty. She'd been asleep little more than an hour, yet she was afraid to lie down again for fear the horrible nightmare would return. She set the candle on the mantel; the wavering flame picked out odd, disturbing shadows in the heavily carved Kent chimneypiece. She sat down on an ottoman, reluctant to go back to bed, chilled by the night air, intensely disturbed by her nightmares.

Was it an omen? Who was the man in the open grave?

A dread filled her, and her spirits were low. She hugged herself, trying to allay the chill which was more than physical. For a moment Georgina was tempted to traverse the long, dark corridors of Hellingham to go to Francis's suite. She could slip into his bed and derive comfort from him. But then she remembered her resolve to do something for Charles. This did not include any furthering of her relationship with Francis. But what to do? Where to start?

Georgina wished that she could command her powers of "finding," but she had never been able to predict any success. Either the vision came, or it didn't. Nothing she ever did changed this.

She would do anything in her power to help Charles, but Georgina knew all too well that her power was limited. Even so, she sat there, relaxed, willing a vision to come to her. Nothing happened. She got more and more chilled. The night air was damp and cold. Finally, weary and very discouraged, she went to bed, snuffing the candle before she crept into the covers. She thought she would not get back to sleep, but surprisingly, sleep came almost immediately.

Again Georgina dreamed. This time the dream was not horrifying, but it still was disturbing. She was in her room at Hellingham, reading her Bible, the one she had brought with her from the vicarage at St. Edmund's. Each verse she read seemed to hint at some great discovery, and soon she was racing through vaguely familiar passages, turning the pages so fast that they became a blur. No matter how much she read, Georgina was not able to find the passage she sought. No matter how avidly she turned the pages, the message eluded her. Then she was floating, floating, going through solid walls. Her levitating body, one arm still clutching the Bible to her, swept in spirals up the winding staircase, faster and faster, until she hovered over the Earl of Margate's bed. For some reason she was able to see through the canopy, although it was as if seeing through a gauzy curtain. The earl was sleeping. A candelabra burned beside him, throwing wavering shadows on the wall and ceiling. Then someone was there, bending over the sleeping figure. A sense of horror filled Georgina. The figure was all darkness, with no discernible detail. It bent over the earl, and there were other shadows which moved in a threatening way. Was that a pillow the figure held over the earl's face? Then the figure moved and Georgina saw that it was Francis, his face twisted with hate. He looked down at his father, smiled a horrible smile, and laid down the pillow. Then he left on ghostly feet.

Some morning sound woke Georgina and she had trouble orienting herself, for the dream in which Francis smothered his father had been so real. She shivered. Had something happened to Peter Hardy, Lord Margate? Had he died while she slept? She picked up her guttering candle and went into the gloomy corridor, for although dawn was pearling the sky, inside it was still dark. Now she felt an awful urgency, a feeling that something tragic was happening. Wavering shadows threatened her as she hurried toward the tower stairs. Her steps became slower and slower as she climbed the spiral to the top. In her dream, she had soared up to the tower suite. What could she tell the nurse? What excuse could she offer for coming in the predawn hours, *en déshabillé,* to the earl's bedchamber? Yet still she climbed until she stood outside the door.

The door was not completely closed, and a single candelabra burned inside, just as it had in the dream. From where Georgina stood, she was unable to see the enormous canopied bed, but a shadow of it wavered on the wall and ceiling. She could see the night nurse dozing in a chair. Softly, so as not to wake the woman, Georgina slipped into the room and eased her way to the bed. The earl lay there, nightcap askew, propped up on his pillows, snoring lightly. Even as she stood there, he stirred, grunted, and went back to his snores.

Feeling foolish, afraid the nurse might wake and find her there, Georgina fled as silently as she had come. There was nothing wrong with the earl; she had let a foolish dream upset her. If she kept up such behavior, someone would begin to whisper that she was mad.

Unable to get back to sleep, Georgina opened the drapes to let in the morning light which increased at every passing moment. With the sun up over the horizon, the vapors of the night disappeared, and she felt cheerful instead of uneasy, happy instead of terrified. Lizzie brought her early tea and helped her dress in a cool morning gown of palest blue India muslin sprigged with delicate pink flowers and soft green leaves and twigs. She tied over it a fashionable white apron of sheer lawn edged with a deep ruffly lace, matched with a fichu to drape the deep décolletage. Lizzie dressed her hair high and left it unpowdered, topping the coiffure with a dainty pinner of lace and silk rosebuds.

When a footman came to tell Georgina that his lordship, the Viscount Quincy, wished her to breakfast with him in his suite, she was ready to join him immediately.

Francis still lolled on his four poster bed, his robe of green satin piped with black braid contrasting nicely with the cloth-of-gold turban he wore over his dark hair. Their chocolate was steaming, the toast crisp.

Without preamble, Francis told her, "We're traveling down to Kent tomorrow. We'll get a very early start. Do you know Kent, Georgina?"

"No, I've never been there."

Kent. That was where Charles's grandparents now lived, in a cottage provided by Francis.

As if reading her mind, Francis said, "I know that Charlie told you all kinds of nonsense about his claim to the title, Georgina. With his imagination, sometimes I think he is wasted as a coachey. He might rival Swift or Fielding as a novelist." She started to deny that Charles had told her anything, but the viscount waved away her words. "I've heard it all for years, Georgina. And I could probably talk to you until you were bored silly, and not convince you that it is just his imagination. So I intend to have someone else convince you that I am the true Viscount Quincy, heir to the Earldom of Margate, master-to-be of Hellingham."

She smiled uncertainly. Surely he didn't intend to take her to see the elder Collinses, parents of Rebecca.

"I want you to meet Charlie's gran," and he said the word just the way one of the villagers in Trindale would have said it. "Charlie's mum was just a serving girl. You know that. Can you imagine for even a moment that my father would have married someone of such low birth to be mother of his children?"

"She was the mother of one of his sons," Georgina reminded Francis with some spirit.

He scowled blackly. "Charlie is not legitimate. Who cares how many bastards there are? You aren't a little innocent, Georgina. You know perfectly well that every country house in England has its satellites of bastards. Charlie isn't the only non-Hardy redhead in this area. Unfortunately, his mother lived here, so Charlie was always underfoot, from the moment of his miserable birth."

What could Georgina say? She now realized that if she were to do anything to help Charles, she must be very circumspect about her activities. Furthermore, it would be wise to keep Francis in a pleasant mood, which was not always easy.

Meanwhile, would she see Charles soon again? He was on the road so much of the time that Georgina despaired of getting more than a glimpse of him as he careened by, driving the stagecoach at a breakneck speed. Since that dreadful night when she last was with Charles, he had apparently not been at Hellingham, although there was no way for her to know if he had been in touch with Olivia Nugent.

She could always send him a letter, leaving it with the innkeeper at Ye Grape; but after Francis's warnings, she was almost afraid to attempt this, even though Lizzie had volunteered to act as mail deliverer. The letter would have to be smuggled out of Hellingham, of this Georgina was positive. Francis might only have been joking about having the butler search the bag of mail to be sent, but Georgina was never sure about her cousin. He just might give the butler such orders, if he thought she were trying to write to Charles. There was no point in these speculations now, though, for she had no news for Charles, and she didn't think, after his sojourn in her wardrobe, that Charles was eagerly awaiting a letter from her. If she were a clever young woman, she would forget Charles Collins, accept that his claims to the inheritance were bogus, and concentrate on this handsome cousin who lolled on his bed, sipping chocolate with her.

"Charles told me that you had given his grandparents a cottage in Kent for their declining years."

Francis raised one black eyebrow. "Did he."

"Yes, and I thought it quite handsome of you."

He grinned wickedly. "Charlie doesn't think anything I do is handsome. He feels that I always have an ulterior motive. What do you think, Georgina?"

She poured more chocolate for herself from the squat silver pot. This gave her time to think of a suitable answer.

"I have no way of knowing what your motives are, Francis. But I insist that it was generous to pension off Charles's grandparents this way."

"You will find them quite content, I think." Francis was very casual in his arrogance. "They have no worries. They are comfortable, with a little garden in which Collins can work. Maybe they'll have some early strawberries for us. Collins raises splendid strawberries."

"Strawberries with clotted cream would be lovely."

"And after our visit, you'll forget Charlie." It was more a threat than a statement. Then he smiled, erasing the threat. "Ah, Georgina, I know how you feel about Charlie. I've seen him turn every woman's head he met since I was born. He has a fatal charm. But you aren't a parlor maid—you aren't even Olivia. You are my distant cousin, with Hardy blood in your veins. You would make a suitable wife for me, Georgina—provided you could get this nonsense about Charlie out of your head. But I warn you—I will not take Charlie's leavings. If you want to please me, if you think you might like to become the mistress of Hellingham, then you must prove to me that you have no interest in Charlie."

Marriage to Francis! It was what she had hoped for. It was more than she had expected. Why wasn't she ecstatic with joy at his words? Why did she still wish —but no, she must forget Charles, even as Francis had warned.

"Don't answer me now, Georgina," Francis went on. "First you must prove to me that it is I you truly love, not that bastard, Collins." His face darkened with rage just thinking about his half brother. "I want you to be sure in your own mind. We'll take the trip to Kent, see his humble origins. After you meet his grandparents, you'll see that Charlie's brain has been addled by his ambitions—ambitions far too high for one of Charlie's low birth. Father should have sent him packing long ago, for Charlie's sake. By keeping him on here, he allowed all of those highflown ideas to grow. It did Charlie no good. Now he feels above himself, unwilling to be a superb coachman—which he is. I would not suggest for one moment, Georgina, that Charlie isn't a good one with horses. He is fortunate to have been given the kind of training he had here at Hellingham. It serves him in good stead now, so that he can earn an honest living on the stages. But father spoiled him for so many years that it turned his head, made him ambitious for the wrong things. When you see the grandparents, Georgina, you'll see that Charlie has come a long way from his humble origins."

She forced herself to smile, forced herself not to reply to her cousin, bit back the words she wanted to shout. Charles came from good stock! He and Francis had the same father. How could Francis keep saying that Charles was of low birth, as if denying his own aristocracy?

Yet she must learn to hold her tongue if she expected Francis to make her his viscountess. She must forget Charles Collins. She must make the trip to Kent, planning to see only what Francis wanted her to see when she met the Collins couple. Charles had indeed turned her head; yet although she often yearned for him, Georgina knew that the time had come for her to forget Charles and make sure that Francis had reasons aplenty to think her a suitable wife.

CHAPTER 24

It didn't rain on the day they traveled to Kent, a good omen in Georgina's eyes. The road was dry, the sun shone warm and soft on them, and the roadside was green and lush with flowers blooming everywhere. Oh, it was good to be young, loved, and alive! She and the viscount traveled in a landaulet with his coat of arms on the varnished door, while Lizzie and his man, Isher, followed with the boxes and bundles in a small chaise which Isher drove himself. Georgina wore a new traveling suit of bright blue velvet, her hair confined under a cunning little matching bonnet with a row of pink silk roses circling the crown. Her gloves were of the softest Spanish kid, and her slippers were also of the fine leather, but dyed to match her velvet basque jacket and full overskirt.

Francis was more subdued in his attire than usual, traveling in a garb more like a pheasant than a peacock; but his coat of cinnamon brown was of the finest twill the Exeter mills could produce, and the buttons were hammered copper, of a design both exotic and eye-catching, having been copied from designs of the red Indians brought over by explorers of the New World in the earlier centuries. His waistcoat, plain for him, was a rich brown velvet with gold lacing, although the copper motif was continued in the buckles of his fawn trousers and also of his highly polished brown calf shoes. His tricorne was a dark brown felt laced with gold.

Georgina knew that she and Francis made a handsome couple. She was determined that he should be proud of her so that he would soon regularize their relationship by taking her for his wife rather than his mistress. If she was to continue with Francis, forget her passion for Charles, she wanted to be more to her cousin than a passing fancy. She dreaded the possibility that he would tire of her as he had obviously tired of Olivia Nugent. Lizzie had whispered, as she dressed Georgina for the trip, that Olivia was highly incensed not to be included in the outing to Kent.

Was Olivia even now sending a message to Charles Collins to let him know that he was welcome in her bed tonight?

I hate her! Georgina thought, stunned at the vehemence of her feelings toward Olivia Nugent. *And I hate Charles Collins, too, with his carefree manner, his blandishments, his seduction of my innocence.* But even as she told herself how she hated the redheaded bastard son of Peter Hardy, Georgina wondered if he would be constant to a woman he loved, or if he, too, would cast her aside as his half brother had rejected the hapless Olivia.

If Charles did find the evidence he so desperately sought, would he make Olivia Nugent his countess when he came into his final inheritance? The thought was so distressing that Georgina fumbled in her pocket for her vinaigrette, feeling suddenly faint.

Before she found the smelling salts though, there was a terrible bump, a lurch, and the carriage listed to one side so suddenly that Georgina was flung from her seat onto Francis, who broke her fall which might otherwise have bruised her badly.

With an oath, Francis disentangled the two of them, then stuck his head out of the window to call to the coachey, "What now, in God's name?"

"Wheel came off on that last bump, milord."

"They are supposed to check things like that before we start," the viscount fumed. "Well," he yelled angrily, "come help us out of this tilted box."

Within moments the footman was wrenching the door open, and with his help from outside, and Francis's assistance in the coach, Georgina managed to get out of the tipped-over coach without ripping her gown. Francis followed on her heels.

"Someone will pay for this," he muttered.

By now the coachey was examining the wheel which had rolled to the side of the road before catching in a haw bush.

"Pin sheared off, milord. The bump in the road did it. Couldn't have been prevented—see, metal's cut clean."

He held the offending pin out in his hand, the cut edge shining in the sunlight, proof of his diligence.

"All right, all right, you couldn't help it," Francis fretted, "but how long will it be to fix it?"

The chaise had now caught up to them, and Isher pulled his horse to a halt to see what was amiss.

"If it's going to be unconscionably long in fixing, Miss Ryerston and I could ride in the chaise, I suppose, and the rest of you could follow in the landaulet when it is repaired."

"Not long to fix, milord," his coachey soothed, laying aside his coat with the multicaped shoulders to work on the wheel. "Here, Fred, give me a hand," he commanded, and the footman joined him to give assistance.

"Do you want to wait in the chaise, Georgina?"

"No, it's such a lovely morning, I think I'd rather stroll along the hedgerow, here, and pick a few flowers." Picking her skirt up carefully, to keep it from being mired by the road, Georgina stepped onto the grassy verge and breathed deeply of the soft air, watching a bumblebee wing his way from flower to flower in the haw blossoms.

Then, faint from far off in the direction of London, she heard the sound of a trumpet playing "Black-eyed Susan," and Georgina's heart jumped into her throat.

Behind her, she heard one of the men saying, "It's the Exeter stage, dead on time." Did the man give his lordship a quick, sharp glance from under his shag of taffy hair? Or was she being oversensitive? Cousin Francis seemed not to notice. He was pacing back and forth, impatient with the length of time it was taking to repair their coach. Lizzie got down from the chaise and joined her mistress. She was wearing a gown of blue stuff for travel, and instead of her usual mobcap, she wore a round cap with lappets tied under her chin, and a flat straw hat over it.

"The stage will be passing soon, miss. I wonder if Charlie'll be up on the box?"

Georgina gave her a quick, tight-lipped look, wondering if Lizzie were being impertinent; but the abigail's face was its usual fresh, scrubbed, pleasant self, with none of the slyness which would be found there if she were baiting her mistress.

"I have no idea," Georgina said shortly. "I don't keep up with the stagecoach schedule, nor with its coacheys."

Lizzie, realizing she'd ruffled Georgina's feathers, dropped her eyes and muttered, "Of course not, miss." Then she went back to the roadside to watch the work on the wheel.

There was the distinctive rattle and jangle as the stage approached, although a slight bend in the dirt road hid it from sight until it was almost upon them. At the very last moment Georgina wished that she had hidden herself from sight in the seat of the chaise, but it was too late now to get into the other coach. There was another long blast of the guard's trumpet —surely no one but Robin Adair played such sweet sounds on the long, brass trumpet—and the coach swept around the bend, out of the concealing beech trees, the four grays galloping hard, their manes flowing in the spring breeze.

Georgina could have ignored the stagecoach. She

could have turned her back on it, or busied herself with picking flowers, she might have bent her head to watch the men replace the wheel, thus hiding her face with her bonnet brim; but she stood as if transfixed, head held high, sun full on her face, watching avidly as the muddy stage rattled by.

It was Adair on the box, trumpet still to his lips. And beside him, his coachey's coat thrown open in the warm spring morning, rode the handsome, dashing Charles Collins, his dark red hair clubbed at his neck, his blue eyes picking her out of the roadside tableau immediately. He didn't stop. He made no gesture of aid to the disabled coach. But Charles did sweep off his black tricorne and bow from the waist, his face sardonic, when he saw Georgina.

She stood as if made of marble, without so much as a wave in his direction. As the coach rolled by in a cloud of dust, Francis came toward her, angrily brushing at his coat. "Trust Charlie to make sure I was covered with dust," he said, disgruntled. "He saw us in plenty of time. He could have slowed the coach to a walk, and I wouldn't be eating half of the county." He made a face and spat. "Fah! It makes my teeth gritty." Then, turning to the chaise, he bawled, "Isher! Where are you? I'm covered with dust, you idiot."

The valet, brush in hand, came at a dead run, babbling about having to get into one of the boxes.

"Yes, yes, well, brush me off! Don't just stand there nattering."

The man brushed vigorously, so that Georgina had to move back a few steps to keep from being enveloped in a new cloud of dust made by the overzealous valet.

"All right, all right, that's enough, man!" Francis snapped. "Isn't that wheel on yet?" he called.

"In a moment, milord. Just making sure the pin is well set. Don't want to lose the wheel again."

"If you do, you'll be looking for another position," he threatened. "Come, Georgina, if the coach is level again, we might as well get in. Less chance of being covered with dust by another passing coach. I think Charlie did that deliberately."

She didn't answer. Georgina wanted to defend Charles. The way their disabled coach was situated, there was no way Charles could have seen it in time to rein in his team, and Francis knew this as well as she. He only wanted a chance to put the blame on his hated half brother.

Instead she smiled her prettiest at Cousin Francis, hoping to distract him from his anger at Charles. "Yes, let's get in and be ready to drive on the minute they've finished working on the wheel," she agreed. "I'm dying to see London, Francis, even the bit we'll pass through getting to Kent. Bath and Exeter are the largest places I've ever seen."

His smile was soft, all anger gone. "Ah, little country mouse, someday I'll show you the sights of the city. You will never want to leave."

"But Hellingham is so grand!"

"True. But it is a different world, Georgina. There is a grandeur in all of the great country houses, so after Hellingham, you'd find accommodations in London crowded, even at the finest addresses."

"But there's all the excitement, so much going on, the theaters and opera, the bear baiting at Hockley-in-the-Hole, the coffee houses and the gambling hells."

"You must have been reading all the gossip in *The Gazette,*" the viscount said, amused at her excitement.

"No, Olivia was telling me about it one day, bragging that you'd taken her to London many times during the Season."

"Well, today I'll whisk you through the city and on to Kent. Olivia was so furious that she wasn't invited on this trip that she was saying malicious things about you."

Georgina didn't know what to say, so she wisely kept silent, just smiling at Francis. She knew why

Olivia was being malicious—she'd lost her place at Hellingham. Francis no longer was interested in her. *Will he do that with me, someday?* she wondered. That would mean the end of life with Francis, and no prospects of a lovely time as the mistress of Hellingham.

Fortunately Francis wasn't looking at her just then, so he didn't see the cloud on her usually sunny face.

"I do believe they've finally gotten the wheel repaired." He stuck his head out of the window.

The coachman and the footman climbed back up on the box, Georgina heard the grate as the brake was released, and then the singing sound as the coachey's long whip cracked over the backs of the four horses. There was the creaking as they settled into their harnesses, pulling forward to start the coach moving. The landaulet lurched once, twice, and then they were moving again, bumping along on the dusty, rutted road toward London.

Soon Georgina, peering eagerly ahead through the window, saw a black pall in the sky.

"Oh, it's going to rain!" she cried.

"The sun is shining brightly, Georgina. How can you be predicting rain?" he cousin asked, amused.

"I see a dark cloud in the sky ahead."

Francis peered out of the coach window, then laughed. "Ah, Georgina, that is the Big Smoke. London. The smoke from the many chimneys mixed with the fog that lies over the city has given it this picturesque name."

She looked again and realized that it was not rain clouds she was seeing. *The Big Smoke.* She almost tasted the words on her tongue. "What an apt name for the city."

Now they were on the approaches to the great London, with houses crowding in close to the road, and chimney pots as far as the eye could see. The roof tops blurred in the distance, and the road was crowded with vehicles of all sizes and shapes, from ornate private carriages to the great, lumbering waggons with wooden wheels two feet wide. They began to see numbers of sedan chairs, even though they were still in the outskirts of the city.

"So much traffic!" she cried, astounded. "How will we ever get through the streets?"

"It won't be easy. Our coachey is quite skilled; but even then, the streets are so full of carriages and waggons, chairs and linkboys, and pedestrians, that it takes hours to go only a short distance in London."

Georgina felt like a youngster at her first fair, gawking at the sights, marveling at the crowding of houses, although they were entering at the West End, the newer part of London, where streets were wider, and houses were far apart, with lovely parks surrounding some of them.

"We could have crossed the Thames at Kingston, but then you'd have missed seeing even this little bit of London," Francis told her. "We can go back that way, missing the city altogether. Today we'll cross on the Horse Ferry, and you'll see the Lambeth Palace at the other side."

Being a vicar's daughter, Georgina knew that this was the residence of the Archbishop of Canterbury.

"Once we're south of the Thames, we'll stop at an inn for a break from our journey. We'll have to wait for the chaise to come across on the ferry after us, so there'll be time for tea and something to eat."

It was a far cry from the crowded, rushed trip that Georgina had taken on the stagecoach. She caught herself just in time, and didn't mention that trip. No point in bringing up the subject, for it was sure to make Francis surly.

They were now riding through Millbank, a new and exclusive section of the city, full of elegant townhouses. The coachey turned them onto Horseferry Road, and they clattered down onto the Middlesex landing stage of the Horse Ferry. They were in luck, as the ferry was at their side of the Thames, and there was no coach waiting to cross. With the help of the footman, they dismounted from the landaulet, allowing the coachey to make the tricky maneuver of driving the skittish team of four and the coach onto the ferryboat. Then Francis escorted Georgina on board. She decided, as it was such a lovely day, to stand on the ferry, rather than sit in their carriage while the polemen propelled the flat ferry boat across the wide river. There was much traffic on the water, little water taxies being rowed or poled from one side to the other, while larger boats created almost as much traffic as there had been on the London streets. Looking back, she could see the Parliament Houses, as well as the towering gray abbey further down the river.

"From the opposite bank, you get a splendid panoramic view of London," Francis told her. "That's why I had the coachey route us this way. If it's not too smoky, you'll even be able to see the huge dome of St. Paul's. We could have driven right on through London, and crossed London Bridge further down the Thames, but with the streets so crowded these days, it would take us forever."

"You'd think they would build another bridge across the Thames somewhere along here. I can see that there is now a line of coaches waiting behind the chaise Isher and Lizzie are in, wanting to cross the Thames."

"Politics, my dear, politics. All of the revenue from this ferry goes to the Archbishop of Canterbury. He's not anxious to give that up, so he exerts much pressure to keep the ferry. And the Thames boatmen, the ones who ply the river with their water taxies, don't want a bridge, for they see it as an end to their livelihood. Who would bother to be rowed across the river if he could cross on a convenient bridge?"

"So there won't ever be another bridge in London?"

"Never's a long time, Georgina. With the way the

city is growing, with the surge of building in the West End, the time will come, probably within the next decade, when the need for a bridge will supercede all of the objections."

They now had reached the Surrey landing stage, and there was a good view of Lambeth Palace, as well as the sweep of London from Westminster to the Tower. Before they got back into their carriage, Georgina stood with Francis on the landing stage as he pointed out buildings of interest across the Thames.

They drove on then a short distance, stopping at a half-timbered inn with a thatched roof, The Pig and Acorn, to wait until their servants arrived in the chaise.

CHAPTER 25

Leaves Green was a tiny village southeast of Croyden. There were a handful of gray stone cottages with reed thatched roofs, a squat Norman church with its graveyard framed in ancient yews, and a triangular patch of village green. Oak trees towered over the entire village, shading it from the summer sun.

The Collins cottage was at the edge of the village, a small cottage like all the rest, set back from the road, with a low stone wall in front of it. Francis sent the coachey and footman on to the local tavern to wait for them. He escorted Georgina in through the wooden gate and up the worn path to the front door of the stone house. Knocking loudly, he stood there, arrogant in his assurance, while Georgina had mixed feelings about the proposed visit.

The viscount was raising his hand to pound on the plain oak door again, when it opened. An elderly woman stood there, peering out nearsightedly, her eyes squinted against the sunlight. She had gray hair, dressed very simply, and covered with a snowy mobcap with a full ruffle. Her dress was of simple dark green cotton, the plain skirt covered with a full white apron trimmed with a bit of embroidery at the hem. A white lawn fichu and white lawn frills at the elbow were all the ornamentation she wore.

Plainly astounded to see the Viscount Quincy at her door, Mrs. Collins dropped a low curtsy, exclaiming, "Milord! Will you come inside?" She was clearly flustered, and rushed about the dark little room, pulling up two plain wood chairs for her guests, and putting a black iron kettle on the fire. "I'll brew some tea, if you would like, milord."

"That would be very kind of you, Mrs. Collins. And if you have any of those delicious strawberries which Abner raises so skillfully. . . ."

"Oh! Abner! Yes, milord, just a minute, your lordship. My man is in the back garden just now, picking berries, no doubt." She rushed out a back door, closing it carefully behind her.

"Oh, Francis, we've upset her, coming in unexpectedly."

He gave a careless shrug. "How could a visit from her benefactor upset her, Georgina? You do have the strangest ideas, sometimes." He smiled indulgently. "I'm sure she feels it a great honor to entertain us."

Georgina looked about the tiny room, with its plain oak table, scrubbed almost white, the oak chairs, and the low, rough bench against one wall. There was an old-fashioned walnut dresser against one wall, with two inexpensive china plates stood on edge in the plate rack, and a few cups hanging from under the shelf.

"It's—so small," she murmured, remembering the spaciousness and luxury at Hellingham. "After living all their lives in a big country estate, how do they like this?"

The minute she'd said the words, she regretted them. Francis scowled, a look she was learning to fear.

"And what's wrong with this cottage, may I ask? It has two rooms, Georgina. Do you see their bed in here? Of course not. They have a separate bedroom. And a wood floor. Most of the houses here in Leaves Green have beaten earth for a floor—or, if the people are lucky, pebble. This cottage is floored with oak. Neither of the old people will ever have to complain about rheumatism. And I allowed them to load a waggon with household furnishings. Everything you see here came from Hellingham. This—a pension—

they are very lucky. Many old servitors who have less charitable masters than I wind up in the workhouses or the poorhouses. The Collinses realize how lucky they are."

Just then Mrs. Collins hurried back inside, dropping another curtsy to Francis and his lady. Behind her was an old man, grizzled hair clubbed back with a bit of string, clad in the usual linen smock of a farmer, still wearing muddy boots over his britches of dark blue. He snatched off the flat round hat he wore and bowed.

"Milord," he muttered.

Mrs. Collins was carrying a small wicker basket piled high with luscious red strawberries which made Georgina's mouth water just to see them.

During the next fifteen minutes, while Mrs. Collins bustled about making tea for the company and capping the berries so they could eat them, Georgina got the feeling that she was not so much grateful to Francis for this home, but fearful of him, working very hard to keep him happy, as if afraid of his wrath.

Collins, himself, was wary. That was the only word Georgina could think of. He kept eyeing his lordship as if expecting some unpleasant surprise.

Francis was pleasant and expansive, chatting away with them as if they were dear friends, not old servants.

"And how is Charlie?" he asked, all solicitude.

Georgina could see Mrs. Collins stiffen. "He's well, milord. We see little of the lad. He drives the stage, you know."

"London to Exeter, Exeter to London. Back and forth," Abner Collins muttered. Was he resentful? Georgina could not be sure.

"Yes, excellent work for him. He always was good with horses. My father, his lordship, the earl, did see to it that Charlie learned to handle a team."

"Yes, milord. The earl—he was always good to Charlie."

"Miss Ryerston knows Charlie," he said, and Georgina knew that sly manner all too well. "She rode as a passenger in his stagecoach all the way from Exeter to Hellingham."

Charles's grandmother gave Georgina a quick look, then looked away as quickly, her face blank and inscrutable. It was that look Georgina had learned to recognize early in life in the vicarage—that closed look the country folk used when they didn't want to give away their thoughts.

"Miss Ryerston is my cousin, distantly removed," Francis went on in a chatty manner so unlike him with servants. "She was on that long trip with Charlie, sitting up beside him in the box, as there was no room inside the coach for her. Wasn't that so, Georgina?"

Georgina nodded, not trusting her voice.

"So Charlie talked a lot to her in those long, tiring days as they traveled over the terrible roads between Exeter and Staines."

"Roads be summat bad, milord," Abner Collins muttered.

Georgina sensed that the old couple were quite at a loss to explain this sudden, unexpected visit from their erstwhile benefactor, and were very wary of his motives.

"Do you know that Charlie is still telling that old tale about how your daughter, Rebecca, was legally married to the Earl of Margate. Silly of him, isn't it?"

Georgina saw the moment of distress that showed on Mrs. Collins's face before it closed. "If you say so, milord."

"I do indeed say so," and Francis's voice was sharp. "I wish you'd tell Miss Ryerston about this nonsense Charlie was spouting to her. You know that your daughter wasn't married to the Earl of Margate."

Georgina felt like crying. She could see the look on Hattie Collins's face, knew what the woman was feeling. When the older woman spoke, though, it was with suitable deference to the viscount.

"My daughter, God rest her, was a foolish young girl. The earl turned her head with his attentions. I tried to tell her, but she wouldn't listen. 'He loves me, Mum,' she'd say when I tried to warn her."

"And this so-called marriage," Francis prompted.

Mrs. Collins seemed to shrink into herself, but she answered, as if afraid to deny the viscount anything he asked. Even, Georgina realized, as Rebecca Collins hadn't dared deny Peter Hardy, the Fourth Earl of Margate, when he wanted her in his bed.

"Rebecca told me they was married," she said quietly. "Showed me a paper that was supposed to be the marriage lines. I didn't believe it then, milord. An earl doesn't marry a housemaid. You know that. But my Rebecca was so sure she was married to him."

Georgina thought she saw the glint of tears in the woman's eyes, but Mrs. Collins turned away to see to the kettle which hung on a crane over the fire.

"You see, Georgina, even Charlie's own grandmother knows this tale is nonsense." The tone he used was one you would employ when speaking to a child, or a half-wit, and Georgina resented it, but, like Mrs. Collins, she worked to keep that resentment from showing on her face. Then, as she realized what she was doing, Georgina had an insight into the responses made by the elderly woman. She was living on a pension provided by Francis. The cottage was part of his largesse. No matter what she thought, no matter what the truth of the matter concerning her daughter, Rebecca and the Fourth Earl of Margate, Hattie Collins would hold her tongue lest she and her husband lose what they had here.

So Georgina smiled at Francis, careful not to say what was in her heart, pretending she believed that the matter had been satisfactorily settled, that she no longer thought Charles Collins had any claim on Hellingham or the earldom.

"How is the garden growing, Abner?" Francis asked, as if he were vitally interested in the few strawberries and peas that the old man raised in the bit of land behind his tiny thatch-roofed stone cottage.

"Very good, milord. Berries are comin' nicely. And I have in some turnips and peas. And a patch of potatoes." Then, almost shyly, "If your lordship wishes, I could show you the plantings I have out back."

"Very well. It isn't time to pick up our coach yet. The horses need a good rest before we start back. Are you coming along, too, Georgina?"

A quick look passed between Mrs. Collins and the young woman.

"No, thank you, Francis. I am so comfortable, sitting here after bouncing along on the rough roads—and if I could prevail upon the good Mrs. Collins for another cup of this invigorating tea. . . ."

"Oh, indeed, miss, there's plenty tea in the pot."

Francis and Abner Collins went out the back while the older woman poured more amber brew into the cup for Georgina.

First the woman hurried to the back door, peering out to make sure the men were out of earshot. Then she came back and said, in scarcely more than a whisper, "Charlie was here day before yesterday, miss. He told me about you."

Georgina's heart gave a lurch. "What did he say?"

"Told me all about the lovely young woman who sat alongside him on that trip from near Exeter. Told me you were to help him find his inheritance." She looked cautiously toward the back door, then leaned forward until her mouth was at Georgina's ear. "My poor dear dead daughter always swore on the Bible, miss, that she was truly married to the earl. Thank God she died before he married the other one." Then she added sadly, "Me grandson is much taken with you, miss. Said he thought you loved him truly—but that now you've taken up with his lordship, Viscount Quincy." She laid a gnarled hand on Georgina's, clutching with a clasp so strong that the younger woman winced. "Charlie's a good man, miss. He's had troubles you can't imagine, being raised the way he was. With his expectations. And then to be thrown out of the only home he's ever known by his own brother." She sighed. "He's the true viscount, miss. I feel it in my bones." She moved away from Georgina, going to the walnut dresser. "He told me to give you this, if ever you was to come here, miss. Charlie seemed to know that his lordship would bring you along, to convince you that he was the true heir to Hellingham, not me Charlie." She opened a drawer, reached inside, and drew out a small package wrapped in linen. Carrying it carefully, she handed it to Georgina.

Suddenly fearful, Georgina tried to draw back and not accept it, but Hattie Collins caught her hand and thrust the small packet into it. "Open it," she commanded. "It is all I have left of my daughter, but Charlie insists that you must have it."

With reluctant fingers, Georgina carefully undid the bit of white linen, until there lay in her hand a small, inexpensive locket of silver. It was burnished with much handling.

Again the old woman commanded, "Open it. Open the locket."

The catch yielded to Georgina's delicate touch, and the locket sprang open. Inside, coiled into a tiny curl, was a lock of light brown hair.

At the question in Georgina's eyes, Mrs. Collins nodded sadly. "It's a curl I cut from Rebecca's own head. It's all that is left of my darling daughter—with the exception of my grandson, Charlie."

With one finger, Georgina stroked the soft hair. As

she touched it, once again she experienced that un-
earthly sensation she'd had before. She left her body.
She floated under the thatch of the cottage, and below
her she could see herself still sitting slumped in the
chair, while the old woman caught at her shoulders,
holding her so that she did not fall onto the oak floor.
Then Georgina was no longer in the cottage. She was
in a chapel. It was night, for tapers lighted the room
only a little, leaving the corners in shadow, touching
the gothic windows lightly. Someone was there—a trio
of people. There was a young woman. She recognized
Rebecca Collins from Charlie's miniature. And Charles
was there. No, not Charles. It was the Earl of Margate,
young and vigorous, his resemblance to Collins remarkable. The other person stood so that Georgina
could not see his face, but he wore the robes of a
cleric, and there was something familiar in his stance.
It was as if she should know him, although Georgina
couldn't place this young priest.

There was a wedding ceremony, and the young Peter
Hardy put a ring on Rebecca's finger. Then the cleric,
his face still obscured, wrote on something and handed
a paper to the earl, who laughed and gave it to Rebecca.

The scene faded, and once again Georgina was in
the little Collins cottage in Leaves Green, looking down
on herself, watching a frantic Hattie Collins fan her
with her apron, then run to the back door and call to
someone outside, all in dumb show, in complete silence.

Again there was a swift change of scene, so rapid
that Georgina felt disoriented, as well as disembodied.
The man who had performed the marriage ceremony
she had witnessed was sitting at a table, a quill in his
hand, writing in an open book. It seemed urgent that
she see who the man was and what he wrote, and
Georgina tried to float forward so that she could see the
cleric's face and read the page on which he penned his
message; but he became smaller and smaller, as if

viewed through the wrong end of a spyglass, and even as she reached out a hand to detain him, the whole scene, room, table, inkwell, book and writer, disappeared entirely. She was back in the cottage, and then everything went black.

"Miss Ryerston! Miss Ryerston!" Someone was patting her cheek, the taps so sharp that they stung her skin. Georgina groaned, moved her head to escape the pain, and then opened her eyes. A face hovered so close to hers that she closed her eyes momentarily, against the blurred features. Again the voice, familiar, calling, "Miss Ryerston!" and immediately after, Francis, saying, "Georgina! Are you all right?"

This time when she opened her eyes the scene was in focus. Hattie Collins, her face worried, hovered over Georgina, while Francis was in the background, his face a mixture of concern and annoyance.

"Are you all right?" he demanded again.

"I'm fine," she said breathlessly, hoping to forestall any embarrassing questions from Francis. Her fingers closed protectively over the silver locket with the bit of brown hair in it. If Francis didn't see it, he wouldn't ask questions which she preferred not to answer. "I guess it was the excitement of the trip."

"And no doubt Lizzie laced you too tightly again." His voice was dry, and Georgina sneaked a look at him to see if he was angry with her.

"She just sort of fainted," Mrs. Collins was saying. "Maybe a cup of tea? Or a bit of wine? I think we have a sip in a bottle."

"No, thank you, I'm fine," Georgina insisted. All she wanted to do now was to get away from this cottage with its reminders of Charles Collins, and the strange effect it had on her.

"Do you feel like going on to Croyden?" Francis asked, as if divining her wish to be gone from Leaves Green.

"Whenever you wish," she said, unable to keep the eagerness from her voice.

"Then if Abner would go to the local tavern and get my carriage. . . ." He looked at Mrs. Collins, who jumped up like a grasshopper.

"I'll tell him, milord. He'll hurry right over to the inn, milord, and get your coach."

Surreptitiously Georgina slid the locket into her pocket. Charles had meant for her to have this memento of his mother, so she would keep it. As Charles had just been here, he still loved her—he must, or he would not have asked his grandmother to give up such a precious remembrance of her daughter.

There was a flurry of leave-taking, and then the clatter of the coach in the road. Georgina was almost discourteous in her hurry to get away from the Collins cottage and back into the Hellingham landaulet.

"And now that you've met the grandparents of Charlie, do you still think he's the rightful heir to the earldom?" Francis asked, following close behind her.

What could Georgina say? Obviously his grandmother still thought Charles was the true, legal son of the earl, but she had offered Georgina no proof whatsoever that this was true—only her faith in her grandson. Georgina was still so upset by the strange visions she'd had that she did not even want to discuss Charles. She sensed that her love for him was somehow at the bottom of these upsetting occurrences.

"Mrs. Collins told me nothing new," was all she was willing to say to her Cousin Francis.

He smiled, smug in his knowledge that Georgina must now believe that he was the one, only, and true heir to the title.

"There's nothing new to tell you, Georgina. I am heir to father's title when he dies, and Charlie is not. It is as simple as that."

Her mind told her that what Francis said was true,

but her heart was very recalcitrant. As the coach jounced along over the rutted roads, Georgina's mind kept returning to the hallucinations she'd had while she sat holding the lock of hair from Charles's mother. What did they mean? Was it only her own idle fancy, brought on by knowledge that Charles had given her about the supposed marriage between his mother and the Earl of Margate, that produced the visions? Thoughts of madness entered her mind once again.

Georgina resolved not to tell Francis what had happened. If he chose to think she'd fainted again, then well and good.

"Georgina, I must ask you again. You aren't expecting a child, are you?"

"No!"

He frowned. "Then you must see a doctor once we're back at Hellingham. These fainting spells of yours worry me. Perhaps you need bleeding—I know, I know, you hate the leeches. Well, we all do. But sometimes they are necessary. Perhaps the doctor will only dose you with some exilir or some special pills. I don't want my dear cousin to be constantly ill."

Forcing gaiety into her voice, Georgina assured him, "I'm really quite healthy, Francis. I don't know what got into me there in the cottage. Perhaps it was because it was such a mean, drab little place, after the luxury of Hellingham. It depressed me. That's all." Then, meaning to turn his thoughts elsewhere, she quickly changed the subject. "I wonder what Olivia is doing today? She was so annoyed that you didn't include her in this outing."

"Did you want her to come along, Georgina?"

"No. I'm sorry, but she's been so hateful to me of late, Francis. She still gossips to the servants about me. Her French abigail, Marie, loves to tell Lizzie all the nasty things that Olivia says about me. She kept that witchcraft gossip alive until you stopped her and the others. Is it any wonder I don't like her?"

Francis put his arm about her shoulders and drew her close to him. "But I agree with Olivia on one thing, my dear. You are a witch. You have completely bewitched me." He kissed her with passion, and Georgina felt all of her resolves disappear. When Francis kissed her this way, all she could think of was going to bed with him. "But it was most unkind of Olivia to say such things about you," he agreed. "Would you be happier if she were somewhere other than Hellingham?"

It opened pleasant new vistas for Georgina. "It would be so much nicer if she weren't there all the time, saying horrid things about me behind my back."

"Then don't worry your little head, dear Georgina. I'm as tired of her carping as you are. I think it time that Olivia moved on. Perhaps Charlie will set her up in some grubby little room where he can see her whenever his stagecoach is in the vicinity. He'll tire of her, of course. Olivia can be very boring after a while. Then Charlie can make a bit of extra money selling her to Moll Bailey."

"Francis!"

"It's done every day, Georgina."

This was not the solution she wanted to the problem of Olivia Nugent; but with Francis's arm around her, and his hand cupping her breast while his hot, eager lips were on hers, Georgina could think only of the immediate future, which included Francis, not Charles. As his caresses grew more intimate, she begged him, "Please, Francis, don't kiss me that way."

His lips were even more demanding. "I thought you liked the way I kissed you, Georgina," he murmured.

"I do, oh, I do," she moaned, "but not here, Francis. Not in the carriage."

For answer he reached up and rapped sharply on the roof of the landaulet. When the footman leaned down to see what his master wanted, Francis, pulling Georgina into an even closer embrace, ordered, "Tell coachey to whip up the horses. I want to get to The Owl in Croyden as fast as possible."

CHAPTER 26

Olivia Nugent couldn't wait to tell Georgina her news when they got back from Kent.

"You should have stayed here at Hellingham," Olivia bragged. "You missed an important visitor."

They were in the morning room, both ostensibly working on embroidery. Olivia had followed Georgina there, and Georgina realized that Marie must have been spying for her mistress, keeping track of where Georgina went after breakfast, for she'd scarcely settled herself in the pleasant, light room to do her needlework when Olivia came sweeping in, still wearing her negligée of mauve weighted silk trimmed with ermine tails.

Georgina felt like a baby hare confronted by a snake. She didn't want to ask Olivia any questions; she knew all too well who the visitor had to be, but there was an hypnotic air about the older woman which dragged the question from her lips.

"Charlie was here, of course. He asked about you, Georgina. I told him that you were so occupied with Francis, keeping his bed warm, that you had little time for me."

Georgina could have wept, but she wasn't going to give Olivia that satisfaction. Instead she struck back. "I'm sure he came to see me, and only bothered with you when he learned that I wasn't at Hellingham."

The minute the words were out of her mouth, Georgina knew she'd said the wrong thing, for the look on Olivia's face was pure triumph.

"Oh, he knew you were off with Francis," she said smugly. "He passed you in the stagecoach."

"Then how did he have time to stop here?" Georgina spat at her nemesis. "He's very conscientious about his work."

Olivia shrugged. "One horse went lame, and they didn't have a suitable replacement at Ye Grape. It took some time to get another horse in from a farm. So he came to see me."

"Francis might not be too happy to learn you'd entertained Charles while he was away."

Olivia only laughed at this. "Poor little Georgina. Can't make up your mind which of the brothers will inherit, can you? What a pity if you choose the wrong one."

With this parting jibe, Olivia picked up her needlework and swept imperiously out of the morning room, as if to show Georgina that she was already the lady of the house.

It was galling. Georgina longed to see Charles, even though she was practically betrothed to Francis. It was stupid of her, she knew. Her prospects were infinitely better with Francis. Surely she would come to love him in time.

Later, though, while Lizzie combed and powdered her hair, Georgina said, in what she hoped was a light, casual tone, "It seems we missed a visit by Charles Collins while we were away, Lizzie. I'm sure that Marie has told you about it."

"No, miss, she didn't say a word. It's strange, too. Usually she brags about such things. Where did you hear about this visit?"

"From Miss Nugent."

"Well, miss, I'd not bother my head about what she says. I think she's just trying to make you jealous. She's that annoyed that she didn't get to go to Kent."

So perhaps it had all been a lie, as Lizzie suggested, used only to pique her.

In the next week, though, the situation changed so drastically at Hellingham that Georgina was beside herself. Suddenly Francis stopped coming to her room, nor did he send his footman for her at night, as he sometimes had done in the past. He began paying all kinds of attention to Olivia and she made it her business to let Georgina know each and every time that he spent in her bed.

"You were just a passing fancy," Olivia whispered to her as they left the dining hall after a sumptuous repast at which the Marquis of Amesford had joined them. "You are much too innocent for Francis, even though he's been bedding you all this time. He prefers a sophisticated, more mature woman of the world."

What could Georgina say? She was desolated, for now she had lost not only Charles, but his replacement. Even Amesford seemed to know what was going on.

"My dear Georgina," he murmured as they repaired to the Red Salon for a game of whist, "I'd be most happy if you smiled on me as you've been smiling on Francis. I think he's made a poor choice." He slid his arm about Georgina's waist in a more intimate embrace than she cared for. The young marquis was not to her liking, but she was so annoyed with Francis, who had spent the evening flirting with his late paramour, that she allowed Amesford the liberty without her usual protest.

The whist game was a disaster. Georgina was so incensed with her cousin that she lost all track of which cards had been played, forgot which suit was trumps, and played her hands abominably.

Amesford, her partner, only grinned slyly and said, "It's a good thing we aren't playing for the stakes we play for at White's, eh, Francis?"

The viscount laughed and told him, "Your partner doesn't seem interested in the game, Amesford. Perhaps she prefers other amusements."

Georgina was infuriated, but not to the extent that she was willing to spend the night with Amesford, as he later suggested. She went to a lonely bed and cried herself to sleep. What had happened to Francis? He'd been so loving on the trip to Kent. Their night in Croyden had been one of blazing passion, with Francis as ardent as any woman could desire. He'd talked of marriage. Then this!

The next day was even more miserable for Georgina. Olivia spent every moment they were together —and she went out of her way to be with Georgina— hinting that something special was going on. "London is so nice at this time of year," she murmured. "But you saw nothing of the greatest city in the land when you went to Kent. To see Charlie's old gran! In her grand house! I expect to be seeing a much grander house than that soon, and in London. If you wish, I might even invite you there for a morning soiree."

"I'll be too busy here at Hellingham with Francis," Georgina snapped, not at all sure that she was telling the truth.

That night as Lizzie disrobed her, the abigail said, "Marie's telling that she and her mistress are going to London. She as good as said that someone is setting up Miss Nugent in a lovely house in the fashionable West End."

"How nice! Then I won't have to listen to her at meal time, will I?" Georgina said, fighting back tears.

"No one knows which man it is, miss. The attention his lordship's been paying her, some of the maids think it is he. But others think it will be Charlie. Isher says his lordship sent an urgent letter to Charlie. And he thinks there was money in it. But he's not sure."

Next morning, however, things looked much brighter. While Georgina was breakfasting *en déshabillé,* Francis came to her room. He was already dressed in a coat of pale green which was most becoming to his dark good looks. His hair was unpowdered, the dark locks pulled back and tied with a ribbon which matched his coat, while his waistcoat, embroidered in gold thread, was of a dark forest green.

"Ah, lazy slug-a-bed," he chided, smiling fondly at Georgina, "not dressed yet for the village fair?"

"I didn't even know there was a fair." She tried to be distant with her cousin, to punish him for neglecting her so outrageously of late, but Georgina was so happy that he had come back to her, she smiled in spite of herself.

"There is a fair, and we are going in my gig. Just the two of us. We'll spend the whole day there, mingling with the common folk. We'll watch the puppet show, and see the strolling players. We'll play the games, and drink the ale. Come, it is a lovely day. We must be off! Call Lizzie and have her dress you in that new yellow India muslin—and wear a straw hat to keep the sun off your lovely white skin." He dropped a kiss on her cheek which set her tingling.

The day was a resounding success. The fair was on the village green, with booths of saplings and thatch set up all around, and peddlers selling their wares everywhere. Georgina watched jugglers in motley keep colored bottles flashing in the air; she joined in the folk dancing with Francis, and she tossed braided straw loops over pegs, winning a crown of flowers which she wore with delight.

"There's a gypsy fortune teller," Francis said, gesturing with a mug of beer. "Have your fortune told, Georgina."

He handed some coppers to the bold-eyed, hawk-beaked woman in her colorful gypsy rags. Georgina, suddenly reluctant, sat on a three-legged milking stool in front of the fortune teller, who reached out and caught Georgina's soft, white hand in her coarse, brown one.

Immediately the woman's face was transformed from the sly, cunning look characteristic of her trade to something frightening. Her whole body stiffened, her eyes rolled up in her head until only the whites showed, and she moaned in such loud tones that Georgina tried to snatch her hand away, but the gypsy clutched the white fingers so tightly that Georgina couldn't escape.

"You have the gift!" The words came in gutteral tones, chilling Georgina's blood. "It can be a curse!" Then the gypsy shook as if she had ague, her chains of brass coins rattling. "Beware!" Her voice went up an octave. "Beware the coach!" Then the woman slumped back, her grip loosening.

In terror, Georgina sprang up, crying, "Let's get away from her, Francis. She frightens me."

Even the usually insouciant viscount was glad to be quit of the gypsy. "I'm sure she puts on such a show for everyone," he hastened to reassure Georgina, but there was a note of uncertainty in his voice which was most uncommon.

"How did she know about my gift?"

"No doubt your fame is known. All of the servants at Hellingham know about it, as do Amesford's. You should know that kind of story spreads more quickly than the plague."

All too well Georgina knew. She tried to regain the innocent gaiety of the earlier hours of the fair, but the horrifying predictions of the gypsy had spoiled the day. Soon she and Francis drove back to Hellingham in the gig.

A footman was waiting with a note for the viscount which he opened immediately, glancing at it and smiling.

"You have one less worry now, my dear," he said to Georgina, crushing the note in one hand. "Olivia has gone to London. I gather that Charlie's charms outshine my own." Then he grinned. "Although I must admit that I did help matters on a bit, by sending Charlie some money and suggesting that Olivia might like a change of scenery."

The pang she felt, the desolation, stunned Georgina. "She's gone to Ch—Charles Collins?"

"So it would seem. But he'll tire of her, as he did before." He sighed. "I really should feel sorry for Olivia, but she is such a gullible little fool. Mark my words, she'll wind up in one of Moll Bailey's brothels yet. Once Charles tires of her—" He left the terrible fate unsaid.

It should have been pleasanter at Hellingham with Olivia Nugent gone, but it wasn't. The very fact of her absence reminded Georgina that the other woman now was enjoying Charles's attention, and it nearly broke her heart. Although she still enjoyed Francis's favors, and knew she should be grateful that he still was interested in her, she longed to see Charles one last time, to rid herself of the hold he had on her emotions. She never seemed to be alone in the tower suite so that she could safely search the earl's desk for some proof of Charles's claim to the inheritance. Maybe, if she did find this elusive proof, she would free herself of the sense of obligation she felt to the coachey.

Sometimes Georgina hated herself, felt she was truly a whore, selling herself to Francis in the hope of a brilliant marriage. Georgina would vow never again to allow her weak flesh to betray her; but Francis would come to her room, his lips eager and hot on her own, his hands compelling a passion she could not deny, and again Georgina would succumb to his virility.

Then, several weeks after the village fair, Amesford came to dine with them. It was during the main course which that day consisted of a saddle of lamb, a lovely rare joint of sirloin, and a tasty game pie which the cook embellished with roast potatoes, early peas, and turnips cooked with onions from the kitchen garden, that Amesford casually remarked, "By the by, I saw the lovely Olivia last week in London."

There was a moment of waiting silence, then Francis said, "I trust she is well." A look which Georgina could not interpret passed between the two men.

Amesford gave that sly little laugh, cut a healthy bite of beef, and said, before he forked it into his mouth, "As well as might be expected, considering where she is."

Georgina was dying to know what he meant, but she was determined not to ask. Both of the men laughed. She supposed that Amesford knew all too well that Olivia had left her home here at Hellingham to be with Charles Collins. Well, if the marquis expected her to ask anything about her late rival, Georgina wasn't going to give him that satisfaction. She picked disconsolately at her meal and drank more wine than she usually did. Finally, after the pudding, she asked to be excused, pleading a headache. For a wonder, Francis didn't make any fuss. It was almost as if he wanted to be rid of her so that he could discuss some private business with the master of Paladino Manor.

As she approached her own bedchamber, Georgina saw her abigail peeking out of the door as if waiting for her.

"Oh, miss," she whispered, "come inside so that I can tell you something special." Lizzie's eyes were snapping with suppressed excitement. Wondering if it would be some gossip about Olivia Nugent, Georgina was almost of a mind to tell her little maid that she was in no mood for gossip. But the abigail didn't give her time to say anything. She leaned close to Georgina and said, so low that Georgina had to strain to hear the words, "Charlie's here, miss, and wants to see you."

Charles! Was he going to tell her that he and Olivia were to be married? Why had he come to Hellingham?

Against her better judgment, Georgina asked, "Where is he?" her eyes involuntarily going to the huge wardrobe.

"In an empty bedchamber in the east wing. I'll show you, miss, if you wish. Or I can take a message to him."

Message. No, there'd be no message. Georgina was drawn to him as a moth to a candle flame.

"I—I had better see him—warn him that the viscount will be furious to find him here at Hellingham."

With a mischievous smile, Lizzie said, "Of course, miss."

Then they were hurrying down long passageways, through the gallery where long-dead Hardys looked down on her with disapproval from their gilt frames, and finally they turned into a wing which was not known to Georgina. Lizzie stopped in front of a carved, white-enameled door and said, "He's waiting inside, miss. Can you find your way back?"

Wanting to be rid of the abigail, Georgina assured her that she knew the way, although she wasn't at all sure she did. Well, Charles knew every inch of Hellingham. He could guide her back to her own bedchamber later.

Tapping lightly, Georgina turned the heavy silver knob and opened the door. Stepping into the room which was lit only by the low rays of the sun which crept in through long windows heavily draped in deep blue, she did not at first see Charles. Then he stepped toward her, out of the shadows, and without hesitation, Georgina went to him, arms lifted in love, and he folded her into his embrace. It was as if they had not parted in anger and dismay on that dreadful night of the masquerade, nor as if he'd passed her so blithely on the road to London. All of her love, all of her longing, went into the kiss she gave him.

What happened next was inevitable. Charles caught her up in his arms and carried her to the high, blue-canopied bed. She offered no resistance when he quickly and skillfully disrobed her. She helped him off with his clothes and held his body as eagerly as he wanted hers. Georgina had thought that lovemaking with

Francis was all that a woman could ever want, but tonight was like that first time when Charles had her on the bearskin rug before the fire at Ye Grape. Her body responded to his, her passions flamed, and she was carried to heights of ecstacy never before reached. Her body reached dazzling heights in a blaze of sensation which left her almost faint, and she clung to Charles in a kind of desperation, willing him never to leave her.

"Georgina, my dearest, I have been mad to have you in my arms, to love you the way we just have loved," he breathed. "When I left you that other time, I was so jealous that I could have killed you, and myself. And Francis." The last name he said so coldly that she shivered.

She lay there with him for a long time as he whispered endearments. Later, passion rising again, he made long, slow, wonderful love to her, so that she finally lay in his arms, sated, happy, drowsy, willing to do anything he asked of her.

It came as a jolt, though, when he suggested, "I want you to try to use your gift again for me, Georgina. Try to see where the proof of my legitimacy lies. Will you do this for me?"

Disillusioned once again, sure now that Charles had made love to her only to use her this way, she still could not say no to him.

"Do you need the miniature of my mother, Georgina? I keep it with me all the time."

"And I have the locket your gran gave me, with the lock of your mother's hair. It's in my pocket." She reached for the rumpled pile of clothing which she had cast aside with such abandon earlier, found the satin embroidered pocket, and drew out the locket. "Let me dress first." It seemed wrong, somehow, to try to use her gift when she was nude. Again there was a little pang of regret when Charles made no protest. He, too, dressed as she put on her clothing.

Finally she could delay no longer. Opening the locket so that she could actually touch the fine brown curl, Georgina stood quietly, eyes closed, hoping for some sort of vision.

When it came, it was so intense that she moaned and swayed. With part of her mind, Georgina realized that Charles had caught her with a strong, supporting arm to keep her from falling. Again she left her body, and looked down on the tableau from above, watching the frantic man plead with her to stop, that nothing was worth this. There was no way, though, for Georgina to control the vision, once it came to her. The scene below faded, and was replaced by the one she'd had in Kent. The cleric, back to her, wrote again in his ghostly book—and as before, Georgina could not see what the man wrote. Then the vision was gone; she was back in the bedchamber with Charles, and he was frantically begging her to forgive him.

"Georgina, what happened? You didn't do this at the tavern in Salisbury."

Still badly shaken by her experience, she thrust the locket into his hand, saying, "I don't want this, Charles. I—" She shuddered, unable to go on.

"What happened? What did you see?"

Knowing she'd have no peace until she explained, Georgina told him about the vision, which was like the one she'd had in Kent.

"Someone writing in a book? What does it mean? Is it—"

"The wedding couple were your mother and the earl. I don't know who the cleric was, nor what he wrote, nor where. Please, Charles, don't ask more of me! I've done all I can to help you. I cannot control these visions."

"I know, I know." But he was far, far away. "Georgina, I have to talk with father. I shall demand an explanation of this vision. He must tell me—"

"You are mad. To risk going there—what if Francis—"

"I must! Your vision has some explanation, and only father can tell me what it is. Go or stay as you wish. I am going to the tower room now."

CHAPTER 27

As Georgina and Charles approached the winding stairs which led to the tower suite, they heard descending footsteps.

"Hide!" she hissed, afraid it might be Miss Twistle.

Charles slid into a small closet at the foot of the stairs, leaving Georgina apparently alone. It wasn't the companion, but his lordship's nurse.

"Is Miss Twistle with his lordship?" Georgina asked, false brightness in her voice to cover her nervousness.

The stolid woman's faced altered just a fraction to show what she thought of Miss Twistle. "She never comes near him this late, Miss Ryerston. But he's asleep now. I'm hurrying to brew myself a cup of tea before he wakes and needs me."

"I'll go up and sit with him for a while. Don't rush. Enjoy your tea."

The nurse dropped a sketch of a curtsy. "Very kind of you, miss."

As soon as the woman had bustled off, her dark skirts rustling with many starched petticoats, Georgina whispered, "It's all right, Charles. The nurse is not upstairs."

They hurried up the spiral staircase, past Miss Twistle's door which seemed to be closed, and into the earl's bedchamber. Charles went immediately to the bedside to look at his father who lay in a deep sleep, drugged with laudanum.

"Poor father. Is he like this all of the time now."

"More often than not."

302

"Did he say more about acknowledging me as his heir?"

"Not in my hearing, Charles. I'm sorry."

Charles sighed deeply, then said, "I'd better try to find something he wrote just before he got sick. If he had decided to legitimatize me, he might have written to Sir Barnaby Kane. Have you looked through the desk, Georgina?"

Feeling she'd let Charles down, yet defensive when he expected her to jeopardize her place here by doing such overt spying, Georgina said, voice sharp, "No, I haven't." She felt betrayed again. He'd made love to her only for this.

He took the candle from beside the earl's bed and went to the desk. Pulling up a plain Kent chair of walnut, Charles went through the contents of the desk systematically, looking for what, he didn't know. Reluctant to be associated with this invasion of the sick man's private papers, Georgina stayed on beside the bed. It was she who heard the sound of footsteps on the stairs, the rustle of skirts.

"Charles! Someone's coming!"

He raised his head, listened. "It's the nurse returning."

It was, however, Miss Twistle, her entire body held in an attitude of righteous indignation.

"So!" she cried dramatically, "the bastard and the vicar's daughter!"

Charles looked up from what he was doing and frowned at her. "Watch your language, woman." His voice was mild enough, but his blue eyes were cold as ice.

"We've all tried to tell his lordship that he was taking an adder into the nest," she went on, oblivious to the threat Charles's manner posed to her. "But he was seduced by your innocent face and your naked bosom, Miss Ryerston."

With one controlled movement, Charles was on his feet, towering over the hapless Twistle.

"Get out of here, woman," he commanded, voice curt.

"How dare you? The dear earl is my responsibility. Where is that nurse?" she sputtered. "I shall report her to his lordship for dereliction of duty. It is a good thing that I heard footsteps on the stairs—"

"Do you always stand with your ear to the door?" Charles asked. "You may hear more than is good for you one day."

Then he turned away from her, sat back down, and went right on with his search, as if Miss Twistle didn't exist.

This was the final affront to her, and she swept out of the room announcing, "You'll see who is in charge here."

Georgina, silent through the exchange, now went to Charles, put a supplicating hand on his shoulder. "Leave now," she begged. "Twistle will send word to Francis that you are here. Get away before he arrives. Please, Charles."

He paid her no more heed than he had Miss Twistle. And, just as Georgina predicted, there was soon the sound of booted feet running up the spiral stairs.

"Too late!" Georgina moaned, looking about frantically for some hiding place as Francis erupted into his father's bedchamber like an avenging demon.

Charles looked up from what he was doing. He did not seem at all perturbed to find Francis there, for he shrugged and went on riffling through a stack of papers he held.

Francis stalked across the floor, and the air around him crackled with his fury. Georgina shrank back from the intensity of Francis's emotion. On the bed, the old man stirred and groaned in his sleep, as if he, too, felt an overflow from the savagery of his son's passion. The viscount stood over his brother, glaring at him.

"What are you looking for, Charlie? Surely by now you've realized that there isn't any proof of your legitimacy. You are a bastard. You've always been a bastard. You will die a bastard." The words were icy, bitter, brutal.

"Then why worry about me, Francis?" Charles actually smiled at his nemesis. "If I am, indeed, illegitimate, you should have no concern at all about my finding anything to help my cause. Methinks you protest too much, brother."

For answer, Francis reached out and snatched the sheaf of papers from his brother's hand. "Nothing in this desk is of any concern to you," he grated. "Nothing!"

"On the contrary, dear Francis," Charles said quite reasonably, "everything of my father's concerns me. And even you will not deny that the man lying over there on that bed, that poor, sick hulk of a man, is my father."

"You are his bastard!" Francis's voice rose, now, and his eyes blazed madly.

"You heard him—I heard him—Georgina heard him. He acknowledged me as his oldest son and heir."

She cringed when she heard Charles's words. It was true, but Georgina didn't want to be drawn into this quarrel. It was too terrible, too soul-searing, to be forced to say anything which would put one man above the other. On the one hand there was Charles, whom she truly loved. On the other, Francis, her lover, the man who provided all this luxury for her, who might make her his titled wife. Why did Charles insist on dragging her into this?

"Charles, no one on earth would pay attention to the maunderings of a sick old man. If you think any court of law would give you my rightful title just on the basis of his babblings, you are as mad as he." The viscount's face darkened with rage, and he yelled, "I told you the last time to get out and stay out, and

I meant it. Now I intend to have you thrown out bodily
—or do you prefer the constables, Charlie? And jail?
Or worse!"

Georgina shrank back against the draped post of the
earl's bed, not sure what was going to happen now.

When Charles did not move, Francis turned and
stalked to the bellpull. Before he could ring for the
servants, however, Charlie was beside him, catching at
Francis's arm and twisting it behind the younger man,
so that the hand was forced up between Francis's shoulder blades. The viscount gasped, for it was cruelly
painful, but he didn't give way before his brother. Instead he lashed out with his high-heeled shoe, catching
Charles a sharp blow on the shin against which even
his high boots couldn't completely protect him.

Charles loosed his hold on Francis's arm, then the
two men were at each other, trading blows as if they
were the principals in a prizefight. Charles was taller,
heavier, with a longer reach, but Francis was wiry and
lightning fast, darting in to lash at Charles, then escaping the most punishing of the blows the heavier man
aimed at him. There was a crash as the men fell into
a heavy Kent chair, knocking it over into a small drum
table.

"Stop it!" Georgina moaned. "Oh, please stop!"

If they heard her, they gave no indication, but kept
pummeling each other, the thud of the blows making
her wince and hide her eyes from the onslaught.

Then, behind her, Georgina heard, over the sounds
of the fight, the earl, making those strangled noises
which sometimes presaged speech. She turned to look
at the sick man and discovered that he was awake and
aware, his ravaged face turned to watch the fierce battle which raged between his two sons.

Eyes bulging with the effort to speak, the Earl of
Margate finally managed to say, quite loudly, "Charles!"

Instantly, as if his inner ear was tuned to his father's

voice, Charles stopped hitting Francis and covered the distance to the bed in three giant strides.

"Father!" he cried. "You must acknowledge me before witnesses." He turned and saw Georgina clinging to the drapes which hung about the sick man's bed. "Call someone, Georgina," he ordered. "I want witnesses here!"

But Francis posted himself in front of the bell and glared his anger at Georgina, so that she quailed before his wrath. He was battered, his wig askew, and a red bruise on one cheek seemed to darken and become livid even as she looked at him. "There are to be no witnesses to anything here tonight."

"Father, do you want to legitimatize me?" Charles demanded, but the old man's lucidity faded as the question was asked, and he slumped back onto the pillows as Charles frantically caught at the old man's shoulders.

"Leave him alone, Charlie!" the viscount ordered, his voice cold and iron-hard. Once again Francis was in command of both himself and the situation. "Now, for the last time, do you leave quietly, or do I have you thrown out?"

Charles turned to Georgina, pleading; but she was too terrified of Francis to do anything to help Charles.

"Maybe it would be better if you did leave now," she whispered, her lips scarcely moving. They felt numb and wooden.

The look Charles gave her was shattering. "You always choose Francis when the chips are down, don't you?" His voice was more sad than accusing. "Come away with me, now, Georgina," he pleaded. "I promise that you'll soon be mistress of Hellingham."

"Mistress of Hellingham, indeed!" Francis sneered. "If she goes with you, Charlie, she'll be mistress of naught save a common coachey."

Then the old man on the bed moaned loudly, and he seemed to be having difficulty getting his breath.

Georgina caught up the glass of medication which always stood on the earl's nightstand, ready for such emergencies. She'd been in the room enough times when this happened to know what to do. Lifting the sick man's head, she tried to pour some of the drugged wine into his mouth. Although much of it dribbled down the corner of his mouth and onto his chin, he swallowed noisily, so she hoped some of the drug went down his throat.

"See what you've done!" Francis taunted. "You've caused father to have a crisis with your demands on him. Get out, Charlie. Get out now, or I shall tell the king's men that you killed our father with your importuning ways."

Georgina, frightened that the old man seemed so gray and haggard, even worse than usual, begged Charles, "This is no time to try to talk to his lordship, Charles. He is much too sick. The fight upset him terribly. Please leave. . . ."

She felt she was betraying the man she loved; but she was truly afraid that the earl might have another stroke if the tension between his two sons continued in his presence.

"Very well, for father's sake, I'll go. Are you coming with me, Georgina?"

"I can't come now," she said in scarcely more than a whisper. "I may be needed here to look after his lordship."

She could see the smile of triumph on Francis's face, and her heart felt as if it would break when Charles left without another word, but she couldn't leave Hellingham now.

In a few minutes the nurse returned, not even knowing that Charles Collins had been there. She took one look at her patient, and quietly asked Georgina, "What happened?"

It was the viscount, though, who answered. "The bastard, Collins, was here disturbing his lordship. If he should by chance return, I am to be summoned immediately, nurse, no matter what the hour. Come, now, Georgina, it is time to go to bed."

He didn't follow her to her own bedchamber, though. He only said, "Don't try my patience too far, Georgina. If I find you one more time with Charlie. . . ." The threat hung there, unuttered.

Lizzie took one look at her mistress and kept very quiet, not asking about her visit with Charles. She got her ready for bed, snuffed the candle, and scurried away. Georgina expected to lie awake for hours, yet she fell asleep almost at once, to a sleep troubled by dreams. Francis and Charles fought again, and the earl rose from his bed and struck them both so they fell down dead. She awoke with a start, feeling the same awful sense of impending disaster she'd had once before. It would be silly to go up to the tower again, as she'd done the night she had the strange vision. The nurse would call Francis if anything happened to the earl during the night.

Georgina turned over, tried to plump up her pillows, and lay quietly, hoping for sleep to return, but to no avail. She thought in quiet desperation of Charles. Even thoughts of him couldn't keep her from thinking that something was wrong with the earl. Her heart pounded, her head ached abominably, and something squeezed her throat so she couldn't breathe. Finally she threw back the covers, slid off the high bed, and donned robe and slippers. She lighted a candle with trembling fingers and started another lonesome walk to the tower. The other time, she'd had the odd sensation of floating up the stairs and seeing Francis smother the old man. There was nothing like that now. She had none of the peculiar visions which had been plaguing her. There was only this intense sensation of disaster, this dreadful feeling of apprehension, which could not be dispelled until she saw, with her own eyes, that the earl was all right. She took the last few winding steps in a state bordering on panic. The door was not completely closed, and a candelabra burned inside. It was as if she were repeating the other visit to the tower. From where she stood, Georgina was unable to see the enormous canopied bed, but she could see the night nurse asleep again. This time she lolled back in her chair, snoring, with an empty wine glass still held loosely in her fingers. Shocking! What if his lordship awakened and needed help?

Indignant, Georgina went into the earl's bedchamber. She went across to the nurse and shook her shoulder, but the woman's slack face didn't change. She gave a little snore, then seemed to slump even deeper into the cushions of the chair.

"Nurse! Nurse!" Speaking sharply didn't wake her. Again Georgina shook her shoulder, but she could not rouse her from her drunken sleep.

Worried now, Georgina hurried over to the huge bed which was shrouded in shadows. Oddly, the curtains were not drawn. The earl lay back on his pillows, nightcap slightly askew, eyes closed. He looked as he did so often when Georgina visited him. There had been occasions when she'd thought he was dead, but close inspection always showed the shallow rise and fall of his chest. Now she wasn't sure that she could see that slight disturbance of the bedding made by his breathing. The flames of the candelabra wavered, and the shadows from the bed curtains moved. Was he breathing or not? She remembered that dreadful vision she'd had when some shadow of disaster hovered over the earl's bed. In a fit of fright, Georgina reluctantly reached out, touched the old man's cheek. It was warm. He must be alive. Yet there was something so still about the figure on the bed that she went to the lampstand and carried the branched candlestick closer to the bed. It was while she stood there, leaning over the bed, that the voice spoke behind her.

"What are you doing here?"

Georgina turned so quickly that the flames from the candles streamed long tails of fire. In the doorway stood Viscount Quincy, with Miss Twistle peering around his shoulder, her hair a bird's nest, her short body robed for the night. Did the dreadful woman do nothing but spy? Didn't she ever sleep? Georgina's heart was thudding from the fright the companion and Francis had given her, for she had not heard them ascend the spiral stairs to the earl's bedchamber.

Ignoring Miss Twistle, Georgina said, "Francis, you startled me."

"You didn't answer me." Cousin Francis came into the room, shutting the door in the face of the ever curious Miss Twistle. "It is five in the morning, Georgina. You should be in bed asleep, instead of wandering about. Why are you here with father?"

"I—I can't explain it, Francis. I woke with this dreadful feeling of disaster—and I associated it with his lordship."

He looked at her as if she were mad. "So you came creeping up here? What did you expect to find, little cousin?"

"Find?" Her voice shook with emotion. "I—I don't know. Truly. It was an impulse, nothing more. But when I did get here, I found the nurse asleep. I shook her, and called, but she didn't wake. And there's the smell of wine on her breath."

"And father?" There was a waiting quality in Francis which Georgina didn't understand, a wariness.

"I—he seems to be asleep." Then her concern for the sick man took over. "Cousin Francis, I—I'm not sure that he's breathing. I touched his face, just now, and it is warm, but I can't tell. . . ."

He crossed the room with swift, fluid strides, pushing past Georgina to the bed. "Hold that candelabra closer," he snapped, as if she were a serving girl. "Closer! So I can see him."

Quickly he pulled down the coverlet and sheets from his father's still form. Then he leaned down, placing his ear directly on his father's chest. Francis stayed there what seemed a long time, but it must have been only about a minute. Slowly he stood erect, not speaking. Georgina longed to ask, but dared not, whether or not he could hear the old man's heart still beating. The silence stretched between them, taut, ready to snap. Then Francis took hold of the bedclothes and pulled them high, covering the earl's face.

"My father, the Fourth Earl of Margate, is dead, Georgina," he announced, his words formal in the night. "I am now the Fifth Earl."

"I'm sorry, Francis," she murmured, remembering her great sorrow when her father died. "I had hoped that perhaps he would recover."

The light from the flickering white wax candles danced, sending shadows across the new earl's face, obscuring his expression.

"Go to bed, Georgina," he ordered. "There's nothing you can do now."

"But the nurse—"

He walked to the chair, leaned close to the snoring woman, sniffing as if he were one of the hunting hounds on the trail of a hare. "Drunk. Just as you suspected. Well, I won't have the distasteful task of dismissing her. Now that my father has finally died, she no longer has a job to do here. She can leave Hellingham as soon as she wakes and sobers up."

Hesitantly Georgina turned, picked up her single candle, and walked away from the bed. She was at the door when Francis asked abruptly, "Have you been here long, Georgina? Miss Twistle said she heard footsteps, and saw you on the stairs. She called me, thinking something must be wrong with father if you were going to his room."

"No, I just came into the bedchamber a few moments before you did." Why was he asking? All too well Georgina remembered that other night, the strange vision she'd had in which Francis killed his father. If anything had hastened his father's demise, it was the fight he and Charles had earlier in the earl's presence.

Francis dismissed her without further quizzing. "Go to bed, Georgina," he said kindly, considering the circumstances. "There's nothing you can do here now."

Did Miss Twistle's door move slightly when she passed, or was it an illusion caused by her flickering candle? Georgina wasn't sure. Obviously she had spied on her earlier, and probably the odious woman again had her eye to a crack in the door. At the bottom of the staircase the Marquis of Amesford appeared in front of her, silent as a ghost. He smiled that hateful smile when she gasped, startled.

"Sleepwalking, Georgina? I shouldn't have kept Francis away from you, should I? Or did Charlie entertain you before he and my good friend, the viscount, engaged in their fisticuffs?"

So he knew. Georgina said, coldly. "The Earl of Margate is dead," giving no explanation, feeling that after his words, the marquis deserved none.

"So the earl is dead—long live the earl? Francis will not be desolated with sorrow when he learns of his father's convenient demise."

"Francis is up there now. He knows."

Did Amesford give her a particularly piercing look? Suddenly the emotional impact of the earl's death hit her. It had come at a most opportune time for Francis, just as his friend had suggested, and at a terrible time for Charles. Would the Fifth Earl of Margate even notify his brother that their father was dead? If not, Georgina knew she must, somehow, get word to Charles, no matter what Francis had said earlier about having him arrested if he came again to Hellingham. It was, however, too late now for Charles. With the earl dead, there was no way to acknowledge his legitimacy.

The Marquis of Amesford still stood blocking her way.

"Please excuse me," Georgina said. "I wish to retire to my bedchamber."

He gave a supercilious bow, but stood aside so that she could pass. Just as she was beside him, he said, in almost a whisper, "This puts paid to your Charlie."

Georgina refused to be drawn, but swept down the corridor as if she had not heard those hateful words. The sound rang in her mind, though, for what Amesford said was true. Poor Charles. With the old earl dead, his cause was lost.

Back in her own room, Georgina did not ring for Lizzie, but sat down beside the window to watch the dawn which was now lightening the sky. Her thoughts were very troubled. The vision she had experienced, where Francis held a pillow over his father's face, was very real to her. And Francis's attitude just now only made her more uncomfortable. She wished that she were not cursed with such hallucinations. Were they true pictures of the future?

If only there were someone she could talk to, voice her suspicions. But there was no proof, not one iota, that Francis had deliberately killed his father. Had the nurse's wine been drugged? She shuddered. How was she going to be able to act naturally with Francis, now that she suspected him of such a black deed? What should she do? Should she try to leave Hellingham—to go where? Charles was through with her, for she had refused to help him against Francis. She couldn't go to him now. And there was no place else for her to go. She would just have to stay on here, and try to forget her suspicions. Even if she did voice her fears, she'd be laughed at. And once she told anyone that she thought Francis had murdered his father, she would be answerable to him. The thought chilled her.

Francis could be pleasant, charming, passionate; but he could also be nasty and cruel. If her vision were true, then he was a killer. And if he had killed one person, he might also kill her.

CHAPTER 28

Lizzie got out the black mourning dress Georgina had worn when she arrived at Hellingham. Although Francis did not approve of mourning, Georgina found that her cousin had bowed to the proprieties enough to have put a black band on the sleeve of his coat, and instead of wearing his usual peacock finery, he was dressed in a somber coat of a very dark gray, with black trousers. He'd even left off his fashionable red-heeled shoes, wearing a plain pair of black calf with no ornamentation except for silver buckles.

All that day there was a steady stream of visitors from the surrounding estates. By tomorrow friends would begin to arrive from London, for Francis had sent out special messengers by swift horse to spread the news of the earl's death.

"He's even dispatched one of the footmen to the Court of St. James to tell his majesty, King George," Lizzie said, awed by a master who was a friend of the king.

Georgina longed to ask if a message had been sent to Charles. She thought Lizzie was loyal to her, but as the abigail's livelihood came from Francis, she didn't care to test Lizzie's loyalty too far.

As if the young maid realized Georgina's worries, Lizzie lowered her voice and said, "All the servants think it is a sin, miss, that his lordship hasn't informed Charlie of the old earl's death. After all, everyone knows about Charlie. All you have to do is see him to know he's a Hardy."

"He'll read it in the papers, Lizzie."

"No doubt, miss. But it's not the same as being told personally." She was dressing Georgina's hair in a severe style to be in keeping with the mourning gown. "Will Charlie come to the funeral, do you think, miss?"

Georgina started, so that Lizzie inadvertently pulled her hair. "I doubt it. He's not welcome at Hellingham."

Lizzie giggled mischievously. "And when has that ever stopped our Charlie, miss? He'll be here. Mark my words." Then she lowered her voice in that way Georgina recognized as a prelude to juicy gossip. "Miss, have you heard what happened to Miss High-and-Mighty Nugent?"

It was a painful subject; she was so sure Olivia had left Hellingham for Charles. Reluctant to say this to her abigail, Georgina just said, "I've heard no gossip about Miss Nugent."

"One of the stable boys was talking to an ostler from Paladino Manor, miss. I just heard this today in the kitchen. Last week Lord Amesford went to London, and his coachey swears on his mother's grave that Miss Nugent is working in one of Moll Bailey's brothels. Says that his lordship went calling at one of them, and his coachey actually saw the snooty Miss Olivia at one of the windows."

"But I thought—" Georgina stopped herself just in time. She'd been about to say that Olivia Nugent had left to live with Charles. Now she was in a brothel? It made Georgina feel ill. Francis had slyly suggested that if Olivia did go to live with Charles, this might be her fate when Charles tired of her; but to know that it had happened. . . .

"I—that's a terrible thing to happen to her," Georgina said, forcing the words from a throat almost numb from emotion.

"I can't say I'm sorry," Lizzie said defiantly. "She was snippy to me—and horrid to you, miss. Surely you don't feel sorry for her after the way she treated you—calling you a witch, trying to make trouble for you."

"But one of Moll Bailey's brothels! Oh, Lizzie, no woman should suffer that fate—not even Olivia."

The day of the funeral dawned bleak and cheerless. The skies were overcast, and it threatened rain. Hellingham was full of guests who had come to pay their last respects to the dead earl whose body lay in state in the great hall, resting on a black-draped catafalque. Huge tapers as thick as Georgina's arm burned in tall candlestands which were wound with black and purple ribbons.

Francis expected her to act as hostess, as she had done on the night of the masked ball. When lords and ladies came to pay their last respects, her eyes searched the crowds, wondering if Charles would try to slip in, unnoticed, to view his father's body for the last time, but no tall, dashing figure appeared. Perhaps he had not heard the sad news, or he might be off on a coaching run, unable to get back to Hellingham in time for the obsequies. King George II did not come from London, but he sent the Duke of Dorset and his Duchess as personal emissaries from the Court of St. James.

Late in the day Georgina saw her abigail slip into the great hall and come close, motioning that she wished to speak to her. When she could get away from the assembled guests, Georgina followed Lizzie out into an antechamber.

"What is it, Lizzie?" Yet even as she asked, Georgina knew that Lizzie's message concerned Charles.

Looking around to make sure no one was within earshot, the abigail whispered, "He's here, Miss Georgina."

Georgina didn't need to ask who "he" was. Conflicting emotions washed over her. She was terrified lest Cousin Francis see Charles and make trouble; yet at the same time, Georgina was filled with longing to see the coachey once again.

"Where is he, Lizzie?"

"Hiding in the minstrel gallery." Lizzie glanced about self-consciously. "He's watching, miss."

"If his lordship finds him here. . . ."

"Our Charlie's too clever by far, miss. Don't worry. He knows Hellingham—all its nooks and crannies and hiding places."

But so did Francis!

"Did he ask for me, Lizzie?"

For one moment Georgina thought her abigail wasn't going to answer. Then, turning beet red with embarrassment, and twining her hands in her snowy apron, the girl muttered, "Well, miss, he didn't say much—he's having to be so careful, you know—on the lookout. That horrid little toad of a Miss Twistle, or Mrs. Pruning—they'd report him in a minute."

"I—I think I'll slip up to the minstrel gallery."

Lizzie's eyes widened with fright as she murmured, "Behind you, miss," as she was dropping a curtsy and saying, "Milord!"

Georgina knew without turning that it was the new earl.

"What are you doing here, Georgina?"

She had learned all too well the signs of his anger, the slightly narrowed eyes, the tiny vertical furrows between his black wings of eyebrows, the tightened jaw muscles. He had one face for love, another for showing her his displeasure. "Our guests—"

"Just a minor domestic matter, Cousin Francis. I'm coming right back into the hall."

No time now to run up the narrow staircase to the minstrel gallery where Georgina could see Charles unseen by the visitors below, screened behind the carved wood. And no chance to send him a message by Lizzie. Francis stood there, waiting for her.

"That's all, Lizzie," Georgina said, as if it had been

she, not the maid, who had initiated the encounter. Lizzie flashed her one despairing look, then bobbed a curtsy, picked up the hem of her green striped over-skirt, and hurried off down the passageway. Georgina laid her fingers on Francis's extended hand, and let him lead her back to stand beside the catafalque. She would not look at the corpse of the Fourth Earl. Even in death, the Hardy look was there, reminding her vividly of Charles. Was he still behind the fretwork of the minstrel gallery? Whenever the new earl moved from her side to talk quietly with respectful friends, Georgina glanced up toward the hiding place, careful, though, that Francis should not see her do it. If he suspected, he'd have Charles forcibly ejected from Hellingham, or, worse yet, call the king's men and have him arrested for trespass.

A sumptuous buffet was laid in the dining room, with great joints ready for carving, fresh breads, cakes, game pies, and a variety of wines from the cellar. The cook had prepared special sauces using spices and fruits and the side dishes were turnips and potatoes together, boiled peas in butter, and cabbage with a ham hock. The butler welcomed all to the board. With the constant coming and going of people, she half expected Charles to try to slip close to the catafalque for a last look at his father; but Francis must have been expecting this, too, for he never left the great hall for more than a few minutes at a time. When he was away from the bier, his friend, Lord Amesford, took his place, ogling Georgina in a fashion not at all in keeping with the occasion. She almost wished Olivia were back at Hellingham, so Amesford's attention would have another target. Could Lizzie's horrifying story be true? Was Olivia Nugent now working in a London brothel? If so, Charles had tired of her very quickly. Had he sold his paramour to Moll Bailey?

The funeral was to be held the following morning in the Hellingham chapel, so some of the visitors were invited to stay the night. Georgina had hoped to escape, to slip up to the minstrel gallery alone, but Francis never gave her a chance. She was sure he suspected something.

Finally, when she was ready to drop from fatigue, he said, "Call your abigail, and retire for the night, Georgina. I want you at the funeral tomorrow, and it wouldn't do for you to faint. It might be dramatic, but there'll be plenty of drama from the archbishop who is conducting the service. Tell your woman not to lace you too tightly." Sarcasm was heavy in his voice.

"I am indeed excessively weary, Francis, and I thank you for excusing me now." She ignored his heavy-handed references to the times when she'd had the fainting spells brought on by her visions. Georgina turned away from him eagerly. Obviously Francis did not intend to spend the night with her, for which she was thankful. It probably was much too late to see Charles, but she knew she had to look into the minstrel gallery before she slept.

As if able to read her mind, Francis added, his voice sharp, "Georgina, Charlie may try to get into the house. Let me warn you, my dear, that I shall take a very dim view of any attempt on your part to communicate with him, or to help him slip inside. I have told one of the footmen that, because you are so overcome with grief, you have been sleeping poorly, and have been sleepwalking. He is to patrol the passageway outside your bedchamber to make sure that you do not wander about in your sleep and fall down the stairs."

It was a fiendishly clever ploy, and Georgina knew she couldn't counter it. There was a triumphant little smile on her cousin's face which she hated.

"Goodnight, dear, lovely cousin," Francis said.

Georgina curtsied and left. What else could she do?

Lizzie was all agog when she came to Georgina's room. "Oh, miss, it was ever so exciting to have

Charlie slipping about the house again today." Then she clapped a hand over her mouth and her eyes widened with embarrassment as Lizzie remembered the time Charlie had sneaked inside and hid in the wardrobe. To cover her chagrin, Lizzie asked, "Did you ever see him today, miss?"

"No, Lizzie, I was busy with the guests."

Georgina wasn't fooling her clever little abigail for one moment.

"But you'd like to see him, wouldn't you, miss?"

It was too much. Georgina lost her temper and snapped, "Let's not talk about Mr. Collins. I'm very tired and I wish to go to bed."

A very subdued Lizzie helped her into her sleeping gown and snuffed the candles. Tired as Georgina was, she lay for hours, hearing the little ormolu clock on the chimneypiece tick the endless minutes away. She could write to Charles, but what could she say? His chances of becoming Fifth Earl of Margate were now gone.

The most dismaying thought of all was that Charles had used her as a means of getting information on the events at Hellingham, even as the new earl had suggested. This last time when they had made love only to have him insist on seeing his father was all the proof she needed. He pretended he wanted her to leave and be with him, but on that he did not insist. Perhaps he had no real feeling for her at all.

Georgina slept, at last, to dream vague, disturbing dreams. When she awakened, it was morning, gray and gloomy as yesterday. Lizzie, still subdued from the scolding Georgina had given her last night, attended to her dressing but didn't regale her with her usual tidbits of gossip, which she missed. If Georgina were to try to contact Charles, she might have to use Lizzie as a go-between; yet she was reluctant to involve the abigail, for if Cousin Francis learned of the girl's complicity, he might dismiss her. Being in a very pre-

carious position herself, Georgina was loath to subject
her maid to any such dangers.

The funeral was conducted with much pomp and
ceremony by the Archbishop of Staines, a well-fed,
florid man full of the dignity and solemnity of the
occasion and himself. The chapel was packed with
mourners. If Charles Collins had smuggled himself
into the crowd, he was well-disguised; Georgina did
not see him, though she scanned every face. She
grieved that he could not be here for his own father's
funeral, and chalked it up against her cousin, one
more of a growing list of transgressions.

Finally the service was over, the guests had de-
parted, and the Fourth Earl of Margate was laid to
rest in the family crypt beneath the chapel.

"The masons will be along as soon as the chapel
is cleared to seal father's tomb," Francis told Georgina.

Now that the funeral was over, and Peter Hardy,
Lord Margate, late of Hellingham, was in his grave,
her cousin relaxed his vigilance. He must have thought
that there was now no reason for the hated Charles
Collins to come to Hellingham. Georgina drifted about
restlessly, pretending that she was supervising the
clean-up in the great hall and the dining room. She still
thought that Charles might be here, somewhere, waiting to see her. She saw a trio of workmen come
through en route to the chapel, carrying their wooden
pails of mortar and their trowels. One man, bent almost double, seemed too old to be laboring. Wondering why Francis would hire such a man to work for
him, Georgina followed after the masons into the chapel
and from there to the narrow stone steps leading down
to the crypt. To her amazement, the stooped, elderly
man went down the spiral steps as spryly as his fellow
workmen. As he stood erect to negotiate the worn
stone steps, he presented a familiar silhouette. It was
Charles.

Georgina scarcely knew what to do. Quickly she slipped down the steps, to see a moving tableau. The two masons stood together, heads bowed respectfully, while Charles knelt on the cold, damp stones before his father's crypt. Finally he rose and murmured something to the two men who began their task of sealing the tomb.

Charles, turning away, caught sight of Georgina on the stairs. With two swift steps he was beside her, his face bitter.

"Spying on me, Georgina?" he asked fiercely, his voice rough with anger.

Stunned speechless by his words, Georgina could only shake her head. Something in her face must have reassured Charles, for he glanced back over his shoulder to see that the two men were hard at work. Then he motioned for her to go back up the stairs to the chapel. There, with the late afternoon sun slanting low into the chapel through the stained glass windows with their gothic arches, he stopped her with a hand on her arm.

"Georgina, are you with me or against me? I must know." It was as near to pleading as Georgina felt Charles would ever get.

"I'm with you, of course." She stilled her conscience which was reminding her that she had decided to marry Francis. But that was before she had the vision in which he killed his father.

"And Francis? Dear, thieving brother Francis? You stood by that other night and offered no defense for me when you'd heard with your own lovely pink ears my father's words."

He had to understand her position. "Charles," and now it was Georgina who pleaded, "he gives me a home here. If he drives me out, where can I go?" She didn't add that Charles had made her no offer, but she knew he sensed her thoughts, for the silence hung thick about them, tension-filled, palpable.

Then he flicked the cuff of her mourning gown. "You wore this when I first met you, and I've seen you in the silks and satins bought with my father's gold. They suit you better than this, dear Georgina. What can I say to you? I can offer you nothing but life as the wife of a coachey, when you deserve to be mistress of Hellingham."

It was in Georgina's heart to tell him that she would prefer life with him, no matter how poor, to any life without him, but she was not sure this was strictly true. Life with Charles as Earl of Margate was really what she wanted.

"You know as well as I that father meant to make me his heir. I won't ask you to be a witness, Georgina, but I intend to take my story to Sir Barnaby Kane, tell him how father wanted him, but Francis refused to send a summons. If there's any written record anywhere in all of England which proves my claim that my mother was legally married to the Fourth Earl, Sir Barnaby will find it."

Georgina sighed. Every chat with Charles always came to this—how he was truly the earl, not Francis. She knew that Francis was a formidable adversary. Now that he was Fifth Earl of Margate, he had the title and the money which went with it—and the power of the Margate name. Would Sir Barnaby even listen to Charles? And would he ask her to verify what Charles said?

This brought a new worry to Georgina. What would she do if the solicitor questioned her? Would she have the courage to tell him the truth? And what was the truth? A sick, dying man, paralyzed, mentally erratic, had mumbled words which might mean he intended to declare Charles his legal son. Again they might have been only the ramblings of a damaged brain. If Charles went to court to claim his title, and lost, then Georgina's position at Hellingham would be untenable if she appeared as a witness for him against Francis.

And what would Francis do to her? He had already struck her several times when she displeased him. If he knew that she suspected him of murder, what might her fate be?

Deep in her heart Georgina knew that there could be no other man for her but Charles Collins. As long as there was a chance for her to see Charles, even in such circumstances as today's, she would stay on here at Hellingham. She knew, of course, what that staying would mean in terms of Francis. He would still expect to share her bed. Very well, if that was the price she had to pay, she would pay it. Her body might betray her on occasion, but her heart was constant to Charles.

CHAPTER 29

It was the next evening when the footman brought
Georgina a summons to wait on his lordship in the
top suite of the tower where the Fourth Earl had died.
The door into the bedchamber was ajar, and the footman knocked discreetly, saying, "Miss Ryerston, your
lordship."

One look at her cousin and Georgina knew that
something momentous had happened. He seemed to
give off an aura that crackled with tension. In his
hand was what looked like a letter. He beckoned for
her to come to him as he stood beside one of the long,
narrow windows.

Handing her the paper, he asked, "Is that from your
father? He was Jonathan, wasn't he?"

Georgina took the letter, and her eyes filled with
tears when she saw the familiar handwriting, wavering
as it had toward the end of his life. "Yes, that's Papa's
writing. When he got so sick, his hand often shook,
and his writing was not easy to read."

He took the letter back before she had a chance to
look at it and then he scrutinized it as if trying to
decipher a code.

"It is legible. You said your father wrote to mine
about your coming here to live." Georgina nodded.
"This is the letter." Francis waved it, and still there
was that air of wildness, recklessness, which she
couldn't understand. Why should Papa's letter have
such an effect on Francis?

"I never saw it until today," he went on. "Apparently it came just before father had his stroke. It lay

327

in his desk with some other papers which I started to sort. I just remembered how interested Charlie was in the papers on father's desk when I found him here with you the night father died, so I decided to look them over myself. And I found this letter."

"So that's why Papa had no answer from the earl."

He scarcely heeded her, seeming in a different world. He read the letter avidly. What had her father said to the Fourth Earl to have such an effect on the Fifth?

Abruptly he asked, "Georgina, do you know what this favor was which your father mentions? He sounds as if my father owed him something—not money—but it's as if your father had done some important service for mine and now wanted something in return. Listen." He paced the floor as he read, too restless to sit. Georgina stood, listening sadly to her dear Papa's words.

Dear Peter, It has been many years since that ball when you asked the favor of me. I have tried to forget it, forget my complicity in such an ugly affair; but circumstances now make it imperative for me to remember, and to remind you of how I helped you. I am dying, Peter. The doctor doesn't try to hide it from me. I have a tumor eating away at my bowels, and I pray for the end of the suffering. Yet I must live until I can provide for my daughter, Georgina, nineteen, alone in the world except for me. I beg that you will take her into your house and under your protection when I am gone, in expiation for what you did—and, God help me, for what I did, too, for you—so long ago. I tell you now that when I learned you were betrothed to Lady Agnes Bouchard, I trembled at what I had done without telling you the truth. I learned, though, that the poor girl had died. I admit I was relieved that I would not have

to make public my misdeed, and yours. God for-
give me. And you, Peter, and you. Take my
child into Hellingham and care for her. You owe
me this.   Jonathan.

· Poor Papa. Georgina knew that something preyed
on his mind those final months. This must have been
it, yet she did not know what Papa was talking about,
and told her cousin so. He stared long and hard at
Georgina as if he didn't believe her.

"Georgina, this favor your father mentions. Could
he have been the cleric who performed the mock marriage ceremony on which Charlie bases his claims to
Hellingham? Charlie's story always has been that someone close to father, some connection, performed the
rite."

Georgina had to sit down, the thought was so stun-
ning and so disquieting. And she felt quite stupid for
not having made the connection sooner. Suddenly the
strange vision she'd had in the cottage in Kent made
sense. The wedding ceremony between Charles's
mother and the Fourth Earl—the cleric who seemed so
familiar. It was her father, a young man she scarcely
recognized; but the set of his shoulders, the way he
stood—it had been Papa. If this were true, no wonder
Papa was in such bad conscience toward the end.

Francis stood over her, slapping the letter with his
hand. "Well, I never knew your father. Would he have
done such a thing, been in on a hoax of this kind?"

Georgina thought of dear, good Papa, a man so
kind and gentle that he was, in her eyes, a saint. But
when he was younger, might he have done such a thing
for his cousin?

"I—I don't know, Francis. Truly I don't."

As she said the words, she remembered! That terrible night when Papa had waked and cried out, "It was
a true marriage! I wrote it down!"

Her face gave her away, as usual. Francis caught her

wrist in an iron grip, just as Papa had done that night. Now Francis was shaking her, as if to force her to remember.

"What is it, Georgina? Don't try to fob off some nonsense on me. You know something. Don't lie to me and say you don't."

Georgina had learned to fear her cousin. Convinced now that Francis was a murderer, yet bound to him with gold chains, she knew that if she displeased him too often, Francis might force her to leave Hellingham, send her away as he had sent Olivia Nugent. Then what would she do? So she told him Papa's words, but she didn't mention her vision to Francis.

"What else did he say?" He shook her arm painfully.

There had been something else, but Georgina didn't remember the words. "He was distraught, Francis— and in great pain. The doctor kept him drugged with opiates. Often he rambled, made no sense, hallucinating from the effect of the drugs."

"It was a true marriage—I wrote it down," Francis quoted. "That sounds quite lucid to me. What else did your father say, Georgina?"

"Truly I don't remember. Something about being ashamed, of profaning his calling. He was delirious, Francis."

"Was there anything more?" His eyes glittered.

Georgina tried to think. "There was something about going to make amends—I'm not sure," she wailed, almost in tears. "Maybe that was another time. He wasn't himself those last terrible weeks."

"Making amends. That doesn't make sense."

"He said he'd read about some betrothal in the paper, but that someone—she—had died, and he'd kept quiet." Georgina was at a loss to understand why Francis was so concerned. "What interest is this of yours?"

"What interest is it of mine?" He almost screamed

the words. "You little fool, you can't see it, can you? Your stupid father maunders on about a true marriage —and says he wrote it down!"

It was as if she had been peering into a heavy sea mist, trying to see the landscape, and then the mist blew away abruptly, making the scene plain before her. So that was what her Papa had meant! She had seen, in her vision, the young cleric writing in a book. The revelation stunned her.

"The marriage of his lordship and Charles's mother."

Georgina could see that Francis regretted bitterly that he'd made her see the truth. "There's no proof of that."

But there was! There was! She'd seen it so clearly. A wave of happiness swept over her. "Then Charles is right." She completely ignored Francis's disclaimer. "His mother's marriage to your father was legal, and that makes him—"

For one terrible moment Georgina thought that Francis was going to strike her. She shrank back into her chair, aware that she had said too much.

"That makes him nothing, do you hear, nothing!" Francis raged. "There's no proof. Even Charlie says that the license was burned."

But he saw the fallacy in his argument, even as Georgina did.

"There must be a record somewhere." In her mind's eye was a younger Papa, writing in a book. A stubborn little flame of hope burned brightly in Georgina's mind.

"Yes, a record." He read the letter again, his face black as a summer thunderhead. "Listen to what your father says. *When I learned you were betrothed to Lady Agnes Bouchard, I trembled at what I had done without telling you the truth. I learned, though, that the girl had died.* What does that mean to you, Georgina?"

She didn't want to say it, for it put her dead father

in a bad light—or did it? "Your father meant the wedding to Rebecca Collins to be a mock one, just to get her in bed!" Georgina spat at Francis. "He was the wicked one, not Papa. But obviously Papa did something to make that marriage legal."

It was a true marriage. Those words rang in her head.

"Yes, your father wrote it down." He walked to the window, looked out into the darkness with blank, unseeing eyes. Then he turned and pounced. "Where did he write it down, Georgina? Where?"

"I don't know," she cried. Georgina guessed, of course. She hadn't been a vicar's daughter for nineteen years without learning intimately the workings of the vicarage, and the church. It would be entered in the church register. That would be the book she'd seen in the strange, disturbing vision, the book in which the young cleric, Papa, wrote with the goose quill.

"I'll go to—what was the name of your village?"

Georgina wanted to scream, "I'll not tell you!" but she knew that such resistance was futile. It would be easy enough for her cousin to find out the name of her village. "Trindale," she muttered angrily.

"Ah, yes, Trindale. Near Exeter, I believe." He smiled like a huge tomcat ready to pounce on a trapped mouse. "The Exeter to London run of the stagecoach—that's where you met our dear Charlie. How fortunate for him that he should turn the head of the one person who could provide the clue to his legitimacy, the elusive clue he's been pursuing all of his adult life." Francis grinned, then, as if at some funny joke; but the joke was on Georgina—or on Charlie. Why hadn't she tried to find Papa's letter to the Fourth Earl when she'd had the chance? Now it was too late. "Too bad that you are here with me, and thus unable to give Charlie this vital clue." Waving her Papa's letter under Georgina's nose, he taunted her. "Well, little cousin, shall we make a pilgrimage to Trindale? Pay our respects to your poor dead father who has wrecked my life? Shall we?"

She said nothing, for nothing she could say would help.

"Ruined my life, Georgina! Your father has stolen my inheritance from me, reached out his dead, corrupting fingers from the grave to wrench my title from me, and steal Hellingham. Well, I'll tell you something, little churchmouse cousin, I won't stand still for it! No dead village parson is going to drive me from Hellingham, deprive me of my earldom."

This was the last straw for Georgina. She had loved her father dearly. To hear him maligned by Francis was too much. Nothing was worth this. She'd acted like a little fool, a bough in the wind, swaying to Charles when the breeze blew that way, to Francis when it veered. If she had to give up all hopes of being mistress of Hellingham, she would. Marriage to Francis no longer appealed to her. He was cruel and murderous. She must have been out of her mind to stay on here once she had the vision in which Francis murdered his father. No wonder he'd been so curious about what time she had arrived in the tower suite to find the earl dead. No doubt Francis feared she had seen him leaving the room after doing the dastardly deed. Poor nurse. Francis probably offered her drugged wine, or put it where it would be a temptation to her to have a glass. It might be possible to prove something there, if the dismissed nurse would talk.

Silently Georgina regarded Francis in his unholy glee; but he had not reckoned with her love for Charles Collins! No— Charles Hardy, true Fifth Earl of Margate. She'd get word to Charles. Lizzie would be only too glad to enter into the intrigue and carry a note to Charles, leaving it with the landlord of Ye Grape. With Georgina's message in his hands, Charles could go to Sir Barnaby Kane and beg him to plead the case before the king's judges. With the nurse to testify about where she had obtained the wine which had put her to sleep, there might well be a case against Francis.

"I shall take you with me, dear little loving cousin. We'll go to Trindale, where you shall introduce me to the poor little vicar in current residence. With your blessing on me, and a generous contribution of gold to the probably empty coffers of—what's the name of the church?—no matter—the vicar will allow me to examine the old records. Let me see." He paused, pursed his mouth in thought. "A logical reason—of course." She didn't like his laugh. "We wish to trace the exact connection between our two families." He winked at her as if they shared some joke. Then Francis paused, nodded, and smiled smugly. "Of course! As beautiful as you are, dear cousin, the perfect solution. I'll tell the vicar that we wish to wed." Georgina was stunned by his words. This was what she had hoped for these past months. Now, however, the idea was abhorrent to her. "And," her cousin went on, "we must trace our bloodlines to make sure we don't violate the Church's laws on consanguinity. Then, a little sleight of hand, a missing page in a years-old church register, later a bit of paper on a blazing fire—and I remain Fifth Earl of Margate, while Charlie remains the laughing stock of the county, the bastard son who would be earl."

"I won't do it."

"Of course you will, my dear. You have no choice, and you know it. If you decide to oppose me, you will no longer be welcome here. Where would you go? How would you live? Not qualified to be an abigail, could you learn to be a housemaid?" He tipped up her chin with a finger and studied her face as if he'd not seen it before. "You really are quite lovely, cousin mine. Perhaps you could become a famous courtesan in London! With the skills you have learned pleasing me, you would be much sought after. You are very interesting. I might even decide to marry you after all. I do enjoy you in bed. Perhaps it would be a good idea to make you the Countess of Margate."

Before Georgina realized what he was about, he caught her up in an embrace of iron and rained hot kisses on her face and throat. Knowing what would happen, what this always led to, no longer willing to be Francis's lover, yet fearing the way her own body usually betrayed her, Georgina decided to repulse her cousin. She put her hands on his chest and, with all her strength, pushed herself out of his encircling arms. Francis was so stunned by this show of resistance that he stood perfectly still for a moment, eyes blazing. Georgina then saw his arms about to grab her once again and she slapped him hard on the cheek, leaving a mark and knocking loose the bag wig which sat askew on his head. The loud crack of skin against skin hung in the air.

He looked at her as if she were a firebrand. Again Georgina feared he was going to strike her, but he didn't. She had been expecting physical violence from him. The look he gave her, though, was murderous. "You'll pay for that, dear cousin. After our trip to Trindale, you'll pay. But I wouldn't want a mark on that lovely face. The vicar might not understand if you came there with your eyes blackened and your mouth minus several of those pretty little white teeth."

With great deliberation he walked across the room to where a small fire glowed in the fireplace. Twisting her Papa's letter into a long spill, he thrust it into the glowing coals. As it caught, the sudden burst of flames turned his face into something satanic.

Then he walked back to where Georgina huddled in the chair, his intent plain in his flushed face. Francis caught her up to him and with most ungentle hands deliberately ripped her gown from her, tugging at the ties of her petticoats, unfastening the waistband of the bell hoops she wore so that they fell in a heap about her feet. Her chemise fared no better.

"No, I don't want to!" she cried.

"But I do. And it is what I want, my dear Georgina, not what you want that is the rule here at Hellingham."

She fought him then, fiercely, managing to claw his smooth, olive cheek with the nails of one hand before he caught both hands and pinned them behind her with one of his. He did little disrobing himself, shedding only essential trousers as a final insult to her, as if she were some cheap rural maid he was violating. Francis didn't even bother to carry Georgina to the huge bed in which his father had died, but he wrestled her to the floor and took her by force, brutally, with none of the tenderness which he had always shown after that first time when he had forced himself on her. This time she did not respond.

CHAPTER 30

Afterward, Francis waited until she had at least partially covered her nakedness with her tattered clothing. She felt degraded, defiled. How could she once have submitted willingly, even eagerly, to his passion? Georgina walked past Francis with as much dignity as she could muster, careful not to get close enough for him to touch her again, and went down the spiral stone stairs. Again there was a spying crack in Miss Twistle's door, which eased closed as Georgina passed. Georgina was surprised that the woman hadn't already been dismissed, now that the earl was dead and there was no further need to employ a companion for him. Georgina guessed that Miss Twistle was loath to leave such an easy post.

Even as she descended the stairs, Georgina was planning what she would put in the letter to Charles. He must understand the truth, that his mother had been the Fourth Earl's legal wife, married by Georgina's father, and that there was a record somewhere, probably in the church registers at St. Edmund's. He must also realize that if Francis got there before him, the record might be destroyed—would be, unless Georgina managed somehow to prevent it. How could she do that, how could she manage? She didn't know. If ever Charles had made the trip between London and Exeter in record time, it must be now.

"Pack whatever you'll need for the journey to Trindale."

It was Francis, right behind her, having followed her

to her bedchamber. Georgina could only pray that he would not force himself on her again.

"I'll ring for Lizzie," Georgina told him.

"Never mind Lizzie. I'll see that you have help." He closed the door to her bedchamber, and she heard a click. Trying the knob, Georgina was appalled to find that Francis had locked her in.

Quickly she took quill in hand, dipped it into the German crystal inkstand on her desk, and penned an explanatory note to Charles, not dwelling on details, but putting the facts as concisely as she knew how. She folded it, held the sealing wax over the candle flame, dropped a blob on the edge of the paper. Georgina had just finished when there was the sound of the key in the lock once more, so she thrust the note into the sleeve of her torn gown for safekeeping.

Instead of Lizzie, Miss Twistle came in, a gloating look on her face. Francis stood in the doorway.

"Miss Twistle will stay with you until we leave."

He made quite a show of giving Miss Twistle the key. She was to be Georgina's live-in jailer, and how she loved it! The companion had never liked Georgina from the first moment she'd laid eyes on her. Now she had her triumphant revenge. The hated Miss Ryerston, favorite of the late Fourth Earl, was now her prisoner.

"I'm very tired and wish to retire," Georgina said coldly to her. "I'll ring for my abigail."

"That won't be necessary," Miss Twistle said, matching Georgina's icy tone with her own frigid ones.

"Then you may help me undress." Georgina didn't ask, she commanded. If there was anything she'd learned here at Hellingham, it was the alacrity with which servants responded to the tone of command.

Georgina saw Miss Twistle waver, and her lips thinned with anger. The companion was in a dilemma. If she didn't allow Georgina to ring for Lizzie, she might be reduced from her status as companion to the late earl to the lower one of abigail, and abigail to Georgina, her hated enemy.

"Very well, ring for your woman." Miss Twistle's sense of importance won, as Georgina hoped it would. Not for her the unlacing of Georgina's stays!

Georgina pulled the embroidered bell tape. "You'll have to let her in, Miss Twistle."

The companion waited until Lizzie tried the door, then made a show of unlocking it. Lizzie checked for one moment, then came in as if nothing untoward were happening.

"Yes, miss?" She totally ignored Miss Twistle.

"I want you to pack for me, Lizzie, enough for a week or two." Georgina, too, ignored her unwelcome guardian. "I'm taking a brief journey back to Trindale tomorrow with his lordship." If the abigail wondered, she asked no questions but simply obeyed. When the cases were packed, Georgina said, "I am tired, now, Lizzie. I wish to retire."

Again Lizzie, although she had to notice Georgina's torn clothing, made no comment. Carefully Georgina maneuvered herself so that Lizzie's body was between her and Miss Twistle. Then, as if pulling on the lace frill of her sleeve, Georgina slipped the note out so that Lizzie could see it, then slid it out of sight again in her sleeve. Not a word passed between them, only a look, but Georgina knew that Lizzie understood.

Very carefully the abigail undid Georgina's ripped dress and slipped it from her arms, drawing the sleeves down over her hands, carefully slipping the note from the lacy hiding place and concealing it in a capacious pocket under her apron. She brushed out Georgina's hair, chattering away about inconsequential things, and finally had her mistress in her nightrobe. As Georgina climbed into her high, curtained bed, she said, with all the authority she could muster, "You shall have to sleep in the chair by the fire, Miss Twistle. I cannot abide anyone in my bed with me."

Then Georgina motioned for Lizzie to draw her bed curtains, something she never did. "And snuff the candles, Lizzie. I cannot possibly sleep if there is a flickering candle in my bedchamber."

Georgina heard the door open, then close, and the lock catch. From the darkness she heard Miss Twistle's indignant voice.

"I'm sure his lordship didn't expect me to sit up all night."

Footsteps sounded, and the door opened and closed again, this time with the key turning on the outside of it. Miss Twistle had locked Georgina in, but at least she had left her in peace. In the morning Lizzie would take her letter to Ye Grape. Then it was out of Georgina's hands, and into the more capable ones of Charles Collins.

She had been asleep when the noise at her bedchamber door woke her. Someone was unlocking her door. Before she had time to call out, the door opened, and Lizzie came in, balancing a tray which held a candle and a squat silver teapot and a cup and saucer of fine china. Quickly she closed the door behind her and moved slowly toward Georgina's bed. Georgina had been peeking through the bed curtains and now, seeing that Lizzie was alone, she pushed back the curtains and sat up, surprising the abigail into a little shriek.

"Is it morning?" Georgina asked, groggy and confused. She'd been sound asleep, and it was the first thing she thought of. Lizzie was waking her for the trip to Trindale with Cousin Francis.

The abigail set the tray down on the stand by her bed. Her hands were trembling so that the cup rattled in the saucer.

"What time is it?" Georgina insisted.

"Gone half after four, miss." Her eyes were wide and troubled.

"What's wrong, Lizzie?" She tried to keep her voice

kind, but Georgina had had too little sleep, and the question came out sharper than she intended.

"Wrong?" Lizzie's voice rose and cracked on the word. "Nothing, miss." The words tumbled out much too fast.

Georgina reached out to catch one of the maid's trembling hands in her own. "I know that's not true, Lizzie."

Georgina could feel a little tremor run through the girl, and Lizzie glanced back over her shoulder as if she expected to see a ghost behind her. "Miss—it's—I—I took the letter to Charlie!"

"Lizzie! You didn't!" Georgina was overjoyed. "Then what's to be frightened about?"

"I—his lordship—"

"He'll never know, Lizzie."

With her letter in his hands, Charles could get a headstart on Francis, get to St. Edmund's before they did. Georgina didn't worry about his not getting the records from the Reverend Mr. Owens. Charles didn't have his lordship's gold, but he had his own natural charm—

"Don't be afraid of the Earl of Margate," Georgina tried to reassure her frightened abigail. "Soon there'll be a new earl here. And with me as the countess, you've naught to fear."

"Yes, miss." But Lizzie still shook as if with ague.

"And Charles—what did he say? Did he read the letter while you were there?"

Lizzie gave Georgina a long, beseeching stare. "Yes, miss. Immediately I told him who it was from."

"How brave of you to go out in the middle of the night to deliver it. I thought you'd wait until morning."

Georgina thought she saw tears in Lizzie's eyes, but she must have been mistaken. The maid turned from her, pulling her hand away from Georgina's, and poured a cup of steaming chocolate from the china pot into the cup.

"But what did Charles say, Lizzie?" Georgina prodded impatiently, becoming a bit provoked with her. Usually Lizzie was talkative to the point of being garrulous, particularly if she scented romance in the air. Why so quiet now? Well, Lizzie'd had even less sleep than she, delivering the note after Georgina had been comfortably in bed. No doubt she was weary.

"He wants you to go with him, miss." Her words were almost a whisper, so fast and low that Georgina had trouble understanding them.

"Go—with Charles? Where?"

"To your village, miss. Where you were to go with his lordship later. He said something about a church —you'd know, Charlie said. Just get you ready quickly. And give you this hot chocolate to warm you, as it'll be a long, chilly ride before dawn breaks. The night air is damp."

Quickly Lizzie soaked up some spilled chocolate with the linen napkin on the tray, then offered Georgina the drink.

"And I'll help you dress as soon as you've drunk your chocolate," she said.

Georgina took the proffered cup and sipped.

"Drink it down quickly, miss. He's waiting!" Lizzie sounded frightened again, no doubt worried that Francis might learn of her complicity in the matter and dismiss her without a letter.

"Don't worry, Lizzie. My traveling suit is ready." Georgina took a gulp of the chocolate and almost choked. It was so strong it was bitter. It made her cough, and Lizzie glanced at her from the wardrobe where she was taking the skirt from the hanger.

"Drink it now, miss, while it's hot. I—I made it special."

Georgina longed to dump the rest of the cup back in the pot, as it really wasn't good; but with Lizzie's anxious eyes on her, she couldn't hurt her abigail's feelings. Taking a big breath, then holding it, she gulped down the rest of the cup as if it were some nasty medicine. The dregs were dreadful. For one horrid moment Georgina was afraid the chocolate would come back up, but she breathed with her mouth open, and the nauseous feeling left.

Lizzie helped her out of her nightdress, and into her chemise and petticoats. As Georgina leaned down to pull on the silk stockings Francis had imported from France for her, she felt momentarily giddy. She must have made a little sound, for Lizzie caught her head and held it against her starched apron.

"I—I felt ill for a moment, Lizzie."

"It's the early hour, miss, and the lack of sleep. I'm so sorry, miss," she added, so low Georgina almost missed the final words. Then Lizzie quickly finished dressing her, urging her to hurry. "Charlie's waiting with a coach, miss. I'll take you down to him."

Georgina was feeling very peculiar. Waves of dizziness swept over her. "I—I don't feel—I'm sick, Lizzie."

The abigail gave a little moan. "Hurry! You'll be all right in the fresh air." She flung a traveling cape about Georgina's shoulders.

Georgina slumped down onto a chair, but Lizzie half-lifted her, one strong arm about her waist. Maybe she was right. She needed air. So Georgina forced herself to move as her abigail half carried her from her room to the passageway.

"My cases . . ." Georgina muttered, tongue thick.

"Never mind. Just come to the coach, now, miss." There was a panicky note in Lizzie's voice.

Georgina seemed to be floating, although it wasn't the same as the other times when she'd left her body. She was still in her own body, but it skimmed along the passageway, and Georgina wasn't aware of her feet touching the floor. The stairs plunged down, down, down, and she thought she'd fall; but Lizzie clutched her in a vise-like grip with one strong arm while she held tightly to the bannister with the other.

"Easy, miss, don't rush, we'll make it in time." Her voice sounded as if it were coming from the end of a long tunnel.

"Sleepy . . ." someone was complaining. Familiar voice. Whose? "Want . . . lie down. . . ."

Then Georgina was on the white checkerboard marble floor of the great hall. The floor revolved in a dizzying manner, and if it hadn't been for Lizzie's help, Georgina might have slumped onto that spinning kaleidoscope. Then she was skimming over the marble squares, and suddenly they were outside. When the cold night air hit her face, Georgina revived enough to ask, groggily, "Why do I feel so sleepy?"

"I'm sorry, I'm sorry," she thought Lizzie whispered.

There was a coach in front of them, a small closed body into which Lizzie and someone else—Charles?— Georgina couldn't see—lifted her, putting her in one corner. Her head fell back against the cushions, and she drifted again, conscious only that the coach was moving. After that, Georgina descended by ever narrowing spirals into a thick, velvety darkness. Her final thought was, *The gypsy fortune teller warned me about a coach . . . coach . . . beware a coach. . . .*

CHAPTER 31

Georgina's head was throbbing and her mouth felt dry and vile, as if it were lined with mangy fur. She was in bed, but it wasn't her familiar bed at Hellingham. Her eyelids weighed a ton each, yet she finally managed to lift them. The room in which she lay was completely unfamiliar. Georgina started to sit up, but was assaulted by such a wave of nausea that she fell back onto the pillow, moaning.

As she started to retch, a woman's familiar voice said, "Here's a basin," which Georgina thankfully used. When she felt better, she sipped water from a goblet the woman held for her. Georgina still had not looked to see who her nurse was, for after the nausea, it was too much effort to hold her eyes open.

After a few minutes, she slowly raised her eyelids and saw the room. It was small, decorated in a florid rococo style, with many gilt-framed mirrors showing the canopied bed from all angles. The hangings were a rich plum-colored satin, very gaudy. Although all of the furnishings were expensive, they lacked that certain touch which spells good taste.

Georgina lay on an ornate bed, and found she was clad in a rich silken nightdress of palest violet, so diaphanous that she felt naked. She turned her head slightly to see who it was who was taking care of her. It was Olivia Nugent. At first Georgina was not sure she could believe her eyes, for the woman was terribly changed in the short time since she had left Hellingham. Olivia wore a negligée of a rich yellow velvet, cut so low in the bosom as to be immodest.

"Feel better now, Georgina?" It was Olivia's voice, true, but even that had coarsened. There were still some traces of her former beauty in Olivia's ravaged face; yet even the heavy layer of white lead paint she used, and the bright spots of carmine on her cheeks, could not hide the lines and shadows of dissipation and degradation Georgina saw there. Her dark hair was down about her shoulders, the powder not carefully brushed out of it. The woman Georgina had known at Hellingham had been fastidious. This creature was slovenly, blowsy, and she smelled sour.

Georgina, confused and somewhat frightened, still feeling logy, closed her eyes, wishing only that she could go back to sleep. She felt this must be some kind of nightmare.

Olivia, though, would not keep quiet. "One of these days he'll put one drop too much of his sleeping draught in some girl's wine, and he'll have a corpse on his hands."

Then it all came back to Georgina in hammer blows; the earl's death, the true marriage, her warning letter to Charles, and the curious flight from Hellingham, of which she remembered only vague bits and pieces.

"Where am I?" she cried, and fear made her dread the answer.

"London, Georgina."

"London! But we were to go to Trindale."

"I don't know what lies he told you. He didn't bother to mention it to me—just ordered me to keep you safely here until his return."

"Who told you . . . ?" Georgina asked, her head aching with confusion.

"Just who do you think? Your escort here, of course." Olivia laughed in a way that chilled Georgina's blood. "Your lover!"

Charles? Had Charles brought her here. "I don't know what you mean," Georgina said indignantly.

"Oh, Georgina! Lie if you like about your relationship with him. Remember, I was at Hellingham. Do you actually think I didn't know everything that went on? With old Twistle spying and reporting to me? And Pruning, too, if it suited her purposes." Her coarse voice was cynical as she went on, "I never made any such pretense. I was his mistress, but I was stupid enough to think he'd make me his wife. He wasted no time in replacing me, and now you, too, are discarded."

Now her words penetrated Georgina's mental fog. "You made me sound like a—a—dollymop!"

Olivia laughed mirthlessly. "Dollymop! That's a polite word for what we are."

Furious, Georgina sat up, spine stiffening. "I don't like being put in the same category as you, Olivia."

She smiled that sly smile Georgina had learned to distrust. "We're in the same boat, just as we've always been, Georgina. Vicarage raised or no, you were just as much a whore as I, and don't forget it. Oh, you weren't paid in gold guineas——but you were paid well, nonetheless. And don't go all innocent on me and deny it." Olivia leaned nearer Georgina, and her green eyes glittered. Spitefully she said, "He's brought you to the same place he brought me—to Old Moll."

"Old—Moll?" Georgina's worst fears were realized. Subconsciously, since opening her eyes on this opulent, tawdry place, she had known, but would not acknowledge it.

"Where did you think you were? The Court of St. James?" Olivia mocked. "You're ensconced in one of Moll Bailey's bagnios. You have heard of Moll Bailey?" she asked as an afterthought.

Georgina could stand the suspense no longer; she had to know the answer to her most burning question. "Did—did Charles Collins bring you here, sell you to Moll Bailey?"

Olivia's eyes widened with surprise. "Charlie? Did Charlie bring me here? Whatever gave you that idea?"

"Francis told me——"

"Francis! He said that Charlie. . . ." Her laugh was wild, hysterical. "Oh, Georgina, if only you knew how funny——" She shook her head. "Not Charlie, Georgina. He'd not do that to any woman. He'd bed everyone he could—well, he's a man. But sell a woman here, into whoredom? Charlie? Never!"

"But—but it was Charles——" Georgina's head was bursting now. Lizzie had said Charles wanted her. And what had Olivia said about drugged wine? Could the chocolate have been—of course! That explained it. She remembered how bitter it had tasted, how she had gulped it down because Lizzie said Charles wanted her to drink it. Drugged chocolate. But the more that was explained, the more confused Georgina became. "If Charles didn't bring you here, Olivia, then who did?"

Olivia looked at Georgina as though she were the prize ninny of England. "Why, Francis, of course. He was tired of me. Said I had become a bore with my whining about marriage. Wanted you at that moment, Georgina. It was as simple as that, really." She shrugged, and her bosom threatened to escape entirely from the low-cut negligée. "Francis had been furious with me since he learned I'd slept with Charles, too. Francis has a long memory, Georgina. He's willing to wait for his revenge." She shook her head ruefully. "I made a poor choice, didn't I? Thought I'd get to be Countess of Margate if I chose Francis instead of Charlie. So Francis packed me up, without even the benefit of a drugged drink, and brought me here to old Moll, because you didn't want me around, once you'd taken him into your bed. He told me he was tiring of you—that you were too countrified—that we'd have a marvelous time in London, as soon as he got rid of you. And fool that I was, knowing him as well as I did, I still believed him." She threw back her head and laughed, a harsh, bitter sound. "Oh, how I gloated, Georgina. I had triumphed over you—over little Miss Wheyface." She looked about her, her mouth twisted in regret. "I lost—but then, so did you, it would seem."

"Francis brought you here?"

"Not in person. But he sent me here from Hellingham."

Georgina's eyes widened in amazement. "Then who brought *me* here? Lizzie said that Charles was waiting in a coach. . . ."

"You thought it was Charlie? How much of the drugged wine did you drink?"

"It was chocolate. And I drank the whole cup."

"Well, you must have been seeing things if you saw Charlie in that carriage."

"I didn't see anyone. I could scarcely walk. My abigail—oh, how could she have been so treacherous?"

"Francis pays her wages, my dear. Don't blame Lizzie."

He must have found out about the note. Georgina couldn't believe Lizzie told him. Miss Twistle must have seen her pass the note to her abigail and tattled to Francis.

"But why would Francis bring me here?" Georgina wailed.

Olivia shrugged. "He just told me to keep you here. He and that nasty friend of his, Lord Amesford, were off to some parish church. I can't imagine why."

Georgina's spirits plummeted. Charles hadn't been warned, and Francis would get to Trindale unhindered.

"Olivia, what else did Francis say? It's vitally important that you tell me everything!" Although what she could do about this dreadful situation, Georgina didn't know.

"That's all I overheard. Frankly, I was too busy with you, and not awfully interested in what they said.

At least his lordship paid me to look after you," she added bitterly.

"I'm sorry to have been such a bother, Olivia—but, oh, you must help me!"

Her face changed instantly, a wary look coming into her green eyes. "Help you? I can't even help myself."

"I have to get out of here."

Olivia's laugh was raucous. "That's what we all say, at first! At least you aren't to be put to work until Francis returns. You have that consolation, a little reprieve."

Georgina understood her words, but they had no emotional impact on her just then. She had a far greater worry than being forced into a life of shame by the notorious Moll Bailey.

"Olivia, I have to get a message to Charles!"

"You think he can rescue you? Little chance of that my dear. Charlie's a favorite here—even old Moll has a soft spot in that rock-hard heart of hers for Charlie, but she'll not go against his lordship, not for a bastard pretending he should be master of Hellingham."

"But it's true, Olivia," Georgina cried. "That's what this is all about. Francis is already en route to destroy the proof that Charles is the legitimate heir to the title."

"Georgina, that drugged drink has addled your brain—or Charlie's been even more persuasive than usual. Everyone knows he's old Peter Hardy's bastard son."

Georgina reached out and caught her hand. "It isn't so. My father was a vicar, and Lord Peter's cousin. He performed the marriage of the old earl and Charles's mother. It was legal, and I know where the proof is. Unfortunately, so does Francis." A sudden thought struck her. "What time is it?"

"Nearly ten."

"In the morning?" There still might be time.

"Do you think his lordship's coach has wings? It's

ten at night. You were brought here some hours ago. From what they said, you'd been on the road several hours."

"It was the middle of the night," Georgina murmured. "They couldn't make very good time in the dark, I suppose. How long has it been since they left?" She had visions of a mad race over rough roads with Francis and Amesford taking turns driving, stopping frequently to change horses to keep up the pace.

"Two hours—maybe longer. They're long gone, Georgina."

Two hours or more! And she hadn't any idea how long it would take for her to get a message to Charles. Georgina groaned. "They'll get there, tell the vicar some lies, give him money for the church, and he'll let them look at the registers." Tears streamed down her face. "Too late!"

"You're telling me the truth?" Olivia demanded. "Charlie's really the old man's legal heir?"

"It's true, Olivia. I swear it. And somewhere it's written down. Francis guesses my father entered it into the church register at St. Edmund's, the church near Exeter."

"Exeter! It'd take days to get there, Georgina."

"As many as six—maybe more." Then she remembered. "Charles made it in three days by stagecoach once."

"The horses must have died in the harness." Georgina knew she'd gotten Olivia to thinking. "Georgina, if his fancy lordship gets there, will he destroy that record of his father's marriage—the wedding that makes Charlie legitimate?" Georgina nodded. Then Olivia shook her head. "No, it doesn't make sense. The old man always favored Charlie, but he didn't think he was his legal heir, or he'd certainly have acknowledged him."

Georgina explained the complications, how her father was involved.

"But the Fourth Earl, not knowing the license was valid, destroyed it," she finished. "Papa, though, said he'd written it down."

Olivia's eyes narrowed, and a positively vicious look came over her face. "I'd love to see Francis Hardy, Lord Margate, thrown out of Hellingham. Oh, how I'd love that!"

"Can you get a message to Charles through the landlord at Ye Grape at Hellingham?" Georgina begged.

"Ye Grape, indeed! Nearly a day away." But she thought about it. "If Charlie's still coaching, he might be caught at The Bull and Mouth at St. Martin-le-Grand."

Hope flared. "Could we get word to him there?"

Immediately Olivia's face got that shuttered look. "We? I like how you bandy words about, Georgina. We! If you think I'll risk flogging or worse to try to get a message to Charlie, you're ready for Bedlam. I don't leave the premises unless I have express permission from old Moll, herself, and then I can't go anywhere in London alone. We must go in twos, like Papist nuns, and always with one of Moll's footmen, as she calls them, to keep an eye on us, to make sure we don't do any business on the side—for ourselves—nor try to get out of her clutches. No, I can't help you."

"But then Francis will—"

"I don't want to hear about it!" she cut off Georgina angrily. "So Francis stays Earl of Margate. I can't help you." Then her face softened a bit. "Georgina, you are such an innocent. Don't you realize how much power Francis now wields as earl? And who am I? A woman from one of Moll Bailey's houses. Who would listen to me? There's nothing either of us can do." Then, as if her resolve might falter, she hurried from the room.

Georgina sat up, then found that her head still swam. Certain she could not escape a horrid fate unless she helped herself, Georgina slid her feet out of bed and stood up shakily, holding onto the post of the canopied bed until her senses stopped reeling. She was weak and some nausea remained, but Georgina knew that she must force herself to move. Clothes. She didn't know what had happened to her clothes. The ornate mirrors showed infinite reflections, her womanly curves all too obvious through the sheer fabric flowing from her shoulders. Georgina laughed, near hysteria. What a sensation she would cause if she ventured out onto the streets of London clad this way.

In one corner of the room a tall wardrobe, boasting enough gilt to pave the streets to heaven, stood with doors half open. Georgina was loath to loose her hold on the bedpost, but she ventured forward, determinedly, bare feet sliding over a thick rug. Her steps were shaky, and she wasn't sure her knees would support her. She kept moving and managed to catch the edge of one of the wardrobe doors. Luckily, she found her clothes there, her chemise and silk hose crumpled on the floor over her shoes, her petticoats and traveling costume hanging from the rod. Her hooded travel cape was there also. It would hide her face.

Georgina was not a fool. She knew how dangerous it was to be abroad at night in London. For a woman alone, it was sheer folly; yet if she stayed here in Moll Bailey's house, there was no hope for her. With trembling fingers she collected her clothing and dressed, although when she bent to draw on her hose, Georgina was so giddy she almost fainted. Finally ready, Georgina went to the door, only to discover to her dismay that it was locked. Olivia Nugent might feel sorry for her, she might even want Francis to lose, but she was being paid to keep Georgina here, and keep her she would. Terribly disappointed, Georgina crept to the plush loveseat that stood in front of a heavily draped window, and sank down on it. With her head in her hands, she nearly gave up to despair. But she caught herself up and chided, *Georgina, you must get yourself out of here. No one's going to do it for you.*

The door was locked. That left the window. Georgina pulled the silken cord that opened the purple velvet drapes. The window was shuttered from the outside, and nothing she did would open it. Georgina did not know if she were on the ground floor or tucked high above, under the chimneypots.

When would Olivia return? Perhaps not until morning. Yet surely she would be given food. The thought of it made her stomach rebel, but Georgina realized that it might be the only way she could escape. If someone brought her food, perhaps she could get out of the door when it was opened.

Georgina knew her chances were slim; but her Papa had taught her that people can rise to superhuman feats when they are in desperate straits, and desperate she certainly was. She found the bellpull which was a narrow band of tapestry with a gilt tassel on the end, and pulled it firmly. In a few minutes she heard the rattle of a key in the lock, and the door opened just wide enough for a mobcapped head to pop in.

"You rang?"

"Would it be possible for me to have something light to eat? Perhaps some hot broth and a cup of tea."

"I'll see, miss." And the door was locked again.

Now Georgina had to plan quickly and carefully. She tucked the long bolster under the bedclothes and partially pulled the curtains. At a quick glance it appeared that she'd climbed back into bed. Then Georgina put on her cloak, found her satin pocket with its tiny hoard of coins hanging in the back of the wardrobe and tied it under her skirt. Georgina was now ready for flight. She pressed herself against the wall beside the door and waited. She had almost given up, thinking that the maid had been ordered not to feed her, when she once again heard the key grate in the lock. The next moments were crucial. Unless the maid left the key in the door, Georgina's escape was impossible.

The maid opened the door with one hand, balancing a tray on the other, and did what Georgina prayed she'd do. She peered at the bed, said, "Miss?" and walked toward the bogus figure under the covers. Georgina waited as long as she dared, until the maid was nearly to the bed, before she slid out of the door and pulled it shut, finding the key still there, and locking it. Then she fled, seeing a staircase at the end of the hall. Georgina could hear the maid call out and pound the door.

Georgina found the servants' staircase and flew down, hoping that she'd meet no one. Soon she was looking down into the cavernous kitchen. The fat cook was stirring a huge black kettle which hung over the fire. No one else was in sight. Quietly she crept down the stairs, heading for the kitchen door. She had her hand on the knob when a harsh voice said, "Just a minute! Who are you?" but Georgina didn't pause to answer. She jerked open the door and fled into the narrow, malodorous passageway beside the house. Georgina had no idea where she was, nor which way she should go; her only thought was to get as far away from the house as possible.

Soon she came to a cobbled street, poorly lit. Up ahead Georgina could see the lamplighter reaching his pole to light the flat pan of oil above his head. She stumbled along toward him. There were a few people about, and one rude follow caught at her cloak, but she snatched it away from him and hurried after the lamplighter.

Catching up with him, Georgina gasped, "Sir, please help me. I must get to St. Martin-le-Grand. Is it near?"

For a moment she thought he would ignore her. He muttered, "Young bloods think it's great sport to put out my lamps!" Then he did acknowledge her. "It's too far to walk, miss."

"I must get there quickly," Georgina cried.

"Well, if you've fare for a hackney."

She didn't know what a coach would cost, but Georgina knew she'd use all her money, if necessary, to get to the coaching station in a hurry.

"I can pay."

"Then come along with me to the next lamp. There's usually a cabby at the beer shop there."

Georgina stayed as close to him as she dared, even though he smelled as if he'd never had a bath in his life. At least he had his lamplighters' pole as a weapon against ruffians. There was no hackney at the corner, but there was a sedan chair with the bearers leaned against it, napping.

"Here, wake up!" he said, shaking them rudely. "You have a fare." He turned to her almost kindly. "You have a coach to catch, miss?"

"Yes. Yes—the coach to Exeter."

To her surprise one of the bearers, a youngish fellow with a cast in one eye, said, "Coach leaves at six, miss. You've lots of time."

That meant that Charles should be there. Georgina almost collapsed into the narrow confines of the sedan chair, and pulled closed the curtains so that no one could see her. She was jounced about for what seemed ages, then finally the chair was set down and the young bearer opened the door.

"Coaching office right here, miss."

Fortunately the fare didn't quite deplete her money. She picked her way toward the inn with its galleries running under steep little gables reaching a height of four stories. Even at this early hour passengers gathered around the coaches in the yard, ready for their long, tiresome journeys.

Then, out of the gloom, Georgina saw the tall silhouette she knew so well, and called out, "Charles!" He stopped short, turned, and then ran to her, catching her in a breathtaking embrace, not minding that people were watching them.

"Georgina! What are you doing here in London?"

In a torrent of words, Georgina told him what had happened. She felt his muscles tense as she described Francis's perfidy.

"We have to get to Trindale ahead of Francis, or you have lost your inheritance, Charles."

"It will be the fastest trip ever from London to Exeter."

"I've no luggage, no money, no clothing—"

"Don't worry. Robin is riding guard, and he'll share the seat with you again. Once we find the proof that makes me the Fifth Earl of Margate, you'll have all the gowns and everything you could ever want!"

Georgina wished that Charles had mentioned marriage, but she was going to take him on any terms. If he wished her to be his mistress, she would say yes, she was so in love with him. If she could be Francis's lover-in-residence, surely she could be Charles's. It all hinged, though, on getting to Trindale before Francis did.

Just then Robin Adair called, "Coachey! The team is hitched, and the ostlers await you. The passengers are aboard, and—" His eyes fell on Georgina, and his face was comical to behold. "Miss Ryerston!"

"She's riding with us again, Robin, and we're breaking all records this trip. For there's proof of my claim to Hellingham in Trindale, and I mean to get there before Francis Hardy. Come, Georgina." He held out his hand for her, and she put hers in it willingly.

Georgina had made that first journey in cold, rainy February. Now it was summer, and all England was in bloom, with the sun across the land. It still rained occasionally and the roads were often muddy and rough, but it was midsummer and she was in love. Georgina felt she couldn't be happier.

Once ensconced on the high box seat between her beloved Charles and Robin, they were off. Robin must have passed the word that this was to be a race. As he trumpeted their leaving the yard of The Bull and

Mouth, a cheer went up from the passengers and on-lookers alike. Georgina glimpsed the mighty dome of St. Paul's Cathedral as they pulled out into St. Martin-le-Grand. Her first time in London, except for passing through a few of its streets when she and Francis went to Kent, and all she'd seen of the city was a bedroom in a brothel! Yet, much as she would have liked to see the marvels of London, Georgina wanted to get out of the city and onto the open road as fast as possible. Only in this way could they possibly catch up with Francis and Amesford.

"What was Francis driving?" Charles asked.

"I don't know. By the time they put me into the carriage, I was nearly unconscious." She remembered thinking of the gypsy woman's warning about a coach. "It was a closed coach, one of the smaller ones, perhaps a landaulet."

"They may have stopped off at Hellingham for a curricle," Adair suggested. "With only the two of them, they can take a lighter carriage, make better time."

Her high spirits began to drop. How could this heavily laden stagecoach, with its full quota of inside passengers, and seven or eight outsiders, plus cases, hope to catch Francis?

CHAPTER 32

If Georgina thought the trip from Exeter was long and tiring, this was worse by far. Charles intended to make fifty miles a day, no matter if he had to travel until midnight to do so. The first morning, all of the passengers were excited at the prospects of such a rapid journey; but as the afternoon wore on, and they began to tire, tempers rose and complaints became louder and more frequent. They raced past Hellingham, not even pausing long enough to find out if Francis was ahead of them, or if he had stopped there for a rest.

Charles drove as if possessed, becoming more and more reckless as the twilight began to fall. He had rushed them through their dinner at The Three Horseshoes in Bagshot, and except for brief staging stops, they drove until long after dark, staying at The Boar's Head in Basinstoke. Charles fretted that they weren't making good enough time, although he'd kept his whip cracking the entire day. Facing forward, a grim set to his mouth, he'd scarcely spoken to Georgina. Robin tried to be cheerful, but even he began to tense when Charles careened around other coaches, risking a lost wheel or a broken axle. As afraid as she truly was on occasion, she couldn't bring herself to say anything, for Georgina knew that St. Edmund's parish records were his last hope. If Francis got there ahead of them, he'd remain Earl of Margate, while Charles would still be Charles Collins, a coachey on the Exeter to London stage.

Charles did sup with her in a private parlor at The Boar's Head, an extravagance which Georgina protested, although she had to admit that it was much pleasanter than eating at ten at night in the noisy taproom. The landlord, not expecting the Exeter stage until the next day, was hard-pressed to find accommodations for all of them. He told Georgina that she'd be sharing with two ladies in from Newbury, but she was so weary, she'd have roomed with old Moll Bailey, herself, without demur. Charles did not suggest that she spend the night with him, for only group accommodations were available. It was unheard of for a lowly coachey to engage a private room for himself while on a coaching run.

While Georgina relaxed in the parlor, sipping a glass of claret, she asked, fearfully, "Any word of Francis?"

At first she thought Charles hadn't heard. Then, seeing the scowl on his handsome face, Georgina was sorry she'd asked. He got up, threw a small chunk of apple wood on the fire, and waited until it was blazing nicely before he answered.

"He and Amesford staged here and ate supper about six. One of the ostlers remembered them, because Francis paid him a shilling to mend a cracked wheel spoke in a hurry. They're in a curricle. The lad said the pair of bays were ready to drop in the harness, they'd been driven so hard." He kicked at the brass andiron. "Francis always was hard on horses."

"They're not staying here?" Georgina was horrified at an immediate confrontation.

"No, no, they left as soon as the wheel was mended. Told the boy they might make it to Salisbury before they stopped for the night."

"Salisbury? Oh, Charles, we'll never catch them."

He dropped to one knee beside her and caught her hand in his. For the first time that day, she saw his marvelous smile. "Don't worry, dear Georgina, we'll catch him. One thing's in our favor. Francis doesn't know we're on his trail. And I know Amesford. He'll get tired of such an arduous journey, insist on stopping at every inn for a glass of wine."

"I wonder what Francis will say to Mr. Owens? He was taking me along to smooth his path with the vicar at St. Edmund's. He was to introduce me as his future wife and say we needed to search the old records for our bloodlines."

Charles looked deeply into her eyes. "Would you have done it? Would you have married Francis if he asked?"

Georgina wanted to say no. But in truth it was something she once hoped for. Finally she said, "Charles, you know what Francis can be like. I'm terrified of him. When I tried to warn you, he packed me off to Moll Bailey."

"I'll see him dead and in hell for that!"

"Charles, you mustn't say such a thing!"

"He takes you to the most notorious brothel keeper in all England and I'm to sit by quietly with folded hands?"

"Nothing happened to me—and you're with me now."

He caught her to him, murmuring, "You are mine —and thank God you escaped before being pawed by half the men in London. It was bad enough to know that you were lying with Francis." He groaned. "Oh, Georgina, how could you have done that to me?"

It was too much for her. The experiences of the past two days had been so horrible, and she was so tired, that Georgina, dissolved in tears. She couldn't explain why she had taken Francis for a lover. True, the first time he had forced her, yet she had enjoyed his sensuous lovemaking. It would be a lie to say otherwise; Charles knew this all too well. Now she sobbed bitterly.

Charles held her in his arms, caressing her, murmuring to her that he loved her. Soon Georgina felt the swell of passion which closeness to him always created. His lips sought hers, and her response was almost overwhelming. It had been too long since she'd been in his arms. There was no fire in the fireplace, there was no bearskin rug, but Georgina didn't care. Once their clothes were cast aside on the worn carpet, she and Charles lay on the floor, unaware of anything except each other. His hands caressed her breasts, rousing her to extraordinary heights. With frantic urgency, she opened her thighs to him, moaning as he entered her. Their lovemaking had a wildness, a kind of desperation, which Georgina had never experienced before, even with Charles. The rhythm of their response quickened and she was conscious of nothing except the exquisite sensations of her body as she matched Charles's ardent passion with her own. Afterward she clung to him, enjoying each blessed, peaceful moment. All she knew was that she loved him desperately.

"I shall win!" he murmured in her ear. "I shall win. I'll be the Earl of Margate, not Francis. I'll own Hellingham."

"Charles, I don't care whether you are the earl or the best coachey on the stage run between London and Exeter," she told him, caressing him, smoothing his red hair from his face, loving him.

They didn't stay much longer in the parlor, as Charles wanted to be on the road again next day by six. They dressed quickly, and Charles caught Georgina to him in one last passionate embrace, then he let her go to her crowded little room where she found she was relegated to the trundlebed. The two ladies from Newbury had taken the bed. She didn't care. After her blissful interlude with Charles, nothing mattered. Georgina slipped off her gown and shoes and fell into bed in her petticoats, as she had no other clothing with her.

Next day they were making splendid time, racing along the plain with the spire of Salisbury Cathedral a beckoning finger, when disaster struck. A farmer driving a flock of sheep to market was in the road, filling it from one side to the other. Charles shouted at him, and Robin blew blasts on his trumpet, to no avail. The man, linen smock dirty and tattered, boots muddy almost to the knee, turned and shook his crook at them, then turned back, making no effort to get his sheep out of the way of the stagecoach.

"Get around him, Charlie, lad!" an outsider encouraged.

Georgina could see Charles chaffing. The road was very narrow here, with a high hedgerow on one side, a deep ditch on the other. Again Robin blew his trumpet. As before, the shepherd ignored him.

One of the outside passengers was a young lad, not more than fifteen, off to Exeter to work in the woolen mills.

"Let me drop off, coachey," he said. "Raised on a sheep farm, I was, on the Kent downs. I'll move the beasties."

"Watch yon shepherd," another man cautioned. "That crook's a wicked weapon; and he looks like a mean 'un."

Without actually waiting for Charles to agree, the lad slid down from the roof of the coach. He ran ahead and began to force the flock to one side, to the ire of the shepherd. Charles, seeing the way open before him, whipped up the team of four, moving right into the bleating flock. They were almost through when one lamb, separated from its mother, made a little leap ahead, right into the path of the wheel horse.

Although it got only a light, glancing blow from the horse's hoof, the irate shepherd came screaming up to the coach, pouring abuse on Charles.

"I'll have the law on ye!" he yelled. "I've as much right to this road as a bloody stagecoach."

He caught at the harness of the lead bay, hauling it almost to a stop. Now it was Charles's turn to be angry. He pulled a penny from his own private money pouch and tossed it to the man, saying, "Here's pay for the bruised lamb."

The man left off holding the harness, eager to catch the penny, but as he turned to pick it up from the mud, his crook caught the horse a sharp blow across the flanks, causing it to rear. Then it lunged forward. The team, out of control, followed the lead of this horse. Not all of Charles's skill could save them. They wound up with one back wheel in the ditch, the coach mired in the mud almost to the axle.

"Lucky the axle didn't break," Robin said, but Charles was furious at the delay. The coach was stuck so badly that Robin had to climb down, get the mounting stairs, and empty the coach of all the passengers, both inside and out. There was a lot of grumbling about muddy boots, but not until the coach was lightened could it be gotten out of the ditch.

By this time the flock was long gone, the shepherd richer by his penny, while Georgina and Charles were in an agony of impatience. She knew that each minute meant that Francis was nearer to Trindale, and success.

Finally Charles managed to get the coach back on the road, and a quick inspection by Robin proved it to be safe for continuing the journey. However, the enthusiasm originally held by the passengers for a record-breaking trip was now tempered with caution. "Better to get there whole and a day later," being the expressed opinion of the group.

Charles still forced the team, determined to make up the lost hour on the relatively smooth roads of the Salisbury Plain. They had dinner well past noon at The Red Lion in Salisbury, with no time to admire the great cathedral by daylight, and no chance for Charles and Georgina to dine alone at The Fallen Angel. He kept rushing the serving girls, until even the passengers rebelled, wanting time to chew the game pie instead of swallowing it whole.

"Any word of Francis?" Georgina asked fearfully.

"Spent the night right here at The Red Lion."

Her spirits plummeted to her slippers. "Then they're hours ahead of us."

"It's not as bad as it sounds, Georgina. Remember I told you that Amesford would begin to tire? According to that buxom serving wench," pointing to a red-haired girl who was carrying four pewter mugs of ale to part of their group, "the two of them sat up until midnight, drinking. Francis was up early, but Amesford refused to leave his bed until nine. Finally Francis threatened to go on alone, so the marquis, with great reluctance, breakfasted and they left just before ten."

Nearly three hours' lead. Georgina was sure Charles was trying to keep up her spirits, but she feared defeat. Francis, when determined, was fully as stubborn as his half brother.

"All aboard the Exeter coach!" Charles called the moment they had bolted their dinner. There was general grumbling, but Robin reminded the passengers that they'd save money by staying at fewer inns for the night. This brightened their spirits again, and once more the passengers were behind Charles as they raced toward Shaftesbury.

"Sherborne tonight!" Charles called, and the outside passengers echoed the cry.

By now Georgina was so tired that she thought she couldn't ride another mile, let alone all those long, rough miles to Sherborne. The road should have been familiar; but it was a blur, village after village of thatched cottages merging in her mind, a series of village greens monotonous in their sameness, a parade of squat Norman churches an endless litany of saints. The earlier enthusiasm began to wane as the road roughened. The outside passengers were in danger of being jolted off the roof, while those inside opened the door each time they changed horses, to get fresh air into the horrid, crowded box in which they were being jostled black and blue. At Shaftesbury, the passengers rebelled, demanding supper, for it was dark and the road was endless.

"We have to push on," Charles insisted.

Finally Georgina spoke up, timidly; she knew she must. "We all need the rest, Charles. If we sup here, we can travel later and spend the night in Sherborne."

It didn't work quite as she'd suggested to Charles. The taproom of The Castle and Falcon was so comfortable after so many weary hours of coaching, that the passengers dawdled over their supper, calling for more ale and cheese while Charles grew more angry.

"Francis didn't even pause here to dine," he muttered to her, glaring at his rebellious passengers. "Ordered up a basket of food and wine while they changed horses, paid extra for the service, hauled Amesford out of the taproom almost bodily, and pressed on."

"Maybe the Reverend Mr. Owens won't let Francis see the records," Georgina suggested, knowing even as she said it that he would. He'd be impressed with the Margate coat of arms on the body of the curricle, and with the money Francis would so cleverly offer him for charity. Not a blatant bribe. Francis was much too clever for that, dangerously so.

Charles, knowing Francis far better than she did, just looked at her until Georgina dropped her eyes, her cheeks hot with embarrasment.

Finally, with much groaning, Charles got the coach loaded. It was full dark, now, so late even the long twilight had been swallowed by night. There was a moon in a blessedly clear sky, a great orange circle showing the road ahead. Unfortunately it also made shadows from the hedgerows and trees, and was poor lighting for the potholes. They jolted along, not able to keep up the breakneck speed at which Charles had driven all day. Hours later, when they limped into Sherborne, Georgina couldn't get down from the seat. When Charles lifted her to the ground, her feet were so numb that she couldn't feel the cobbles of the courtyard. She seemed fated to see Sherborne only after dark, almost dead with fatigue. Georgina knew they'd stayed at The Unicorn and Maiden on the trip to Hellingham, but by now the building was just one more inn. Clinging to Charles, she was trying to force her aching legs to carry her across the courtyard to the darkened inn, when Charles stopped her with an oath.

"What's wrong? Charles, I'm so tired I don't know if I can climb to the bedchamber. Will they have beds for us at such a late hour?"

"Not here. I can't let you go inside."

"That's not a very funny joke, Charles."

"See that curricle over in the corner of the yard?"

"Just the outline."

"It's the Hardy curricle! I'm sure of it!"

Charles turned in the darkness and called, "Robin?"

Adair came from the coach where he'd been getting down a small case for one of the passengers.

"Be a good fellow and see if that curricle over there has the Margate crest on the door."

Robin took one of the lanterns from the stagecoach, then crossed the cobbles to the carriage. Back in moments, he asked, "A great black falcon on a field of blue?"

"It's Francis, then, spending the night here." He let out a shout of boisterous laughter. "We've caught up with him, Georgina! We can beat him yet. But I can't let you go inside The Unicorn and Maiden. If he sees you, he'll know he's undone."

"What do you expect me to do? Sleep in the coach, or bed down with the horses in the stables?" She was near tears.

By now the landlord, alerted that a stage was in at this unlikely hour, had lamps going inside. Georgina was sure she could smell the pungent odor of mulled wine, and her body ached for the comfort of the fire he'd be blowing to life with the bellows, for the night air was damp.

"There's another inn nearby, off the main highway. The Plough. I'll get you a room there."

The days since Francis had found her father's letter to Peter Hardy had been a constant strain on Georgina. Now this mad dash of a journey to Trindale, with the final blow that she must go elsewhere to sleep when she was too tired to put one foot in front of another, was too much. She was far too exhausted to think clearly.

"I will not do it."

"But Georgina, you must. If he sees you—"

"He'll see *you!* Unless he's deaf and blind, he'll see the stage. Francis isn't stupid, you know. He'll hear all of the serving girls greeting Charlie!" Georgina sounded like a jealous fishwife, but she didn't care. Her body was bruised from jolting over these execrable roads at a rate of speed unbelievable. The horses only had to make it to the next staging post, but she had to endure mile after dreary mile. Now, weary to death, Georgina burst into tears.

"I cannot walk to another inn," she wept.

"No need." Without any warning, he picked her up, cradling her as he would a child. "I'll carry you to The Plough."

It seemed Georgina had scarcely gotten to sleep in the little room under the sagging slate roof of The Plough when someone was shaking her shoulder, whispering, "Get up, miss. Your coachey's here for you."

Creeping out of the bed which she'd shared with a mother and her child, Georgina pulled on her dress and splashed water from the pottery pitcher into the basin, bathing her face, wondering what the hour was. In order not to disturb the other sleepers, the maid had left the candle outside the room, with the door partially open so that the light kept Georgina from bumping into the plain wooden chair which was, with bed and washstand, the only furniture in the room.

She stumbled downstairs to find the cook just getting the fire started. Charles was there, impatience stamped on his handsome face.

"What time is it?" Georgina mumbled, only half-awake.

"Four-thirty."

"Four-thirty! Charles, have you lost your mind?"

"No, but I may lose my inheritance. I gave one of the ostlers a penny to warn me if Francis left early. He called me at four, to say that the curricle was ready to go."

The maid had hastily brewed a cup of chocolate for Georgina, and she drank it standing in the cold taproom, nibbling on a crust of bread. "I thought you said that Amesford was a late riser." If she sounded cross, it was because she was cross. "Does he know you're driving the stage?" she added, swallowing the chocolate too fast, and almost choking.

"I don't know. All I know is that we have to be on the road as fast as possible."

"Charles, the other passengers won't get up."

"They're already up and breakfasting." Then he grinned, the volatile Charles Georgina knew so well. "I won't lie to you, Georgina, love. They're not happy —but they're up. I've promised them Exeter for bed tonight."

Georgina finished her breakfast, and Charles settled her bill. As he hurried her along the muddy street, lighting their way with a torch he'd thrust into the ground outside the entrance to The Plough, she asked, "But what are your passengers going to say when they find you've rushed them out of bed in the middle of the night, only to make them wait while you transact private business in Trindale?"

"Ah, yes, that. Well, Georgina, I haven't much choice. I'll have to take the stage on to Exeter. You do understand that. Only an hour more—less, the way we've been going. I thought I could drop you off at the vicarage. Surely the vicar, a man of goodwill, wouldn't mind that. As soon as I get to the booking office in Exeter, I'll get a private carriage, something light and fast, and come back for you."

Georgina stopped dead. "You expect me to confront my cousin alone?" She was appalled. "Charles Collins, you have no heart. You are every bit as bad as your brother." Georgina was close to tears. "You know how Francis treated me. Just what do you expect him to do when he sees me at St. Edmund's when he thinks he has me tucked safely away one hundred fifty miles to the east?"

"Georgina, do you for one minute think that I'd let you go to the vicarage alone if I thought you'd not be safe?"

"For your inheritance, yes." Charles still did not know her suspicions that Francis had turned murderer. She would not tell him these now, dared not, for in her heart Georgina knew that even this knowledge wouldn't stop Charles from asking her to confront Francis.

Charles took her arm, urging her along the narrow street as he exerted his utmost in persuasive powers to win her.

"You're unkind to me this morning. The vicar will be there, Georgina, and his good wife. What would Francis dare to do? Nothing. And if you are there, you can thwart him in his attempt to destroy the record of my legitimacy. You know why he's dashing to Trindale." He paused. "Georgina, it isn't just for me. It's for you, too. You deserve to be mistress of Hellingham, but not with Francis as the earl."

Still he did not mention marriage. Yet how could she be cross with Charles? Just being this close to him drove all reason from her mind. Georgina was one mass of seething emotion. Before she could answer him, though, there was a clatter of hooves and a rattle of wheels on the cobbled street. Out of the gloom ahead of them came racing a familiar curricle, pulled by matched grays. The two figures on the box were only silhouettes in the early dawn, but Georgina knew that Francis and his friend were en route.

Charles pushed her, not gently, into the doorway of a draper's shop, and stood in front of her; but even with that solid protection, some of the mud from the carriage wheels spattered Georgina's gown. Francis drove like one demented, without a thought for those on foot.

Scowling after him, trying to brush the globs of mud from her skirt, she said, "Very well, I'll do it, Charles. I'll help you, even if it means facing Francis alone."

CHAPTER 33

Georgina aproached St. Edmund's fearfully, not knowing what to expect. Although Charles had made incredibly fast time from Sherborne, they had not caught up with Francis. They saw evidence of his passing at the staging inns where the horses he had driven were in a dreadful condition. Even though Charles pushed as hard as he could, he still did not drive the horses beyond the limits of their endurance.

Charles had stopped the coach just within sight of the squat gray stone Norman church which Georgina had known since childhood. "Just letting off a passenger," he said to queries from the outsiders who had grown cross with fatigue. "Exeter next, within the hour. My word on it."

To Georgina, as he lifted her down from the high seat, he whispered, "I'll be back within two. I promise. Try to delay Francis. Enlist the aid of the vicar. He knows you, will listen to you, when you explain what my brother is up to. And above all, don't let him get his hands on those church registers. Knowing Francis, he'll burn them on the spot, then pay off the vicar in gold."

She shivered with fright. "Can't you just come in with me for a moment, Charles?"

"Enough lollygagging there, coachey," one rude fellow called from atop the stage. "On to Exeter!"

"It'll be all right. Nothing can happen to you with the vicar there. I'll be back as fast as a team can bring me, Georgina."

Then he was gone, swinging up into the driver's

seat, taking the reins from Robin, and saluting her with the long coachey's whip he held. A crack of that whip, and the horses leaned into their collars, moving the heavy coach into the road again. The last Georgina saw of it, Robin had just lifted his brass trumpet to his lips, and she heard the notes ring out to warn The Bee and Thistle that the coach was in.

Reluctantly Georgina walked from the road to the lych-gate of the church, going in onto the side porch and entering the sacristy. The verger, old Jonas Philby, was replacing the volumes of the church register, muttering as he worked. Hearing her footsteps, he looked around, peering shortsightedly at her from beneath a ragged fringe of gray hair. When he recognized her, his mouth dropped open, and the volume he was holding fell from his hands to the worn stone floor.

"Miss Georgina! I—it's you, ain't it, miss? Not a ghost?"

Georgina walked quickly to the old man, took his hand, and assured him that it was, indeed, she.

"But I don't rightly understand, miss. The lord who was just here a bit ago—he said he came from you."

Her heart fell. Too late! "Tell me, Jonas, did he find what he was looking for?" The scattered books told her a frightening story.

Old Jonas stood there, shaking his head. "Right mad he were, miss. Terrible angry. Threw the books down and frightened the reverend."

She could well imagine that mild little Mr. Owens would be frightened by an angered Francis Hardy, Lord Margate.

"Said the book must be hidden away—insisted that he hadn't seen all of the years."

Hope peeked cautiously through the gloom, and Georgina asked, "Did my father hide one of the church registers, Jonas? Would you know that, if he did?"

The old man's face twisted as he tried to think.

Jonas was a dear old lamb, but not too heavy with brains. Papa was used to him, and so was she, but Georgina knew that he was slow of wit, particularly when disturbed.

"I don't think so, miss. They were all here. I dusted them sometimes. Clear back into history, your dear father, God rest his soul, used to say to me. Backbone of England, its villages, he'd tell me."

"Yes, I know, Jonas. But the lord who was here. Did he find the book he wanted?"

"No. Mr. Owens showed him they was all in order. None missing. I don't allow anyone in here to steal."

"I know you don't, Jonas. You are a good and faithful servant to the parish." Then Georgina tried to get him back to his account of Francis. "But the Earl of Margate, the lord who was here, didn't find what he wanted?"

"Afraid not, miss. That's when he got angry and threw the books about. Mr. Owens was very distressed. But then the lord, in his fancy coat—looked like silk, it did—stopped being angry and said he was sorry. He gave the church a gold piece. I saw it. And he gave me a penny to pick up the books."

Georgina didn't know whether to be sad or glad. If Francis hadn't found what he was looking for, then it meant that Papa hadn't written the marriage in the register here at St. Edmund's, which made sense, when she thought about it. He had not performed the ceremony here, but at Hellingham. Did that mean the record was there? Impossible. In all these years, Charles would have found it. Georgina was sure he had searched every inch of the place looking for proof of his legitimacy. Perhaps the marriage license which the Fourth Earl had burned was the only written proof of the validity of his marriage to Rebecca Collins. If this were so, then Charles would never prove his claim to the title. In a way she was relieved. If Charles did find proof that the marriage had been legal, it would

mean a terrible battle with Francis for the title and
Hellingham. Everything would be against Charles. He'd
been known too long as Peter Hardy's bastard son,
while Francis was a friend of King George.

"Where is the lord now?" Georgina asked Jonas.
"Has he been gone long from St. Edmund's?"

"From the church, miss? Not too long. I've not
finished putting the books back on the shelves."

Knowing how slowly Jonas moved, that didn't mean
much.

"His carriage isn't out in front of the church," she
mentioned. "But we didn't pass it just now as the stagecoach came from Sherborne."

"You in Sherborne, miss?" The face, brown as leather
and a network of fine wrinkles, twisted as Jonas
thought, an obvious process. "I thought you went some-
ers near London."

"That's right—Staines. But the coach from London
to Exeter passes through Sherborne, Jonas. We spent
the night there."

"At an inn? Inns do be dear, I understand."

"Do you know where Lord Margate went?" she
persisted.

"Lord Margate? Is that the young lord what was
here?"

It was as painful as having a tooth extracted, prying
information from Jonas. "Yes, that was Lord Margate,
my cousin."

This brought a big smile, showing the gaps where
Jonas's teeth had been. "Said he was your cousin. The
vicar welcomed him as he would yourself." Then he
frowned. "But when he got mad and threw the books
about, Mr. Owens was unhappy."

"I'm sure he was. But where did my cousin go,
Jonas?"

"Do you mean in his fine coach? Lovely, it was.
Light. Fine team of grays, too, but turrible sweated,

they was, and blowin' hard. T'other one took 'em off to The Bee and Thistle to change horses."

"Then where's my cousin, if he didn't go along?"

"Went to the vicarage, of course, to get your books."

"My what?"

"Your books, miss. Said he'd deliver 'em to you."

"But I didn't—what books, Jonas?" She knew, though. With an appalling clarity, Georgina realized what he meant.

She heard the rattle of a carriage outside, and the old verger lifted his head to listen. "Must be t'other one now, miss. The lord's friend—is he a lord, too? Dressed up in silks and satin, never saw the like. Squire don't have such fancy clothes."

"I have to run to the vicarage, Jonas." Fear ran through her veins like icewater. The only "books" of hers at the vicarage were the rest of Papa's journals, which Mrs. Owens had agreed to store for her until she could send for them. She'd been too busy to think of it until now. Papa's journals! Could that be where he'd written down the marriage? Yet, if that was it, would it stand in a court of law, an entry in a private diary? That would be for a judge or solicitor to say.

Francis mustn't get his hands on Papa's journals! They were hers, and if there was anything in them about the marriage of Peter Hardy and Rebecca, it was for Charles to read.

Georgina picked up her skirts and ran from the church, leaving poor Jonas open-mouthed. The vicarage, built of the same gray Devon stone as the church, was set back from the road in a lovely garden. A narrow lane led from the main road back to the house, and she could see the curricle standing there with some-one on the box. From here she couldn't tell whether it was Amesford or her cousin.

There was a path through the churchyard which she'd taken so many times that her feet flew along, missing the leaning gravestones, without her even having to look. This path ran along the low stone wall surrounding the churchyard, and there was a gap in the stones leading to the kitchen garden of the vicarage where she'd spent many hours cultivating her herbs, vegetables, and luscious strawberries.

Georgina ran so fast that she got a stitch in her side and had to stop and lean against one of the ancient yews planted in the churchyard, sheltering the graves. After catching her breath, she hurried on, lifting her skirts scandalously high to get through the break in the wall. Then she went around the edge of the garden and came to the door leading into the scullery. As it had always been when she lived here, the door was on the latch. Georgina gave a perfunctory knock, lifted the latch, and went into the slate-floored room which led to the kitchen.

"Mrs. Owens?" she called. Not waiting for an answer, Georgina hurried into the large kitchen where an iron kettle bubbled over the fire. A girl of twelve, the Owens's Marie, was mixing bread in a large wooden bowl. Her eyes grew round when she saw her visitor.

"Is it—Miss Georgina?"

Georgina smiled at the child and nodded. "Where's your mother? I must speak with her privately."

"We've a guest, miss. A lord! Mama let me peek through the pantry door to see him. Oh, what a fine suit he has!"

"I know, I know. But whisper to your mother that I'm here. Don't let the fine lord hear you."

Doubt was on her face, and she pushed a lock of blond hair away from her forehead, leaving a streak of flour in its place. "Mama might be cross with me."

"I'll make sure she isn't. Please, Marie, it's important."

"Very well. If you promise Mama won't scold."

"I promise. Hurry!"

Georgina didn't know what Francis was doing. It was all very well for Charles to tell her to walk right in on him, that he'd not dare do anything to her in front of the vicar, but she didn't trust her cousin.

Marie slipped through the door into the passageway leading to the parlor, while Georgina waited, afraid of what might happen. If the child mentioned her name so that Francis could hear, he'd be in the kitchen so fast they'd think a whirlwind had swept through the ancient house. A plain clock stood on the wooden dresser where Mrs. Owens displayed her few pieces of china, and the ticking reminded Georgina that time was running out for her and for Charles. Where was that child? Had she balked, once out of her sight, afraid to interrupt her mother who was entertaining a lord? Georgina took a step toward the door, then stopped. If she confronted Francis, what would he do?

Then Mrs. Owens, her weary face puzzled, came through into the kitchen.

"Georgina, is it really you? But why didn't you come to the front door? Your cousin's here. . . ." Her voice trailed off uncertainly, and she made a vague gesture toward the front of the house. "Lord Margate. He said—but why did he ask for your books, when you're here?" She frowned, trying to figure it out. "He told me you were in London."

"I was." The bitterness in her voice reached Mrs. Owens, for she looked at Georgina quite sharply with those gray eyes. "My books—Papa's journals. You've not given them to him yet, have you?" Georgina prayed for her to say no.

"He said you wanted them." Her voice rose, accusing. "You hadn't sent for them."

"I know—I'm sorry. I have been busy, and I forgot."

"He said he'd take them to you."

"I know, I know. But there's been a mixup. You couldn't know, Mrs. Owens—I'm not blaming you. But I don't want my cousin to have those books. It's extremely important."

She flushed bright red, indignant. "Well, I've already given them to him. If you don't want him to have them, you'll have to go tell him yourself. I can't say yes to a lord one minute, then say no the next, can I?"

"No, no, of course not." Georgina took a deep breath. There was no alternative. She'd have to face Francis alone. It was too late to try to explain the situation to Mrs. Owens, or to the vicar. Too late to do anything except confront Francis, and try to prevent his carrying off those precious journals. "I'll go talk to Cousin Francis myself."

Mrs. Owen stood aside, to let her go through the door to the passageway, making no move to follow. Georgina was on her own. But she was too late, for she met Mr. Owens hurrying back toward the kitchen.

"Who—Georgina! What a surprise! Your cousin was just here. A fine man—a bit of a hasty temper, but he was very contrite. Made a contribution to St. Edmund's—a very handsome gift, I might add. But I thought he said you were in London."

"I'm here. My cousin—he's gone?" Mr. Owens nodded, his face as puzzled as his wife's had been. "I must catch him!" Georgina brushed past the vicar and ran to the front door, flinging it open and rushing outside. She was too late. The curricle was at the end of the lane, just turning into the London road and traveling at a great rate of speed.

Georgina sank down upon the doorstep, appalled at what she'd done—or hadn't done. If she'd gone right into the parlor, instead of hiding in the kitchen while Marie went to fetch her mother, she might have stopped Francis somehow. Now it was all over, and she'd ruined everything for Charles. What would he say when he got here from Exeter?

Georgina sat there and sobbed, letting all her fears and frustrations build until she thought she could never stop crying. Then she felt a hand on her shoulder.

"Georgina, my child, come inside. Mrs. Owens is brewing tea for us. Have a cup and calm yourself. Then tell us how you happen to be here when we were led to believe you were in London." He helped her up and led her back to the kitchen. "I do hope we've not made a mistake in placing your books, your dear father's journals, into the hands of your cousin. The Earl of Margate." He said it with reverence.

"It's my own fault. I should have come right in and stopped him. But I'm deathly afraid of him," she admitted.

"Afraid of your own cousin?"

Georgina noticed Marie, all round eyes and eager ears. Her mother realized that the child was taking this all in.

"Marie, go out to the Wilson's cottage and see if they have any fresh eggs. And wipe the flour off your face."

"Yes, mother." Marie left reluctantly, knowing she was being sent away so she couldn't hear the story.

When the child was gone and Georgina had been put into a rocking chair by the window and given a cup of tea, Mr. Owens said, "Now, Georgina, what's going on?"

She told him the whole story, beginning with her coach trip to Staines. She carefully omitted the fact that both men had been her lovers; Mr. Owens and his good wife would never understand such a situation. Now that she was back in the vicarage at St. Edmund's Georgina had difficulty understanding it herself. How far she had strayed from her gentle upbringing! She didn't hurry her story, for she knew there was nothing she could do until Charles got back from Exeter. Georgina didn't leave out anything else. She told of the mock marriage of Peter Hardy and Rebecca, her father's part in the shabby affair, everything, including her forcible transportation to Moll Bailey's brothel.

"A brothel! Thank the good Lord I sent Marie out. The fine young man who was here—he took you to such a place?"

"After forcing drugged chocolate on me, Mrs. Owens." The tears came again. "And I was too cowardly to confront him. Now he has Papa's journals, Charles's only hope to prove his legitimacy. What will he say, when he gets here?"

"I shouldn't worry about that, dear," Mrs. Owens said, voice indignant. "Any man who'd leave you to face such a monster as that—that—"

"He had a coachful of passengers for Exeter," Georgina reminded her. "He couldn't ask them to wait, tired as they all were, while he settled private problems here, could he?"

"Mrs. Owens, Georgina is right," the vicar said, siding with her. "A man's job is his responsibility. When others depend on him, he must not shirk."

"But to leave Georgina here to face that man! With his smooth talk and his money for the church." Now she was bitter.

Georgina saw anguish on the vicar's face. "My fault," he said. "When he became enraged in the sacristy, threw the church registers about, I should have realized he was unstable. But I was impressed by his rank, prostituted by the gold he offered." Reluctantly he drew the gold coin from his pocket. "Tainted money. What shall I do with it?"

Georgina's good sense took over. "Use it for St. Edmund's, Mr. Owens. That's what Papa would have done. My cousin's motives were bad, but his money, in itself, isn't good or evil. It's the way you use it that matters." She wiped her eyes with her kerchief, took a deep breath. "Sitting here weeping won't help anything. If I'd just marched into the vicarage and confronted Francis, I'd still have Papa's journals."

Mr. Owens paced the scrubbed boards of the vicarage kitchen floor. "Those journals—somehow, Georgina, I can't see how they could help you. A man's diary is just private writing. If your late father wrote of this marriage in his diary, I don't think it would mean anything in a court of law." He paused, scratched his head, setting his wig askew.

It was a terrible blow to Georgina, who had thought the registers were the answer, and then that it was the journals. She felt faint. Mrs. Owens, noticing how pale she was, caught at the teacup before Georgina let it fall onto the slate floor. Once again Georgina had the strange sensation of leaving her body. She was against the low ceiling of the vicarage kitchen. Below her both of the Owenses hovered over her, Mrs. Owens clucking and waving her apron in Georgina's face, Mr. Owens patting her hand. Then she was somewhere else. As before, she saw the man she now knew to be her father writing in that book. This time Georgina forced her floating body forward in the room, so that she hovered over the man. From where she was, she could see the page on which he wrote. It was the registry in the family Bible. Even as Georgina recognized the page, the young cleric finished writing, blotted it carefully, then closed it firmly. She recognized the binding of the holy book, although it now was much worn with use over many years. It was the Bible she had taken with her to Hellingham, the Bible she had been holding when she had the first of these strange experiences.

As she thought this, Georgina was back in her body, with the vicar and his wife attending to her. There was the sharp odor of sal volatile, and she moved her head away from the vinaigrette which Mrs. Owens held under her nose.

"I'm all right," she murmured: "I'm all right. I—I just felt faint for a moment. All the excitement." Not for a minute would she tell Mr. Owens and his good wife what had happened. The vicar would probably insist on exorcising evil spirits from her. Instead, she said, as if she had just thought of it, "Could Papa have written down the marriage in his Bible? Would that be legal?"

"Yes, the Bible record is accepted. Do you have his Bible with you?"

"Not here. It's back at Hellingham—or I guess it is."

Mrs. Owens smiled, glad the terrible tale had a happy ending. "Then it's simple. You'll just go back, get the Bible, and see if the marriage is recorded in it."

"You've never examined your family Bible?" Georgina thought the vicar spoke reprovingly.

"I have my own Bible which Papa gave me when I was confirmed. I remember that Papa showed me the record of my own birth which he'd written in the large family Bible, and Mama's death. My birth started a new page. I never read the other entries."

"So you don't know whether or not the marriage of the earl and this unfortunate woman is recorded?"

Now Georgina had more to worry about. "I don't know."

Charles, hurry! she pleaded silently. *When Francis reads Papa's journals and doesn't find what he wants, he may search my room at Hellingham and find the Bible. We must get back there at once.*

Yet the thought of that journey frightened her, and the prospects of contronting Francis filled her with dread. Georgina remembered the wag who'd joked about the "coach to hell" that first time she'd seen the gates of Hellingham. Truly, that was what the home of Francis Hardy, Fifth Earl of Margate, seemed to be. Hell, itself. But she must be brave and go back, or all hope for Charles was lost.

CHAPTER 34

Charles drove with consummate skill. If Georgina thought they'd flown over the road in the stagecoach, it was mere plodding compared to their journey in the light carriage he'd hired in Exeter. Yet they did not catch up with Francis, who drove as if possessed.

When Charles came to the vicarage, Georgina admitted that she had bungled everything. There was one moment when she thought he would blame her, but then he gave that light-hearted laugh and vowed, "We're not done in yet by my half brother. He'll never think of looking in your Bible, Georgina. Francis's mind doesn't run to religion."

With the blessings of the vicar and his wife, they set off for Hellingham, Georgina's weariness gone at the prospect of success. Charles thought they might even pass Francis at some inn where he and Amesford stopped to rest.

"He may decide to read the journals en route, Georgina. Stop at a cozy inn, hire a private parlor, and try to find the entry he hopes is there."

Somehow she didn't think so. No, Francis had the bit between his teeth. Hellingham represented so much to him, it was the visible symbol of his station in life, that Georgina felt he'd want to return there now. He'd leave the books packed in their cases until he could read them in the comfort and security of his study. Hellingham was where it had started, and Hellingham was where it would end.

The journey was a blur. Village merged into village, the brief stops to change horses were all alike, Charles drove long after dark, until it became dangerous and foolish to continue, before they found an inn for a few hours of rest. She fell into bed with other travelers, not even knowing who they were, nor caring. There was no question of sharing a bed with Charles. They both were far too exhausted for anything but the merciful oblivion of sleep.

Francis was always just ahead of them. They got news of him from ostlers and stable boys, from landlords and serving wenches, but they couldn't reduce his lead.

"Never mind, my dear, we'll get to Hellingham in time," Charles assured her. "All we need is your family Bible. Francis is welcome to the journals." Then, realizing how this must sound, he apologized profusely. "I'm so tired, I'm not thinking straight, Georgina. Of course we shall get your father's journals back from Francis. They are yours. He has no more right to them than he has to the title he flaunts, and to Hellingham."

When Charles talked that way, Georgina was convinced that they were destined to succeed; but in the long, silent stretches between villages, when the roads were bad and Charles had to concentrate on driving to make time without tipping them over in the ditch or breaking an axle, Georgina had many moments when she despaired. They were only guessing. The strange vision she'd had might mean nothing. Papa might not have written the marriage in the Bible at all. Maybe, when he wrote that final letter to his cousin, Peter, his mind was already clouded by the opiates he was taking. Perhaps when he told her he'd written it down, he was only crying out in his delirium, his mind filled with pain and drug-induced hallucinations and fantasies.

Yet, whenever Charles seemed to doubt their eventual success, Georgina tried to hide her own misgivings in order to bolster his flagging hopes.

"I'm sure we'll reach Hellingham ahead of Francis."

"How can we fail, my dear Georgina? For I am the finest coachey on the London to Exeter road."

"Modesty is not one of your faults, sir."

"I have never been retiring by nature. You have to fight for what you want in this life, Georgina. Sitting back, meek and mild, is not my way."

Georgina loved him just as he was. If they succeeded, if he was able to prove that he was the true heir to the title, she would be happy for him; but if it was all a will-o'-the-wisp they followed, if Francis remained Earl of Margate, then she would be happy with plain Charles Collins.

They drove into Staines after dark, and like the first time she'd come here, it was raining. The gig was open, so both of them were drenched, but it took more than a summer shower to dampen Charles's high spirits.

"Almost there, my love. We'll slip into Hellingham, get the Bible from your room, and then go to Ye Grape for late supper and bed." He touched her cheek gently, his intent naked in his eyes. "Until I have that Bible in the hands of Sir Barnaby Kane, I won't rest comfortably. I might even drive on to London tonight, after we have some time together, to make sure Kane gets the Bible at once."

They rattled through the muddy streets and then were once again on the open road with Hellingham only minutes away.

"How shall we get in through the gates, Charles? I don't think that Francis would welcome us if we drove up to the gatekeeper and demanded admission." Tired as Georgina was, just thinking about this made her laugh nervously.

"Ah, but there's a little door in the wall."

"But it's kept locked from the inside."

"And I just happened to keep a key when my brother invited me to leave Hellingham. How do you think I got in to the masked ball? I haven't wings to fly over the wall."

Jesting, yet a tiny bit in earnest, Georgina said, "I thought one of the maids, stricken with love for you, unlocked the door and let you in."

"Ah, jealous, Georgina?" He laughed uproariously.

The time for laughing was soon over. The gates of Hellingham loomed dark in the rain, but Charles drove on past, not even pausing. "We'll leave the carriage at the inn. The horses are tired and deserve a rest. I know you are exhausted, too, my dear Georgina, but I dare not take you into Ye Grape even for a cup of hot wine, until after we've breached the walls of Hellingham. The landlord is my friend, but there could be others there who owe their livelihood to the false earl. I wouldn't want him to be expecting you."

"Nor I. If I never see my cousin again, I shall be very happy."

He arranged for the ostlers at the inn to care for the horses, then he hurried her along the road to the little door in the wall. He carried his coachey's whip with him, "just as a bit of protection, love." From one of the deep pockets in his greatcoat, Charles produced a brass key which opened the gate. Inside, he picked a way through the gardens with the ease of long practice.

The house loomed huge and black in the rain. There were lights in some of the windows, and Georgina wondered where Francis and Amesford were.

Then Charles checked her advance, his arm tightening about her. "There's a light in your room, Georgina."

"Perhaps it's Lizzie—unless Francis dismissed her after forcing her to drug me for that horrid trip to London."

"We'll hire her back as soon as I possess Hellingham," he promised. "The mistress of the house must have her abigail."

Mistress of Hellingham—never once did he call her his countess. "Will I have to keep on Mrs. Pruning and Miss Twistle, Charles? They have been my enemies from the start."

"Once I'm earl, my first act will be to dismiss them."

Georgina whispered, "I'm frightened. Let's give it up. Go to Sir Barnaby, tell him about the Bible, let him make arrangements for getting it from Francis. If we go inside, and Francis finds us, I don't know what he'll do. He might kill us both and claim he thought we were intruders."

"I'm hard to kill, Georgina. But if you wish, I'll take you back to Ye Grape and come here alone. Just tell me where the Bible is to be found, what it looks like."

The resolve in his voice strengthened her own. "No, I'll come with you. It's my Bible. And it's my cousin who is trying to cheat you of your inheritance." She didn't add that it was her own dear dead Papa who had been a part of the fraudulent marriage in the beginning, but it was true, and Georgina had an obligation to Charles to help him. Finally, she loved Charles with all her heart. If she waited at Ye Grape while he burglarized Hellingham, Georgina would die of fear for his safety.

They moved on to the dark, wet brick walls which towered over them. Again Charles produced a key which opened the side door, and they slipped into the house. Now it was going to be a question of luck. If any of the servants saw them, if Mrs. Pruning got wind of their arrival, all was lost.

For a man as large as he was, Charles moved as silently as a cat, peering around each corner before they showed themselves, making sure that no one was around. There was little light in the great hall, a few candles on candlestands only deepening the gloom.

"Maybe Francis isn't here yet," Georgina whispered.

"I'd guess he is. We'd have seen him en route. I looked at each inn we passed, but he was always ahead of us. We can be out of here before he knows we're around."

Slowly they crept up the main staircase and moved through the long gallery, two ghosts joining other ghosts from the past. They traversed it safely, and then they were in the passageway leading to Georgina's room.

Even from the end of the corridor, she could see the line of light under the door. "Someone's in there, Charles." She was very nervous. "What are we going to do?"

She saw mischief glitter in his eyes. "Trick them, Georgina." He tried the door next to her room, found it unlocked, and the room unoccupied.

"Inside, Georgina. Leave the door open for me."

Then he crept along the passage and tapped at her bedchamber door with his long coaching whip, darting back inside the room with her only an instant before her door swung open and Francis's valet, Isher, poked his head out. Seeing no one, he moved back into her room, and left the door open. When Charles moved to try the tapping trick again, she whispered frantically, "He'll see you."

"Trust me, Georgina."

He was extra nimble this time after tapping sharply on the door jamb with the whip held at arm's length, but Isher almost caught him. Georgina held her breath for fear the valet would see the crack in the door through which they peeked.

For a second time Isher went back inside; but he came out again almost immediately, candle in hand, with the last of the journals tucked under his arm, the only one Georgina had brought with her from Trindale. He was nervous, for he kept peering back over his shoulder as he hurried away. Georgina was so indignant that she almost protested aloud, but Charles sensed her emotion and clapped a hand over her mouth to keep her silent. They waited, tension mounting, until Isher's elongated shadow melted into the dark at the end of the passage before they slipped into her room.

"He has no right to that journal!"

"Softly, softly, Georgina. Where's a candle?"

There was no fire laid, so her room was chill and dark. Georgina groped her way to the stand beside the canopied bed and found a candle which she lighted. "He didn't get the Bible, did he?" Charles asked.

She knew Isher had carried only one volume, so Georgina moved to the small French desk where she had kept both books. It was empty. "It should be here."

Charles took the candle from her and lighted a second one which stood on the chimneypiece. With this added light, they now could see that the room had been searched. Drawers to her chest stood open, with her intimate garments hanging from them, and her desk was a jumble.

"I'd say, Georgina, that someone put your books away for safekeeping, and Isher was searching for them."

Then it all came back to Georgina. The last time she'd seen the journal and the Bible, she had that strange seizure. Later, when Lizzie asked if Georgina wanted them left on the desk, she'd begged the abigail to store them out of sight.

"Lizzie put them away somewhere, Charles. I don't know where. I didn't want to see them right then."

"Obviously Isher found them as we saw he had the journal. That means that Francis is back—and has probably not found what he's looking for in the earlier journals. No doubt he realized from the dates that there might be one more. Mrs. Owens might have told him you took one with you when you came here."

"Surely she didn't mention my Bible to him."

"We can't take any chances, Georgina. We have to find that Bible ourselves. If only we knew where Isher found the journal—the two books were kept together?"

"Yes, but on the desk. When Lizzie put them away, she might not have left them together."

They divided up the room to save time, with Charles going through her desk, while Georgina tackled the chest. It was she who finally found the Bible, just as she despaired of success. She had opened the large wardrobe, standing on tiptoe to see if it was on the shelf. There it lay, just above her normal line of sight.

"Charles, it's here!"

He was beside her in two strides, reaching up to take the precious volume from the shelf. He'd tossed his whip on her bed when they'd begun their search. Now, his hands free, he leafed through the first pages of the Bible, looking for the family register.

"It's there, Charles." He had turned to the page on which her birth was recorded as the first item. "It would be on an earlier page."

He leafed backward through the pages, checking dates, and then they both saw it, at the same instant. There, in her father's hand, was written: *Married on this day my cousin, Peter Hardy, to Rebecca Collins, at Hellingham.* And the date.

"He didn't use your father's title," Georgina whispered. "Will it be legal?"

"He says his cousin, Peter Hardy. And he specifies Hellingham. I'm sure Sir Barnaby Kane will be able to use this Bible to prove my right to the earldom," Charles said confidently.

"Somehow, dear brother, I think Sir Barnaby will never see that Bible," came a voice from the doorway.

CHAPTER 35

Francis stood in the doorway to Georgina's room, a sardonic smile on his face, and a wicked-looking pistol in his hand. The pistol pointed at Charles. Behind Francis, holding high a lighted candelabra, was his friend, Howard Dubonnet, Marquis of Amesford.

"I've been expecting you," Francis said, his voice languid but his eyes alert, "and when Isher told me of ghostly tappings, I knew you had arrived." His grin was evil. "There was a message for me when I returned tonight, a note from a London friend, Moll Bailey." His laugh chilled Georgina. "She said you left without thanking her for her hospitality, sweet coz." He clicked his tongue, shaking his head at her in mock reproof. "What shocking bad manners, cousin dear." Then he said, "A pretty pair of rogues, aren't they, Amesford?" Georgina could see that the marquis was enjoying every moment of their discomfit. "Shall I shoot them—caught red-handed—as though they were burglars?"

Amesford snickered, and Francis smiled that frightening smile which Georgina knew so well.

"Killing me with that pistol will buy you a one-way passage to Tyburn, Francis," Charles said, his voice as calm as if he were at some drawing room soiree.

Imperceptibly Charles edged away from Georgina, all the while chatting with his brother. Francis, knowing he had them trapped, just stood there, smiling that terrible smile. Although he appeared relaxed, Georgina noticed that the pistol never wavered from its aim at Charles's heart. When Charles moved, so did that black, lethal eye.

"He's up to something, Francis," Amesford warned. "Better shoot him."

"And bring all the servants running? Francis is much too clever for that," Charles jibed. "Murder's murder—it wins you a hempen neckcloth on the Tyburn gallows, remember."

Georgina could see Francis's eyes narrow. If he thought he could get away with killing Charles, he'd do it. A cold terror froze her there, unmoving. If he killed Charles, then she was a witness to murder, and Francis would not allow a witness to live. Within moments, they both might be dead.

The fear for Charles gave her courage to cry, "Give him the Bible, Charles. What good will it do you when you are dead?"

Francis nodded. "Well said, little cousin. She's quite right about it, Charles. Give me the Bible, and you escape with your life. No title, no Hellingham, but you'll be free to drive the stage back and forth from London to Exeter until you grow too old to manage the horses. You've always excelled in handling horses. I'll be the first to admit you do it even better than I." Then he laughed, an ugly sound, which made Georgina even more afraid. She knew that even though Charles should surrender the Bible, he'd not live to tell anyone of it. She opened her mouth to cry out a warning, but before she could form the words, Charles acted.

"Catch, Francis," he cried, tossing the Bible underhanded to his half brother, and simultaneously lunging past Georgina, knocking her to the floor while he threw himself onto the bed.

Caught off guard, Francis took his eyes from Charles momentarily as he automatically tried to catch the Bible. In that crucial moment, Charles rolled from Georgina's bed, back onto his feet—but he was no longer unarmed. In his hand was the long coachman's whip.

While Francis fumbled the Bible, dropping it to the floor, Amesford, behind him, cried out, "Careful, Francis!"

Alerted, the new earl took in Charles's position with one flick of his dark eyes, then swung the long-barreled pistol so that it pointed not at her beloved, but at Georgina as she huddled on the floor where Charles had thrown her in a vain effort to protect her.

"One move, Charlie, and I put a bullet through Georgina's lovely forehead," he warned, his voice crisp and cold.

A chill ran down her spine, and she tried to vanish into the wide floorboards. There was madness in her cousin's eyes, a controlled madness more dangerous than any flare of temper. Georgina knew that within minutes she could be dead, a corpse before she'd been a bride.

Charles stood perfectly still, frozen in place, the whip ready. When he spoke, his voice was as calm as before.

"If Georgina dies, so do you, Francis. My word on it."

It was an impasse. She huddled there, almost dead of fright, while these two brothers faced each other in what Georgina knew was a final contest for Hellingham.

"Pick up the Bible, Amesford. And keep that light where it shines on Charlie. I don't trust him." His laugh was high and wild.

Moving with great caution so that he would not get between Francis and Charles, the marquis dropped to one silken knee, holding the candelabra high, while with the other hand he picked up the precious Bible.

"Make sure that entry is in the Bible. Charlie is a tricky one," Francis ordered.

Amesford had to set the candelabra on a candle-stand in order to free his hands to leaf through the Bible. Georgina could hear the rustle of the pages, and she knew that if neither of them did anything, they'd both soon be dead. Her fear left, consumed by a rage that startled her with its intensity. She loved Charles. She was not going to let Francis kill him. Drawing herself together, Georgina eased her feet under her, hidden by the wide expanse of skirt which billowed on the floor. Then, tensing her muscles, she lunged upward, right at Francis, her hands flung forward, fingers stiffened into claws. A shriek came from somewhere, and Georgina realized that it was she making the horrible noise.

But even as she was in motion, Georgina knew she had made a terrible mistake, that she had misjudged her cousin's control, for he wavered not an inch, but kept the pistol pointed at her. From where she was, in one of those split seconds which stretch on and on in the peculiar way time does during crisis, Georgina could see his finger whiten as he tightened it on the trigger. There was a flash and a terrible noise, and something struck her shoulder a clublike blow. There was a second noise, then, one she'd heard over and over again during the long, tedious miles to and from Trindale. It was the sharp crack of a skilled coachey's whip.

She seemed to be once again lying on the floor, viewing the scene through the wrong end of a spyglass. The long, black whip sang through the air, and it curled about her cousin's neck like a black snake. There was a curious snapping noise, Francis's face contorted, and then everything went black.

She awoke to a terrible throbbing pain in her shoulder, so intense that Georgina cried out, rousing herself. She opened her eyes and saw, before her, the beloved face of her darling Charles, his eyes dark with worry.

"Georgina, dearest, it's going to be all right," he murmured.

As he spoke, some of the worry left his face.

"What—what—?"

"Shh, don't try to talk now," Charles said softly.

Someone else was there, a middle-aged man with wise eyes and firm hands.

"I'm Doctor Smalley," he said. "You must rest quietly, Miss Ryerston. You've been wounded—not seriously. Just a flesh wound in that shoulder. Painful but not fatal." He held a goblet to her lips, raised her head. "Drink this. You'll sleep."

Georgina didn't want to sleep. She had to know— but the draught flowed down her throat, and she felt it begin to take effect immediately.

"What happened?" she murmured; but if anyone answered, Georgina didn't hear it.

When next she woke, it was daylight. Her shoulder still throbbed, but the pain was not so intense. As her eyes opened, a familiar face bobbed into view— Lizzie, eyes wide as saucers.

"Oh, miss, I was that worried. Thank God you are all right."

Had it all been a dream? Frantically Georgina looked around her room. Charles was no place in sight. Terror seized her. "Charles?" she said, her voice weak. Then, as the terror grew, so did her voice. "Charles? Charles?"

"Hush, miss," Lizzie said, "don't try to sit up!" Gently but firmly she held Georgina's shoulders down. "You'll break open your wound. Charlie's just in the next room, napping. He wanted to stay in here, but Dr. Smalley said you must rest undisturbed. Charlie—" Then a hand flew to her mouth, as if she'd said something terrible. "Oh, excuse me, miss—his lordship said I was to call him the minute you woke."

His lordship? Francis? Her head was awhirl, and Georgina didn't know what to think. She'd had this terrible dream—or had it been real? Or perhaps it had been one of those strange visions she'd been experiencing. Her shoulder throbbed suddenly—then memory swept back with frightening clarity. They'd all been in here—Charles, holding the whip—Francis with the pistol—Amesford with Bible and candelabra. She'd been sprawled on the floor where Charles had flung her to keep her out of the line of fire; but something —yes!—she'd lunged at Francis to try to get that deadly weapon from him. She'd thought he might flinch, give Charles a chance; but Francis's finger had tightened on the trigger, there'd been a flash, a loud explosive noise, and the blow to her shoulder which threw her back onto the floor again. Then, clear as if she were once more seeing it, came the memory of that long, coachey's whip curling through the air—the familiar crack it made—the curl of black around Francis's neck—and the final, horrid, dry snapping sound as the Fifth Earl's neck broke. Yet Lizzie had said his lordship. . . .

All a dream? A horrendous nightmare?

Then the door opened and Charles, unshaven, disheveled, was there. The old Charles, the one Georgina loved; for he stood a moment just inside her room, then he flung back his head in that gesture she knew so well, and laughed with joy.

"Georgina! You're going to be all right!"

Crossly she said, "Not if you don't tell me what happened."

Instantly contrite, he hurried to her bedside, kissed her forehead gently, and then took her hand in his.

"As the true Fifth Earl of Margate, lord of Hellingham—" Charles began.

"It's true, then? I didn't dream it? Francis is. . . ."

He added the word she couldn't say. "Dead. Yes, Georgina, I was trying to flick the pistol from his hand; but you sprang at him just as I snapped the whip, he turned—truly, I did not intend to kill him,

Georgina. I just wanted to get that pistol away from him before he killed you." He shuddered. "When that pistol fired, I went a little mad. I didn't care, then, that the whip had wound around his neck. When I heard his neck break. I only wished it had been my hands around his throat. You remember it, don't you?"

Georgina shuddered. "I'd thought it might have been a nightmare." Then fear washed away her happiness. "But the law—Charles what will they do to you?"

"Nothing, Georgina. Amesford will tell the truth." He laughed, harshly this time. "A born turncoat, Amesford. When he saw that Francis was dead, he couldn't get the words out fast enough. He assured me he'd been duped by his false friend. He deplored the fact that my miserable half brother had wounded me, and told me he would swear before the judge that Francis had tried to murder you, and to cheat me out of my rightful inheritance."

"And Francis killed his father." Finally she could say it to someone.

He caught her hand in a painfully hard grip. "He what?"

She told him of the strange vision she'd had, and his eyes widened.

"You saw this the night he died? After the fight Francis and I had?"

She shook her head. then wished she'd not, as it made her wounded shoulder hurt more. "No, it was earlier. But I know he did it, Charles, although it could never be proved."

"Francis was so afraid I'd be able to establish my claim, once father tried verbally to acknowledge me as his heir."

"Then it is true. The Bible—will it be accepted as proof of your legitimacy?"

"There'll be no trouble, now that Amesford is on my side. The Bible has been sent by guarded rider to Sir Barnaby Kane, with a letter of explanation. Only one problem remains to be solved, now."

Georgina felt fear clutch at her throat. "Another problem? Is it I?" Dismay flooded her. "But you said I could live at Hellingham. You did, Charles. You said I deserved to have gowns of silk and satin—to have my own abigail as mistress here. I suppose now that I've done what you wanted me to do, now that I've provided you with the proof you've looked for all your life, you won't want me around." She gave a bitter little laugh. "Francis mockingly called me his little country cousin. I'm your cousin, too, remember. Now that you're earl, I guess I'm not elegant enough for you." Tears rolled down her cheeks. It had been such a terrible week. Two mad trips across the whole of England, almost. She was bone weary, she'd been shot, Francis lay dead—and now Charles saw her only as a problem. "You don't want me, now, because Francis was my lover, yet you've bedded every serving wench between London and Exeter." She remembered the vision in which she'd seen Charles lying with that girl, loving her. It had earned her a slap in the face from Francis, had that particular vision. "It's all right for you, I suppose. You're a man. You seduced me, just to get me to help you win an earldom. But you hate me because I lay with Francis." Now she sobbed so much she couldn't continue.

Charles let her say it all, not interrupting, not trying to defend himself. Now he took out a lace-edged kerchief and gently wiped away her tears. "We've both done things we'd prefer to forget, Georgina. Don't cry, now, my dearest. Where could you have gotten the idea that I would not want you here at Hellingham? Where else would I want my wife?"

"Your—your—wife?" she gasped, hope surging through her entire being.

"My wife." Then that devilish grin she knew so well

lighted up his face. "Tell me truly, my countess-to-be, am I the best lover you've ever had?"

"Charles! How dare you suggest I've had a succession of lovers. You were the first—and there was Francis—"

"You haven't answered me, Georgina."

Her left arm hurt too much to move it, but she slid the other arm around his neck, pulling his face down to hers.

"You were the most wonderful lover a woman could ever want. And I can't wait to have you make love to me again."

His lips sought hers in a passionate kiss, although he held her gently.

Then Lizzie came in, all happy smiles, and shooed him away, reminding Charles that Dr. Smalley said her mistress must rest.

When he'd gone reluctantly, Lizzie begged, "Can you ever forgive me, miss? His lordship—the other one —found the note you wrote. Horrid toad Twistle saw you pass it to me and tattled. He threatened me, said if I didn't coax you to drink the drugged chocolate, and lie to you about Charlie—'scuse me miss—his lordship!—he'd claim I'd stolen from him and have me hanged."

"It's not your fault, Lizzie," Georgina assured her. "It all came out all right, as you can see."

Georgina dismissed her abigail, and lay there in her bed at Hellingham, the happiest woman in all England. She remembered that first coach ride here, when the wag had said they'd all ridden the "coach to hell." How little he knew. It had been, for Georgina, the coach to heaven.